Will Munday

A Reluctant Warrior

A NOVEL
BY

Richard Beougher

To Erin,
A deserving grand daughter
who I love.
GRAMPS

Richard Beougher

PublishAmerica
Baltimore

ISBN: 1-4137-4516-4
PUBLISHED BY PUBLISHAMERICA, LLLP
www.publishamerica.com
Baltimore

Printed in the United States of America

To my treasure trove; my children,
Sandra, Julie, Lauri, Richelle and Richard II.

Acknowledgements

I am grateful to so many people. It would be impossible to cite all of them. Here are just a few of the many who held sway during my journey through life.

I want to thank the late Sara McBride, my English teacher at East High School in Des Moines, Iowa, who had enough foresight to give me a failing grade because, as she explained it, "You can do much better. You are a talented young man who is not trying, but one who does have a flair for creativity. I could've let you slide by but I would be doing you an injustice to pass you with an adequate grade when I know that you can do much better." How right she was.

Years later I encountered another person who influenced me to follow my creative dreams; Ann Ragsdale, a motivator extraordinaire, who appointed me to ply my talents as an editor and writer for a newsletter distributed by the organization she chaired.

Just recently, when I had all but given up the notion that I would ever succeed, another talented lady, Loree O'Neil, gave me a swift kick in the rump that spawned a resurgence of determination to keep trying until I could see my story, *The Reluctant Warrior*, in print. LOOK! Here I am. Here it is.

I want to pay a special tribute, in lieu of the endless bouquet of roses she deserves, to my bride of almost fifty years, June, who suffered with me through the agonizing years of rejection. She's always been there when I needed her.

And finally, I appreciate how the editorial and management staff of PublishAmerica gave me an opportunity to present my manuscript, with special kudos to my editor, Anne Meiners, who then waded through this tome and fine-tuned it into a worthwhile read.

I am beholden to them, one and all.

Every time we fail, every time we do not do our best,
we don't just let ourselves down,
we let down all of the others that we might help
if we did our best and if we did succeed.
                                                    —Eleanor Roosevelt

Prologue

This is Will F. Munday's story. It tells about his goings-on during World War II, and about the apple of his eye, MaryLou, an elusive maiden who was always a skip and a hop beyond his grasp. It is a tale about people who influenced him, for better and for worse, and tells how those persuasive pressures helped to chart his course through a war not tailored to his likings.

Will was an only child, a nonconformist, who didn't fit the mold of a brotherhood such as the Army. But the blame wasn't entirely his. His father, a domineering tyrant, had to share the responsibility along with Will's mother, who had always assumed the role of the obedient wife in matters pertaining to Will's welfare.

When Will was eventually caught up in the war's wake at the end of his junior year in college he was running from his parents, as well as from himself. And as he stood on the precipice staring down into the unholy abyss of global war, he might've copped out of the military service by either evoking the *only son clause,* or could've sought another educational deferment. Why he didn't was as much a mystery to Will as to anyone else.

Will reported for duty and was inaugurated into an alien society far removed from that to which he was accustomed, and before his tour of duty was to expire he would suffer the agony of crawling across war's threshold to keep a general's promise, "I shall return." It would be then that he would witness the gates of hell swing open and would see his comrades offered up as sacrificial lambs to the pagan gods of war.

The reluctant warrior would finally meet destiny face to face in a place of someone else's choosing, committed to a strategy planned by his superiors, leaving him to accept the blunt reality of dying in a war he had, theretofore, held in contempt. It would be judgment time for Private Will F. Munday, the reluctant warrior.

Chapter One

"...and that," the sergeant exploded, staring in disgust at his motley mob of misfits, "was the biggest fuck-up of the entire war since Dunkirk." He was furious. His screams would've roused the dead. Actually, the ass-chewing wasn't deserved. None of his new charges were dead as a result of the disaster that befell them when they washed ashore like a bunch of buffoons in the life rafts they'd never been trained to pilot. It was obvious to Will as he copped a peek through the corner of his eye, first left, then right, that the new sergeant was indeed in control. He had shivers creeping up near everyone's backside. Will supposed it was his way of dealing with stateside commandos who'd not yet felt the proverbial sting of battle. They were, to a man, fresh in from the States, all of them having been plucked from a replacement depot a few hours earlier.

The sergeant's outburst was probably foreboding enough to scare the average GI half to death. But it barely fazed Private Will F. Munday, who had acclimated himself to such indignities during basic training back in Camp Hood, Texas. "Awe, c'mon, Sarge," Will scolded his new boss under his breath, "comparing this inept dry run with a colossal disaster like Dunkirk, where the Germans overwhelmed the remnants of the English and French armies and forced them to retreat into the sea, is a travesty." Today's ordeal had nothing to do with the embarrassing withdrawal from Europe, where a flotilla of privately owned watercrafts snatched the floundering soldiers from certain death. This little fiasco was nothing more than a training maneuver, a kick-off stunt to inaugurate them for the upcoming assignment. It had no bearing on the outcome of the war. He thought his sergeant was overreacting. He was a rookie, but he did already comprehend that whenever the Army saw fit to throw a green bunch of boneheads together to form a new unit—especially draftees who could never measure up to the standards expected of professional soldiers in the regulars— Murphy's law would prevail. He softly chuckled to himself when recalling that one of his new comrades lost his rifle over the side of the raft on the testy trip ashore. He suspected there'd be hell to pay when the big man up front caught wind of that. But Will figured that would take the heat off of the rest of them while the sergeant addressed that problem.

In all fairness to everyone in the formation, Will confessed that his performance was no more outstanding than that of the others in the group. To describe it briefly, he mused, he had participated in an *ill-fated, simulated, amphibious assault* for which neither he nor any of the others had been trained, which was almost a guarantee they would end up being underachievers. He figured everyone did their best. Will had hunkered down in the raft as soon as he left the LCI's deck, holding an oar he didn't know spit about using, and then just hung on for dear life while the rubber boat bounced and pitched and tossed its way to shore, where, upon arriving, it flipped sideways and dumped him and his comrades onto the sand. The ocean had been a fickle bitch. He had overheard one swab-jockey say the sea was "pretty damned choppy to try launching these rafts." He halfway suspected his superiors knew the outcome in advance and were just testing everyone's skills for encountering the unknown. Will was thankful to still be alive. Had it not been for an onshore flow that just naturally delivered them onto the beach, they'd have all drowned or floated out into oblivion on the high seas.

It was just natural for Will to ignore much ado about nothing. He was soaked to the skin, as were all of his buddies, water still dripping from the cuffs of his fatigue jacket. Being wet was one of his prime concerns; he hated it. When he glanced at the sergeant, who was dressing them down, he couldn't help but take notice that his uniform was spic and span, as well as dryer than a popcorn fart. The brand-new captain, and a brand-new corporal, were maintaining their distance as observers. They both wore subtle grins on their kissers and were garbed in equally dry attire. Will figured they were really enjoying every minute of this spectacle. In his humble opinion they should have been blushing with shame for engineering an operation that was doomed before it ever began. They needed their asses chewed out, but as usual, it was the private in the rear rank who ended up with an acute case of hemorrhoids.

The lad who'd lost his rifle came back to mind. Will pitied him. There would be, Will decided, a lot more dialogue about the loss of a rifle; the unpardonable sin for a foot soldier.

His hands gripped knuckle-white behind his back, Sergeant Baker pranced to and fro along the beach, playing a game of tag with the surf, its bubbly foam stopping just a tad short of the sergeant's shoes each time it crept onto the sand. This guy was, Will surmised, a cool cucumber. He'd tread back and forth, throwing intimidating glances across his shoulder, chiding them all with one snide remark following another. It was the routine reaming, curt oldies such as, "I've gotta hand it to you jurblowfs. You are definitely in a class all by yourselves. What in the hell were them guys up in GHQ thinking about when they saddled me with a bunch of jack-offs like this? Jack-offs, yes. Jurblowfs, no. You couldn't qualify as jurblowfs."

Will had heard the term *jurblowf* any number of times since being inducted. He never really understood its meaning but did figure it to be less than complimentary. If it was a negative label, he guessed they could all qualify as jurblowfs. He stole another glimpse at the other guys in the formation and after viewing their dowdy appearance decided they were definitely jurblowfs. It would've been an understatement to say he wasn't overly impressed with the clowns he, like Sergeant Baker, had been saddled with. On board the LCI he met a hillbilly named Tillie, who at the moment was fidgeting around on Will's right flank in the ranks. On Will's left stood another lad, a much less forceful individual than Tillie, who said when Will asked his name, "Awe … everyone just calls me Farmer. You can call me Farmer." Will had taken a shine to him for some unexplainable reason. He didn't much care for Tillie, but then he had a hangup with hillbillies in general, all of whom he thought harbored an arrogant opinion of folks who weren't reared in the boondocks. He conceived his opinion from a solitary hillbilly who once told him, "You can't trust city folk. They buy yore squeezins from the cooker, then call the revenuers." Will knew nothing about squeezins, or revenuers for that matter, but it sounded like a bum rap to him, and he just naturally took a disliking to back country people.

But Will promised to be Sergeant Baker's big surprise package. It wasn't that Will was unique, or one of a kind. There was no such thing in the Army. He was more of a few and far between—a Walter Middy of sorts who could hole up within his inner self and daydream his troubles away, much like he'd been doing throughout Sergeant Baker's elongated evaluation of the body of boneheaded conscripts GHQ had blessed him with. Fantasizing was Will's way of coping with command.

Sometimes, if the brass did scream loud enough, they might shake Will back to reality, just as Baker did that very moment, jarring him into the present tense with a shout loud enough to be heard at GHQ, wherever that was, "AND I'll tell you jurblowfs this! Thirty days from right now you are going to be the United States Army's best seamen … OR … I'm going to know the reason why."

It was just another siege of threats, Will supposed, which would give him time to revert to Never-neverland to shield him from the brutality of those with rank. He began to analyze Farmer, the kid to his left, who had been

11

boggling his mind since they were still on board ship. *Why,* he asked himself, *do I like this farm boy?* Customarily, he kept his distance from clod-hoppers. He realized he couldn't help but share the Army with them, but he wasn't very keen about listening to their atrocious palavering—the "Y'alls" and the "Youse guys" with their "Yups" and their "Nopes." They rarely offered a simple "yes" or a "no" when asked something. Will had almost flipped his lid back aboard the LCI while seated on the deck between Tillie and Farmer for a spell. Listening to them decimate the English language was hard to handle. Will did admit to himself that Farmer had a better handle on the national language than Tillie, but even then, his communication skills were frightful.

So Will found himself wondering what there was about this illiterate hayseed that stirred his curiosity. For one thing, Will had spent a lifetime as a loner who needed no one. His mom and dad had seen to that. He was coddled, pampered and brutalized all at the same time during his growing years. His mother deplored street fighting, while his father threatened to "tan" his hide if he ran from a fight. He had no friends because no one wanted him as a friend. To compensate for the disparity he became a bookworm who would hole up in his room hour after hour, his nose pinched between the covers of a textbook, while other lads were shooting marbles, pitching yoyos, and sitting on the curbing under a street light late in the evening telling dirty stories to one another.

Will had no girlfriend. He'd never kissed a girl and wasn't even sure he'd have the nerve to try if an opportunity arose. He did have a secret love, his fantasy—MaryLou, the sensuous, tantalizing blonde he had savored since the beginning of his freshman year. He'd never ask her out. He figured she would only reject him. He was a reluctant suitor as well as a reluctant warrior.

Unable to shake Farmer's image from mind, he paused to consider that he and the sodbuster might strike up a relationship, then shook his head from side to side, and mumbled, "No way. That would be temporary insanity."

"SEVENTEEN YEARS," Sergeant Baker again aroused Will from his stupor. "SEVENTEEN YEARS in this man's army," he repeated. "When this goddamn war is over, provided one of you jurblowfs doesn't get me killed, I'm going to retire. Just three more years to go. So, to prevent that dismal possibility from occurring, gents, let's talk about teamwork. Yeah, TEAMWORK! Teamwork will prevent a re-occurrence of this misfire we just experienced. D'ya want to know what went wrong? Here it is, plain and simple, gents. Every damned one of you guys were pulling in a different direction. I saw it as soon as you hit the waves. That's going to change.

Beginning today, WE ARE A TEAM." Sergeant Baker pivoted on his toe, wheeled about and summoned the corporal who'd been observing from a distance, asking him, "Is there anything you want to add, Corporal Schuster?"

The corporal sauntered to the front of the formation, hanging his head with a disgusted expression locked on his face. He glanced left, then right, then center, eyeballing each and every man in the detachment. "Let's start off on the right foot. Everything ... and I do mean everything ... that Sergeant Baker just told you ... goes double for me." He scanned the row of beleaguered soldiers, made a left pivot, and walked away. Will wasn't overly impressed with him. He was a sawed-off runt with a profound beer belly that overhung his waist belt. A narrow mustache adorned his upper lip. It was too painstakingly trimmed, appearing almost artificial, as though it was painted on his face. Will had an ongoing problem with corporals, too, so his not being impressed with Schuster was par for the course. He'd been victimized by a corporal or two since he took the oath. All too often, he'd noticed, they were also hillbillies, much like Tillie; not overly bright but dedicated. Corporal Hackmore, the non-com he answered to back at the replacement depot, was a prime example of the disparity. He had a one-word and a one-phrase vocabulary. He could say, "yup," and could justify every order he gave by explaining, "'cause this here's the Army. And that's the way the Army wants it did." Will recalled one evening when he was put on perimeter guard at the depot how he'd asked Hackmore, "Are there any Japs around close?"

"Nope," Hackmore assured him. "There's not a Jap closer'n forty miles of here."

"Well then, Corporal, that being the case, why are we walking guard instead of sleeping?" Will asked.

"'Cause this here's the Army, soljur," Hackmore curtly informed him, adding, "An army hasta have guards on duty. It's SOP. You do understand about Standard Operating Procedures, don't you?"

Again, Will's reverie didn't last long. With Schuster's departure, Baker returned to face the unit. He approached the kid who'd lost his weapon, barking, "YOU, PRIVATE, HAVE SOME EXPLAINING TO DO!" He shook a crooked finger in the lad's face, then asked, "Is Davy Jones a friend of yours? Maybe King Neptune's your sidekick?"

The kid responded with a negative shake of his head, mumbling something about not understanding the question.

"Ahem," Baker cleared his throat while he casually scratched his chin on a pretense of deciding how to deal with the problem, "old Davy must be a bosom buddy, because you're going to pay for that weapon you lost over the side, Private."

"Pay, sir?" the befuddled soldier asked in a meek tone of voice, obviously in shock over the possibility of forfeiting a half a month's pay.

"Yeah," Baker calmly replied, informing him that "You're going to sign a statement of charges and the finance officer is going to deduct the cost of one M-1 rifle from your pay as a subtle but constant reminder in the future to keep a tight rein on your rifle."

The lad was actually trembling, his chin quivering, while he fought to hold back tears that would've exposed him as a crybaby in front of the other guys. But he said nothing.

"You understand," Baker chided him in a patronizing manner, "there's a lot of things a soldier might survive without in the field ... such as his helmet, his shoes, his gas mask, even his goddamn pants ... and the worst possible scenario might expose him to be bitten on his lily-white cock by some malaria-infested mosquito ... but a soldier never ... let me put some emphasis on the *NEVER* ... misplaces his piece. *NEVER!* I'm a fair individual. I'm willing to compromise. I'm going to order you a brand, spanking new rifle from ordnance; a rifle that you'd best keep a tight grip on. Every time I glance in your direction I wanta see the rifle first and you second. If I catch you without it on your person, you'll be digging a six-by-six-foot hole so deep into the ground that you will think you're tunneling your way to China. However, if you follow through with my demands and don't screw up, I'll conveniently disregard that statement of charges."

That was enough said. Digging a six-foot-by-six-foot hole in the ground regardless of its depth, the Army's age-old reprisal for rubbing against the grain, had proved to be an effective tool for keeping the hardiest of non-conformists in line. Will supposed Baker would have no further problems with this timid soul. The guy appeared to Will to be terrified into a compliant state of being.

Baker, having finished his session of dispensing a dash of discipline to the lad, wheeled about and turned the formation over to the new captain.

Will had prematurely, as usual, formulated an opinion about the new commanding officer who'd introduced himself while they all were still on board of the LCI as "Captain Roul," and then advised them, "that's spelled R-O-U-L and is pronounced as though it contains a 'W,' like in Captain Rowell." He was, he told them, of Filipino birth, and he had been one of the men evacuated from the Philippine Islands along with General MacArthur in 1942. Will was a trifle impressed with his diction and laidback manner of speech but was, of course, still suspect of him as an individual, if for no other reason than his being an officer; meticulous linguistic talents notwithstanding. It did boost Will's outlook on the future, which was a shock to his dissenting attitude about the military, because he'd finally crossed pathways with someone in the Army who could verbally express himself with a slight touch of class. There had to be a rub, though, or Will would've been totally out of character. He decided the problem with Roul was his native background. The captain being a Filipino, bugged Will. He wasn't sure he could motivate himself to respect and to follow the leadership of a Filipino aborigine who might well have taken the swinging-vine route to the recruiting station. He shrugged off the idea as ridiculous, scolding himself for even harboring such a foolish thought. The very suggestion of a man of Captain Roul's demeanor evolving from a loin-clothed, cannibalistic society was remote, at best. Will's immediate problem was that he'd served under Caucasian officers in a segregated army that allowed color barriers to divide the troops by race, and he looked on this as a break in tradition. It was a switch in custom that he would have to deal with.

The captain put them all "At ease, gentlemen," an almost casual order that shocked them. It was refreshing for a change, especially coming on the heels of Baker's abusive tirade. "Each of you were assigned to this unit traveling under sealed orders. I'm sure you've been inquisitive about the procedure. It is time for you to open the envelopes and discover what's in store for you." The sealed orders that the smelly, cigar-puffing captain back at the replacement depot had passed on to Will when he departed the base had completely slipped his mind, disputing Roul's suggestion about them all being inquisitive. The crude send-off from the depot hadn't been forgotten, though. It was etched in Will's mind. "Don't leave any gear behind. You ain't comin' back, 'ceptin' maybe in a body bag," the captain had cautioned him. The very suggestion of being stuffed into a body bag sent a shudder up Will's spine at the time. He fished the soggy envelope from his pocket and peeled the wet flap open, then slid the folded paper from its cover and quickly read the brief communiqué. It simply stated that he had been "reassigned to Stopwatch," where he would receive further orders. It meant nothing to him. *Stopwatch?* he silently wondered. *What the hell is Stopwatch?*

The captain took his time waiting for each and every man to read their orders, then summoned their focus back onto him with "Are you curious?" He paused to study their reactions. "I, too, was curious the day they sprung Stopwatch on me at headquarters. Stopwatch, gentlemen, is a symbolic name that refers to a finely tuned, perfectly executed commando raid that, hopefully, will play hell with a major Japanese communications system on another island. It is symbolic because it's a synonym to a twenty-one-jewel

15

Swiss-made watch that has a time-tested reputation for keeping perfect time. The ultimate goal of this mission hinges on perfect timing."

This bit of news was an unexpected kick in the ass to Will F. Munday, the ultimate reluctant warrior. *A secret mission?* he quizzed himself. *A Swiss watch?* They might've been synonyms to Captain Roul and to his superior officers in some bombproof bunker at headquarters, but to Will the words "commando" and "Will Munday" were definitely antonyms. He didn't have much time to mull over the assignment, however. Roul continued, raising his voice a pitch, "STOPWATCH! SURE, you're puzzled. You are asking yourselves, 'who nominated me for this risky undertaking?' Let me assure each and every one of you that you're not here by accident. GHQ carefully perused the service records of many, many men to single out this team. I'm not going to bore you with the minute details of our eventual mission at this time, except to say its success is vital to the war effort in the Pacific Theater of Operations. AND, I'm obliged to advise you, the mission is classified *top secret,* so for the immediate future you are all quarantined. You may get lonesome out here in the back country of New Guinea in coming weeks, but I can promise you that there'll be little time to dwell in your solitude. Sergeant Baker pretty well defined our immediate goal; teamwork. As he pointed out, teamwork is the primary ingredient in our pot of guerrilla stew. Discipline is the spice that makes it palatable. Teamwork and discipline are the recipe used by every victorious army in the history of warfare. Again, teamwork, discipline combined with secrecy and timing must be utmost in your minds from this moment forward."

Having laid out a sketchy blueprint of their immediate futures, the captain summoned Corporal Schuster to front and center, then suggested that he "Give this unit a short break, after which they must pitch their tents and turn this clearing into a military installation that will serve as their quarters for the coming weeks." Falling into step beside Sergeant Baker, Roul joined his sergeant, hustled across the beach and scampered up the ladders and onto the LCI that had beached its bow while they were being critiqued by Baker, and Schuster, and Roul. The new corporal took center ring in the circus that Will had inherited.

"Take ten," Schuster barked, adding, "smoke if you've got 'em. Don't wander away too far, except to find a shade tree. There'll be work aplenty for everyone when the break's over." Will was first of the thirteen men to break ranks. He had a hankering to be alone, all to himself, someplace where he could catch up on his daydreaming. There was, he'd taken notice, an inviting glade just a short distance up the beach where the trees embraced the sand to greet the foamy tides that crept ashore. After reaching the spot, he plunked his carcass down onto the ground in the shade of some towering palm trees that were gently swaying in the breeze.

Staring out across the seemingly endless ocean, he withdrew into his mentally detached Land of Oz, trying to rationalize the circumstances that had delivered him to this precise location. It was difficult for him to fathom that he was actually sitting on an isolated island, almost halfway around the world from home—a godforsaken island that he had already predetermined was *the asshole of the creation.* Being there was, however, a fact he could not alter. Why he was there piqued his curiosity even more. He wondered where it all began. Was it Pearl Harbor? Not necessarily. Did the beginning go back even further, to when the Japanese invaded China to hone their talents in anticipation of one day attacking the United States? He dismissed that idea. Was he to blame? Yes. He could have obtained another educational deferment. He didn't. He could have tried to invoke the *only son* clause to get off the hook. He overlooked that, as well. He halfway suspected his present predicament was his own doing by not evading military duty when his summons came to report for a physical at Camp Dodge, a pre-induction facility in Iowa. Memories of that day were engraved in his mind—his discomfiting waltz, in the buff, through an infirmary that was, in his opinion, overstaffed with pompous ninety-day wonders who'd been commissioned as officers as a result of their medical expertise, and not because they'd earned the berth. They weren't much different than he, Will guessed. They were glorified civilians with uniforms who knew nothing about military protocol. It would be those clowns who would decide who went to war and who stayed behind.

It was a god-awful day, especially when the shrink in charge of interviewing the new conscripts inquired, "How long since you masturbated?"

The unexpected query flustered Will to no end. He was totally embarrassed and he realized that his face was red as a beet, because the skin on his cheeks was sizzling. He was momentarily tongue-tied and just stood their like a nitwit, staring at the major who made the inquiry. In fact, it angered Will. He thought the question was out of order, that it invaded his privacy and should be stricken from the guidelines for interviewing recruits in the future. That, of course, was the beginning of his indoctrination into the Army. It was only a preview.. He did get some consolation, though, when the man next in line approached the major, who bluntly asked him, "Married?" He said that he was. "How is your sex life?" The man just stared at the major but did not reply. "How long since you screwed your mother-in-law?" the major smugly asked. The man in line paused a moment, weighed his reply carefully, then inquired of the major, "How long since you screwed yours?" There was a rash of laughter in the room, which embarrassed the major equally as much as the major had shamed Will a moment earlier. Will was beholden to that clever draftee's retort for days to come. His rash comeback was Will's only pleasant recollection of that dreadful experience.

But, Will soon discovered, Camp Dodge was only the beginning of his disconcerted military career. His next assignment was Camp Hood, a sprawling facility in Texas where Will was infixed with "right face, left face, about face" and "shut your goddamn face." His second day at Hood, he was again shuffled through the dispensary routine where he was inoculated with countless doses of serum to give him immunity over diseases he knew nothing about. His upper arms throbbed all day because of a half-dozen needle perforations performed by two overzealous medics who actually appeared to enjoy the task. The third morning he was rolled out of his bunk at three o'clock in the morning for his first *pecker check*. It was, to him, a revolting development, being forced to stand in the nude in front of his foot locker and squeeze his pecker while some bleary-eyed medical officer, who was paying little or no attention to the procedure, barked, "Skin her back and milk her down." The unscheduled event was, Will learned that day, a common occurrence; a three a.m. rise and shine to exploit what little modesty he had retained since his first antagonistic insult during his physical back at Camp Dodge.

Those disparities were the root of Will's incorrigible attitude about the Army. They were, in his way of thinking, illogical inequities employed to catch one or two careless whore-hoppers who'd caught a case of the clap at the expense of every innocent man in the United States Army. He regretted he'd ignored the opportunity to catch another deferment.The war had derailed his personal plans to pursue a scientific vocation. The truth of the matter was, Will hated the Army, with all of its trappings, simply because he didn't feel he was cut out to be a soldier. His suspicions were probably more right than wrong. He wasn't a very good soldier by any standard.

"OKAY!" Schuster shouted at the top of his lungs, summoning them to formation with "Let's go. Off'a your asses and onto your feet. Outta the shade and into the heat. Move it. Move it. On the double."

Will hated to budge. He had so enjoyed his short respite. But he wasn't surprised. "Leave it to a corporal to screw up my visit in reverie," he moaned under his breath. He did spot Sergeant Baker back on dry land, conferring with Schuster. Will did look upon sergeants with more esteem than corporals, although he had to agree with Tillie's assessment of Baker while they were still on board of the LCI that morning. Tillie had remarked, after Baker held his critique with them on deck, "Them sergeants ain't nothin' more'n a pain in the prat, if'n you ask me." He cautioned both Will and Farmer, "This here sergeant's gonna be a ball-buster. Y'all can bet a month's pay on that."

As much as Will detested hillbillies, he halfway agreed with Tillie's assessment of Baker. New sergeants, Will had learned from past experiences, were like trying to break in a brand-new pair of shoes. A guy had to wear them a spell to break them in. When a guy finally got comfortable wearing them, they transferred him to some new command where he had to break in another new pair of shoes. Where Baker was concerned, however, Will had decided to take a wait-and-see approach before formulating any opinions. He wanted Tillie to be dead wrong about Baker for some unexplainable reason.

Schuster brought Will back to reality. He reassembled the formation, put them at ease, pointed to a small vale that crept back into the depths of the jungle, and said, "There's your new home." But before he could continue, Baker stepped to the front, apologized to the corporal for intruding, then approached Tillie in the ranks. He stared into Tillie's face, long and hard, finally asking, "Okay, soldier. Where are they?"

"Wal, Sarge ... where's what?" Tillie countered.

"First off let's have an understanding. It isn't Sarge, it's Sergeant," Baker dressed him down for not properly observing his rank.

"Wal..." Tillie stalled, a dumbfounded expression twisting his homely face, before inquiring, "Sarge ... er ... I mean Sergeant ... what'cha lookin' fur?"

"Your teeth, soldier. Where's your teeth?" Baker asked.

"TEETH, SARGE ... er, I mean ... Sergeant? What teeth?" Tillie responded with a puzzled tone of voice.

Baker shrugged. He was displeased because he thought Tillie was toying with him and he didn't hesitate to let his discontent show. "The teeth that aren't in your mouth. That's what teeth. You know what teeth I'm talking about. Don't play dumb with me, soldier," he roasted Tillie.

Tillie snickered, then grinned, revealing a toothless gap in his upper jaw. "Oh..." he acknowledged Baker's curiosity, admitting, "I see whatcha mean. These here teeth." He pointed at his toothless upper gums.

"Yes. Those teeth," Baker retorted.

"Wal, cheezus ... as best I can recall, them thar teeth was'a laying on a barroom floor in Salinas ... you know, that there town where all the Fort Ord rookies get their R&R," Tillie replied with a chuckle.

The men in the ranks surrounding Tillie broke out with a boisterous roar of laughter, which didn't please Baker. "Quiet in the ranks," he scolded them. He was getting exasperated with Tillie. He, obviously, wasn't much on tomfoolery. "I know where Salinas is. Salinas, the last I heard, wasn't missing. I don't know where your teeth are. They appear to be missing. I'm referring to the dentures you were issued. You were fitted for dentures, weren't you, following that mishap in Salinas?" Baker explained.

"OH-H-H-H," Tillie played coy, "them teeth. You're talkin' about my store teeth."

"Yeah, soldier. Your store teeth. Where are your store teeth?" Baker demanded to know.

"Wal, sir," Tillie confessed, patting his right hand on the cargo pocket of his fatigue trousers. "They's right here in my pants pocket. Y'all see, Sergeant, they fit my pocket better'n they fit my kisser. I done told that dentist fellow right off when he shoved them in my mouth that they didn't fit, but he paid me no never-mind. So, you see, that's why they's in my pocket and not in my mouth."

Will thought he detected a tad of amusement creeping across Baker's face when he heard the explanation. The sergeant turned his head aside, then about-faced and walked several steps away from the formation, pressing the forefinger of his right hand across his lips. Will figured he was actually laughing. If he was amused, though, his joy soon vanished. He whirled about and stepped back to face Tillie down. "I see," he said. "It's not rare for someone to be issued an item that doesn't fit well. But they wear it, or they use it, which ever the case might be. It's a crying shame your store teeth aren't a custom fit and I must apologize on behalf of Uncle Sam for any inconvenience or discomfort it's caused. However, so long as you are in this man's army you will wear whatever is issued to you whether or not it is a proper fit. Which means, soldier, put those goddamn teeth into your mouth. NOW!"

Tillie glared at Baker for a moment, trying to decided whether or not to tangle with Baker this early in the assignment, then meekly protested to no avail, "Wal ... Sergeant, they're a mess." He pulled them from his pocket. The partial plate was covered with fuzz and lint. "Them there teeth has been in there for a coon's age." He figured Baker would give him an opportunity to clean the denture prior to placing them in his mouth. He was in for a big surprise. Baker had already made up his mind to have the final word concerning the matter as a show of force for the benefit of the observers. He shook his head from side to side, grimaced, then tossed a glance at each and every man in the formation.

"Put the teeth into your mouth. NOW," Baker repeated. "There's a object lesson to be learned here. It's the rule. You will use and wear and carry all issued gear and equipment and clothing at all times. There will be no exceptions. Those teeth are GI issue. You will wear them during all of your waking hours while on duty, which means, having been assigned to this unit, that will be twenty-four hours each day because there will be no passes, no leaves, no malingering during this training cycle. I had best not catch you wearing a toothless grin on your face again. Put the teeth into your mouth, NOW!"

Tillie wiped the denture across his sleeve, trying to dislodge as much foreign matter as he possibly could before inserting the partial plate into his mouth. It almost nauseated Will when Tillie finally worked up the courage to plant the plate onto his upper gums. Tillie gulped, gagged, and swallowed hard but managed to keep the teeth in place in spite of the horrid taste they spawned. Will turned away, lest he puke. A ball of fur was tickling his tonsils. But the exchange between Tillie and Baker had also been an object lesson to Will. Baker did rule the roost. He was a no-nonsense non-com. Although Tillie had the edge going into the dispute, Baker re-established his credibility as the leader, reminding each and every man that he was king of the hill. Baker pivoted, then turned away, telling Schuster, "Okay, Corporal. Get these jurblowfs cranked up."

Schuster left the troops standing at ease and began to assign them, two by two, to certain projects pertaining to setting up camp in the ravine. He pointed to several rolls of canvas that the navy personnel had brought ashore while Baker and his men conferred. He sent all but two of the men to fetch the tents and instructed them to "Tote them up the draw and start breaking them out. I have another chore to tend to, after which I'll be coming along to supervise the project." After the others were assigned their duties, that left Will and Farmer the only survivors still standing in formation. Schuster glanced in their direction, pointed to several shovels piled on the beach, and said, "Grab a shovel apiece and follow me."

Will was immediately suspicious. Shovel details were bad news. Being the last man assigned also was an ill omen. It was kind of like when he was a kid and the neighborhood gang chose up sides for a ball game, leaving Will until last because no one wanted him on their team. He sensed that same feeling about this detail.

Farmer broke the silence while they trudged along behind Schuster, who headed directly into the wildwood. "Have you got a gal friend?" he asked.

"Why? Does it make a difference?" Will quipped in return.

"Nope. Not a bit. Just asking," Farmer nonchalantly replied.

"Well ... I sorta have a girlfriend," Will lied, not wanting to admit he wasn't exactly considered a lady's man. What Will actually had was a one-sided romance with a girl who rarely acknowledged he existed.

"Me neither," Farmer reproached him, suggesting that he didn't believe Will had a girlfriend at all. Farmer was, Will realized, a clever clodhopper, not a country bumpkin.

Will said nothing further after Farmer upended his philosophy about plow jockeys being lackluster hicks. Prior to meeting Farmer Will had always looked down on farmers. He thought of them as being uncouth clods who slopped hogs, milked cows and dug furrows in Mother Earth's crust. As for Farmer having no girlfriend, Will couldn't have cared less. He wasn't surprised. The country boy was timid, almost withdrawn at times. That was, at least, the conclusion Will had reached concerning him while they chatted back on board of the LCI. Will suspected he was devoted to his mother; almost reverent, in fact. He recalled to mind how Tillie and Farmer had disagreed when the hillbilly made his premature judgment about Sergeant Baker. Farmer actually scolded Tillie, accusing him of being unfair. He told Tillie that his mama always said, "First notions cause commotions. One should never judge a person until they are well acquainted."

Trying to analyze the few men he'd already met who were assigned to this mission, he was confident that it would be he, and no one else, that would become Sergeant Baker's surprise package, just as Farmer had suddenly loomed up to become Will's revelation. And a startling revelation the country boy turned out to be. Will had suspicions that Farmer was probably pretty damned good at anything he tackled; a excellent hog slopper, a gentle cow milker and he could probably boast of plowing the straightest furrow in ten counties.

"Right here," Schuster halted his patrol, pointing a finger toward the ground. "Start digging. A two-holer will do," he suggested.

"A two-holer? A latrine? We drew the latrine digging detail?" Will protested.

"Yeah. You got a problem with that? You're getting off easy. Those other guys have to wrestle those big tents to erect them, then pound in the stakes, and tie them down. If you dislike the idea of a two-holer, perhaps I could find it within my heart to make it a three-holer," Schuster informed them.

"No," Will hedged. "A two-holer's fine. There's no need for you to get overly generous by making it a three-holer."

Schuster grinned. Turning around, he vanished into the trees, shouting over his shoulder as he left, "I'll be back to check up on you stateside commandos and I better see nothing but assholes and elbows when I do."

Schuster's order to dig a slit trench that would serve as their unit's outdoor privy in the coming days didn't benefit Will's already dour image of corporals. Grumbling to himself about the disparities of the Army, barely audible, but just loud enough to be heard, Will thrust the shovel's point into the ground, planted his foot on the blade, and paused a moment to offer Schuster a patronizing stare as he faded out of sight. He pressed down, tilted the blade backwards, lifted a scant shovel of dirt out of the tiny hole he'd made in the ground, and informed Farmer, "Some shit, huh? Digging the crapper. Will it ever end?"

Farmer chuckled, informing Will that "Turnin' the soil is an everyday chore for me back home. T'ain't nuthin'. Just dig in, lift out, pitch it aside, and dig in again 'til you figure the hole's deep enough to satisfy the corporal." He commenced digging and pitching at a furious pace, moving twice as much dirt as Will, and before long they had penetrated the earth to a depth of about twelve inches. Farmer stopped, leaned on his shovel handle, and grinned at Will, suggesting, "Guess we'd best take a break. A man could fetch himself a heat stroke in this climate from working too hard."

Will paused, leaned on his shovel handle and agreed, explaining between labored breaths, "I'm tuckered out. How deep to you suppose we need to dig this trench, Farmer?"

The country boy glanced around, then down into the hole they'd carved out of the earth, and told Will, "I reckon if'n we dig it about hip deep that oughta do. I gotta be honest with you. I've seen latrine trenches before, but I ne'er actually stared right down into the bottom to see how far my shit was falling."

Will laughed. It was a valid point. He'd never bothered to look either. But their brief break did cost them. Schuster came darting out of the foliage, shouting, "I told you to dig a ditch, not stand in a ditch and shoot the bull. Quit leaning on them shovel handles before you break them, and start digging."

"Wal, Corporal, we was just taking a breather. We just quit diggin' a minute afore you walked up on us. Honest Injun!" Farmer claimed.

"Well, the break's over. I'll be back," Schuster advised them, and again he left them to their duties. And he did return more than once, but each time reappeared when they were digging and not loafing.

When Farmer and Will finally reached a depth that satisfied the both of them, Will leaned his backside against the freshly cut earthen wall of the trench and slowly slid down onto his rump, informing Farmer, "That's good enough for me."

Farmer didn't hesitate to join him on the floor of the hole. He had no sooner sat down than he scooped up a hand full of the loose crumbs remaining in the trench, then slowly let the soil filter between his fingers and fall back onto the ground. "I'll tell you one thing, Will. A man couldn't get twenty bushels to an acre farmin' in this loam," he commented.

"A man couldn't what?" Will shouted, an expression of surprise twisting his face.

"I said that man couldn't—" Farmer tried to reply, but Will quickly interrupted him.

"I heard what you said."

"Wal, then why'd you ask me—" and again Will cut him short.

"I can't believe you're for real. Your name fits you to a tee. You're a farmer, all right; a stupid, dumb farmer."

Farmer grinned. Will's tirade rolled off of his back like water off of a duck's back. "Now, why'd you go and say them things?" he asked.

"Because," Will replied. "Here we are, digging a crapper in a war zone, where we might get ourselves killed anytime now, and you're fretting over the quality of the soil and its prospects of growing a bountiful harvest."

"Wal, it's a fact. I know about plantin'," Farmer rebutted him. "You city boys just stuff your gullets with grub and never once think about the work some farmer did to grow it."

"I don't really give a shit, Farmer," Will verbally skewered him.

Farmer reached down again, scooped up another handful of dirt, shook it above Will's head, and threatened to "plant you, so's you'll know something about plantin' and farmin'."

"You wouldn't dare," Will provoked him.

Farmer dropped the fistful of soil atop of Will's helmet, then laughed as Will squirmed to shake the dirt from his shoulders. But Will wasn't going to let the country boy badger him. He swept his hand down across the ground, scooped up a fistful of dirt and pitched it onto Farmer, who responded in kind just about the time that Schuster returned to the scene.

Crimson faced, the embarrassed diggers glanced up when Schuster shouted, "And what the hell is this all about?"

He was standing directly above them, his toes hanging off of the trench's top rim, fists planted firmly on his hips, arms akimbo, just shaking his head back and forth, a disgusted expression aglow on his face. He slowly meandered around the hole, glancing first down, then at the mound of dirt they had piled on the ground beside the hole.

"It'll do. Could'a been a tad deeper, but it'll pass. Get out of the hole and shake the dirt off of your uniforms, then report back to the bivouac area. On the double."

The corporal pivoted on his toe, then strutted away, paying little mind to his latrine diggers. He knew they would follow behind, because there was no other place for them to go in such a godforsaken wilderness. Will did, however, overhear Schuster mumble to himself as he drew away, "Now, just how in the hell do they expect us to fight this goddamn war with a bunch of lain-brained kids?"

Chapter Two

The first day of Will's new assignment was finally drawing to a close. Twilight's creeping tentacles of shade quickly engulfed the meadow where their camp had been hastily pitched in a draw between two hills. The relenting sunlight faded behind the crests to the west and the thicket was veiled underneath a swarthy gloaming that obscured the view of the island's extensive, unexplored interior. The landscape's unbridled vastness intimidated Will. He was, in fact, almost spooked by the sprawling, numinous hinterland. It dredged up recollections of his childhood; of ghosts, of goblins, and such. A cold chill hopscotched up his spinal column and sent a shiver seething through his entire body. He shook the sensation off, trying to bolster his courage, lest he appear skittish to his newfound friends. He did pause to wonder, though, if any of the others were leery of the jungle's uninviting depths. Did the thought of it make their blood run cold, as it had his own? Would it be unusual, he asked himself, for Will Munday to be an oddity, being the only *chicken liver* in the unit? Yeah! He'd been an outcast many times in his life because he was different. Therefore, he reasoned, he could be a solo sissy.

Will had always handled daylight hours better than the dark of night. He was definitely not a nocturnal creature. He found nights unending, and lonely. He desperately wanted a smoke, but military restrictions that banned smoking after dark were rabidly enforced. Being in a combat zone was a new twist, too. Back in basic training during the war games, he recalled, he'd caught hell one night for lighting up after dusk. He begged off, insisting it was a mere oversight, that he'd inadvertently broke the rule. His sergeant bought the alibi, advising him in no uncertain terms to "Butt that smoke, Goddamnit, and don't let me catch you smoking after dark again." New Guinea figured to be a different environment than being stateside. He needed to watch his P's and Q's. A flick of light could invite a sniper's bullet, which would leave him cold and dead on this island purgatory. The urge was too much to overcome, however, and he elected to take a few quick drags before total darkness enveloped the bivouac area. There was, he justified his urge to smoke, still a trace of daylight. It was a borderline thing. He could, being an optimist, say, "It's not quite dark." Or he could take a pessimistic view, forego the cigarette and say, "It's not quite light." He opted to be an optimist, fished his pack of butts out of his breast pocket, turned his back away from the campsite, flicked his Zippo lighter into a flame, and torched the tip of his cigarette. He inhaled a deep puff, let the smoke filter back from between his lips ever so slowly, and flopped down onto the ground to relax a few moments while he recapped the activities of that day.

Smoking, he determined as he carefully stole another drag on the cigarette, was actually a blessing. It was an analgesic, he told himself, that would calm his nerves. It had also proved to be a labor saver now and then. He recalled how, back in Texas, the cadre, all of whom smoked, would assign shit details to the non-smokers while the smokers sat on their duffs taking ten. He recalled one incident in particular where a buddy who didn't smoke was ordered to walk perimeter guard, parading in a circle around the others, who were huddled together having a cigarette. He'd thought at the time it was actually discriminatory, but he was helpless to do anything about it. He figured he'd best shut his trap and not infuriate one of his non-coms, most of whom weren't particularly fond of him anyway. He might find himself walking guard right along with the poor slob who didn't smoke.

Taking a final drag, he remembered they'd once been told that lighting up after dark was like sending an open invitation for some incoming fire. A guy could, they were warned, end up having his head split wide open like a ripe watermelon by ignoring the orders. He smashed the smoldering tip of the cigarette into the dirt, tore the remaining paper apart, and let the tobacco trickle down onto the ground from between his fingertips, then sprawled out, leaning his head on the trunk of a downed tree, and stared into the night sky. It was a magnificent sight; a speckled sea of endless stars, all waltzing in three-quarter time around a pale, lemonade-colored moon. He was almost mesmerized by the extravaganza, to a point of dozing off to sleep. But, recalling they'd been told there would be a meeting before bed check, he jerked himself awake and sat up. It wouldn't do to miss roll call. There would be a roll call. Being a no-show the first night in camp was definitely a no-no. He'd seen Baker on the prowl for someone's ass already—the kid who'd lost his rifle coming to mind—and he believed it would be frugal on his part to NOT offend the top soldier today, tomorrow, forever, for the duration of the war, give or take a day or two.

Will shuddered to shed the thought and focused his mind back to the evening mess. The evening meal, he recalled, left a little to be desired. *NO!*

28

he corrected himself. *It left A LOT to be desired.* It resembled a pile of previously eaten grub that had been regurgitated in the center of his mess kit. When he winced, the navy cook curtly informed him that it was "Beef stew. The navy's specialty to welcome new arrivals."

"You're shitting me," Will rebuffed him. "I looks more like the navy's gastronomical surprise package."

In retaliation for Will's dissenting barb, the moody mess attendant laced the main course with a generous topping of fruit cocktail, informing Will, "Okay. You wanta be a wise ass, this might help you to keep your bung hole open and your face hole closed."

Figuring any further complaint would fall on deaf ears, Will decided to do exactly as the sailor had suggested, shut his mouth. It appeared that he would be dining in this outdoor mess hall manned by the crew of the LCI for quite a spell, and he didn't think it would be prudent on his part to antagonize his hosts. Leaving the chow line behind, he ventured across the beach to the row of tables the navy had provided for their comfort, sat his mess gear down, then stared long and hard at the intermingled potpourri he'd been served. Farmer, who'd beaten him through the chow line, was already seated close by, and the two of them were soon joined by the unfortunate lad who'd forfeited his rifle to Davy Jones.

The young man introduced himself to Will as "Duffy. The name's Duffy." After the brief introductions were over the threesome struck up a conversation while they ate. The exchange did finally evolve around to the lost rifle, and Duffy's ass-chewing. Will tried to comfort him, suggesting that he adopt a philosophy of "don't let the bastards wear you down." He told Duffy that maintaining such an attitude did help him counter grievances that he could do nothing to change. Based on Duffy's reaction when Baker chewed him out, he suspected the kid was shy, if not shyer, than Farmer. He assured Duffy, "If you don't allow the brass to wear you down you can cope with this army life a lot better. I know. It works like a charm for me. Try it."

The chat did elevate Will's spirits a tad. He was almost elated in discovering that he'd found two new friends, two separate individuals, who might share some of his beliefs. That would be an unexpected, if not unbelievable, development for Will. Garnering two new buddies in one afternoon, which added up to a grand total of two buddies, was a vast improvement of his previous record of having no friends.

The trio of young would-be warriors jaw-boned between bites, laughing and joking with one another, making the most of their first break away from duty since they'd debarked from the LCI early that afternoon. Talking did help Will to take his mind off of the disagreeable chow, which in turn probably aided his digestive system. The verbal chitchat might've lingered on for a spell had a commotion not erupted at the far end of the tables. Someone shouted, "Well, deal them pasteboards, Gambler, and let's see if you can shuffle cards as fast as you flap your gums."

A card game always seemed to take center ring whenever there was both time and opportunity to play poker, or twenty-one. Some guys were participants, others just onlookers, those being the men who had already lost the last month's pay in previous games. Will knew about poker. He learned his lesson the hard way back at Camp Hood when several shysters in his training battalion sucked him into a "low stakes, friendly game" of Jacks or better, five-card draw. After forfeiting his dough, and being forced to drop out while holding a queens over fours full house, he had never played again. It was a realistic lesson he hadn't forgotten. Figuring at the time that the only remaining player would either fold, or call, he was devastated when the guy bumped the pot another sawbuck. Unable to cover the raise, and having no friend to borrow from, he turned over his hand, stood up and said, "That's it. You've got all of the money you'll get from Will Munday." He kept his vow, swearing he would never again be goaded into a game against those bastards with the Bicycles.

He turned his nose up at the remaining grub in his mess gear, got to his feet, and moseyed over to the sanitary station the navy had rigged for rinsing out their mess gear. He gave it a fast shuffle in the water, then ambled over to observe the festivities of the card game, from a spectator's vantage point, of course. Farmer tagged along beside Will, also keeping a safe distance from the game. A kid Will hadn't yet met, the one everybody was calling Gambler, appeared to fit his nickname to a tee. He was a typical huckster. Will had seen many of them his first few months in the service. They were, more often than not, eight-balls whose uniforms were shoddy by military standards. For some unexplainable reason they always seemed to wear their fatigue cap slouched down across one eye and had a two-day growth of whiskers. While he watched, though, he began to understand why the man was appropriately called "Gambler." He was a virtuoso with the deck—a nimble-fingered maestro conducting his pasteboard symphony with an allegro shuffle of slippery cards. And just like most every other cardsharp Will had seen, he came off as being a conceited, cocky, outspoken asshole. He was definitely a shill, pretending to be a novice when, in fact, he was a pro. His unkempt appearance and capricious manner should have served as a warning to the naïve gulls who'd gathered around the table to make their contribution. Will marveled just watching them. It was as though they could hardly wait to lose their dough to this dandy dude. Will halfway suspected that Farmer, like he, was not a player. Nearly everyone else teemed like a swarm of angry bees around the table to get a piece of the action. Figuring that, when the night was over, most of them would get precisely what they deserved, Will couldn't offer anyone any sympathy. He was, however, almost mesmerized by Gambler's finesse. He fondled each card carefully, methodically distributing them around the circle of contestants. "It's five-card peek. Nothing's wild, A quarter ante." He paused, took a head count, then proceeded to inform them, "Three raises. Final card down and dirty." Although a quarter didn't sound like a lot of money, Will knew that before the game was to end the stakes would go up, the bankrolls would go down, and as sure as shooting, Gambler would have the lion's share of the stakes. With nothing to gain by watching any longer, Will turned his back on Gambler's extravaganza and wandered off to get away from the racket. He just moseyed around the primeval outpost, trying to contemplate what prospects the hinterland had to offer in a way of entertainment during their tour of duty. Being, as he was, incarcerated in the wilderness, he couldn't imagine anything developing that would tickle his fancy. It looked as though there would be but two options; a Hoyle holiday or a grand Bicycle tour in days ahead. He knew for sure there'd be no surprise visit by a USO troupe. They didn't cater to small units in back country. They favored the big installations where thousands of soldiers could be entertained with a single show.

Their surroundings promised Will nothing but an austere lifestyle. Even essentials, such as drinking water, would be rationed, probably allowing each man only two canteens of water every day. Daily showers would be a thing of the past. There was, he'd taken note, no such facility in the draw where the camp was hastily pitched. It would be a bath in a stream whenever and wherever they could find suitable water. Home sweet home meant sharing a squad tent with several other guys, most of whom snored, talked in their sleep, or farted with a great deal of gusto. He had heard from guys back at the replacement depot about the jungle crawling with varmints that sometimes crept into bed while men slept. One man had warned Will, "Check out your shoes afore you put them on come morning. There's apt to be a leach or a centipede hunkered down in the toe. Once't saw a snake crawl outta a guy's shoe; a little green snake no bigger'n a pencil. The sergeant said it was deadly poison. He said it customarily lived in the trees and dropped on unsuspectin' folks whenever they passed underneath." This was, Will decided after taking his short tour of their quarters, not the Waldorf-Astoria. At least he didn't think it was. Then again, he mused, it might be. Truth be known, Will had never seen the Waldorf. Will had been totally obsessed with his recollections of chow and of the card game that followed while he half-dozed near the outer perimeter of the bivouac area. He'd ventured off into La-la Land for a good half hour he figured. It sounded from a distance as if the poker game was still in progress. He could hear Tillie, the hillbilly, chattering above the other voices. He guessed it was some more of his homespun rhetoric, which made him suspect that Tillie adored being the center of attraction and would never pass up an opportunity to make a fool of himself just to garner some attention. Will had met a couple of others much like him in training. They were clowns with a storehouse of amusing tales to tell, all performed with slapstick gestures—hardly a repertoire of a professional entertainer, but something to break the monotony of camp life. The Tillies in the Army were a contradiction to customary military procedure. They got away with murder playing the part of dunces, doing less than their counterparts, but getting more attention.

The moon went on French leave behind a bank of seething clouds. It seemed as though day faded to darkness in almost an instant. Will glanced up and found a patch of clear sky floating aimlessly about in a sea of clouds. It was lined with a legion of tinsel-coated stars, sparkling like a host of diamonds in the depths of outer space. How awe inspiring it was. Will stared at the spectacle until it spawned a sensation of dizziness; a giddy perception that reminded him of looking through a kaleidoscope when he was a lad. He felt nauseated, but Corporal Schuster saved him from upchucking his unsavory supper by paging the Stopwatch detachment to report for the meeting. "OKAY, troops," he shouted from the bivouac area. "LET'S GO! FRONT AND CENTER, ON THE DOUBLE!"

Will shook his head, trying to reclaim his boggled mind from the stupor that had held him captive the past hour or so. It was important, he figured, to report for duty with an up-and-at-them attitude, not half dazed. He heard a noise nearby and glanced in that direction. Two shadowy figures were hustling toward the campground along the edge of the timber. It was, he discovered as they passed close by, Captain Roul and Sergeant Baker. "Hm-m-m-m," he hummed to himself. "The long and the short of it. The Mutt and Jeff of Stopwatch." He thought the pair did make an excellent analogy; Baker tall and slim, Roul short and stumpy, closely resembling the comic strip characters from the Sunday funnies. But he purged the characterization from his mind fearing he might negligently smart off sometime in the future by calling one of the other of them by the cartoon identity and land himself in a heap of trouble. It was, he reconsidered, a nonsensical idea anyway. He'd already procrastinated too long. He could hear Baker's voice, impatiently calling roll from a distance. Will picked up the cadence and hotfooted it to the meeting site just as Baker called his name from the roster. "Here," Will answered.

The captain, standing at Baker's side, commented to his sergeant, "We have but eleven men present."

"Correct, sir," Schuster cut in. "all men present or accounted for."

"We have thirteen men. There are two absent," Roul announced.

"Right, sir," Schuster replied.

"If I recall correctly I made this meeting mandatory for the entire unit. I wanted every man present. This will be our get-acquainted session, Corporal," Roul reminded him of his previous orders.

"Yes, sir," Schuster answered, reminding the captain, "I know you did. But it is S. O. P. to have sentries posted on the perimeter after dark in this zone, sir."

"That was taken care of," Roul informed him. "The Navy is taking the watch until this meeting ends. Perhaps I didn't make myself clear on the point. Go find the two men on post and bring them back to attend this critique,"

"Yes, sir," Schuster barked in return. Will sensed he wasn't very happy over being reproved in front of the men. But the corporal quickly vanished into the night to fetch the sentries as he'd been ordered to do.

Will actually felt a bit sorry for him. That was a switch in character. He could sympathize with Schuster for feeling miffed after being upbraided in such a manner. He'd felt that sting before himself. He was, in fact, a trifle curious over the breakdown in communications. First off, he decided that it was actually more Roul's fault that Schuster had erred, than the corporal's. Secondly, he wasn't overly pleased that the captain singled the corporal out in front of him and the others. But he also considered that it might all be a result of the first day jitters that normally accompanies mustering a new squad of men that, heretofore, were all total strangers to one another. He decided to disregard it for now, mumbling to himself, "That's once, Roul. I'm keeping tabs on your conduct from here on in. I thought you were a cut above average for an officer. Maybe I was wrong."

Schuster wasn't long fetching the two sentries from their posts and returning with them to the meeting. With everyone present, the captain pointed a finger toward a man standing in the rear of the assembly. "Gooch. Front and center," Roul said.

A dwarf-sized lad, who had deliberately maintained a low profile throughout most of the afternoon—in spite of being the only Oriental in the group, which made him actually stand out like a sore thumb—sprung forward to the captain's side. His fleet obedience to orders, along with the fact that

33

he'd been paged by a name that sounded more like a sobriquet than a surname, tended to stir Will's curious nature. *Could these two individuals have had a previous relationship?* he silently wondered.

Will sort of wished now that he had intermingled more with the entire gang that day, instead of keeping more to himself as usual. Now that he'd had an opportunity to take stock of Stopwatch en masse he saw several guys he hadn't even noticed prior to now. The only thing that he had previously established was a head count while they were all lounging around on the deck of the LCI hours before. At that time he had counted thirteen people and had mused that, because their sergeant's name was Baker, one might refer to them as a *Baker's dozen.*

Will's suspicions over a previous association between the kid named Gooch and Roul were soon rewarded. His hunch was right. The captain introduced Gooch, saying, "Gentlemen, this is Gooch, our interpreter and our chief scout."

Actually, the news was welcomed by most everyone, because no one wanted the job of scout, anyway. It was a hazardous occupation. Will had heard stories from combat veterans that warned him about the brevity, or life expectancy, of those who took the point. They were the valiant souls who led the parade trying to ferret out the enemy in advance of the main column approach. Will didn't want the job, so Gooch's talents were fine with him.

Roul, then, reiterated his and Gooch's familiarity. They had met the first time during the battle of Buna. "As the fight was reaching its climax," the captain explained, "I inherited this young man from headquarters. Much like all of you, he was fresh in from the States. The Japs had us pinned down with a mortar barrage. We had victory within our grasp if we could break through and flank their positions. That was where Gooch came into play. The plan was to advance a column along the left flank as a pretext of the main assault, while we infiltrated the right flank, which would customarily be under-manned under those conditions. We were warned to expect light resistance along the proposed route and they hoped we might also take some prisoners in the deal. Under questioning a Nip prisoner might divulge enough information about the strength of their unit to gain us an edge. I had no interpreter to interrogate prisoners. They assigned Gooch to my command. When we were first introduced, Gooch snapped to attention, clicked his heels, and saluted, blurting out, 'Private Seisuburo Yamaguchi, sir.' He was nervous. It showed in his demeanor, so I tried to cool his anxiety, saying, 'That's a pretty long handle for such a short guy.' He grinned, a cheek-to-cheek smile, suggesting to me, 'Well, sir, if it's all the same to you, most of my friends call me Gooch.' So, to make a long story short, gents, he's been

34

Gooch since that day."

Will had to give Roul credit for one thing. He kicked off the meeting with a human interest twist that sat well with everyone. He had their attention in the palm of his hand with the Gooch tale. But Roul did add, in a way of warning to the others, "Think it is vitally important to clear up the matter of Gooch's heritage. While he does stem from Japanese stock, we should all remember that he is Nisei, that is to say, he is American-Japanese, born in the United States just like all of you, with one exception." He pointed a finger at a young Mexican lad who sat in the front row on the ground. "We'll get around to you later," he added. But getting back to his original theme, he advised them that he would consider it a personal affront should he hear anyone treat Gooch in a derogatory manner. "He is, like you," he said, "an American soldier. He is not one of the common enemy, so do not refer to him as a 'Jap.' Gooch accepts his obligation as a soldier with a great deal of pride." That said, Roul tapped Gooch on the shoulder and said, "You're excused. But before you return to your perch I would like to say I'm sorry if my method has embarrassed you. The success, or the failure, of any venture is measured by the sum total of mutual trust among its participants. Racial narrow-mindedness is a formidable foe. We have a common foe. The Japs lurking around out there in the jungle. Now that you all know, and hopefully understand, my sentiments on the subject, we'll get on with the meeting."

Gooch was excused. He was, Will imagined, also embarrassed. He quietly slipped back to the rear of the group and leaned against a tree trunk, trying to blend his humiliation into the shadows of the forest. Roul, however, had made his point understood. Several of the men patted Gooch on the shoulder as he passed by them in his hasty retreat. Will even sympathized with him. He thought that Gooch had been put on display like a cheap piece of dime store jewelry, and if his assumptions were correct, it was a forecast of things to come. Before this was to end, Will feared, they would all be put on a pedestal to be scrutinized by all of their peers. It appeared to be Roul's way of introducing the men to one another.

"I should add," Roul added to his commentary about Gooch, "that Gooch's linguistic talents are only overshadowed by his ability to scout. You can rely on him. He can guide you in, and he can guide you safely out of any predicament."

Roul paused a moment and scanned the faces of his men, glancing left, then right, as if trying to cull out a certain individual, then seemed to change his mind and told them, "Let's take a short break. You can smoke, if you've got them. There is nothing to fear from the Japanese at this location. It was secured weeks ago."

35

After a few moments had passed, he knelt down, rolled sideways onto his rump, and said, "Now, it's time to get acquainted. When this meeting is over all of you are going to know more about the others than your imagination can comprehend; such things as everyone's likes, their dislikes, their fears, perhaps even their favorite brand of chewing gum. You'll know if the guy sitting next to you prefers blondes over brunettes, and possibly some revelations that might even shock your modesty, if indeed there is such a thing as a soldier afflicted with modesty."

To a man, they were now sitting on a bed of pins and needles, anxiously waiting to see who would lead off Roul's version of *true confessions*.

Chapter Three

The casual get-together was original by most military standards. Captain Roul was the antithesis to the degenerate major back at Camp Dodge who was more concerned with Will's sexual deviations than his blood count. While it was true that both Roul and the major were commissioned officers, that was where the similarities ended. Will could already tell that Roul had a knack with enlisted men which he made work to his advantage. It was apparent that this meeting was intended to serve as a self-incriminating tell-all and that, one by one, the captain planned to pry into each man's soul to measure his worth.

It all began with Farmer, who was momentarily shocked to be the first man summoned to toot his own horn. He wasn't accustomed to being the center attraction so was a tad bashful until Roul said, "Come on, soldier. Speak up. Where were you raised?"

"Shucks," Farmer complied in his countrified, laidback manner. "I'm a farm boy. Everyone knows that. Farmin' is about the only thing I know'd something about 'til I got drafted." He paused, glanced at Roul, and fell silent, figuring he'd had his say.

"You can do better than that. This is a get-acquainted session. We would all like to know a little more about you," Roul coaxed him.

"Wal, back home I used to do my share of hunting wild game," Farmer opened up, recalling fond memories with "It was fun and folks around said I was a crack shot with my rifle. Rabbit is a treat that city folks never eat. I'd bring in the bunnies, or the squirrels, sometimes a duck, if my pappy let me borrow his twelve-gauge come fall. Yes, sir, mighty good eatin'."

"Now you're getting the idea. How about you training record in the Army? What was your specialty?" Roul urged him to continue.

"Wal, sir," Farmer continued, appearing more at ease as time went on, "I done took my basic trainin' in the Infantry. Qualified expert on the M-1. But I got a surprise when basic ended on account'a I figured I was shipping overseas. Wal, sir, someone decided I needed some more training, so the next thing I know'd I was up and transferred to another post where they trained us to be Medics. And, wal, here I am."

"Let me ask you a question that's on everyone's mind. Do you ever get homesick?" Roul asked.

"Yes, sir, I do. I sorely miss my mama and papa and my dog, Sport. And I miss going to Sunday school and church every weekend. I once't got me an award for havin' perfect attendance six years running. I won a beautiful Bible with my name printed in gold on the cover," Farmer told them. "My pappy's all crippled up. I had to drop out of school at the end of eighth grade on account'a he got busted up real bad in a runaway horse-drawn wagon. Someone had to do the chores and field work and it fell my lot in life, I guess, to keep the farm a'going."

Farmer glanced at Roul again as if to ask, *Is that enough?* Roul excused him, saying, "That's what I need in this outfit. Men like you who do what needs to be done. That was an excellent report, soldier."

Duffy's turn came next. His was an extreme case of hardship if compared to Will's sheltered upbringing. Duffy did not raise his head or even look up at the others when he related his tale of woe. His eyes were glued on the new rifle Sergeant Baker issued to him shortly after the evening mess; the rifle he'd spent an hour's time to scrub off the rust inhibitor, Cosmoline. Duffy's raising was a real tear-jerker. He had been abandoned, he said, as a baby in a basket; left on the steps of a church in East LA. He knew nothing of his biological parents. To hear him tell it, he'd lived in "so many foster homes I quit counting. I'd run away. They'd fetch me back and they would punish me. But I kept running away until I finally made it when I was turning sixteen. The threat of war caught my attention. When the Japs attacked Pearl Harbor I trotted right down to the recruiting office to join up. I was too young. They said to come back in a year or so. I went back and here I am. I've been thinking about making a career outta the military if some Nip doesn't put me out of my misery. You guys mostly don't like military life but, d'ya know what? The Army is the only place I've ever been that compares to having a real home."

To a man, his comrades were sober faced after hearing Duffy's offering. Roul reached a hand out and patted his shoulder, saying, "You were a committed youngster who went after what he wanted, regardless of the hardship you endured to seek your freedom. There again, you are the kind of man we need. Committed! But what are your military qualifications? You never mentioned them."

"Oh," he added as an afterthought, glancing up, then around at each and every one of his new brothers in arms. "I didn't, did I? I wanted to be the best. I qualified sharpshooter on the M-1, expert on light machine gun, mortar, rifle grenade, and won the *Expert Infantryman's Badge* at the end of training."

Will could hardly believe his ears. Duffy had, perhaps, completely fooled him. He might've been shy in a social sense, but he had the heart of a lion when push came to shove. He would be a handy guy to have around, Will confessed, when the going did get rough.

Roul called on Tillie next. Tillie was the ultimate party-pooper. He chided Duffy's disclosure about making the military a career, telling him, "You musta stayed out in the sun too long. Only a guy with a fried brain would make a home outta this here army."

Of Course, Tillie had overlooked the fact that there were two, possibly three, members of the regulars on hand; Roul, Baker and maybe Schuster. Roul frowned at Tillie's mockery, suggesting, "Why don't you concentrate on your qualifications and knock off the BS."

Tillie wasn't offended. Guys like him never were. They couldn't be embarrassed, or humiliated. They were just yoyos who had a way of weaseling their way out of most any predicament. "Wal," Tillie drawled, "thar ain't much to tell. I'm a mountain man. Love the outdoors. Coon huntin'. That's my favorite. Don't mind sippin' a jug of corn squeezin's now and again." He paused, as if trying to decide how much he wanted to reveal about his background, then continued, "I reckon y'all know I'm a BARman on account'a I'm holding a BAR in my hands. Qualified expert on it. And y'all should ought'a know that Tillie ain't my actual name. It's a nickname. Now, y'all gotta promise not to laugh if'n I tell y'all my rightful name."

There was a mumble of agreement from most everyone. "Wal, my given name is Attila. Now, you gotta understand. I didn't have nuthin' to say about my christenin'."

"ATTILA?" a voice shouted from somewhere in the crowd. "Is that ATTILA, like in Attila, the Hun? How many L's and how many T's?"

Another voice sounded from out of the dark to further aggravate the hillbilly, suggesting, "Aw-w-w-w-we, go on. Can't you spell? There ain't no L's and T's in BARman."

The captain raised a hand to shush the outburst, figuring that Tillie had suffered his share of indignities for this session. To take the heat off of the hillbilly, he called on another member of the squad, who he paged with the name *Perkins*, asking him to "enlighten us about yourself."

Perkins, it turned out, was seated next to Farmer. He managed to squirm when his name was called, obviously loathing the task at hand. "Perkins?" Roul repeated.

He finally replied, "Yes, sir. I'm Perkins. But except for roll call I answer to the name Perk." He was obviously not a conversationalist. He claimed he had never actually done anything worth telling about. He suggested that Roul "Pass over me, sir. I had a very boring life. Suffice it to say I'm a combat medic. Anyway, I'm probably the only guy in the Army that has his own mouthpiece to speak for him." He pointed at another man, telling Roul, "This is my buddy, Slycord. He knows more about me than I know about myself."

Roul was skeptical but decided to play along with the ruse. "Should your mouthpiece's testimonial on your behalf fall short of requirements I will call on you later. Get on with it, Slycord."

Slycord wasn't at all bashful. His and Perk's relationship did extend far back into their pasts. They grew up together in the same neighborhood. "I think we were in the sixth grade the first time we met. Old Perk never did have much to say. The gang used to called us *Sly* and *Shy*. I'll be damned if we didn't get drafted in the same contingent. Took our basic together, and we both were sent on to Med training. We make one helluva team, though. Should anyone of you guys get shot, or injured, you'll be in good hands. We've had our indoctrination on the finer arts of dressing wounds, wrapping splints, vaccinations, amputations, medications and sanitation."

"Two more pill rollers?" someone exclaimed.

"Yeah," Slycord barked back. "You got a problem with that? Listen up. We're both experts with most every firearm issued to you ground pounders, too. So, tape your mouth, wise guy, before I dig some suture outta my kit and sew it shut." That revelation puzzled Will no end. So far three of the men had professed to being medical personnel. He couldn't help but wonder if this mission was doomed to disaster. Why else would there be so many medics? More surprising, he believed, was the fact that all three of them had been trained as infantrymen prior to their medical schooling. All three were experts with weapons, a feat customarily considered taboo for pill rollers, because medics did not bear arms. All three of these self-proclaimed healers were armed, and not one of them wore the emblem customarily displayed to identify medical personnel; a bright red cross.

Roul cut Will's curious appraisal short. "Well, Slycord, I'm going to allow your testimony on Perkins' behalf, but only this time. In the future Perkins will speak for himself. There'll be no Edgar Bergens and Charlie McCarthys in Stopwatch." He glanced around, decided on his next victim, and invited Gambler to mount the stump.

Gambler was quite matter-of fact with his presentation. "Bobby Belton's the name, gambling's my game," he boasted, claiming to be "from Reno, Nevada, a town that has a lot in common with the Army in that no one gets much sleep." He didn't mention, of course, that in Reno loss of sleep was voluntary, where in the Army it was mandatory. His military specialty was, he said, "Demolitions. I can hardly wait to ply my talents. I think that blowing a Jap bunker to smithereens would be as exciting as hitting a royal flush, just after you've bet the farm. I love BIG BANGS and even BIGGER pots, as some of you losers already discovered tonight in the seaside diner. Most everyone calls me Gambler. I like the name."

That answered one of Will's questions. How had everyone fared in the poker game following mess? They lost. Gambler won, just like Will had anticipated the sharpie would.

But as the meeting progressed Will discovered that Gambler was but one of three powder men. The next two men to spill their guts were a guy named Seiverson and another named Foreman. They had attended demolitions classes with Gambler. That accounted for the name recognition that puzzled Will early on. He knew there had to be a connection prior to this new assignment. As it was turning out, this was the second occasion where some of his newfound comrades had known one another previously.

According to their claims, both were also experts with an M-1 rifle. Seiverson boasted, "I can split a cunt hair at a hundred yards," to which Foreman added, "Yeah, and I taught the kid everything he knows."

O'Hare was next in line. He was another surprise, explaining he was the son of American parents who operated a huge coffee plantation in South America. "Joining up," he told them, "really vexed my mom and dad. I thought that, being an American, even though I have lived down south since I was a small boy, made joining the fight an obligation. Besides, have you ever lived on a coffee plantation? What a drag. I wanted some excitement in my life. It was beginning to look as though the war was going America's way and might not last very long. I was afraid if I didn't get into the thick of things now, I would miss it entirely. My spec is rifleman. I qualified expert on the range. And, I guess, that's about it."

Sergeant Baker, who had remained silent throughout the meeting, suggest to O'Hare, "Well, if you wanted to get into the thick of things you certainly came to the right place."

Everyone laughed. They needed a little humor. The interval was short lived, though. The young Mexican lad named Barrentos came in on O'Hare's heels. He was, he claimed, seeking "revenge." His older brother had been killed at Pearl Harbor. His use of English was atrocious, but his motives were sincere. "You see, Capitán, old Juan he get even with zee bastards what keel hermano," hermano being Spanish for brother. To emphasize his anxiety and gnawing penchant for vengeance he sprung to his feet, slung his BA sweeping arc, and verbally imitated the sound effects of his weapon, offering a "Rat-a-tat-tat-tat" that caught everyone, including Roul, off guard.

The captain reached out a hand and grasped the barrel end of the BAR, pulled it down to where it was pointing at the ground, and cautioned Barrentos, "Careful there. We don't want any casualties before we start training."

Barrentos laughed, assuring the captain that he was thoroughly trained to handle the gun. "You see, Capitán, old Juan eez, oh what'chu say in Inglés, maybe he make very good soldado." He was, he complained to Roul, disappointed that they were not armed with Thompsons like, "you know, sir, zee commandos in zee cinema. Everybody, he has a machine gun."

Barrentos' use of a Spanish word now and then gave Roul a melancholy feeling. Although English was customary in the Philippines, along with the native tongue Tagalog, some Spanish was still spoken by families that descended from early explorers who'd put their roots down in the island nation. And the captain was amused by Barrentos' reenactment of a commando in action. But he had to face the facts. "I'm afraid," he explained to Barrentos, "that you are not a Ranger, and secondly, actual raids in war are not exactly as they are portrayed by Hollywood producers. In addition, you are holding one of the most effective weapons in the Army's arsenal. The Browning Automatic Rifle is the old reliable. It's been around awhile. Its muzzle velocity, its range, its accuracy are unmatched. On a mission of this nature, range is a determining factor when selecting weapons for issue. I'm afraid you're doomed to tote that piece of hardware until our objective is reached and destroyed."

Roul decided it was time to allow Gooch to take the stand, giving him an opportunity to toot his own horn. The unit's official scout and interpreter came forward in a reluctant manner. He did, however, enlighten them all about how his people were interned at the war's beginning. He recalled them being "rounded up like animals, then transported to a staging area at Santa Anita racetrack in Arcadia, California, only to be sent on to an internment camp in the Owens valley."

This was an eye opener for the lot of them. They all had heard about the mass round-up but had never actually been told the facts. And they'd never bothered to ask, because the media made all Japanese in America suspect in their reporting. They were Japs. That was good enough for the average American. Finally, O'Hare asked, "Aren't you bitter about that? I mean, you're being treated like an enemy of your own country."

He admitted that at first he was. But it faded with time. Then an opportunity arose for the young men who were interned to get away from the camps by enlisting in the Army to serve as interpreters and such. The turnout was numerically greater, he thought, than they anticipated. Before long the Army was forming entire units of Nisei. "I joined, I guess, because I wanted to prove that all Nisei were good Americans," he explained, admitting, "I suppose, in a way, it was a reverse protest, but here I am, doing my thing, and I'm really glad to meet all of you guys."

Will wasn't surprised when Roul called his name following Gooch's eye opener. He wasn't overly enthused about the tell-all but could hardly renege. He started out on the wrong foot with his opening line, telling them one and all that he wasn't "wild about being in the Army." He complained that his educational pursuits had taken a backseat to the war. He'd have been wise to have taken a different approach, because Slycord didn't waste any time firing a response. "Who'n the hell do you think you are? I don't think any one of us are here out of choice. You're a goddamned crybaby."

"You had your turn," Will rebuked him, reminding Slycord, "and I'm entitled to mine."

But he'd sparked a flame that he couldn't easily douse. Gambler chimed in where Slycord left off. "Hey, clown. Where do you think I'd rather be right this minute than here?" he asked, adding that he had rather be in "Reno. That's where," he continued. He bemoaned the fact that he "could be rolling a natural at the crap table, or drawing to a gut straight in a poker game, or even feeding my dough into those hungry slot machines. I could be making a helluva lot more scratch than the lousy fifty bucks a month I get paid."

Will was miffed. "I'll just bet you would. You'd waste your life in some gambling casino, not applying yourself at some useful profession. You've got a lot of nerve comparing my college ambitions with that mediocre metier of yours," Will shouted in return.

Roul thought it wise to intercede at this point and let tempers cool, but Gambler wanted the last word. "YEAH?" he screamed, shaking a clenched fist in Will's face. "You're cute, all right. You've got them two-dollar words to talk down to guys like me. And ... what the hell is a metier, anyway?"

"It's French," Roul intervened on Will's behalf, trying to defuse the dispute. "It means one's occupation, a line of work someone is suited to."

"Yeah. He talks French. Big deal. I'll bet he was the big man on the campus," Gambler insisted on being last to speak.

"Tell us, Munday," Roul inquired. "What's you spec?"

"Oh! I'm a 745, a rifleman. I did qualify as expert on the M-1," Will replied in a subdued tone.

"Fine," Roul said, then moved along quickly to put the argument behind them, calling on a slightly older member of the unit named Williams. I

43

the last, but he did prove to be the most revealing contributor with an admission that garnered everyone's attention. "I'm glad I'm not superstitious," he said with a grin, "because according to my count I drew the thirteenth slot on rotation."

Roul assured Williams it was quite by accident. "It's where your name landed on my duty roster," he said. "Tell us about yourself."

"Well, sir," Williams cautiously began, "I've been sitting here throughout this entire session trying to decide what I should say when my turn came. You know, guys, it appears that we've been picked by the hand of fate for some mysterious mission that might not have a happy ending. I recall that this afternoon the captain said that the success of this mission depended on mutual trust. I suppose that's why he went to all of the trouble to set up this critique. It is important that we know and trust one another. I could sit here and tell you I'm a BARman. I am, and a good one. And just let it go at that. But I think it's important for me to level with all of you about my past. This confession might knock your socks off. I know it would have me barefooted if I were in your shoes right now. I think it is appropriate for me to inform you that I was, at one time, a preacher who, incidentally, fell from the Bishop's good graces and was defrocked."

To a man they were stunned. They were also speechless for a moment, exchanging glances with one another, trying to digest this scrap of damning information. Tillie, loudmouth that he was, finally broke the impasse. "Cheezus! D'ya mean y'all was a genuine preacher man ... like folks calling you the Reverend Williams?"

"Yes," Williams calmly replied, reminding them, "the former Reverend Williams. Like in has been."

Gambler was puzzled. "You know ... you didn't have to tell us that," he suggested with a sympathetic gesture.

"I know," Williams countered. "I'm telling you this story because I think it's important for every one of us to understand that we are human beings, not saints. I was defrocked because I fucked up big time. That doesn't make me any less a god-fearing man. I might have lost my credentials, but my heart is still with the ministry and I thought there could come a time when someone in this group could use a friend—an understanding friend—to seek council. If that need arises I would be honored to oblige. I have a sneaking hunch that, considering our ultimate destination, a bona fide chaplain might be a trifle hard to find."

Will kind of admired Williams, even though he, himself, was a diehard agnostic. He doubted he'd ever need to take advantage of William's offer. But Tillie latched right on to the portion of the confession where he said he'd "fucked up big time." The other men, for the most part, would just let the subject drop, but Tillie stuck his big nose into the revelation. "Wal, I've gotta ask. What did y'all do to make that Bishop fellow give you the old heave ho?"

Williams lifted his helmet, scratched his head, dropped the metal hard hat back onto his head, and admitted they were entitled to an explanation because, to hear him explain it, "I guess I opened a can of worms. It's like I said before. We're all human, all mortals, subject to temptation. We've all sinned. My greatest sin was taking certain liberties with the Bishop's daughter that a man of the cloth should have been able to refuse. I was younger then. Fresh out of school. I suppose that most of you think preachers never get horny. You're wrong. And that Bishop's voluptuous daughter made everything much too easy for me."

"Wow," Foreman shrieked. "D'ya mean you went all the way with her?"

Williams nodded, saying, "I'm afraid so. It was just one of those things that came naturally. Peggy was there. I was there. Not another solitary soul was there and, at that particular moment, it just seemed like the thing to do."

"Where'd you do it?" Tillie asked. He was all ears.

"In the study, of all places. It was Sunday, just after the services were dismissed. Peggy stopped by to, she claimed, seek some private counciling. It started off innocently enough. She said that she wanted me to help pave her way into heaven; that she didn't fully understand religion and wasn't moved like the other people in the congregation. Well, it was a difficult task, because I couldn't keep my eyes off of her resplendent body. And then I realized she was staring at me equally as inquisitive. It was spontaneous. The next thing we knew we embraced, then we kissed, and then I did exactly what she asked; I paved her way to heaven right there on the carpeted floor of the study."

"Holy shit," someone exclaimed, followed by Tillie's, "Cheezus! You fucked her?"

"Hey, dimwit," Gambler interceded. "Yeah, he did. That's what he's been telling us. He inserted his holy key into her holy lock and opened the gates to heaven, right?"

Williams laughed at Gambler's all too accurate description of what actually did happen. "Yes, as a matter of fact I did. We were in ecstasy."

"How'd the Bishop find out?" he was asked.

"Well, that was the bummer. Never count on people being creatures of habit. They'll fool you. The custodian normally came in Monday morning, tidied up the study, then the church, and finally the rectory. He'd been doing it in that precise order for years. Well, he wanted to go fishing bright and early Monday, so he opted to do his chores that afternoon instead of the next day. He stumbled right into the study just about the time Peggy reached a climax. The old guy was in a state of shock. He dropped his carpet sweeper and high-tailed it right back outside to, of course, spread the word about this awful thing he'd seen," Williams woefully explained.

"Kinda shameful, if you ask me," Farmer cut in. It figured. Will had him pegged as a pious sodbuster. "Doing such a thing in a church. It's blasphemy."

"It wasn't in the church," Williams tried to defend his actions. "Don't make it sound any worse than it was. The study is in the rectory."

"So, what come of it?" Slycord wanted to know.

"It's like I said. The Bishop, who was also Peg's father, turned out to be a typical dad from the old school of thinking. He insisted that I marry her because I had violated her. It would've done little good to base my defense on the possibility that every guy in town had taken a few liberties with her. I took the philosophy that it was a small town, so it wasn't like she'd bedded down with every Tom, Dick and Harry in seven counties. Our marriage was, to be right down honest about it, a shotgun affair. To set the record straight, though, we went through the motions and did get married and then something odd occurred. We discovered we were actually in love with one another. She is still my wife, I'm happy to report. We tried very hard to put our shame behind us, and I think we managed to succeed," Williams summed it up, adding, "and that's about all there is to it. I might add that, compared to my civilian achievements, it would be fair to say that my military background is almost phlegmatic. Had I walked the straight and narrow in days of yore I would have been commissioned a chaplain. But fate delivered me here to serve as a BARman, which might fall into the category of the Lord working in strange and mysterious ways. Perhaps my being here is by His divine design."

Roul glanced around from man to man, trying to appraise the fall-out from his diverse approach toward melding thirteen men into one close-knit group. It was quite dark, but the moon had broken through the clouds to shed a little light on the congregation. "Why don't we take a short break, gents, before we conclude this critique," he suggested.

Will, for one anyway, had the need for a breather that would give him time to digest Williams' unique resume. Prior to this he hadn't expected to meet another enlisted man who commanded the English language so effectively. He was delighted that there was one of the flock who he could carry on an intelligent discussion with, depending of course on Will's acceptance of another pious footslogger in the unit. Concentrating on

Williams' explanation that he was a mortal first and a saint last left Will almost admiring him. And considering that Will skirted the fringe of being an infidel, he couldn't quite explain the feeling of comfort he felt just knowing they had their own chaplain. *Oh, NO!* he told himself. *I'll never need him. I'm in control. But it's a nice feeling just knowing he's around to minister to the other guys.*

All in all he was troubled more by numbers than individuals. What he did glean out of the meeting was the numeral "3." There were, according to his score sheet, three medics, three BARmen, three riflemen and three powder men. Equally puzzling was the fact that each and every one of the men was qualified as experts on the range. *Why three demolitions experts,* he wondered. The table of organization, or T.O. as it was called, for Stopwatch was a bit unusual. He wondered if Roul would be able to transform this diverse contingent of jurblowfs into a competent team of commandos.

He recalled his own short dissertation and decided he might have erred with such a belligerent outburst. He didn't figure to get a standing ovation for his remarks, but he hadn't anticipated the negative vibes he spawned either. He would probably have to mend some fences in the next few days if he wanted the other guys to accept him

Duffy's tale of woe pestered him most. He couldn't begin to fathom the plight of an orphan's lot. He'd never known one. He had been lucky to have two parents, even though his dad was hardly a role model. But he was a father figure of sorts. There had been some continuity in his raising, but he could see where Duffy was coming from. Abandoned as a baby, never having felt the joy of motherly love must have been a dreadful existence. As for Williams, who came to mind once again, he figured no one could've concocted such a cock and bull tale from his imagination. It had to be true. Will didn't envy Roul's challenge to stitch this group into a patchwork quilt. After everything he'd just heard in the exchange, Will figured that whipping this group into shape would be a tall order. It was one thing, he admitted, for GHQ to cull out this gang of screwballs, but it would be quite another to convert them into an elite fighting machine.

Roul cut Will's melancholy moment short, suggesting, "Finish up your smokes. We still have a few thing to consider tonight. But before we do I would like to explain to each and every one of you why I said the things I did on the beach this afternoon. After hearing all of your new comrades in arms bare their soul, you must've also realized that, as I said earlier, your being here wasn't by chance. I'm satisfied, after hearing your short autobiographies, that we have the necessary makings of a unit with the caliber needed to accomplish our mission. I know some of you might be wondering why this job wasn't given to a Ranger unit. Normally, it would've been. But this operation is so special that GHQ didn't want to take any chances on its very existence being betrayed. You are special even if you don't think so. There are probably less than a half dozen men outside of this campground who know what we are preparing to do. It is that top secret, as I told you earlier. Now, I think it's time to hear a few words from our non-commissioned officers. Sergeant Baker! Would you lead off?"

If Sergeant Baker's presentation was supposed to be an actual glimpse at his inner self, he was obviously a very modest man, or so it seemed to Will. His laidback style came as no surprise to anyone, including Will. "I joined the Army when I was a kid not much older than most of you," Baker said, recalling, "It was the year 1927. There has been a lot of water go over the dam since then." He went on to explain that he hadn't intended to make the Army a career, but when his hitch was up in 1930 a man couldn't buy a job. So, he re-upped, then re-upped again, and finally re-upped himself "right into this goddamn war. Twelve years of service and I finally made Corporal. The war changed everything. The conscripts began to arrive on base and it fell our lot to train them, so lucky me, I was promoted to Sergeant. It wasn't long after the attack on Pearl that I was transferred to Australia. I also spent some time in New Zealand and ended up on New Guinea in time to test my fangs at the battle of Buna. That was when I met Captain Roul."

Baker paused and stared off into space as though he was in an entirely different world for a moment. Perhaps he was, Will allowed, given his record as a soldier. Finally, he grimaced, turned his attention back to the men, and told them, "That was my introduction to war. My baptism, as it's often called, and what a ceremony it was. We were getting a bloody nose from those goddamn Japs. They were dug in like moles in fortified bunkers and we had to pry them out, one position at a time, catching hell from their mortars without letup. I snagged myself a flesh wound to the leg before it ended, but I did learn the art of survival, and that, gents, is what I intend to teach you in the coming days. A dead soldier isn't worth a plug nickel. But a live soldier who has been properly trained to survive is worth his weight in gold. A few weeks hence you are all going to be twenty-four-karat guerrillas, because that is what you must become if we are expected to kick some ass on our next assignment." That was all he had to say. It was enough. He did prove to Will that he had the magic potion necessary to transform these stateside commandos into ultimate warriors. The fact that he had been wounded in battle tended to re-enforce those credentials. Will F. Munday was impressed.

Captain Roul, however, didn't let Baker get away with such an abbreviated biography. He deemed it necessary to illustrate Baker's courage as a lever to command respect. "If the modest sergeant won't tell you, gents, then it is the duty of his commanding officer to oblige. Sergeant Baker was decorated with a Bronze Star Medal for his bravery during the battle of Buna." It was just another one of Roul's calculated risks. He flaunted Baker's medal so that his new charges could learn to associate valor with duty. Having hand-picked both Baker and Schuster as his aides, he wanted them held in everyone's highest esteem.

It then came time for Corporal Schuster to toot his horn. Baker's resume was a tough act to follow, so he kept his past brief. "At Buna," he recalled aloud, "we lost twenty-two men, all of them youngsters like you. A couple of them died because they were careless. Several died when they zigged instead of zagged to dodge some incoming fire. The others were casualties that just go with the territory. Those can never seem to be avoided. It's the ones resulting from foolish whims I'm concerned with tonight. If nothing else good comes out of this training session I hope I am able to teach each and every one of you some common sense for staying alive. Men die when the going gets rough. And it will get rough. I don't want to collect the dog tags from around your necks to post a roster of the dead." He shook his head as if disgusted and fell silent. Will suspected he had recalled the climax of a Christmastime battle at Buna a tad too vividly; things he probably would rather have forgotten. Having nothing further to add, he took his feet and sashayed away from the gathering, disappearing into the dark of night that engulfed the camp.

Schuster did more than he'd anticipated with his testimonial. It urged Will to do some soul searching. The corporal had actuated Will's suspicions that war in general was anything but fair. His reasoning centered on two men, Baker and Schuster, who had already waltzed around the arena with the maiden of death, both of them probably lucky to be alive. Somehow it seemed to him that asking a man who'd already performed such a duty for an encore performance was grossly unfair. They had managed to cheat the Grim Reaper once. Did the odds turn against them for running the gauntlet again? But, he also concluded, if the old-timers like Baker didn't teach the recruits, then who would train an army for combat? He amused himself by looking for common denominators, such as *war* and *warranty*. They began with the same three letters, then quickly parted company because, based on what he'd just heard, war had no guarantees. He visualized the brass-hats huddled around a table, pondering their strategy, marking the grids, discussing the options, and concluded that in the end all that really matters are the stats, the projections, the faceless casualty lists. Every man was, in reality, akin to the unknown soldier until such a time as he distinguished himself or was killed while trying.

Recalling for a moment some happier times back in school, he remembered what his science teacher once said of success or failure. Somehow it seemed to apply to warfare as well as to the laboratory. "There is always a fly in the ointment," Mister Edmundson warned the class. "Science is research; a journey through unexplored jungles trying to locate, then to unlock, doorways to marvelous miracles. A dedicated scientist must be able to deal with defeat, then to turn the lessons from the defeat into success, for it is in defeat that we discover the obstacles barring a route to success. Once identified, obstacles can be displaced." Will's mentor had paused then, glanced about the room, then outside through the windows, and back toward his students, who were perched on the edge of their seats awaiting his summation. "I did say *dedicated* scientist. One cannot be successful unless he is also dedicated to his endeavors."

Dedication was Will's primary problem with being a soldier. He realized it but didn't really care if he confronted the problem, or not. He could not motivate himself to his surroundings, because he could not accept ridicule. Whenever he did manage to sense that he was on the verge of subduing his hangups, he'd be wronged by someone of rank and would then fall into a tailspin back to square one. He was, however, about to make some drastic changes in comportment. He would soon comprehend the meaning of his role as a patriot; one who is dedicated—yes, dedicated—to duty, to honor, to country. He had overlooked a rudimentary rule his mother had taught him at a young age. She and Will oftentimes whiled away the evening hours piecing together jigsaw puzzles. He was impatient. His mother was steadfast. She would find the proper piece for the proper place, while Will floundered to find a single fragment. Then, his mother would reach out and take hold of his hand and explain to him, "First you must study the shape and the colors. Then you sift through the pile carefully and you will find them." That had been Will's first introduction to dedication. Why, he wondered, had his mother and Mister Edmundson popped up in his thoughts? They should've been the last thing on his mind while residing on such a godforsaken piece of real estate in the middle of nowhere. But then he made a startling discovery. His mother and his teacher were the key. In a sense, Will had inherited his own jigsaw puzzle, or perhaps a labyrinth. He needed to locate a passageway through this quagmire, this endless tunnel of emptiness. The obstacle he finally observed was Will F. Munday, and only he could open the doorway to earn his rewards for being a good soldier. He needed to change his ways.

Will had no idea of how long he'd commiserated with his thoughts, but

Roul reclaimed his sanity by shouting, "MEDICS!" Will shuddered, shook himself back to reality, then glanced around to see if anyone had caught him napping. He doubted they had. "You are wondering why there are three medics assigned to this unit. I must confess," Roul continued, "their MOs as medics will not be their primary purpose on this mission. I know what you're thinking. Medics wear a red cross on their helmet, sometimes on an armband, and are supposed to be provided safe passage because they bear no arms and mean no harm. But this mission is not one of mercy, and their talents as weapons experts will be more beneficial than their knowledge of medicine. However, on the chance that some of you might be wounded, or injured, GHQ thought it advisable to have three medically trained men in this unit."

Baker quickly interjected his thoughts on the subject, warning them, "That goddamn red cross isn't much protection with these Nips, anyway. They're historically notorious for knocking off unarmed medics."

Farmer cringed. His thoughts were back in basic training and med school, where they were led to believe a medic's life was reasonably safe, if properly identified with the customary red cross insignia.

"So, if the numeral three is also puzzling, as I'm sure it is," Roul continued, "there is an explanation for that, too. We have three medics, three BARmen, three riflemen and three powder men, who are also qualified with small arms; four different spec numbers in a single unit of only thirteen men, including Gooch, whose duties have already been outlined."

This was, it occurred to Will, the moment of truth they'd been waiting for; their new duty assignments. It wasn't long in coming.

The captain split his force into three separate squads, designating them as *Able, Baker, and Charlie*. Each squad, he explained, would be comprised of four men; one rifleman, one BARman, one medic, and one demo expert. Without any fanfare, then, he rattled off the rosters he'd prepared for this occasion, assigning the men as follows: "Barrentos, Foreman, Slycord and Duffy are in Able squad. Farmer, Gambler, Tillie and Munday will make up Baker squad. That leaves Williams, Seiverson, Perkins and O'Hare to complete the duty roster in Charlie squad. You will be quartered by squads in three of the tents you pitched today. The fourth tent will serve as our C.P., as well as Gooch's and Corporal Schuster's billet. Sergeant Baker and I will be quartered aboard the LCI."

So at last Will F. Munday's puzzle was coming together, at least an outside framework, leaving a lot of loose pieces to fill in as changes occurred. He need not fret over where he fit into the scheme. He was the rifleman assigned to Baker squad—a reluctant rifleman, but a rifleman nonetheless. He was actually somewhat pleased over how things turned out.

51

Being hogtied to Tillie and Gambler wasn't exactly a delightful prognosis for the future, but he'd ended up with Farmer as a teammate and that was good.

"Now," Roul sought their attention once again, saying, "you all know which slot you're filling, so I believe it is time for you to establish a bit a amity with your new brides."

The remark spawned a roar of laughter, but Roul cautioned them, "It will seem that way. You will see. You are going to sleep together, dine together and even learn to breathe as one, and that's about as close to connubial bliss as any one of you are going to get for months to come." He paused, squinted to read his wristwatch, then remarked, "It's 2200 hours, gents. Customarily it would be time for lights out, but I think you've earned a special treat so, in lieu of a half hour's sleep, I've requisitioned some refreshments as a substitute." He glanced toward the new bivouac site and, seeing Corporal Schuster approaching with an armload of cardboard cartons, told them, "So, let's break out the beer."

Will Munday greeted Roul's gesture with a great deal of zeal. It was a fabulous finale; a social hour set in the middle of a jungle in, of all times, the middle of night. If nothing else positive had come out of the meeting, Will did decide to accept Captain Roul's credentials to command. Perhaps Roul had compromised himself to be one of the guys for only a short while, but his decision to drop his standards suggested to Will that he was both a compatible and a dexterious individual which, in his opinion, made him a great leader of men.

To a man the gang was dead on their feet, but they dived headlong into the frothy foam and mystically made forty-eight cans of beer vanish into thin air. A chorus of delightful moans and groans was reward enough for the captain, but he did give them some sound advice along with the beer ration. "Remember," he cautioned, "for those of you who savor the Devil's nectar, be advised that warm beer in the tropics can have devastating consequences. I will tolerate no sick call malingering as a result of overindulgence."

Will wasn't at all surprised when Farmer didn't consume his beer ration. But Will didn't refuse his offer of two additional cans, which he gave to Will, then one can each to Gambler and Tillie. The cardsharp and the hillbilly exchanged inquisitive glances over the disparity, but the farm boy just shrugged his shoulders and said, "Next time I'll give one of you two the extra can."

Will patted Farmer's shoulder; his way of saying thanks, and then asked Farmer, "D'ya feel like talking?"

Farmer begged off. "Naw," he said, "I'm plumb tuckered out. It seems like it's been a lifetime since sunup this morning. I need some shuteye." He pointed at the corporal, warning Will, "You'd best turn in yourself. That two-striper will be crowing like a rooster about dawn to get us out of the sack."

Will declined to join Farmer. This would give him one last opportunity to be alone. He needed to sort things out. Shoving his cans of beer into the side cargo pockets of his fatigues, he strayed away from the others, trying to locate a sanctuary along the forest's edge. There was, he recalled, a downed tree close by. It would make a perfect bench to stretch out on while he daydreamt. From the distance he could hear Captain Roul chiding Tillie, urging him to "share with all of us your recollections of the scrap in Salinas. You know, the place where you left several teeth on the barroom floor. Your service records indicate that it took something like four MP's to cart you off to the guardhouse. Is that right?"

Tillie needed little encouragement. He gleefully related the escapade, but Will mentally tuned his voice out and elected to retreat to Never-neverland. He sat down upon the log, lay backwards, and heaved a sigh of relief. Closing his eyes, he drifted back into one of his intellectual bogs; a comatose state of euphoria that only Will F. Munday's subconscious could sculpture on such short notice. Drifting back in time, his thoughts floated until he found himself seated at his classroom desk, turning his ear to better hear the professor's lecture while stealing a glimpse of MaryLou in the same instant.

"Pay close attention, students. Many of the answers to the questions in your semester exam will hinge on today's preachment," the learned mentor warned them.

But Will wasn't concerned over the finals. He knew he would get an "A," because he always did. Besides, there were other pressing problems to consider. There was MaryLou, for one thing, and the military draft notice he'd recently received in the mail for another thing. He elected to put the draft notice on the back burner in favor of concentrating his thoughts on MaryLou. The draft notice, being secondary in importance, lay on his writing desk in the dorm. MaryLou was here. As usual, one look at her and he was captivated. The ravishing young lady had caught his fancy the very first day of college, nearly three years before. She had the face of a goddess and ruby-red lips he wanted to taste. He dreamed of sliding his fingers through the golden locks of hair that framed her face, and of telling her about his undying love. He imagined what it would be like to caress her snuggly, holding her bountiful bosom firmly against his chest. He had agonized far too long. His eyes were glued on MaryLou's sumptuous rump that gracefully filled the seat just ahead of his own but across the aisle to his left. He cautiously stole a peek at her through the corner of his eye. The blood began to percolate throughout his body. He was enchanted by her well-rounded breasts; breasts which were blessed with supple nipples that stretched the cashmere sweater she wore—mountainous breasts that swelled, then ebbed, with each breath she inhaled, then exhaled. *It was the sweater,* he scolded his anxieties. *That infernal sweater. Why must she wear it? Oh, yes. She wears it to drive me insane.* What other garment could enhance her voluptuous bosom quite like a sweater? He was breathing heavily and was afraid someone would overhear him, perhaps MaryLou being the one. He tried to force himself to look away, but his eyes came upon her lean, contoured thighs; shapely thighs that suggestively spread the pleats of her plaid skit. Her sensual beauty was a virtual torment, an aphrodisiac that constantly held Will convict to his hungry desire to sample the elegance of her resplendent body.

Will's lust for MaryLou, that had dogged him almost three years, might've been fulfilled had he not been so shy. He realized it, too. He rebuked himself for lacking courage, for pussyfooting around the issue, for making excuses to himself that she might refuse his advances. Now, the *might factor* needed to be dealt with. Today was the day of reckoning. What would he say? How would he ask? When would he wrangle an opportunity to make his play? He realized his approach must be unique. "What're you doing Saturday evening?" would never do. Nor would, "Will you honor me...?" He wouldn't ask her to "accompany me." That was too juvenile, so junior highish, that he knew he'd never make the cut with a redundant come-on like those. But his draft notice came back to mind. Time was running out. He would be gone all too soon, so he had to pose the question today. YES! He would time his steps to reach the classroom doorway when the students were dismissed so that he could pass through the narrow opening abreast of MaryLou.

He glanced up to discover MaryLou staring at him. Flustered, he tried to look away but could not. She was gazing directly into his eyes, her face slightly tilted, her mascara-enhanced eyes insidiously blinking, and an alluring curl twisting the darling dimple that adorned her right cheek. *She knows,* he silently tortured himself. *She knows I lust for her. Why else would she tease me? She is teasing ... isn't she? We shall see. When the dismissal bell rings I will know the answer."*

But, as usual, Will's sudden surge of courage to stalk the object of his affections was scuttled by Dame Fate. From out of the darkness Corporal Schuster's voice echoed across the dell, snapping Will back to camp. "MUNDAY! BARRENTOS! Front and center. Let's go. Move it, move it. You drew first watch."

Will begrudgingly jumped to his feet, agonizing over the aches and pains that the strenuous stress of first day's training syndrome had spawned. He didn't recall drinking his beer, but it was gone. He moseyed across the clearing to where Schuster was waiting near the main tent. Barrentos came into view just a moment later, showing about as much enthusiasm as Will. Will had been looking forward to getting a good night's sleep. It was not to be. Things were running par for the course; guard duty pulling the first watch of the first night.

"LISTEN UP!" Schuster barked. "Post number one is the east perimeter," he explained, pointing to the east, "and post number two is along the west perimeter. Both posts run from the beach to the head of this draw, where you will meet while making each round. Tours of duty will be two hours. You guys really got a break. You'll be relieved at 2400 hours so, well let's see," he said, pausing to calculate the remaining time they faced, "it's about 2230 hours, so you only have to stay on the job for an hour and a half. Be reminded that staying alert is a priority. Although this sector has been secured and for all practical purposes is a safe haven, a guy never knows when Tojo's fanatics might sneak up on him."

Will offered Barrentos his choice of posts, but the Mexican didn't really care which one he trod. "Awe ... Señor Munday, you choose zee post you like. Barrentos ... well, he take, oh what'chu say in Inglés, zee pot lucky."

Schuster chuckled, explaining to Barrentos, "You're warm. It's called pot luck. It means to take your chances."

"Oh, sí," Barrentos concurred, spreading his hands wide apart as if to silently inquire about Will's druthers.

"Okay. I'll take post number two, the west perimeter," Will informed them, suggesting to Barrentos, "Keep your ears and eyes open. I just came from over there, where I was resting on that downed tree drinking my beer and ... well, I thought I heard someone moving about in the bush." Actually, the threat was a heap of horse hockey. He'd heard nothing, but he just wanted to add a taste of mystique to the assignment to see how Barrentos would respond.

Barrentos' response surprised him. "Oh, sí, Señor Munday he pull Juan's leg, huh? But, Señor Munday should be prudente, too. Prudente eez Español. It means to take care, Señor Munday," he explained.

"Oh, sí, señor," Will responded with a grin. His new amigo did have the final word though. "Barrentos he have ... a ... preocupacion for you. Juan think Señor Munday feel pur-r-r-ty bad if Juan come to harm. It eez you what put Juan on post number one after you hear strange noises in zee bosque, so I am at your mercy." He then laughed, a loud, raucous roar that could be heard throughout the campground, and walked away from Will to take his post.

Will's knowledge of Spanish was limited but he figured Barrentos was one up on him, because, although his linguistic talents with English left a lot to be desired, he could bluff his way through. Will could not do likewise with the Spanish language.

"Take your post, Munday," Schuster yelled.

"I'm going. I'm going," Munday replied as he faded from the corporal's view into the thicket of trees along the camp's west perimeter.

"HALT! WHO GOES THERE?" Will was challenged by an unexpected voice. He had forgotten that the posts were already manned by Navy personnel.

"It's Private Munday. I'm your relief man," Will responded to the challenge.

"Well, it's about time," the landlocked sailor complained as Will approached. "I didn't join the Navy to walk guard on dry land."

"Oh, it's you," Will uttered when he discovered the man he was releiving was the mess steward he'd tangled with during evening mess.

"Yeah. It's me," the sailor replied, inquiring of Will, "How's your bunghole? Did that fruit coctail loosen up your bowels yet?" He laughed.

Will didn't see the humor. "No," he replied sarcastically. "Is everything quiet?"

"Nothing to pass on. It's very quiet," the guy replied as he darted away toward the beach, leaving Will alone in the awesome stillness of the nighttime jungle—a quietude that raised the tiny hairs on the nape of his neck. The only distinct sound he recognized was an occasional chaffing of the palm fronds whenever a breeze wafted through the spooky forest.

Now, Will was faced with a dilemma he'd neither anticipated nor experienced prior to then. His obstinate status of being a reclusive loner began to haunt him. He would've preferred to have some company on his lonely assignment. While it was true that Barrentos was but a hundred, maybe two hundred yards away, that was little consolation. The reality of his assignment began to gnaw on his mind; he being a lone sentry, responsible for the lives of his newfound comrades was, in reality, his first encounter with the throes of war. A lot could happen to him while his friends slumbered in the squad tents. He was but one of two barriers between them and the enemy. If, by chance, there were a few Japanese stragglers in the vicinity, Will realized he was no match for them; Imperial Japanese, seasoned combat veterans who knew the whys and the wherefores of killing their fellow man. Could they be, he wondered, out there right now sizing him up? Could they be biding their time, waiting for the opportune moment to pounce upon him with a samurai sword? Would they whack off his head? Or hold him by force and slice off his penis, as he'd been told they sometimes did to prisoners? "God forbid," he muttered to himself, gulping to catch his breath. An inner vision of his head rolling between the trees like a bowling ball terrified him. But even more appalling was the apparition of losing his pecker; a piece of his anatomy that up until then had been little more than a water spout, and not a sex organ. He decided to purge the aggravations from mind and to dwell on something less agonizing, but Corporal Hackmore, the by-the-book non-com at the replacement depot, recaptured his mind. Hackmore had insisted there were no Japs within miles of the depot. Of course, Will was no longer at the depot. He'd been transported some distance by sea to this spooky spot, which in reality could be beyond Hackmore's estimated range for contact with the enemy. And Schuster had touched on the possibility, too. Was, as Schuster had warned, one of Tojo's fanatics lying in wait? That possibility was, Will admitted, *the fly in the ointment. Edmundson is right, as usual. There is always a fly in the ointment.* One or the other of his corporals had to be wrong with their diagnosis of his current status. That was the fly in the ointment. It was a toss-up. Fifty-fifty odds, either way. He opted to go with Hackmore's assessment and put his wandering imagination to rest. Captain Roul had even mentioned that this portion of the island was secured. Banking on their judgment, he muttered, "Not to worry, Munday. Keep a cool head."

Whistling a soft melody, in a pretense of not being afraid, he moseyed up the edge of the draw toward the spot he and Barrentos were instructed to meet during each round of their posts. His feet felt as though they weighed a ton. Each and every step was a agonizing effort. He yawned. He was suddenly very sleepy. The events of his first day with Stopwatch had taken their toll. His toe snagged on a tree root that snaked a trail above the ground, causing him to stumble, then to fall down onto his knees. He clutched both fists around the stock of his rifle and pulled down on the butt plate, jamming it into the dirt to break his fall. The maneuver was almost automatic. He'd been taught to hit the ground in such a fashion back in basic training. It worked like a charm. When he finally did manage to clamber back onto his knees, he spotted a downed tree just a few yards' distance. It was an invitation to screw off for a spell. He needed to slow down his metabolism and catch his breath. It was an inviting spot to rest a moment while he surveyed any injuries he might've suffered when he tripped and fell. Will didn't bother to stand up. He just crawled on his hands and knees to reach the log and then pulled his rump onto its bark-covered shell and heaved a big sigh of relief. As best he could determine there were no injuries. He felt no pangs of pain, excepting those he already had prior to the fall. But sitting down for a moment was a welcomed respite in routine. Will did need a pause to rest. He listened. He heard nothing. He swiveled his head back and forth, surveying the area that surrounded him. He saw nothing except for the trees. He had to admit he'd been letting his imagination run away with his good judgment. Pulling his rifle barrel up, he placed a hand atop of the muzzle and leaned his chin against the clenched fist. He was utterly exhausted, though, and decided he'd best get moving, lest he doze off to sleep. His brief pause to rest made matters worse; it spawned a terminal case of lethargic yawns. This would never do. Falling asleep on guard was tantamount to treason. He recalled how he'd once drifted off while on sentry duty during basic training and of how he slept for more than two hours before awaking to discover his post was being manned by another soldier who obviously hadn't spotted him snoozing in the bushes next to the latrine. He figured at the time he was probably in a world of hurt for failure to properly turn his post over to the new sentry with the routine change of the guard. He never even knew when they came. Surely he was missed. Had no one bothered to look for him? He had no other options than to sneak away and return to his quarters in the guard house. When he entered the room no one even took notice, so he just moseyed over to the rifle rack, placed his weapon in the proper slot, and went to bed. He spent a fretful night wondering what dawn would bring. Would he be dressed down in front of the entire unit? Would they court-martial him? But morning dawned and nothing was said about his unscheduled nap while on post. Relieved from his tour of guard duty, he returned to his unit and the matter of his dereliction of duty was never addressed. But, he reasoned, that was stateside. This was in a combat area. The two locations were hardly parallels. Under the terms of the Articles of War, as he recalled them, a man could be stood up in front of a firing squad for such a careless act. That would never do, either. But a short rest could hurt nothing, he decided, and he let his thoughts drift back to the home front; to the soda fountain in the drugstore near the campus where he toiled his tush off to pick up a buck or two to help pay his college expenses. It was a pleasant remembrance. He could almost hear the faint sound of a jukebox wailing, the noisy duos and trios of students who frequented the place, chattering like chipmunks and the hedonistic coeds squealing like star-struck children every time one of the Goth-like jocks came through the front door of the place. Oh, how well he remembered the soda fountain. It was an unforgettable place, because he landed the job his first week as a freshman at the school, and it was where he'd first laid eyes on MaryLou. Deep in meditation, he sauntered back in time to the day when she waltzed into the room, flanked by several of her less attractive sorority sisters, and swung her tantalizing torso upon a counter stool and asked Will to, "Make me a scrumptious double chocolate soda, will you, honey." She caused quite a commotion. A half-dozen guys tried to put the make on her, but she fended them off with crude insults. She also transformed Will into a bumbling boob. He was all thumbs, as he recalled the encounter. It was next to impossible to take his eyes off of her and pay attention to the chore of dipping a double chocolate soda. He'd dropped the freezer lid on the fingers of one hand, pulled them free, trying to pretend it didn't hurt, then spilled the prepared soda onto the floor. Somehow, as he remembered it, he did finally manage to create a dessert delight that pleased the flaxen-haired princess who had captured his heart. The golden tresses of hair framed the face of a goddess. One of the long bangs hung pretentiously down across her right eye. She brushed it aside, then winked the unveiled eye at Will, and said, "Thanks, honey. Super stuff!"

A gust of wind suddenly rattled the palm trees overhead, shaking Will back to the present time. He wasn't sure of how long he'd day-dreamt but figured it would be pushing his luck to screw old Shep any longer. He took to his feet, slung his rifle over his shoulder, and headed up the draw, hoping to meet up with Barrentos. Seeing that the Mexican had beaten him to the rendezvous spot, he was relieved, but he hoped he hadn't kept him waiting while he was in reverie.

"What's happening?" Will asked on his approach.

"Oh, nothing, Señor Munday. She's ... oh, what'chu say, not a bo-peep," Barrentos replied in his best, but still broken, English.

"You mean 'not a peep,'" Will corrected him. "Little Bo Peep lost her sheep."

"Awe, chingawa," Barrentos exclaimed. "Thees Inglés, she's pu-u-urty hard to comprender, huh?"

"You'll get the hang of it. You do pretty good," Will complimented him, figuring it must be quite difficult for a transplanted alien to master another language without any tutoring. "Have you been waiting long? I got hung up for spell," Will inquired, not bothering to explain the reason for his delay.

"No, señor. Un momento. One minute in Inglès, right?" Barrentos replied, waving a single finger at Will. He was obviously quite proud over making a proper translation.

"Right. One minute. Very good. I told you. You'll get the hang of it," Will reassured him. Will had, for some unexplained reason, taken a shine to this Latin-American import. He momentarily recalled the amusing *rat-a-tat-a-tat* Barrentos uttered to illustrate his familiarity of his weapon during the earlier tell-all briefing.

"Well, it's time to go. We'd best make another round," Will suggested, and the two parted company, heading down opposite sides of the draw. That brief interlude of cordial camaraderie did force Will to focus his thoughts around a sudden realization that he was, whether he liked it or not, now dependent on others. It rekindled his opinion about his long-standing tradition of living the role of a loner. College? Perhaps it was okay! Basic training? Maybe there, too! But over here, after getting a wee taste of solitary confinement in the wilds of the tropics, he began to reshuffle his thinking about making an attitude adjustment. He almost envied Barrentos, whose only real hangup was avenging his brother's death. At least Barrentos could justify his part in the war with a vendetta. But he suspected that, for the most part, all of the others, including himself, were just here because Dame Fate put them here instead of someplace else.

He doubled back along the trail he had taken to the head of the draw, finally coming to the tree root and downed tree he'd used as a perch a short time earlier. Another brief breather seemed in order. Who would know? No one. Barrentos was across the way. He couldn't see Will. Everyone else was fast asleep. "Yeah. It's break time," he mumbled and crapped out on the log once again. And as he'd done last time, he pulled the business end of his weapon up into the air, placed his fist atop of the muzzle, and propped his chin on his fist. It was but a matter of seconds before his thoughts began to wander again, but this time back to his home, not the soda fountain or the college classroom. He was sitting on the couch of his living room, reliving a run-in with his father—a towering man whose barrel chest strained the straps of his bibbed overalls. The old man thrust his long, sinewy arm forward, shaking a clenched fist in Will's face, shouting at the top of his lungs, "G'won, bookworm. Git out on your own and take your highfalutin ideas with you. Do them there books tell you how to earn money? Hardly! My sixth grade schoolin' was good enough to make a home for you and maw. You'll come crawling back, bright boy, if'n you get hungry enough," Will's dad was furious with him. A network of deeply furrowed creases interlaced his brow, accentuating his abysmally sunken, cruel-set eyes. That was Will's memory of his dad; a tyrant, whose spirit had been broken by the devastating depression that wiped out his entire savings and left him without a job and sent him scurrying to hustle daywork, wherever, whenever to keep food on the table. The economic bust transformed him into a boozer, who found solace in a bottle of cheap hooch. "What was it," Will asked himself, "that the captain called our beer ration? Oh, yes! The devil's nectar. An appropriate title," he agreed, for the joyless juice that had raised havoc with Will's life after his dad became bosom buddies with a bottle.

Will had no trouble dealing with the crapulent image of his father. The several thousand miles that separated them just made it easier to digest. The memories of his last day at home were etched in his mind, though. He could still see his mother standing on the rickety, old front porch the day he packed up his personal belongings and left. The tears that streamed down her cheeks weren't that easily forgotten. The sound of the broken screen door slamming against the sill when he walked out still echoed in his memory. His mother's pleading voice beseeching him to write letters and to write often so she would know he was okay. Her pleas continued to haunt him. Will wondered what it was that kept a woman shackled to such a brute. It was beyond his comprehension, but his mother did stay with this man whose cold, cold heart had frosted their relationship many years before. They slept in separate bedrooms. They never embraced or kissed one another. Will looked upon his memories as nothing more than a blackboard that recorded all of his good deeds as well as his misdeeds. It could never be scrubbed clean, only erased. The unforgettable images of his unhappy childhood clung to the ebony slate to re-emerge time and time again; to follow him, he feared, all the days of his life.

Will might've daydreamt until his relief man arrived to assume the post had not an arm reached around his neck from behind, then locked its elbow snuggly against Will's throat, slowly cutting off the flow of air to his lungs. He fought to break loose, trying desperately to take his feet and to twist free of the interloper, but his head began to spin like a toy top. A harsh voice whispered into his ear, "If I was Tojo ... you'd be dead." No longer able to sustain consciousness due to a lack of oxygen, Will passed out, falling into a limp heap of flesh and bones onto the ground.

He finally regained his wits. He had no idea of how long he'd been out cold. He was, in fact, just happy to be alive. Still numb, he raised a hand to rub his neck, trying to gather his thoughts and, finally realizing what had actually happened, quickly took to his feet and eyeballed the area immediately surrounding him. He saw nothing; nothing except his own rifle leaning against the tree trunk that had been his perch. He was flabbergasted. "What the hell?" he barked. If a Jap had assaulted him from behind, why had he left Will's weapon? *So, I let down my guard the first fucking night. I was careless. But it was not the enemy who snuck up on me. If it were, I'd be dead. It was someone playing games; war games. Was it Schuster? Baker? Captain Roul, perhaps, teaching me a lesson?* He considered calling for the corporal of the guard but changed his mind. How could he explain such an incident without admitting his disregard for the general orders pertaining to walking a post; even the first order which stated, "To walk my post in a military manner, keeping always on the alert...?" To tell anyone would be to

61

betray himself. If nothing came of the affair with the morning formation it might just be another lucky break for Will or a tacky trick to haunt him. He'd have to wait it out. It was Camp Hood all over again. He'd have to live with it until such a time as someone fessed up.

Midnight did finally arrive and none too soon for Will F. Munday. He made no mention of the attack to O'Hare, who relieved him, nor to Schuster, who escorted the relief guards to their posts. It was quite dark in the shade of the grove, but Will did think he could detect a smug expression of self-satisfaction glowing on the corporal's face. He couldn't help but wonder if Schuster was laughing on the inside over the cunning deception. Then again, he reasoned, it might not be Schuster. There were just too many possibilities to consider. Will was dead tired and ready to drop in his tracks.

He returned to his tent, crawled into his bunk and tried to catch some Z's, but sleep kept its distance until far into the night. Again and again he heard the caveat whispered in his ear, "If I was Tojo ... you'd be dead." Sheer exhaustion finally dictated that he sleep.

Chapter Four

A primer coating of dew glistened like Christmas tinsel on the drooping flora when the next day dawned. The congruous sounds of calling birds, already winging aloft on their search for food, was a pleasant summons to reveille. Will kicked aside the flimsy mosquito netting that clung to his body and rolled feet first off of his cot. Arms outstretched, he expelled a clamorous moan that awoke everyone in the tent. In fact, he scared Farmer half to death. The farm boy vaulted to his feet, shouting, "HUH? WHAT? What's going on, anyhow?"

Corporal Schuster was up and about, just like Farmer had predicted he'd be, and was making the rounds, slapping canvas with an opened hand each time he darted past one of the three tents. "OKAY! OKAY!" he screamed to arouse them. "Up and at 'em. C'mon. Move it, move it. Drop your cocks and grab your socks," Schuster bellowed.

Will would much have preferred a bugler over Schuster's outlandish call to formation. He was, in fact, glad he'd been awakened by nature's embrace of tranquil tones before the corporal screwed up his day with military jargon. Corporal Schuster's style was actually, in Will's way of reasoning, a contradiction to military protocol anyway. *Where,* he wondered, *are the bugles?* Historically, an army was awakened by bugles. He'd have bet a month's pay there wasn't a bugle anywhere on the island. Only yesterday, did Roul not outline the ingredients for success in military campaigns? Didn't he say something about "teamwork, discipline, secrecy, and timing" being the primary factors? He hadn't mentioned bugles. "Oh, well," Will mumbled, purging the thought from mind. Bugles weren't important. They were apparently a tradition that gave way to progress. That conclusion satisfied his curiosity, which in turn calmed his anxieties, so Will bounded from the tent into the out-of-doors, Farmer just a step or two behind him.

Farmer was finally coming to life after his rude awakening. He groaned, wriggled his lanky torso into the shape of a corkscrew, stretched his arms in a wide arc, and informed Will, "A guy's gotta wake up them lazy muscles." He then planted his fists on his hips and began to gyrate his body like a belly dancer in a harem, explaining he was doing the *funky pretzel;* a routine that caught everyone's fancy, along with a few catcalls from his less than enthusiastic fans who weren't impressed.

"Funky pretzel?" Will barked in disbelief. "What the hell is the funky pretzel?"

"What I'm a'doing," Farmer replied with his big countrified grin. "I call it the *funky pretzel* and I do it every morning. I gotta do the *funky pretzel* to get awake."

"Still tired?" Will asked.

"It was a fast night," Farmer replied, continuing to waltz around on the company street.

"Well, I'll bet you got more sleep than I," Will complained.

"Mighta got more but t'waren't nary enough." Farmer countered.

"Well, you didn't have to stumble around in the damned jungle until the middle of night, like I did," Will argued. He was tempted to relate his encounter with the unidentified voice of a stalker who'd snuck up on him, but he ditched the idea and kept his lips zipped. He figured that, if anyone in this command was the guilty party, they'd get around to cutting him a new rectum before long, probably during the roll call formation.

It was a beautiful morning, this being Will's first opportunity to take notice of the entire spectrum of the sprawling landscape that engulfed the camp ground. The jungle, while still a menace, didn't seem half as intimidating in daylight as it did after dark. It sort of reminded him of a huge oil painting he'd once seen when he was a kid; an endless landscape of growth in the midst of a rain forest. This jungle and that jungle were definitely look-alikes.

"Nice morning, huh?" Farmer told to Will. "Sun's a'shining and the birds are singing a happy song. I don't think it's apt to rain today, either."

The forecast touched one of Will's nerves. He loved the *no rain* part of Farmer's prediction. "Do you give guarantees with your weather forecasts?" Will asked.

"Shore e'nuf."

"But you do know it rains most every day," Will reminded him.

"Maybe so," Farmer admitted, but he stuck to his guns. "I'm a'telling you it won't rain a drop today," he insisted.

"You're a surprise package. The next thing you're going to be boasting about it that the Army also sent you to meteorology classes, too," Will chided him.

"Oh, no. Don't need no classes for this. Look at that sunrise. D'ya see a red ring around the sun?" Farmer asked.

Will glanced at the sun, then turned his head away and rubbed his eyes, confirming Farmer's observation, "No, I don't. What's a red sunrise got to do with the high price of rice in China?"

"There you go again, Will, talking with riddles. It ain't got nuthin' to do with China or with rice. It's got to do with my mama. She always says if'n there's a red ring in the morning it's a sailor's warning, but if'n it's a red ring at night that means it's a sailor's delight."

"SO?"

"Wal, don'cha see? No red ring. It means them sailors don't hav'ta fret about stormy weather today and I'll betcha there'll be a big red ring around the sun when it sets tonight, too," Farmer declared.

Gambler and Tillie had been eavesdropping on Farmer's weather projection. The wheeler-dealer never passed up an opportunity to bet on something as iffy as a weather forecast. He shouted to Farmer, "Hey,! What's this about no rain today?"

"That's right. No rain," Farmer assured him.

"Farm boy, you're as full of shit as a Christmas goose. Did anyone ever tell you that? You damned farmers and your stupid almanacs. I hear that you dumb clodhoppers actually plant potatoes by phases of the moon. Is that right?" Gambler goaded him.

"Yup. That's a fact. We do," Farmer admitted.

"Well, I'll just tell you what I'm going to do for you, hayshaker. I'll give you two to one odds that it does rain today. That's right, my sawbuck against your fin," Gambler offered to warger.

Farmer hesitated a moment. Will didn't figure Farmer to be a betting sort of individual, but he seemed quite sure that the absence of a red ring around the rising sun was a sure thing. "Wal, I ain't normally a man to wager on things," he hedged, stalling for time to make up his mind, then finally said, "but I reckon I'll just see that bet."

"You've got it, sodbuster," Gambler agreed, asking Farmer, "Who's going to hold the stakes?"

"Hold the stakes?" Farmer protested. "Why does someone hav'ta hold the stakes? Don't you trust me?"

"Yeah," Gambler replied. He was baffled over the inquiry because it tended to question his honesty. "I trust you but it's customary for a third party to hold the stakes, that's all."

Farmer would have none of that. "Wal, let me ask you … if'n you do lose you do plan to pay-up, don'cha?" Farmer challenged him.

"Are you shitting me? HELL YES! Gambler always pays up. What d'ya think I am, a goddamned deadbeat?" Gambler shouted, informing Farmer, "I never welch on a bet." He was miffed.

"Wal, farmers always pay their obligations, too, so I don't think we need anyone to hold any stakes," Farmer insisted. "You should be forewarned that my mama's never wrong about the weather. I ain't too worried about owing you, just as long as you've got a ten-spot to pay up with tonight when we're sitting here high and dry."

"Hrumph," Gambler grumped, then walked away. Farmer had made his point. Each man held his own money.

Will laughed over the dispute. In fact, he enjoyed seeing Farmer pin Gambler's ears back. "Hey, you kind of got his dander up a little, didn't you?" he flattered Farmer.

"Wal, I get sorta mad when someone doubts my honesty, Will," Farmer explained.

Will grabbed Farmer's forearm and spun him around so he might look the country boy squarely in the eyes. "What did you just call me?" he asked.

"Wal, I guess I called you Will. Will is your name, ain't it?" Farmer asked.

"Yeah. Sure. It's my name, all right. Heck, I haven't heard my first name spoken since the day I donned these fatigues," he explained himself, claiming he was getting sick of "Munday, go here; Munday, go there; Munday, listen up. A guy loses his identity when he's drafted, you know?"

"Yeah, it sorta feels that way sometimes," Farmer agreed, asking Will if it would be acceptable for him to use Will's given name instead of his surname.

"Are you kidding? Sure it's okay. In fact, it might help me to recapture my ego," Will encouraged him. "I'm sick of being Munday or just plain old 37756079, the damned number they assigned me when I took the oath."

Schuster was nervously prancing back and forth, constantly checking the time of day on his wristwatch, then biting everyone in the ass, reminding them, "Chow's in fifteen minutes." Will figured Schuster was also a victim of the first-day jitters. Nervous tension always accompanied the upheaval of change, and each time a soldier drew a new duty station there were changes galore to deal with; new faces, new locale, new procedures, new officers, new latrines. "Ugh," Will grunted, dreading all of the changes they were facing.

Gambler also took notice of the corporal's apprehensive disposition. He tapped Will on the shoulder and remarked, "He's about as nervous as a whore in church, ain't he?"

"He's got a lot on his mind, I imagine," Will took the corporal's side, which was a twist in comportment.

Farmer, however, disapproved of Gambler's remark. He tossed the cartridge belt he'd been fondling with his hands inside of the tent and spun about on his toe, advising the cardsharp, "You just can't say nuthin' without being disrespectful of the church and God, can you?"

Gambler glared at Farmer, asking, "Do you have a problem with that?"

"Yep! I shore do! It's shameful the way you fault everything. Can't you talk without swearing and tarnishing images that other folks hold sacred?" Farmer asked, quickly adding, "And I don't particularly like someone staring at me like you are, either."

"What did you say, sharecropper?" Gambler fired back.

"I said I don't like to be stared at. Turn your evil eye another direction. Y'know, my mama always sez—" Farmer tried to explain, but he was cut short by Gambler's retort.

"FUCK YOUR MAMA," Gambler shouted.

Gambler would've been better off had he omitted the farm boy's mother from his reply. It appeared Will's suspicions over Farmer being devoted to his mother were right on target. Farmer was aghast. He just stood there for a moment trying to digest the insult, then offered Gambler an opportunity to square things. "WHAT? What did you say?" he inquired.

"I said 'fuck your mother,'" he repeated, turning aside and asking Tillie, "Did you hear what I said? Didn't I say 'fuck your mother'? Tell him, Tillie, what I said. The hayseed has a hearing problem, I guess. Yeah. I said, 'fuck your mother.' And while you're at it, fuck that Farmer's Almanac and those phony weather forecasts, too."

Tillie wasn't about to get himself caught in the middle of this dispute. Being a country boy himself, he understood where Farmer was coming from, so he tried to sidestep Gambler's request, suggesting to him, "Why don'cha just forget it, Gambler?"

Momentarily turning his attention away from Farmer was Gambler's second mistake, the first one being the use of the word *fuck* in conjunction with the word *mother* when he shot off his mouth. It was one thing to damn the almanac, or the weather forecasts, but he'd gone too far down the river of no return when he said "fuck your mama."

What ensued was something akin to a prairie fire fanned by a high wind whipping across the plains. Farmer leaped into the air and landed squarely on top of Gambler, knocking him to the ground, and then straddled him, one leg to each side, grabbed his head by both ears, and began to pound his skull on the hard-packed surface of the soil just in front of their tent. Will could plainly hear the *thud* each time Gambler's head struck the ground, and also the "ughs" and "ouches" and finally, "Uncle. I said uncle," when Gambler tried to cede to save his hide.

By that time several of the guys were trying to pry Farmer loose from Gambler, lest he kill the man in his fit of anger. That was when Schuster again arrived on the scene. "What the hell's going on?" he shouted as he advanced to the spot of the altercation. Of course, the guys already had both men on their feet and were brushing the dust off of their clothing when the corporal joined them. "I asked what's going on here?" he repeated.

"Awe, nothing much," Farmer replied. He was reaching out with a hand to wipe some blood off of Gambler's lip as he spoke.

"Okay," Schuster gave it another try. "You guys are fighting like a couple of bantam roosters and you say nothing's happened. D'ya wanta try again? What's the fight over?"

"What fight?" Gambler asked, still shaking his head to clear the cobwebs out of his cranium.

"You're trying to tell me this wasn't a fight. Right?" Schuster demanded to know.

"Yup," Farmer endorsed Gambler's denial. "'Twarn't no fight. You see here, Corporal, I was just showing him how I won the blue ribbon at the country fair in the hog wrestling contest back home. I guess I kinda got carried away."

"Yeah, that's how it was," Gambler chimed in.

Schuster shook his head from side to side, propped his elbows out to the side, poked his clenched fists onto his hips, and told the pair, "Un-huh. Hog wrestling, huh? I'd like to hear some more about this hog wrestling contest, but it's chow time, so I'll pretend I believe you, which makes me a bigger liar than either one of you jurblowfs." He glanced around at those who'd observed the altercation, then barked, "The show's over. Okay! Fall in. Chow time."

Once again the military code of ethics prevailed. The fight cleared the air between the farm boy and the big-city hustler and no one was held accountable. No one really believed that the drubbing Gambler had suffered at Farmer's hands would change Gambler's ways. He was the type of man who would forget the scrap as soon as the first card was dealt in the next poker game. Whether or not Farmer would carry a grudge, Will could only guess. He hoped for everyone's sake that he wouldn't. Inter-unit disagreements weren't all that rare, but then again, Will had never seen one stem from compelling motives such as religion and motherhood.

They all hustled to get into formation so Schuster could call the roll, which in Will's opinion was a farce when he considered that the corporal could see everyone was there without going through the routine, and he headed them down the draw toward the beach, reminding them while they marched, "This is the Army. It's not the Golden Glove tournament."

Marching along in a column of twos, Will tried to justify the reasons for Schuster's strict compliance with military protocol. It seemed to him that he could simply have said, "Chow's ready. Head for the beach," and they'd manage to meet the deadline for chow without an assist from the ranking man present. It so resembled a full dress parade, he thought, marching to breakfast like schoolchildren. "Surely," he told Farmer, who'd positioned himself in the ranks so as to be by Will's side when the formation moved out, "the birds and the beasts of the jungle must be thoroughly puzzled by just watching us. Have you ever thought about how dumb we must appear to them; God's chosen mammal trampling across their domain, killing one another, obliterating their ecological garden, and hup-twoing like a bunch of juveniles through the coppice?"

"Naw," Farmer confessed. He hadn't given it any thought. The notion wouldn't have occurred to him, because he was a rational granger at heart who wasn't plagued by hangups the likes of which continually hamstrung his new friend, Will.

But Will had given Farmer a good deal of thought. He was, he decided, a Pandora's box of sorts. He'd never thought of Farmer as being a spunky person, so he was shocked when Gambler provoked him into assuming the aggressor's role. Will had hoped that Farmer's religious hangups would set him apart from the other guys. Farmer was an exception; a breath of fresh air that Will needed. He was pious, a rarity in the ranks, and his overzealous devotion to his mother was almost unparalleled. Will sort of figured that Farmer's dedication to his mom was second only to his reverence to the church. In fact, he wasn't at all sure, after seeing Farmer whip the tar our of Gambler, that, perhaps, his mom came ahead of the church in the standings. Farmer was becoming a rock of stability that Will could hang on to if the tides of ambivalence swept him too far out of the mainstream. He desperately needed that.

Another of Will's obsessions were the never-ending lines he had to stand in for everything he needed; to take a leak in the latrine, to get his chow in the mess hall, for medical aid when they reported for sick call, even payday, when they were paid with cash and had no place to spend it—except the floating crap games and poker parties. Here he was headed for another line, so he didn't let any grass grow under his feet when Schuster dismissed them to eat. He darted across the beach to be first in line. Farmer ran a close second in the ration relay. But, as usual, breakfast was a big letdown. Will's appetite ebbed when he eye-balled the bill of fare and he grumbled,

"Scrambled, powdered eggs." He'd reached a point where he had to gag them down, lest he throw them up. He hated them. Holding his mess kit out over the big trays of food on the mess table, he glanced down into the big pan of eggs. He had not doubt they would be too runny, or too lumpy, or broiled so dry that they resembled a sponge more than food. The worst was when they had been cremated into laminated layers that could challenge a man's imagination. He paused, pulled his gear back, and asked Farmer, "Doesn't an egg deserve a better fate than this?" Nary moving a muscle to receive his portion of food while he was making up his mind, the mess attendant asked, "D'ya want some or don't you? You're holding up the line, wise guy, just like you held me up last night by taking your time to relieve me on post."

Will glanced once more at the flaxen-colored mound of eggs, trying to determine whether or not he could deceive his taste buds by persuading them that the gross pile of fixings was actually camouflaged eggs posing as food. He was hungry, though, so he opted to give it one more try. "Yeah. I'll take some. Do you have any hors d'oeuvres for a chaser?" he wondered aloud, his cute way of ragging the mess attendant. The pudgy mess steward grinned, a full-cheeked smirk, and piled the eggs to the brim of Will's mess gear. "I thought you'd never get around to asking, wise guy. Yeah. We've got hors d'oeuvres that you're going to love." He laced the entire pile of eggs with a topping of fruit cocktail, then curtly asked, "Does that suit Your Majesty?"

"Man, what a grouch. I was only funning you. Can't you take a joke?" Will asked.

"Nope. Never could take a joke. Now, you eat your meal all gone like a good little soldier boy. I gave you an extra serving of fruit cocktail ... er, I mean hors d'oeuvres ... on account'a the serving I gave you last night evidently didn't get the job of stifling you mouth done," he curtly informed Will.

Will pivoted on his toe and turned away, trying to find a suitable seat at one of the tables, mumbling to himself as he moseyed across the sand, "I know what these are. They're not scrambled eggs after all. They're a Japanese secret weapon."

Farmer wasted no time getting his ration of grub. He overtook Will just as he was seating himself and plunked down his own carcass across the table from Will. "Can I sit by you?" he asked.

"Sure. Sit. I'll guarantee you that your company will be a darned sight more appetizing than these god-awful, powdered scrambled eggs," Will told Farmer, inviting him to sit a spell.

"I know you city folks don't know sic'em about eggs, like your country cousins, but you're wrong about that pile of grub in your mess kit being

70

powdered scrambled eggs," Framer curtly informed Will.

"What d'ya mean, wrong?" Will bowed up.

"They ain't powdered scrambled eggs, Will," Farmer insisted.

"They sure as hell are," Will retorted.

"Nope. They ain't," Farmer stuck to his guns.

"Okay," Will appeased his friend, pausing to ingest a mouthful of the concoction he'd been served up by the vindictive mess steward. "Let's just say for the sake of argument that you're right and let it go at that." he patronized Farmer, figuring that would end the discussion.

It did not. "What d'ya mean let it go at that?" Farmer protested. "You're just afraid you're wrong, so you're tryin' to get off the hook by dropping the subject."

"I'm not admitting I'm wrong, but there's no point in arguing about it, because it isn't a life or death issue," Will again tried to defuse the disagreement.

"Okay, smarty pants," Farmer fired back. "Since you know so much about it, tell me how they're made."

"I don't know how they're made. I don't even care how they're made," Will countered.

"Wal, I do know how they're made. They takes these eggs and scrambles them, then cooks them, then dehydrates them to make powdered eggs," Farmer smugly explained the process. "So ... that being the case, they are scrambled powdered eggs."

"Big deal," Will fought back. "What's the diff? Scrambled powdered or powdered scrambled eggs are one and the same. It's all a matter of grammar. Fact is, I wonder if they are eggs at all. If you ask me, I think they are goo from a dead Chinaman's ear."

Farmer wasn't about to concede. "Wal, if'n they are, they'd be scrambled powdered goo from a dead Chinaman's ear," he ventured a guess.

"Okay. It's a draw. We're hopelessly deadlocked, Farmer. I suppose you do know more about eggs than I," Will tried to temper the fuss.

"Sure I do. I admit I don't have much book learnin' like you, but I know farmin'. I'll bet you don't even know where eggs come from, do you?"

"Sure I do. From chickens."

"Yeah? Wal, if'n you wanted a dozen eggs in one day, how many chickens would you need to own?" Farmer quizzed him.

"How would I know? One, maybe two. Why?"

Farmer broke out laughing, telling Will, "See? Who's the dummy now? It's just like I said. You don't know spit about chickens. You would need at least a dozen."

"A dozen?"

"Yup. How many eggs does a chicken lay each day?"

"I haven't the foggiest notion."

"One. One a day," Farmer laughed to taunt Will, holding up a single finger and waving it in Will's face.

Will, too, began to laugh. He'd just learned something from this yokel that he didn't already know. "One a day? Do you mean that when I went to the grocer back home and bought a dozen eggs it took twelve chickens an entire day to fill that little carton?" Will asked between snickers.

"Yup!"

"That's incredible!"

"Yup!"

"What d'ya mean, yup?"

"Wal ... I don't rightfully know what that incredi— Oh, what that word means," Farmer confessed.

"Well, Farmer, incredible means it's fantastic. Almost unbelievable. Kinda like you, my friend. You're incredible," Will flattered him to cool things off.

"Hey, you love birds," came a voice from the opposite end of the table row, "are you finally going to kiss and make up?"

"The captain said there'd be days like this," someone else opined. "He said we'd be living like married couples, but you two clowns make a strange-looking bridal party. Who's the hick and who's the chick?"

Will and Farmer tried to ignore the unsavory comments. The disagreement did, however, muddy the water as regarded Will's view of Farmer's character. He was, as things were turning out, a tad coyer than Will had anticipated. And his next gesture proved it. Farmer stood up, leaned across the table, paused a moment to catch everyone's attention, then planted a big kiss on Will's cheek and yelped, "Sorry, my dear."

Pandemonium broke loose. Every last one of the guys began to laugh, to shout and to whistle, one of them yelling, "Ain't you going to return that kiss, honey bunch?"

Unfortunately the entire stunt caught Will with a mouth full of morsels and, although he tried to stifle himself, he couldn't refrain from bursting out with a roar of laughter. In the process he sprayed his breakfast all over Farmer's uniform. In fact, Farmer was decorated from his neckline to his beltline with an unappetizing layer of unsavory food scraps that he began to brush away, shouting, "Now ... look and see what you did?"

Will darted around the table and began to brush off the orts from Farmer's jacket, apologizing over and over again, "I'm sorry. I'm sorry." Everyone else, many of whom had caused the disruption, just stood by laughing at them, not bothering to offer a hand.

Captain Roul and his non-coms had been observing the entire event from a distance. They offered no comment at the time, except for Schuster to shout out, "Chow's over. Everyone report back to the bivouac area. Police the company street. All I want to see, if I come looking, is assholes and elbows pointing upwards, and heads pointed down." The corporal did intentionally chart his course closeby to Will and Farmer, asking as he passed, "What's with you two guys? Every time I glance in your direction, one or the other of you is throwing something onto the other one; first it was dirt, now it's garbage."

Neither Will nor Farmer responded. They turned away and headed for the tent area. Will pondered his relationship with the farm boy while they strolled side by side. *Why*, he silently wondered, *does this guy have such a profound effect on me?* His fondness for the big, clumsy lug was growing with each passing incident. With all of his book learning, Will was unable to explain his emotional upheaval since meeting up with Farmer. It had to be, he guessed, something no one can explain, or he would've read about his affliction at some time or other. Will was being introduced to camaraderie with the living flesh.

Captain Roul, however, must've seen something that he liked about the Baker squad foursome. He remarked to Baker as they returned to the LCI, "Those kids in Baker squad are scrappers. If we can somehow channel that belligerence in the right direction, we might only need one squad to accomplish this mission." Baker agreed. Little did he realize how right he might end up being.

The baker's dozen had the site spic and span when Schuster arrived on the scene and gave it his stamp of approval. The time of day was 07:55. The corporal, much to everyone's surprise, was decked out in full combat regalia, standing at the head of his assembled formation, when Roul and Baker made their appearance. Roul eyeballed his wristwatch and at precisely 08:00 nodded his approval of what he'd seen. Pointing a finger toward the jungle west of camp, he instructed Baker to "Let's get things rolling, Sergeant."

Baker saluted Roul, pivoted on his toes, and announced, "The captain will have a word or two with you prior to embarking on our initial training exercise."

Roul put his men at rest in the ranks. His eyes twinkled like those of a child awaiting Saint Nick's arrival. It was obvious to Will that he was a man with a mission and that he was on the brink of performing that long-awaited task. His manner was almost devious. Will suspected that Roul knew a lot more about the upcoming mission than he'd let on, but was withholding certain facts that might not be very appealing to his new, untested commandos. "Gentlemen," Roul finally said in a compassionate tone of voice, "the Stopwatch is activated. It shall continue to tick off the minutes until we have done our duty. We must prepare ourselves for that final moment—the very moment that the hands on Stopwatch finally come to rest on zero hour. It will be then, gents, that you will understand the purpose of this rigorous training schedule you are about to embark on."

A chill raced up Will's spine. He thought he detected a tone of urgency in Roul's announcement. The chill was discomfiting; an almost scary shiver that upset Will. This training cycle, as things were turning out, was but a temporary reprieve from combat. What they were destined to do might, in the end, be much worse than if he had been assigned to any ordinary rifle company. The fact that GHQ was touted as the culprit by hand-picking this particular group of men was equally as mysterious as the final objective. This had to be, Will finally decided, something really big.

"OKAY," Roul shouted and turning to face Sergeant Baker advised him it was time to "Move 'em out."

Baker called them to attention, gave the command, "Ri-i-i-i-ght, face," and took the point of the column himself as the guide-on. Baker headed them directly into the forest, allowing the formation to proceed at a *route step* pace, which allowed them to talk in the ranks while they hiked. And, as was his custom, Will soon fell captive to his imagination, a practice that invariably victimized him on the long trails of forced marches. Roul was first to invade his mind; the captain's way with words, his flair for dramatics. He was a far cry from any commanding officer Will had served under since entering the Army. Somehow, even though Will realized that he and Roul were hardly peers, he felt that they were at least competitors. They were both intellectuals, Roul being the first officer of that caliber Will had encountered. It was a rivalry Will needed. He began to look forward to matching wits with the man in charge. The ground rules, of course, gave Roul the edge, because Will would have to consider the captain's rank when push came to shove.

Baker awoke Will from his trance, shouting, "Let's double-time it. C'mon! Take it and follow me, or eat my dust."

Baker couldn't lay claim to being the creator of "take it and follow me" because that was an old infantry refrain, but his addition of "or eat my dust" was a new twist. And he evidently meant exactly what he'd said, because he quickly outdistanced his column of men and vanished over a ridge, into a wall of trees. Sergeant Baker, Will thought, was a different sort of shoe than he had broken in prior to now. This shoe was going to take some getting used to, because Baker was pinching Will's toes at the moment. And the worst was yet to come, although Will had no way of knowing what lay ahead.

His two-week wait at the replacement depot, which was preceded by a twenty-eight-day lackluster voyage from underneath the Golden Gate Bridge, had softened his once resilient body considerably more than he had thought. In just the short time of a few weeks the muscles he'd labored to build at Camp Hood had already regressed to flab and his body, in general, was protesting this abuse. The surprising thing was, though, that Roul's game plan at the present time appeared to be a Siamese twin to the schedule in basic training; more running, more jumping, more climbing, more crawling. He had waltzed through the final two weeks of training at Hood, which was dubbed "Killer's Kollege," because he was physically conditioned to the task. The only difference Will could see that separated basic training from this jaunt was geographical. One was stateside, the other in New Guinea. It was, he thought, like trying to play checkers on a chess board. That was, in Will's opinion, what made the Army a contemptible existence. No matter where he went, everything was still the same. Go, go, go, go. Go to nowhere in particular, just go, go, go. They were offered no breaks in the grueling pace, and the only enlisted men in Roul's command who weren't a total wipe-out at noon time were Baker, Schuster and Gooch. The sergeant led them back into camp, their asses dragging the ground when they stood the final formation of the morning. Baker wasn't overly kind to them, either. "You're a pathetic bunch of jurblowfs. I'd call it appallingly out of shape, to begin with, and you don't have any heart, which makes matters worse. But we're going to do something about that in the way of additional morning calisthenics to firm up your muscles. We're going to improve your heart condition, too. Do you think this morning was a tough route?" He paused, chuckled to himself, but loud enough so that each and every man in the formation could hear him. "I wasn't on Bataan when it fell to the Japs, so I'm basing this on hearsay," he added, "but I suspect those men who endured that infamous death march had it easy compared to what you've got lying in store for you if you don't shape up."

Captain Roul agreed with Baker's observation. He suggested that they postpone the regularly scheduled forced march that afternoon in lieu of some classroom training.

Gooch, the nisei scout, obviously not fatigued when Schuster dismissed the formation for chow, flaunted his exhilarated stamina in front of his bedraggled comrades by dancing a ritualistic two-step as he shed his pack and tossed it into his tent. Will envied the midget marauder's stamina. He was a challenge to catch up to and overtake in days ahead. Will decided then

75

and there that he would keep pace with Gooch come hell or high water.

The hour-long break for noon chow didn't restore anyone's get-up-and-go. Will, as one of the twelve dissenters, was pleased that they were to have some classroom training instead of another jaunt through the countryside. The critique Roul suggested prior to the noon dismissal was welcomed news, because it would give everyone an opportunity to sit on their duffs and listen, rather than to be made spectacles of again. Will was curious, though, over how Baker intended to convince any one of them that anything as inimical as the surrounding wall of jungle was an ally. He suspected the meeting was intended to be a sales pitch for the grueling pace that Baker had promised an hour earlier. Will had caught his first really good glimpse at New Guinea's untamed wilderness that morning and he couldn't imagine anything he'd seen as being a synonym to people-friendly.

As usual, Schuster paged them to formation, then herded them into a nearby clearing located just a tad east of the camp perimeter. Then, which wasn't unusual, the *wait* that always followed the *hurry up* to get somewhere began. But it gave Will an opportunity to bat the breeze with Farmer while they waited. "Do you know what?" Will asked Farmer.

"Do I know what? What about what, what?" Farmer coyly mocked him.

"Well, I was just thinking how different this class will be compared to classes in college," Will explained.

"Oh," Farmer came back. "How so?"

"Look at this setting, man. We're out in the middle of nowhere. There is no blackboard, there are no visual aids, not even a podium for our instructor to plant his elbows on," Will complained.

"Wal, what did you expect? This here is the Army, not a college," Farmer chided Will.

"I know. But it would be nice if we could all be transported back to civilization for this class. I don't imagine you've ever seen the inside of a college, huh?" Will asked.

"Naw. Hardly! I was lucky to see the inside of a one-roomed country schoolhouse," Farmer confessed.

"It's really cool, Farmer. So clean, so tidy, so unreal in a worldly sense. There's indoor plumbing, floors, walls, ceilings and reference libraries where a guy can search out almost anything he wants to know. When you are in college you rarely see the out-of-doors, except when springtime came calling. Old Professor Boon invariably came down with an acute case of spring fever every year, and to escape the confines of the lab and classroom, he'd suggest we all take a nature walk to observe the budding flowers that flourished in the beds of blossoms across the campus. We all had our suspicions that he was justifying a break from classroom routines by hyping the change in seasons. He'd say, 'Seeing spring spring gives us the chance to search our inner souls and thus to find our inner selves.' Inner souls? Inner selves? My ass! We'd all roll our eyes around in their sockets, shake our heads, and patronize him, praising the idea with a chorus of, 'Yeah. Great idea.' It was a cop-out, but we enjoyed the breath of fresh air after being held captive by Old Man Winter the past few months."

"Wal, just maybe the captain has a touch of spring fever," Farmer suggested.

"Spring fever?" Gambler questioned him. He'd been listening to the exchange. "You've got to be kidding, sodbuster. It's fall, not spring."

"Who says?" Will cut in.

"By God, I do," Gambler fired back, quite indignantly, "It's September."

"Right," Will agreed. "It's September, which makes it spring."

Gambler grinned from ear to ear. He'd been waiting for an opportunity to put a whammy on Will. He smirked, rolled his eyes around in their sockets, and wobbled his head like a dunce, then asked, "Are you for real? Everyone pay attention. Old Gambler's going to teach the college whiz kid a thing or two. Now, listen up."

But most of the guys spurned his request. They probably understood the reversal of seasons in the southern hemisphere. Gambler also should have, because on the voyage across the Pacific, when the ship crossed the equator, every dogfaced GI was baptized a *shellback* in a ceremony honoring first-timers upon crossing that imaginary line.

"Gambler," Will curtly informed the cardsharp, "if you had paid attention to your teachers back in grammar school, instead of trying to bilk your classmates out of their lunch money, you'd know what the rest of us do. South of the equator the seasons are reversed. Down here our normal summer is their normal winter." Gambler's face burned red. He'd been put in his place by the very person he was trying to embarrass.

Fortunately for the both of them, Baker arrived on the scene and let Gambler off of the hook. "Let's have your attention. Listen up," the sergeant barked. "Let's get this critique underway, if you don't mind me interfering with your childish games and arguments."

The entire gang of misfits were just what Baker called them, with just a couple of exceptions, childish. It fell Baker's lot to guide them into manhood. He was not the type of man who'd wet-nurse misfits, and they were about to get their second lesson from this old war horse, who'd already made fools of them before lunch. Baker's afternoon session, introducing these raw rookies to the finer points of military expertise in the South Pacific, was convened.

Chapter Five

"Whose headgear?" Baker asked, pointing a finger at a steel helmet someone had carelessly left lying on the ground.

"Mine, Sarge," Tillie replied in a subdued tone of voice.

"Mine, SARGE? Did you intend to say, 'Mine, Sergeant'?" Baker scolded him a second time for neglecting to show military etiquette when addressing superiors.

"Yup. Er, I mean, yes, sir, that's right. It's my helmet, Sergeant," Tillie timidly confessed.

"Un-huh. Then I suggest you place the helmet on your head where it belongs," Baker advised him.

"Wal, sir. It was on my head until just a couple'a minutes ago. You see, Sergeant sir, my head gits hotter'n the hubs of hell when I'm wearing that wash tub, so I was just giving my noggin a breather," Tillie crawfished.

"I see," Baker responded, further informing the hillbilly that if he continued to run around a war zone without his helmet, "Some Jap will put a breather right through your noggin, after which time you'll have no need for your helmet. This is supposed to be a secured area, but from past experience, we've learned that very few Nips surrender when hostilities end. They take off into the wilderness to fend for themselves, waiting for another chance to kill off some Americans. There could be a sniper out there watching every move we're making. It isn't likely, but not impossible, either. If I was in a Jap sniper's shoes and you removed your helmet I'd be delighted to puncture a hole straight through your noggin."

Tillie cringed over the thought, then scooped up the helmet, dropped it onto his head and tried to charm Baker by offering his countrified, full-cheeked grin; a very toothless grin. That was yet another mistake.

"Where's your goddamn teeth?" Baker exploded.

Tillie twisted his torso sideways so he could reach a hand into his side pants pocket to fish out his partial plate and quickly insert it, lint and all, inside of his mouth.

Baker was visibly upset over the persistent hillbilly, who was turning out to be just about as disobedient and twice a brazen as Will F. Munday. "Be advised, soldier, that I'm keeping an eye peeled in your direction," Baker said, then paused and directed his attention on Duffy before adding, "and in yours, too, to make sure your brand spanking new Garand rifle is in good hands."

With order restored, Baker called the class to order, informing them all, "Listen up, jurblowfs. Or … should I say girls? I can hardly call you men when you fall flat on your faces because of a little stroll through the park such as we took this morning, now can I? I suggest you throw your silk bloomers away, girls, because it ain't going to get any easier. This morning was but a prelude of things to come. The only positive thing that came out of that fiasco was that we discovered what we needed to know about you and your physical condition."

"STROLL?" Tillie cut in, exclaiming, "STROLL THROUGH THE PARK? Shit, Sarge … er, I mean Sergeant, I've chased a coon hound halfway through the timber, after working a shift in the coal mine, and was never as spent as I was when we broke for chow."

"Tsk, tsk, tsk," Baker patronized him. "You don't look any worse for the wear to me. I'd say you're still alive and kicking."

"Wal … I am, but my ass was'a dragging," Tillie informed him.

"You'd best hitch your ass up a few feet then, because if you don't, both of our asses could end up in a sling. That's what our meeting is about; staying alive and keeping each other alive, so you'd best listen up and pay close attention to details," Baker announced.

Will fidgeted about, changing positions to avoid Baker's stare, which he halfway suspected was focused on him. Baker's words had an ominous ring. Up until now dying in combat had been a possibility that loomed at some future date. Will, along with most of the others, looked upon dying as an event reserved for other folks, not himself. His recollections of people dying always were centered on the elderly. Dying was the natural end of things when the body gave way to the ravages of age. Will's body was neither old nor worn out, but according to the gospel of Sergeant Baker, he was a prospect just waiting for the Grim Reaper to harvest.

"War," Baker continued, "is a game of sorts, but a deadly game. All games have rules. Rule number one is that you cover my ass and I, in return, will cover your ass. Any questions about that?" he asked, taking a short pause to field any inquiries. His comments were greeted with affirmative nods, so he added, "Death is permanent. Prior to now you've been playing soldier, firing blank cartridges, pretending to take out an enemy bunker, and being

80

declared a casualty by impartial referees during staged maneuvers. Over here, gents, the bullets are real. If you're hit, you're down. Back in basic training you were probably reminded time and again to 'Pay attention. What I'm saying may save your life.' You're going to hear that one more time. Right here. Today. The bottom line in combat is ... you kill them before they kill you. Winning requires an edge. As things stand today, the Japs have a definite edge over you. We're going to change the odds by taking away that edge to level the playing field of this game. So, I imagine, you're asking yourself what the edge is. Well, pay attention. The next thing you hear me say can save your life. That edge is simply two basic things; first, it's the jungle, and second it's using your head for something more than an ear rack."

Baker had touched a nerve. Will couldn't recall how many times one of his cadre had boasted that his words of wisdom might save Will's life some day. There'd been plenty of them. It was pounded into their minds day and night. "Pay attention. This can save your life." Will had supposed throughout basic training that Camp Hood was preparing him for combat. Now, after hearing Baker's caveats, he became suspect. Did he have adequate training? The jungle had never been mentioned stateside.

"So," Baker interrupted Will's train of thought, "now you think you are soldiers. Yes, you have uniforms and you have weapons—if you don't lose them, as one of our complement did—and last night during our bullshit session I discovered that you jurblowfs are weighted down with enough sharpshooter and expert medals to qualify as a scrap drive. I was impressed. And that's about as close as anyone of you have come to being a soldier. Down here, without the edge, you're nothing more than cannon fodder. And the edge doesn't just happen. It's not something I can hand to you. It's something you have to understand, and to feel, and to sense, and to know. An example would be whether you are curious enough about land mines to pause and look, or to take a detour, rather than to step on it and get blown to smithereens. You can't buy combat savvy, or beg it, or steal it. You must earn it, like one earns that prized high school diploma. Now, I'll just bet a month's pay that you all just had a great furlough at home before getting shipped out. I can just see you clowns standing in front of the corner drugstore, all decked out in those snazzy uniforms, adorned with all of those sharpshooter's medals. I'll bet you were playing grab-ass with every cute girl on the block. Yeah, big deal."

A snicker filtered through the ranks. He'd resurrected an accurate picture of their furloughs. But he didn't tarry long. "So, here comes the bad news," he informed them after the laughter waned. "When you turned your back on that old drugstore your last night at home, you turned your back on the last glimmer of glamour you're going to see for one helluva long time. There ain't, as you might already suspect, any glamour over here. So, what did Sergeant Baker inherit from the replacement depot? I'll tell you what. He got saddled with a bunch of kids who look like soldiers, but who aren't quite a finished product." He glanced around, then pointed a finger toward Gambler, asking, "What is the primary ingredient in the making of a soldier?"

Gambler avoided his stare by turning his head sideways, then meekly replied, "Beats me. I didn't know being a soldier was an ingredient thing."

"Well, from what I've seen so far around camp, you appear to be the outfit's gambling man," Baker needled him, suggesting, "so perhaps a wager is in order. No high stakes. Five bucks'll do. Yeah. Five bucks says it's not a matter of not knowing, it's a matter of not caring. Would you care to stake your reputation as a speculator on such a wager?"

Gambler shrugged his shoulders, but said nothing.

"Okay. Does anyone want to make the wager with me?" Baker asked.

Gooch raised his hand, but Baker declined, saying the Nisei scout already knew the ropes, which disqualified him.

"Hm-m-m. No takers, huh? Okay. All bets are off. The answer is so simple it defies you to recognize it. The most import ingredient in the making of a soldier is, one of the two things I just pointed out, the importance of knowing, caring and thinking. Yes, thinking, too. You must think at all times. Never quit thinking. Conjure up hypothetical situations and decide how best to master them. Imagine yourself caught up in the worst-case scenario, then think your way through it. Know what you're doing. Care what happens. Think of a plan."

Will was sold. Thinking was his bailiwick. Thinking was a must in college classrooms. It was a twist he hadn't anticipated but did welcome. Somehow, thinking and the Army had, until this moment in time, been antonyms.

"Granted, you've probably never been told about the importance of thinking. Now, you've been told. You must begin to think like soldiers today, and tomorrow, and every day thereafter, if you intend to survive in the jungle. When you think, you gain an edge, because you turn the jungle into an ally. It all begins out there," he said, pointing into the far reaches of the jungle that surrounded them. "Take a good look. Go ahead. Look at the tangled, jangled mass of limbs and leaves. Starting today, you are going to be on the inside of the jungle looking out, not outside looking in. You'll curse the vines and roots that trip your feet," a possibility Will had already encountered on guard duty the night before. "You'll hate the everlasting canebrakes that you must hack your way through," he continued, asking, "Is the jungle all trees? No. There are meadows of head-high grass that stifle your breath, and mucky swamps that swarm with vermin the likes of which you've never seen, and there are snakes bigger around than your forearm, just lying in wait for you to come past. It it's negative, it's in the jungle. If it can kill you, it's in the jungle. If it can frighten you until the piss trickles down you pants leg, it's in the jungle. It's out there, right now, just waiting for you. So, let's have a smoke and take a few minutes to look around ourselves. That's your new home; your new friend, the jungle. When you finally come to grips with the idea of befriending the jungle, such as I once had to do, you'll know why it is one of the few allies you've got working for you in the South Pacific."

Will fished his pack of smokes from his jacket pocket, palmed his Zippo lighter, and lit up. He was surprised to discover that Baker's warning was unnerving. He squinted his eyes and stared at the heavy stand of palm trees that circled their outdoor classroom. He glanced left, then right, and finally swiveled around on the cheeks of his rump for a look behind. It was everything as Baker had said; a formidable foe in itself, a savage flora that completely smothered New Guinea's countryside. It was pristine in nature, awesome in size, and intimidating to its core. Will tried to compare it to the forest back home. He couldn't. They shared nothing common. Parks back home offered stands of stately oaks, mighty elms and leafy sycamores. This was more of a deformed yet flourishing thicket that seemed to have no rhyme, no reason. It was a hodge-podge of overgrowth, strangled by undergrowth, all seemingly bound together by an endless web of vines. It was nature's arboretum, a greenhouse stuffed with plant life that sprang from prehistoric cycads to modern-day ferns and palms. It was a mysterious, half-choked woodland that stirred Will's curiosity, and for one brief moment he felt as though he was standing in the core of the kernel of evolution. Had fate, he wondered, somehow delivered him to his own edify, so that he could get a firsthand glimpse of nature's embryo? Was there a reason for his being there? Did this sidetrack in his educational pursuits have a hidden motive that might benefit his career in days to come?

The cigarette burned short and singed Will's fingers. He dropped it, then quickly picked it back up and field-stripped the remaining butt. A soft, gentle wind had begun to blow, sending a chill up Will's spine—a warm breeze that, for some unexplainable reason, blew cold on the nape of his neck. He tried to dismiss the eerie feeling, thinking the culprit was his overwhelming desire to steal into the primeval wildwood—a place that, prior to now, he had detested with a passion.

"The edge, gents," Baker aroused Will from his subconscious slumber.

"Have you seen enough to be convinced? Do you understand—I mean UNDERSTAND—why an edge is necessary? The Japs have the edge over you now. They're cunning, deceitful and diabolical. They make the jungle work for them. Are they intimidated by it? CERTAINLY! But they put mind over matter and do not allow the jungle to handicap their movements. They devise ways to blend into the background so methodically that you could walk within ten yards of a Nip and never see him until it's too late. They won't hesitate to slip up behind you and slash your throat."

Will was astounded over what Baker said. He remembered all too well how an arm encircled his throat while he was on guard duty the previous night and of how a voice threatened him with, "If I was Tojo, you'd be dead." Yeah, he decided. It was Baker who scared the piss out of him. But he'd said nothing to suggest it was he. Was he looking at Will? He glanced at Baker and saw that he was staring directly at Tillie, not at him. Maybe it wasn't Baker after all.

"Okay," Baker inquired, "does the jungle frighten you? C'mon, now, let's hear it. Be honest, if not with me, with yourselves. Does the jungle frighten you?" He glanced first left, then right, then at the center of the huddle to make eye contact with each and every man. But not a man responded one way or the other to his query.

"I'll buy that. You're reluctant. You're afraid the guy next to you will think you're chicken shit if you openly admit you're scared of the jungle. That's understandable ... but not necessarily wise. Do you want to see a man with a hand raised because the jungle does frighten him? OKAY! Take a good look," he announced as he lifted his own right hand and held it aloft for everyone to see. "I'm afraid of the jungle. You damned betcha I am. Only a fool wouldn't be. It's no disgrace," he admitted, dropping his hand back to his side. "These chevrons don't provide me with any special protection. Sergeants get just as scared as anyone else, but we're acclimated to hide our fear from our subordinates. Now, let's see a show of hands from those who are afraid of the jungle."

Things had changed. Every man's hand went up. "Now we're getting somewhere," Baker said with a trace of pride in his voice. "See? It wasn't that hard to admit you're afraid of something, now was it? Here's a tip for you. Those Japs are equally as scared as you. Even the natives who were born and reared in this jungle don't take a Sunday stroll through the thicket without keeping a sharp eye peeled. So, what's that tell us? It tells us the playing field is level if you learn to make the jungle your ally when you finally begin to play the deadly game of hide-and-seek with those goddamn Nips. Look out at the jungle one more time. It is teeming with natural lairs

84

in which to hide. Those lairs are as much yours as they are the Japs'. Use them. Drive Tojo's fanatics crazy trying to find you, don't wear yourself down to a nubbin looking for him. Make him fight on your terms, not goad you into fighting on his terms. Don't expose yourself to him, make him come looking for you. By admitting your fear of the jungle you've taken the first step to harness that fear. That is the edge. And that's what this critique is about."

Baker paused, gave his men another smoke break, than beckoned the pint-sized scout to front and center. "C'mon, Gooch," he paged the Nisei to come forward. "What would you say if I suggested a little game of cowboy and Indian?"

Gooch sauntered to Baker's side, shrugged, and complained, "It sounds like fun, but I suppose I hav'ta be the Indian again, huh?"

Baker smiled and nodded in the affirmative, and said, "Yup. You're it."

Captain Roul, who had silently observed the meeting from the start, encouraged Gooch, saying, "Excellent casting, Sergeant," then laughed when Gooch began a high-stepping war dance accompanied with an eerie "E-E-E-, I-I-I, YI-YI-YI" to set the stage.

They all laughed over Gooch's antics and laughed even louder when Roul confessed, "Perhaps I was wrong. He's no Indian."

"Well, sir, I must agree. Sitting Bull he isn't. But he's as close as we can come to a backwoods pathfinder," Baker agreed. He pointed to Gambler, asking, "Would you like to make odds on whether any one of you jurblowfs can ferret out Gooch in the allotted time frame ... which will be ... hm-m-m ... let's say three hours." He glanced at his wristwatch to verify the time of day, informing them, "It is now 13:30 hours."

Gambler hedged. "Naw..." he begged-off. "I don't think so. I make it a practice to never bet a man with a smirk on his kisser."

Baker's smirk changed to a wide-faced grin. He didn't figure Gambler was fool enough to see his offer. "Okay, Gooch. Get moving. You are to stay within two hundred yards of the camp perimeter, in any direction. You've got a five-minute head start. GO-O-O-O."

Gooch darted away from the group and was swallowed up in the coppice within an instant. The others just sat there wondering what would come next. Baker glanced at his wristwatch time and again. Finally, he said, "Okay! Time's up. You have two hours and fifty-five minutes remaining in which to flush Geronimo. Move out."

They all took to their feet, pairing up in twos to pursue Gooch when Baker barked, "Oh, another thing I failed to mention. Everyone starts out on their own. No double-teaming. Get going. Report back to this spot when the

85

time is up, or if you should get lucky, bring your prisoner of war, Gooch, in when you nail him."

That was another unexpected kick in the ass. Will was quite verbal over the rule change. "Damned sergeants, anyway," he muttered as he turned on his toe and ventured off across the compound. He hadn't been very enthusiastic about playing cowboy and Indian when he was a kid, and his inclinations hadn't changed. Trying to find Gooch in the jungle, especially as a lone wolf, was child's play. How, he silently wondered as he moseyed into the fringe of trees on the west perimeter of the bivouac area, could this have any bearing on the outcome of the war?

It didn't take Will the full three hours that Baker had allotted to conclude that Gooch was everything Baker claimed. "Hm-m-m-m," he mumbled, telling himself, "that little prick must hold a master's degree in concealment." What had began as a grown-up's version of a kid's game called hide-and-seek had evolved into a game of skill; greenhorns versus a specialist. The afternoon continued to creep by without anyone of the Baker's dozen flushing Gooch from his hiding place. Actually, Will had himself to blame for his failure. He hadn't really tried. He'd just roamed here and yon without seriously trying to find the Nisei scout. After giving it some thought he concluded that, since no one else had unearthed Gooch, he wasn't the only misfire in Stopwatch. Surely, he reasoned, after such a long time someone of the posse must've scoured every square inch of the designated area. Disgusted, weary, his feet throbbing, his back aching, his spirits in the cellar, he decided to screw off a while, telling himself he was wasting his time, because Gooch had somehow melted into leaf and limb. For all he knew, Gooch was out there watching him right now, laughing his ass off.

He paused, plunked his hind quarter down on a large boulder near the crest of the hill overlooking their camp from the west, and bemoaned Baker's prediction that no one would find Gooch. Little did he realize that his fortunes were about to take a turn for the better. Had he not stopped, Farmer probably wouldn't have encountered Will sitting atop of the rock. But the two did bump into one another, with Farmer asking, "No luck, huh? Me neither."

"No. We're wasting our time, Farmer," Will confessed, further complaining, "College sure didn't prepare me for this."

Will's admission was music to Farmer's ears. "Wal, shucks. What did you expect? I knew it right off, the first time I saw you. You ain't got a lick of pioneer stock in your bones," he belittled Will.

"Pioneer stock? What the hell are you talking about, pioneer stock? What you're saying, in your countrified way, is that I'm stupid when it comes to the out-of-doors stuff. Right? Well? Isn't that what you're saying?" Will blustered.

"Wal, sorta, but I weren't tryin' to be disrespectful. You're an all-fired city boy. It sticks out all over you like mold on the north side of a stump. Now, don't get me wrong, Will. I don't hold that against you. It ain't your fault you were born in the city," Farmer tried to let him down gently.

"Oh, thanks a heap. I feel better all over just knowing that," Will countered in a curt tone.

"Wal, don't fret. It's about stompin' grounds, Will. You do know what stompin' grounds are, don'cha?" Farmer asked.

Will wagged his head from side to side, replying, "No. I can't say that I do."

"Wal, I think you city boys call it turf. It means your neighborhood, sorta. See, Will, whatcha gotta do is get the lay of the land first off, that's if'n you intend to survive in the wilderness. A guy's gotta read signs. So, I can see why you're all flustered. I'll betcha they ain't got a single text book about that in the whole college ... do they?" Farmer asked.

"Hardly. So, big deal. If your so smart about the ways of the wildwood, how's come you haven't got Gooch in tow?" Will insisted on knowing.

But Farmer did have the background he boasted. He'd dealt with sly foxes trying to invade the henhouse, and hungry wolves trying to cut calves away from the herd, and gophers burrowing through a field of freshly planted seedlings. "Wal, it would appear you're right, 'ceptin' for one thing,' Farmer admitted. "Hunting is tricky business. Sometimes a guy goes home skunked. Sometimes he's got a game bag stuffed with kills. But just 'cause I don't have Gooch snared as yet doesn't mean I don't know how to do it."

"Okay, Kit Carson," Will chided him. "Let's hear some more of your rural wisdom on the subject. If, and take note that I said 'if', you know how to catch Gooch, what am I and the rest of the jokers doing wrong?"

"Wal, when a man's hunting he's gotta keep in mind that things ain't necessarily what they 'peer to be. So, I was just a'thinking when I ran into you that there's gotta be a parallel between hunting wild game and hunting people. I think our problem is that we ain't seeing what we're seeing," Farmer informed him.

"'Peer to be?" Will barked. "Farmer, you'll be the death of me the way you decimate the English language."

"Might be," Farmer came back, but he did ask Will, "You do want to nail Gooch, don'cha?"

"Certainly. Nothing would please me any more than upsetting Baker's ego trip."

"Wal, for once't in your lifetime forget college, and book learnin' stuff and get practical," Farmer advised him.

"Okay," Will humored him. "I'd like to get practical if you'd quit talking in circles. Just what does 'we ain't seeing what we're seeing' mean? That isn't even logical."

"Oh, yeah. It's logical all right," Farmer insisted, explaining to Will, "It's like this. What we've gotta do is put our heads together, face off from one another, and let Gooch trap hisself."

"Are you daft?" Will exclaimed. "We can't do that. Baker said no double-teaming." He shook his pointer finger at Farmer, admonishing him with a "naughty, naughty" gesture and added a series of "Tsk, tsk, tsk" to drive his point home.

"Wal, sir, he did at that. He said, if'n my recollection is right, we was supposed to *start out alone*. Didn't he?" Farmer reminded him.

"Hm-m-m-m, excellent point of view. We did start out alone and stayed alone most of the afternoon. It's a technicality, but a guy might get away with it," Will concurred.

"So, let's put on our thinking caps and forget them dad-blasted rules," Farmer suggested, informing Will, "What we've got here is an animal, not a human."

"Animal?" Will asked. "What kind of an animal, pray tell me?"

"We've got outselves a squirrel!"

"A squirrel? What kid of squirrel?"

"We've got ourselves a red squirrel, that's what kinda squirrel we've got. I know. You city boys don't know sic'em about squirrels. I'll bet you didn't know that a squirrel ain't got a brain much bigger'n a pea. Did'ja?" Farmer asked him, then fell silent, waiting on Will to reply. After Will nodded and mumbled, "Unh-hu," Farmer continued, telling Will, "You see, that's how they fool us. Folks think squirrels are stupid, but the truth is they're smarter than most of us folks."

"Okay. So how does all of that homespun wisdom help us?" Will asked.

"That's it, Will. This here squirrel's been outsmarting everyone of us all afternoon. Didn't you ever go squirrel hunting, Will?"

That was probably the most ridiculous question ever asked of Will. Squirrel hunting, if graded on a scale of one to ten for favorite pastimes, would have rated a definite zero. The idea of cradling a rifle across his elbow, then traipsing all over the countryside in search of a squirrel, had never been a consideration during his entire lifetime. In fact, Will rarely ventured beyond the city limits of his hometown. "NO, Farmer," he replied in a disgusted tone of voice, "I've never had the pleasure of hunting squirrels.

Hunting squirrel is a pleasure. Right?"

"Yup, it is and that's your tough luck," Farmer needled him. "Gettin' yourself born in the city, where you can go to the market on every whim, was your misfortune. Now us hicks, you see, know squirrels. And I'm about to teach you how to bag one'a them rascals."

"Okay. I'm game," Will joined in. "What's our first move?"

"Wal, you see, he's outsmarting us. He's got us all buffaloed. Gooch is the squirrel. He's been circling us all afternoon, first one guy, then another, slipping around on our backsides, then holing up to wait us out," Farmer explained.

"And you think he's circling us, right?"

Yep. No doubt about it. So, let's play his game. We'll just move on down this slope a tad, hole up in that outcropping down yonder, and wait out Gooch," Farmer suggested, insisting to Will that "Sooner, or later, he'll think we're gone and he'll poke his head out and ZINGO, we've got him."

"ZINGO?" Will shouted.

"Sh-h-h-h," Farmer shushed him. "Gotta be quiet to hunt squirrels."

"What's zingo?"

"Wal, it's like greased lightning. Squirrels are smart, but they're also forgetful," Farmer explained as they reached the outcropping and hunkered down between two large boulders. "Now, y'see, he'll get inquisitive pretty soon and start looking for us, and when he does, zingo. We've got him."

"You know, Farmer, you aren't half a dumb as ... well, what I mean to say is ... well, you know what I mean," Will tried to compliment Farmer, but he tripped over his own tongue instead.

Farmer began to chuckle, advising Will, "Wal, my mama always says a guy shouldn't oughta talk with his mouth full. And I'd say your mouth is full of foot right about now, so shush up." No further explanation was expected. Farmer was not the sort of individual who'd press a man when he's down in the mouth. So, as things were turning out, Farmer was something akin to a box of Cracker Jacks; a surprise in every package. In fact, his demeanor puzzled Will to no end. On the outside he was a good egg with a soft shell, an almost harmless country boy who wouldn't harm a flea. But he was also a contradiction. He whipped Gambler soundly that morning, then when Schuster came on the scene, jerked his handkerchief out of his pocket, blotted the blood he'd drawn from Gambler's nose and lied through is teeth. Now, here he was, sitting on a rock, discussing a scheme that, had it been in actual combat conditions, would end up with Farmer killing another human being. Farmer was, Will began to realize, a blend of many colors, ranging from fire red to tranquil green. And what worried Will even more was the fact that he was afraid he hadn't yet scratched the surface of Farmer's apparent unpredictable constitution.

The duo nestled down to get comfortable in the rugged rock formation. Will welcomed the respite. According to Farmer's logic, the two of them could just screw off and, possibly, accomplish their assignment. Unfortunately, another hour passed with no activity, except when Williams sauntered past their hideout without even taking notice of them. Will began to fidget about. He wasn't an idler. But his constant wriggling disturbed Farmer, who scolded him, saying, "Lay still, Will. If'n you don't that squirrel will spot us for sure."

"Well," Will confessed, "I've been thinking about us double-teaming and then, after I saw Williams still slogging along all by himself, I wonder if we made a proper decision."

"Forget it, Will. We did what Sergeant Baker told us to do. We both started out alone and ran across each other," Farmer stuck to his reasoning.

"Time's about up, anyhow," Will suggested. "Baker'll be calling us home pretty soon, now, so's he can have a good laugh at our expense."

The sun was beginning to arc down across the horizon to the west, but still no one had flushed Gooch. Will was fed up. "Farmer, this is a crock. I wouldn't be at all shocked to learn that we're the only two dumbbells left out here. I'll bet the other guys have already headed in."

Farmer reached out a hand and grasped Will's forearm to quiet Will and whispered, "A crock, huh? Take a gander down there, and tell me old Farmer don't know how to bag a squirrel."

Will glanced down the sloping hill and, sure enough, Gooch was standing right out in the open, swinging his head from one side to the other, trying to pan and scan the surrounding area. He was out of luck. Except for Will and Farmer, who were concealed in the outcropping about fifty yards upslope from where he stood, the other men had, as Will suspected, headed back to camp without their prize.

Baker, however, hadn't actually suggested what one might do if they were lucky enough to find Gooch. He probably figured it wouldn't occur, so there was no need to waste his breath with alternatives. Farmer figured it wouldn't pay to dilly-dally long, lest Gooch vanish again, so he jumped up, aimed his rifle at Gooch, then shouted, "GOTCHA! BANG! BANG! YOU'RE DEAD!"

The expression of surprise on Gooch's face made Farmer's and Will's long vigil worthwhile. The sawed-off scout was in shock. Then, he began to laugh—to laugh so loudly, in fact, that he caught Baker's attention a hundred yards away. By the time Baker did arrive to see what was happening, Gooch was lying on the ground, rolling around, screaming, "I'm dead. I'm dead!"

"Well, I'll be damned," the sergeant muttered when he realized that Farmer and Will had, indeed, caught Gooch with only minutes left before the game of cowboy and Indian would've ended.

Captain Roul was last to arrive on the scene. He broke out laughing when he observed Gooch carrying on like a banty rooster, still shouting between giggles, "I'm dead. I'm dead."

"Wal, Sergeant, we shore outfoxed the squirrel that time, didn't we?" Farmer exclaimed when he and Will finally made their way down the hillside to join the throng of onlookers.

Will shook his head in the affirmative but said nothing. He felt guilty taking the credit for Farmer's unique plan. The incident did, however, bring Will to realize that the knot of friendship he'd been tying with Farmer was drawing tighter with each passing moment. The unbelievable finally had happened to Will F. Munday; he had a bosom buddy, the first one of his entire lifetime.

Baker led the troops back to the critique area and held an impromptu recap of the afternoon's class. "Well," he admitted, "the world, it's been said, is full of surprises. I'd have bet a month's pay this wouldn't happen. But I overlooked a couple of factors. Farmer and Will just flat outfoxed Gooch. It wasn't luck, either. It was a planned effort. They stole Gooch's edge by waiting him out, so the exercise was a real success. What have we learned today?"

Gambler had been doing a slow burn since the moment he learned about Gooch's capture. He didn't try to camouflage his anger, either. "It pays to cheat," he complained. "That's what I learned. They stacked the deck by teaming up in violation of orders. Does the Army give kudos for disobeying orders?"

"OKAY! OKAY!" Baker agreed. "They did, but if you will recall my orders were to start out alone. I made no mention of joining forces later. It's a minor infraction I'll overlook because, had this been a combat situation, the violation would've been the right decision. So, I too learned something. We're off to a flying start. At least two of our group used their noggin; they thought things out. I told you earlier that, to survive in the jungle, you must think. You can see the benefits it reaped. THINK!" And with those words he dismissed them to take a short break prior to eating evening mess, saying, "A half hour till chow time and I'll bet you've all got a hearty appetite, too."

Once dismissed, Will moseyed back toward the bivouac area, figuring to crap out for a few minutes on his bunk before chow. The late-afternoon sun was descending, having evolved into a crimson ball of fire nestled atop the trees west of camp. Will glanced at the sun and, after staring too long, was momentarily blinded by the brilliant glare. He blinked. The glance at the bright sunlight etched the inside of the eyelids, coating them with multi-colored configurations, all of them revolving like the images he'd seen when looking into a kaleidoscope as a lad. He paused a moment, rubbed his eyes, then resumed his trek toward his tent.

The Japanese aviators also knew a thing or two about sunsets, and about approaching from the west at treetop level. That was an edge Baker hadn't mentioned. Swooping over, down on the camp, the sun behind their rudders, was a classic maneuver used all too often by flyers to pounce on the enemy unannounced.

Will heard a distant scream; a voice that he thought was Sergeant Baker's, advising everyone, "INCOMING ENEMY PLANES. TAKE COVER."

Then, all hell broke loose. Will could faintly hear the anti-aircraft gun on the LCI begin to cackle and the roar of engines overhead as the planes thundered across the glen and the *WHA-A-A-O-O-O-M-M* of a bomb detonating near the center of the campground—an explosion that knocked Will's feet from underneath him and sent him sprawling onto the ground. *This is it. I'm dead,* was his first and primary thought. He rolled over onto his back and tried to catch a glimpse of the planes that had returned for another sortie. And he discovered he was the perfect target; lying in the open where one of the Nips could blister him with machine gun fire on their next pass. He wanted to scamper to his feet, to run and to hide in the jungle, but his reflexes would not obey their commands. The war finally caught up with the reluctant warrior. A half-dozen enemy fighter pilots in a menacing menagerie of Mitsubishi Zekes introduced him to reality. Stopwatch was prematurely engaged and inadequately prepared for what befell them.

Chapter Six

Will had always prided himself on his insight of history. From his earliest recollections he was fascinated with man's continued struggle to dominate the world. He didn't agree with the philosophy about the spoils of war belonging to the victor, an adage that was credited to Andrew Jackson, nor did he worship heroes from the past or present. He knew a good deal more than Mister Average about historical legends such as Caesar, and was thoroughly schooled about the Holy Knights and their futile Crusades to redeem the Holy Land. He was well versed on Wellington, and Custer, and John "Black Jack" Pershing. He had concluded that most of history's so-called heroes were in reality nothing more than egomaniacs who were either killed trying to attain magnanimity, or were decorated with a chest full of medals heavy enough to bring their arrogance back down to earth. He didn't subscribe to the theory that some men had a date with destiny, nor did he rule the possibility out. He figured that anything was possible, so he preferred, in the event he might draw a loser's hand, that Dame Fortune would jilt him and pass the curse along to someone else. Now it was apparent that those long-standing beliefs were all being challenged. And altered. Dame Fortune, being the contrary bitch he'd anticipated her to be, was a punctual broad who took Will's hand to escort him through the intersection where life's roadway crosses death's thoroughfare.

Will had been making preparations for this event since the moment he took the oath to "bear truth, faith and allegiance" to his country back at Camp Dodge. Somehow, though, he never actually believed it would come down to him staring directly into the canon's muzzle. And considering the surprise assault came from the sky, after he'd been trained to counter assaults on the ground, he would've preferred to look down that cannon's barrel, rather than face off against aircraft piloted by fanatics who had but one thing in mind—kill as many Americans as possible in the shortest span of time without retaliation from the ill-prepared and under-equipped ground forces domiciled at a training site. He actually thought when the first wave came storming across their campsite that they'd soon be gone, heading back to their bases, leaving him in one piece. And for a moment he believed he was right. The noise abated for a brief interlude because the planes had vanished from view and were beyond earshot. But his vision of peace and quiet evaporated when the Nips returned for another pass. He barely heard Sergeant Baker screaming, "TAKE COVER, GODDAMNIT. ZEKES AT NINE O'CLOCK. TAKE COVER IN THE JUNGLE! MOVE! MOVE! MOVE!"

It wasn't actually Baker's caveat that sent Will scurrying for cover. It was the practicality of doing the obvious. Will was already on his feet, high-tailing it toward the tree line that abutted the west fringe of the campsite. He was caught like a rat in a trap, because there was very little natural cover within thirty, perhaps as much as forty, yards distance in any direction. He'd have made it safely across the clearing had a Jap Zero not come soaring in across the treetops again, honed in on a heading directed at Will. His machine guns peppered the ground with a hail of fire that left Will with no options other than to go prone again, then to hug the ground so as to minimize the size of the target. So, he hit the dirt, face down, digging a furrow in the sandy soil with his nose while scooping up a mouthful of grit in the process. He was, it dawned on him, the perfect bull's-eye if ever one existed. He lay there, spreadeagle, dead center of the clearing, where a blind pilot couldn't overlook him. He was spitting and coughing, trying to eject the grime from his mouth. Being angry at himself only complicated his compromising position. He'd panicked and thrown himself down when he should have kept running to find some cover in the trees. But it was too late. All six Jap aviators bore down on them again, riddling the area with machine gun fire, punctuated by an occasional anti-personnel bomb meant to destroy the camp. One exploded not ten yards from where Will lay. He found himself caught up in a vacuum that seemed to suck the air from his lungs. He was smothered with the scattering clods of dirt that were displaced by the explosion and his head rattled, his inner ear fluttered and the tremendous impact of the explosion hugged his entire body like a vice. An odor of sulfur seared his nostrils and throat as he gasped to inhale a precious breath of air, and his ears agonized with pain, then all seemed to be quiet. He was deaf. For a moment he could hear nothing; not the planes, not the LCI's gun, not even Sergeant Baker, who, last he did heard, was screaming like a banshee to get his men safely out of the target area.

Will was crying. He could hear his own sobs, which was a good sign that his hearing was restored, but they seemed so distant, as though they were coming from someone else. He felt, in fact, as though he was detached from his own body. His head began to spin like a child's top and his stomach muscles seethed, then heaved, then rippled, and his bladder emptied itself in spite of Will's attempt to hold his urine. "OH, GOD," he shouted. He was angry at himself for wetting his pants. He pounded the ground with his fists. He was furious, humiliated, and helpless, all because he had made a bad call when the raid began. He just knew that he was the only jurblowf who hadn't relocated to some spot out of the strafing arena, but he had little time to dwell on the problems, because the Japs struck again, dropping another cargo of bombs in the area. Will's brain went into a tailspin. He was, it seemed, caught up in an endless labyrinth, and death was probably his only way out of the maze.

An inner voice told him, "You're going to die if you don't get up and run, run, run. Get up. Run. Run. Run." His only chance was, he quickly determined, to make a break for the forest, to get himself out of sight, out of the direct line of fire he'd been hopelessly mired in. He managed to get to his feet and, throwing caution to the wind just as another plane swooped down on his position, raced against time to seek refuge in the jungle—his ally, the jungle. Another plane flew past during his dash for cover and he could actually see the pilot sitting inside of the enclosed canopy, staring directly at him, a toothy grin on his face. They were that close to one another. The plane, even though it was soaring three hundred miles an hour, seemed locked in a time warp and appeared to be barely moving. But just as Will reached the sanctuary of the forest he heard Tillie's voice coming from behind and he paused, turned around, and discovered the hillbilly standing flat-footed in the clearing, the butt plate of his BAR propped against his hip, the barrel hoisted high into the air, its muzzle spurting one quick burst of fire after another. Tillie was screaming, "CHEEZUS! GOTCHA! CHEEZUS, YOU'RE DEAD, YOU SLANT-EYED SON OF A BITCH!"

Will was awestruck by what he'd seen, amazed at Tillie's courage, or idiocy, or both, but when he gazed at the plane just leaving the area he saw a trail of smoke coming from the underside of its fuselage. It was descending, and then it crashed into the jungle in a gigantic ball of flame. All that remained for Will to view was a spiral of smoke curling up into the sky. Will believed it was the plane piloted by the very Jap who, only an instant before, was bloated with joy when he looked down upon that frightened American, Will F. Munday, running to save his ass.

"I GOT 'IM," Tillie shrieked.

"You dumb sonofabitch," Baker cursed on his approach from the trees. "Get your fucking ass down. DOWN. DOWN. GODDAMNIT. DOWN!"

Tillie lowered his weapon, spun around, offered Baker a toothless grin, then turned and headed into the trees along the east perimeter.

95

The din of battle had ceased, ensued by an awesome quietude. There were no planes, and there was no gunfire. Will garnered a sudden surge of energy, along with a rebirth of confidence in himself, and darted into the protection of the stately palm trees. He dived headfirst into the first clump of growth he saw, then rolled over and over, backside to tummy, tummy to backside, until he felt he'd found a safe haven. He needed to recuperate his emotions. He looked down at himself; at his feet, then his legs, his torso, then wiped his hand across his brow. There were no telltale signs of blood. He was, it appeared, unscathed. But he was far from pleased with his performance. He had lost his rifle in the shuffle to survive. His web belt, along with his canteen, first-aid kit and several clips of ammunition were also missing, and he had no idea of when or where the belt ripped loose from his waist. He'd wet his pants. That was the worst part. But the Japs didn't let him sit there to wallow in his self-pity for very long. He heard the planes approaching for another run and could already hear the *TAW-TAW-TAW* of the turret gun on board the LCI. Perhaps, Will dared to guess, this was the finale, the last run for those "damned Japs." Didn't it have to end, he asked himself. Wasn't there a time when their ammo ran out, when they had no more bombs to drop, a time for them to return to their base where they could boast of their exploits?

Will miscalculated again. It was only wishful thinking. This time the planes bore down on them from the east and strafed the tree line along the west perimeter; precisely the spot that Will had staked his claim for safety. It seemed that no matter what he decided to do the enemy read his mind. Did they, he wondered, have a personal vendetta? Now, he wished he'd chosen the east perimeter for a hiding place. And then he realized for the first time since the raid began that he was not alone. Gambler came snake crawling from behind the very clump of bushes Will had slid into for cover and he suggested that the two of them should make a run for it to the opposite side of the clearing. In fact, he submitted to Will, "You'd best shift into high gear before they hit us again or you're liable to get your ass blown off."

The remark perturbed Will. "My ass?" he protested. "What about your ass?" he asked, inquiring if Gambler was wearing bulletproof shorts.

The pair jumped to their feet at the same instant to make a dash for the east perimeter, running a zigzag course through the meadow, trying to dodge a furious strafing of machine gun bullets. The Japs had circled a final time to finish off their prey. They caught both Will and Gambler right out in the open and one of the pilots, evidently spotting them running for cover, banked hard left, came about and zeroed in on the duo, spraying them with a parting volley of hot lead that peppered the ground in every conceivable bare spot.

By a stroke of luck not a single bullet hit either of them, even though Will figured he was as good as dead. He prayed to himself every step of the way, even though he was an agnostic, because he didn't figure he had anything to lose by asking for divine intervention. How, or even why, the Jap pilot missed the both of them with every round was unthinkable. But a moment later the menace was gone, and the confused but overjoyed pair of unscathed ground pounders dove headlong into the brush at the jungle edge—the very jungle that Baker had told them could work for them and against the Japs. The jungle was responding much like Baker promised it would; providing cover that might be their life preserver if the planes circled again.

They just lay there for what seemed an eternity, both of them panting to catch their breaths. And then Gambler finally broke the silence. "By God, Munday, I must have bulletproof shorts. They just flat out missed my ass with every round."

Will was amazed to hear Gambler's make such an admission and he asked, "Do you mean to tell me that, after running that hard to save your ass, you're still fretting over my inquiry about your underwear back there?"

"You're damned right I am," Gambler confessed, admitting to Will that, "It occurred to me while we were running like scared rabbits that a professional gambler would never bet against himself, so I figured I just might be wearing bulletproof shorts because I am a professional."

"Some shit," Will countered Gambler's boast. He intended to add a few words of wisdom about Gambler's professionalism when he paused and peeled an ear to listen.

"What d'ya hear?" Gambler asked. "More planes? Are they coming back?"

"No. But I thought I heard someone moan. A painful moan. Didn't you hear it?" Will asked.

"Nope. I didn't hear nothing. Shit! My ears are so fucked up because of the racket I may never hear well again," Gambler replied.

So, Will dismissed the thought and charged it off to his own hearing problem that began when the first bomb exploded just a few yards away. He was, in fact, just enjoying the peace and quiet. It was so quiet, he noticed, that he almost thought he could hear the silence. A blue-gray cloud of smoke was wafting its way skyward from the bivouac area, inspired by an onshore flow of breeze. Finally, Will could inhale a breath of clear, clean air. The fresh air, like the quiet, was a welcomed respite from the assault he'd just endured. But he also got his first taste of a trauma well known by veterans of many wars; *What-if syndrome.* The raid was obviously over and done, but the possibilities of having been killed weren't over by any stretch of the imagination. Questions overwhelmed him. The bomb. It landed but a few yards away. He was saved by a mere measure of minute distance. *What if,* he silently asked himself, *that bomb had veered just a few more yards to the south? It would have blown me to bits.* His inner thoughts were muddled with a score of what-ifs to include, *What if that Nip had've gunned Tillie down like the sitting duck that he was? The toothy pilot would be heading home a hero and Tillie would be dead.* He shuddered at the vast number of possibilities that might've changed everything.

Lying there, resuscitating his lungs, savoring the lull, an amusing thought crossed Will's mind. What would Mister Edmundson say to him, he wondered, if he was to insist that he could hear the silence? He chuckled over the thought, then decided the suggestion would've sparked a classroom debate that would have up-ended Mister Edmundson's apple cart. Will was certain Edmundson would insist that Will's reasoning was "a figment" of his imagination, "triggered by the sudden absence of noise" because "silence can not be heard."

"ALL CLEAR," Baker shouted from a distance, proclaiming that the raid had ended.

Schuster wasted no time paging his men to formation. "Get your asses down to the beach on the double. The captain wants a head count," he barked, repeating the orders, again and again, to make sure that every man, no matter where he was, could hear.

Will rolled over onto his belly, then pulled himself up onto his knees, and finally managed to take his feet. But as he pivoted around to start the trek to the beach he saw Gambler sling his rifle over his shoulder, then start back into the woods in the opposite direction of what they should've taken. Will wondered what the huckster was up to and even considered that he'd lost his bearings and was confused following the anxiety of the air raid, so he followed him a short distance, to where Gambler abruptly stopped, unbuttoned the fly of his fatigues, leaned his rifle against a tree trunk, and then urinated on the roots of the tree, telling Will, "That kinda shit can make a guy's piss run cold ... can't it?" It wasn't until he'd completed relieving his bladder that he turned around to acknowledge Will's presence and, glancing down to take notice of Will's wet trousers, began to snicker. "I guess you didn't wait. You pissed your pants, Munday."

Will had momentarily forgotten the mishap. So much had happened in such a short time. But Gambler's demoralizing jab embarrassed him. In fact, it upset him. He wished it had been anyone but Gambler who'd noticed his wet trousers, because he knew most of the other guys would've been sensitive enough to either ignore it or be a little sympathetic. He also realized

Gambler would be quite the opposite, and for a fleeting moment he recalled an instant in his childhood when he'd had an accident of how his father had called everyone's attention to it, then screamed for the benefit of the gawkers, "You make me feel like a fool, wetting your pants right here in front of everybody." And he had wondered at the time why his dad didn't understand that it was he, Will, who felt like a fool. His dad's words had cut him to the quick that day, but not nearly so much as Gambler's snicker followed by his remarks this day, so many years hence from his childhood. So, for a second time in his life he had been taunted by someone equally as unsympathetic as his dad, and he knew that Gambler was just itching to head for the beach, shouting all of the way, "LOOK, GUYS! MUNDAY PISSED HIS PANTS."

However, Gambler made two errors. His discomfiting snicker was the proverbial straw that broke the camel's back. Gambler's first mistake was leaving his rifle unattended against the palm tree. Will figured this was as good a time as any to straighten out this scurrilous bastard, who he feared he'd be haunted by until the war ended, or until after one or the other of them was dead. If, Will wondered, wetting his pants in a moment of terror and panic was grounds for being unreasonable, then he couldn't see why just shooting Gambler here and now wasn't equally as fair. He hotfooted it over the where the rifle was leaning against the tree. Recalling he had no weapon of his own, Gambler's weapon was Will's only option, so he snatched it up, flipped the bolt to make sure a cartridge was in the chamber, then leveled the barrel directly at Gambler. Gambler was caught completely off guard. He didn't even finish buttoning his fly. He just stared at Will with a puzzled expression locked across his face. Munday was the last man that Gambler figured was lunatic enough to shoot him over such a trivial incident. But he had no way of being certain. It was one thing to call a man's bluff in a poker game where money was the stake, but it was another thing when your own life was table stakes. The cocky twinkle that customarily sparkled in Gambler's eyes dimmed, his face twitched, and Will even thought he could see Gambler's knees trembling. The truth was, Will had the better hand of the two, a loaded M-1 rifle in his grasp, aimed directly at Gambler's heart, which was about the equivalent of holding a Royal Flush. "Shut the fuck up for once in your life, you two-bit four-flusher," Will threatened him. "You're an insensitive, ill-mannered prick. You didn't need to tell me I pissed my pants, because I already knew it. Am I happy about it? Hardly! But it couldn't be helped."

Fortunately for Gambler, though, Will was beginning to have second thoughts, because he was wise enough to realize what the consequences for murdering Gambler in cold blood would be, and murder was what it would've been called. He was also sore at himself for cursing because, prior to being a soldier, he'd considered profanity an unacceptable form of expression, and now he could curse like a stable boy behind the barn. He dropped the muzzle of the rifle a few inches and tried to explain to Gambler that, "I had to piss when we got hit. I was on my way to the latrine when the first plane came roaring in. So, Gambler, you'd best start keeping your wise cracks concerning me to yourself. Next time I won't let you off of the hook." Actually, he lied. It was true he hadn't relieved himself most of the afternoon, but he wasn't on the way to the slit trench he and Farmer had dug as he claimed. He knew, and he suspected that Gambler also knew, the Jap raid just scared the piss out of him. He suspected such a thing just went with the territory.

Gambler heaved a sigh of relief when Will lowered the rifle. Swallowing his pride and complying with Will's demands was no easy task for a man like Gambler, but he assured Will, "Okay, Munday. It's your pot. I fold."

Will swung the rifle to high port, then tossed it across to Gambler, who caught it in midair. And the face-off was defused, at least for now. Will didn't figure he'd ever get along with Gambler, but this did give him an edge. He'd let the cardsharp know he couldn't be bullied. He felt bad inside for having been so brazen and so foul-mouthed. So bad, in fact, that his inclination was to just sit down onto the goddamn ground and have a good cry. But memories of his mother telling him time and again, "Big boys don't cry," quelled the urge.

Will wheeled about and started his journey to the beach, remembering to take a detour to locate his rifle and cartridge belt. It wouldn't do for him to report for duty without them. When he saw the devastated camp ground he could barely believe his eyes. It was blown to bits. He wasn't sure of the precise spot he'd wallowed on the ground but he figured that was where he lost his rifle and belt. He glanced around, then spotted a bomb crater just a few yards ahead. He thought it was the right spot and, dropping onto his knees, began to feverously claw with his fingers, hoping he'd somehow locate it underneath the dirt. It was not there. But he was sure he'd fallen in the vicinity. He swiveled on his knees and prodded the soil a short distance behind himself, then breathed a sigh of relief. "AH-H-H," he uttered when his fingers touched something solid. Digging a little deeper he saw the muzzle end of the rifle poking up through the ground and as he continued to scrap away the crumbs of dirt he uncovered the entire weapon, right along with the cartridge belt. He considered himself to be a lucky stiff. He had already mentally prepared himself for Baker's ass-chewing if he failed to

100

report with his gear intact. Now, he could relax a bit. He pulled the weapon free of the dirt, grabbed the belt, and jumped to his feet to respond to Schuster's incessant barking, "C'MON, DAMN IT! The captain wants a head count."

Will cut across the disshelved campground, veering left, then right, to sidestep the holes left by the Jap aviators. Looking ahead, he could see several of his comrades already on site, clustered around Schuster near the edge of the beach. But it appeared there were a couple of men still unaccounted for, which pleased Will because it didn't make him the last one in. He no sooner got within earshot of the group than he could hear Tillie flapping his gums over his heroic endeavor, boasting to the others, "Ah got that cockwalloper, shore as shooting. Just flat out blew a hole in the belly of that there airplane. Cheezus! It was more fun than coon huntin'."

But when Will did finally arrive to rejoin the unit he noticed a displeased expression on Baker's face. His chin hung low, creases wrinkled his brow, and he was staring directly at Tillie almost with a vengeance. He finally got around to informing the flamboyant hillbilly, who obviously hadn't shut his mouth since the air raid ended, "It was shithouse luck, soldier. Shit house luck."

"What did I do wrong, now?" Tillie asked.

"Everything," Baker fired back. "You didn't follow orders. You could have gotten yourself killed trying to be a hero. If there's one thing I don't need in this outfit it's a goddamned hero. When you've had some time to think about that stupid stunt you'll realize it was a foolish folly to try to bring down a Zeke with a BAR."

"STUPID?" Tillie objected.

"Yeah, stupid," Baker retorted. "I'll give you this much ... you've got guts, but my order when I first heard and spotted those Nips was to take cover and you failed to follow my orders."

Tillie was humbled, almost humiliated. He thought he'd get a hero's reception and Baker had belittled his accomplishment. "Cheezus, Sarge ... er, Sergeant," Tillie protested "I thought we was supposed to kill them Japs. Now I'm catching hell for killing one," he argued.

"You're right, Tillie. That is what we're training for. But heroes more often get themselves killed than those lucky enough to live. We cannot afford to lose a single man at this stage of the game. We have a mission to perform. A lot of planning has gone into this operation and someone a lot higher up than you or I decided we needed thirteen enlisted men, one corporal, one sergeant and one captain to accomplish the task. That includes you. We need you in one piece, not in a body bag."

101

"Wal, sir ... it won't happen again," Tillie assured Baker.

"I hope not. Besides, have you stopped to consider the extra workload you put on me if you get yourself killed?" Baker asked.

"Wal ... no, sir," Tillie mumbled. "Whatever are you talkin about?"

"Well, if you do die I have to sit down and write a letter to your kin folks back home ... and tell them a lot of lies about how proud of you they should be, without mentioning you were also stupid and got yourself killed because you disobeyed orders," Baker explained.

Tillie looked down at the ground, trying to avoid Baker's penetrating stare.

"For everyone's benefit, remember; wars are won by teams. We're a team. Thirteen men strong," Baker reiterated his teamwork theme before pausing to take another head count. He then lambasted Tillie with one more volley, informing him, "You'd better never pull another stunt like that or it'll take a team of field surgeons to remove my number ten shoe from inside of your rectum. Got it?"

Tillie grinned, a modest, closed-mouth smile, because his teeth were still inside of his pocket, but he did inquire of Baker, "Do I get one'a them little Jap flags?"

Baker momentarily ignored Tillie's question while he counted heads. Their was still one man missing from the formation, but he finally took time out to ask the hillbilly, "Little Jap flags. What're talking about?"

"You know, sir. Like them flags on the gunnery tower of the LCI," he explained, pointing to the ship.

"Those?" Baker barked. "You mean those flags on the bulkhead of the turret?"

"Yup. Them. That sailor boy told me they stand for how many kills they've had. Each time they knock down a Jap plane they add another flag,' Tillie explained.

"Why in God's name do you think you should have one of them flags?" Baker asked.

"Wal, on account'a I shot down a Jap plane. That's why," Tillie explained.

"Oh, I see," Baker replied ins a less than sympathetic tone of voice. "So, you think you deserve a flag. And, if you were given such a flag, what would you do with it?"

Tillie patted the side of his steel helmet and announced, "Wal, I'd paste her right here," and then grinned from ear to ear.

Baker shook his head with dismay, sarcastically commenting, "Oh, you'd paste it on your helmet. That is the most preposterous thing I've ever heard.

It's kind'a like how I have to remind you, over and over again, about your goddamn teeth. Again, you are out of uniform."

Tillie quickly jerked the lint-coated teeth from his pocket, shoved them into his mouth, choked to clear his throat, and asked, "Perpos ... what? I never heard that word before in my life."

"Perposterous, Tillie. Is that what you're trying to say? It means unbelievable, or maybe ridiculous," Baker explained.

"Oh ... I see," the hillbilly replied with a dour expression of disappointment on his face. "I take that to mean I don't get one'a them little Jap flags."

"Right. No flag."

Captain Roul, in the meantime, had been just standing alone off to one side, staring back up the draw, hoping against hope that the last straggler would wander in. But he'd waited in vain. "We're short one man, Sergeant," Roul informed Baker, suggesting, "It must be that young fellow who calls himself Duffy. Everyone else appears to be accounted for."

"Yes, sir. Right. It is Duffy," Baker agreed, turning to ask the others, "Did anyone of you see Duffy after the raid? Or even during the raid?"

No one admitted to seeing him since they broke ranks after the critique ended just minutes before the Japs struck.

Will recalled of hearing the sound of moans, or at least a sound he thought was someone moaning, but he didn't mention it. He didn't want to suggest that Duffy might've been the source of the sound. He knew that his ears were also playing tricks on him in the aftermath of the thunderous explosions.

"Okay," Captain Roul sought their attention. "Let's all fan out in a wide arc extending from the east to the west perimeter and comb the entire draw. Check every tent, or..." and he paused to catch a glimpse of the devastated area, then continued, "every possible spot a human being could squeeze into. Move it. I want Duffy found."

Will grabbed Farmer by the arm and said, "Let's pair up. Two sets of eyes are better than one, yours in particular."

But as they began the slow process of searching the ravaged campground, Will gingerly confessed to Farmer, "Some soldier I turned out to be, huh?"

"How's that?"

"You seen my wet trousers, didn't you? I pissed my pants, Farmer. I'm so damned humiliated I could cry. I guess that's what they mean when they say something scared the piss out of someone. I just ran to save my own ass, never really giving a thought to anyone else," Will remorsed. "I totally ignored Baker's advice about covering the other guy's ass."

"So?" Farmer sidestepped the admission. "I didn't do much better. I was a'running for the storm cellar myself, so I can't fault you for doing the same. Besides, I forgot all about everything Baker told us today, too. I mean everything. Covering the other guy's ass? That, too."

Once again, Farmer had extended Will a. verbal handshake out of the goodness in his heart—a wonted gesture he would repeat in the days to come to help quench Will's powerful thirst for companionship.

Will came upon the first tent, Farmer following a step or two behind him. It was a tattered rag, sagging onto the ground, the center pole broken in two. Will almost hated to lift the tarp, lest he find Duffy underneath, but Farmer offered a hand, and the two threw back the canvas to reveal nothing but mangled cots and demolished personal belongings. There was no body.

They were just closing in on the second tent when they heard someone up near the top of the draw screaming, "HERE! UP HERE!" Will thought it sounded like Perkins' voice; a voice that emitted a tone of urgency. Will glanced up the slope and spotted Perkins, already flanked by several guys, standing there, just staring down at the ground. A shiver spiraled up Will's spine. That was the general area from which he thought he'd heard moans just as the raid ended.

"Let's go," Farmer yelped, urging Will to keep pace on a dead run to the head of the lea so that they, too, could see what the commotion was all about. Their arrival on the scene was not what they'd have preferred.

"Yeah ... he's dead," Baker announced just as Will and Farmer reached the spot. Baker was knelt down on one knee and was closely examining Duffy's riddled torso. He pulled Duffy's shredded fatigue jacket down to hide the gaping belly wounds from view, but most everyone caught a glimpse before Baker could finish the task. It was, to Will, the most sickening tableau he'd ever seen—Duffy's body near cut in half, his intestines protruding through the holes in his hide. Baker went about the task of camouflaging the mess in a matter-of-fact manner. He'd been callused to the task. "For whatever it's worth, he probably didn't know that hit him," Baker tried to console his troops, who he knew all too well were aggravated with first-time syndrome. "He was machine gunned right across the middle."

Will knew better, but he dared not say a word. It had to have been Duffy he heard moaning just after he and Gambler found sanctuary in the forest. Perhaps, he considered, he might've helped Duffy by calling attention to the incident, but he doubted it. It was, he guessed, much like Baker described it. He might've lived a minute, or two, but nothing could've saved Duffy. He was positively shot to pieces. But the thing that upset Will more than anything else was when he caught sight of Duffy's hand still clinging to the stock of his brand spanking new M-1 rifle.

O'Hare was last on the scene. He flamboyantly elbowed his way through the crowd, only to turn and spew vomit on the ground when he saw Duffy's remains. His deep-throated regurgitations enhanced Will's overwhelming urge to join him, but he managed to swallow an imaginary puff ball that tickled his tonsils, telling himself, "Breathe slowly, through your nose, Munday. It'll pass." That was, he recalled, what his mother always told him when he was about to puke. Still, Will was compelled to take one more look at Duffy. He didn't know why, he just knew he needed to. He wanted to reaffirm the disquieting observation of Duffy still gripping his precious rifle. There was something bizarre about it. He couldn't kick the image from his thoughts.

Will turned away, paused to inhale a chest full of fresh air, then stood there almost breathless again, trying to recall Duffy's lamentable autobiography during the meeting the previous evening. He had to look one more time, to satisfy his scorn for the Jap who killed him, and to reassure himself that his newfound friend Duffy was, indeed, quite dead. There was no one back home to grieve his death; no one to mourn this lonely individual's departure from a world that wasn't actually very kind to him. He was a roamer, according to his own testimony, and had never tasted parental love because he was orphaned as a babe in a basket. Will was almost overcome with compassion. Duffy, he repined, had died without firing as much as one cartridge from his brand spanking new M-1 rifle—the weapon that Sergeant Baker had made such an issue of the previous day. Somehow, to Will's way of reasoning, this was not acceptable. Will always suspected he'd have to deal, sooner or later, with seeing his first casualty, but he never imagined it would be anything this grotesque. Something down deep inside of his bosom snapped and he lashed out at the establishment; the establishment, in this case, being the handiest participant around, Sergeant Baker.

Will could not just idly dismiss this from his mind. His introduction to war and death was too appalling to just walk away and say nothing. It was madness. Someone, he believed, had to be held accountable and in his haste to pin the tail on someone's ass, he turned back and shouted, "Well, Sergeant Baker, SIR! His goddamned rifle ... you know ... the rifle you chewed his ass over ... really didn't mean spit when it came down to reality. DID IT?"

Will would've been well advised to have followed O'Hare's lead and vomited, rather than to spew his distorted feelings in such an insubordinate fashion. But it was too late to reconsider. The die was cast. Baker didn't appreciate Will's outburst. The dour expression on his face left little doubt over what to expect. He swiveled on his knees, rose up onto his haunches, then to his feet, and just stared for the longest time at the insolent soldier. But he kept a cool head and a lowered voice, warning Will with a military cliché, "As you were, soldier," which was the SOP for telling someone to *shut his goddamned mouth.*

But Will did not comply. He could not accept a simple, "As you were, soldier," in response the his question. His innards were burning and churning, and he couldn't refrain from making matters worse by adding a few words to the already self-destructing exchange. "As you were? Is that it? As you were, soldier? It's all that simple for you, isn't it? You browbeat this poor guy over the head for two days, all for the sake of a goddamned rifle, and now everything's supposed to be forgotten. It isn't forgotten. It's bullshit, Sergeant. Bullshit. Duffy's dead and his goddamned rifle couldn't— scratch couldn't—it didn't, mean shit. This whole fucking war and the army that's waging it is just so much bullshit."

Will had lost control. And he was totally out of character, because, previous to now, he rarely raised his voice and rarely cursed. He was no fool, either. He knew full well he'd just committed a court-martial offense. But at the moment he really didn't give a damn.

Sergeant Baker would have been within his military boundaries, perhaps even his obligation, to destroy Will's entire life. Even more fortunate for Will, Captain Roul, the unit commander, if he so desired could have intervened and sent Will packing to the closest stockade. But he did not barge headlong into the dispute, leaving the sergeant the options to do that which a sergeant is supposed to do, without interference from superiors.

Baker didn't disappoint his commanding officer. He shook a crooked finger in Will's face, then unleashed a verbal assault the like of which no one present had thought him capable of. "I GAVE YOU AN ORDER, MUNDAY. TO STAND AS YOU WERE and by God, I meant STAND AS YOU WERE. Don't try to tie this can on my tail, you untested greenhorn punk."

Will's knees began to tremble. Baker had come on strong enough to intimidate the devil, and for a fleeting moment Will was caught speechless. But he glanced at Duffy's ravaged corpse again, then finally dredged up the courage to continue his tirade. "So ... there ain't a Jap within forty miles of here, huh? If that's true, who in the hell just clobbered us in those planes? Some more Army jingo to bullshit the troops? Why don't you tell Duffy that? Why don't we all join together and tell Duffy there ain't a Jap within forty miles of here? C'mon! All together. Let's hear it for Duffy." Will was crying. He knew it and he didn't give a damn. Tears streamed down his cheeks, streaking his dirty face. He wiped a sleeve across his eyes, then over his cheeks, to blot the teardrops and then he heard his mother's voice calling to him from within, reminding him, "Big boys don't cry."

Baker's initial reaction to Will's tantrum was that of surprise, but he could see that if he ignored such an insubordinate outburst, Will F. Munday would have pinned him to the mat. Even if it had been just the two of them going head-to-head without observers, he could not allow it to stand. To compound the problem, it occurred right in front of the commanding officer, so Baker assumed the military posture of a leader who subscribes to the theory that the best defense is a good offense. Again he jabbed a finger in Will's face, this time pressing the end of the finger squarely against Will's nose. "NO JAPS WITHIN FORTY MILES OF HERE? WHAT THE HELL ARE YOU TALKING ABOUT?" He knew he had never made such a statement and he doubted Schuster had. "Who's feeding that line of crap to you, anyway? There's Japs all over this goddamn island. They're stragglers who didn't surrender when their units were overrun. One, maybe even two of them could be watching us this very minute. Who told you there were no Japs within forty miles of here?" Baker figured he owed Munday that. The forty-mile safety perimeter couldn't have been a figment of Will's imagination.

The surge of anger and nervous energy that had propelled Will thus far began to dissipate. For the first time since he opened his mouth he realized that the eyes of every man were trained directly on him. "Hackmore," he finally managed to say. "It was Corporal Hackmore. He said there were no Japs within forty miles of the replacement depot."

"HACKMORE?" Baker shouted. "Corporal Hackmore, that rear echelon goldbrick who's been dodging combat since he arrived in New Guinea? That's who told you?"

"Yes. Hackmore," Will concurred, explaining, "He told us that the first night he posted us on perimeter guard at the depot."

"Munday, you'd best quit listening to jack-offs like Hackmore, if you don't want to end up with your balls shot off. He wouldn't know a Jap sniper if one fell on him out of a tree," Baker scoffed.

Farmer had been a nervous wreck throughout Baker's and Will's dispute. He knew enough about military codes of ethics to realize his friend was probably in a heap of trouble. He stepped forward and grasp Will's arm, trying to turn him away from Baker, and lead him to safety, but the sergeant quickly rebuffed him, telling Farmer, "As you were, too, soldier. This is between me and Munday. You have no stake in it." Farmer released his grip and stepped back, his face flushed red with embarrassment.

107

But that was a good sign to Will. He thought there might be a light at the end of the tunnel after all. He concluded that if Baker intended to press charges for insubordinate conduct he would already have discontinued the dialogue and would have signaled the epilogue to Will's career in the military. Will realized just how grateful he should be to have Baker and Roul for superiors. They were, he discovered, tolerant personalities who knew how to deal with death in the field. It took Duffy's demise to open Will's eyes. But Baker wasn't quite through with Will. He told him, "You know, Munday, you're an insubordinate bastard. Why am I not surprised? Because I had you figured out the moment I laid eyes on you. You're a crybaby, a whiner, who blames everyone else for anything you can't rationalize. I've seen your kind come and go. It's too goddamn bad this war isn't being conducted to suit your precious, pampered ass ... now, isn't it?"

Will couldn't think of one argument with Baker's assessment of him as a soldier. He already knew he was a whiner, and Baker was right about Will indiscriminately blaming other people. An example might've been his draft board back home who arbitrarily called him up for duty.

"You're barking up the wrong tree, Munday, when you blame me, or anyone else in this command, for what happened here today. A Jap air raid was not on my mind when I awoke this morning. The goddamn Japs killed Duffy, not me. So, get off of my case," Baker informed him.

Will was ready for a checkmate. He nodded in the affirmative but did not reply.

"Do you want to get even for this?" Baker asked Will, then swung his head around, as if to suggest the inquiry included all of them. "Do you want to avenge Duffy's death?" He glanced from man to man. "Take another look, gents, at what those heathens did today," he suggested, pausing to let them each take another gander at Duffy's body. "Hang on to that vision. When we go into combat take that vision with you and then, the first time you have an opportunity to draw a bead on one of those slant-eyed bastards, you won't have any qualms over whether or not to squeeze the trigger." He paused again, swiveled his head around to exchange glances with each and every man, then zeroed in on Will a final time. "As for you, Munday, I've got some reservations over whether you even belong in this unit. I doubt you can make the grade. Unless you screw your head onto your shoulders in the right direction you won't. Somehow, I doubt that you have the backbone or the grit to be the kind of soldier I need on this mission."

Baker pivoted on his toe and spun around to study Tillie for a moment, suggesting to the hillbilly that he "Smile, soldier. I wanta see those pearly teeth."

Tillie forced a smile, offering a subdued glance at each and every one of his buddies, whose eyes were focused on his kisser, and informed Baker, "There they be, Sergeant, right there in my mouth like you done told me."

Sergeant Baker then invited Captain Roul to take charge. Roul, wearing a grim expression across his face, walked to where Williams stood and placed a hand on his forearm, asking him, "Would it be expecting too much if I would ask you to say a few comforting words over our departed comrade, as well as to beef up the spirits of those who remain?"

Will was astonished. First off, he was delighted to duck the spotlight for a change, and secondly he was a trifle surprised over Roul's request. But Williams, being one of God's messengers, appeared to relish the opportunity and, pulling a small, pocket-sized book of the Scriptures from his breast pocket, knelt down beside Duffy's remains and began to spit out the solemn passages of the Lord's Prayer, after which he added, "And Almighty God, bless this comrade who we all knew for such a short time. Take him unto Your bosom, where he might bask in the warmth of Your everlasting love. Give his soul the peace and solitude he sought, but never found, in this mortal life. And, Lord, help those of us who do not fully understand why these things happen to find ways to cope with their grief. Give each and every one of us the strength to deal with those things we cannot change ... in Jesus Christ's name ... Amen."

Williams' missive was short and sweet and to the point; a proper epilogue to Duffy's life, Will thought. He halfway wondered if Williams' special request for intervention to the survivors wasn't solely for his benefit. He had, he realized, made a total ass of himself.

But Captain Roul didn't give them any free time to dwell on the awful mishaps of the day. "Detail a couple of men," he instructed Schuster, "to wrap the body in a blanket, then transport it to the beach. There should be a stretcher or gurney available on the LCI." He paused, then glanced around at the entire crew of men and reminded them, "Busy minds are a must during times like these. You will all make yourself useful in the bivouac area. Hell, it looks like a war zone over there."

A modest, almost forced cackle of laughter filtered through the ranks, and in response Roul concluded, "I think that's because it *is* a war zone." He warned them they'd have to make the best of things until morning, at which time the Quartermaster Corps would deliver some new tents and gear to replace the equipment destroyed in the raid.

Schuster culled out two men for carrying out Roul's orders to remove the corpse. Will was delighted Schuster passed over him. He really didn't think he could arise to the task if summoned to help.

109

The final gloaming of dusk purged daylight from the campsite. Schuster made his rounds inspecting what was left of their accommodations and satisfying himself that his men had done their best to restore the base, informed them, "Not bad, men. Not bad at all. I commend you. I was just told that the waterfront café is re-opened for business. It's quite late. I suggest you all get your asses in gear and get a bite of grub before turning in."

"Cheezus," Tillie exclaimed, "ain't you gonna march us down to chow?"

"I might," Schuster threatened, telling him, "if you're still standing there in about ten seconds."

The stampede for chow was on, but Will didn't try to be first in line this time. He even hesitated, letting the others get ahead, and then stopped for a moment to turn around and survey the damage to their camp. He peered up the draw to the downed palm tree, at the spot where Duffy met his maker. He refocused his attention on the ravaged tents, rent with tears and holes, and hoped it wouldn't rain during the night. There was one bright spot. He believed he could lie in the tent and look up at the stars through the openings in the canvas. He was very tired and was looking forward with a great deal of anticipation to hitting the sack after chow. He needed that time alone to commiserate with his conscience over the disobedient stunt he'd pulled that afternoon. And he needed to unwrap his roily mind, to fantasize to his heart's content about more pleasant things and nicer people; MaryLou for one. The air raid changed many things that afternoon, but it didn't change Will's selfish inspirations to dream about everything he left behind when he was conscripted into the military service; his home, his mother, his college, his professors and mentors, and his love affair with an unresponsive maiden he worshipped.

He was late getting to chow. Everyone else was already seated and there was a commotion at the far end of the table where Tillie was seated. Several sailors were clustered around him, pasting a decal of a little Japanese flag on his helmet. The awkward hillbilly verbally protested but inwardly loved every minute of the presentation. And when they had finished the task, the sailor boys all stepped back, formed a line, and shouted in unison, "Welcome to the South Pacific, pollywogs. You are now veterans." And a roaring cheer echoed throughout the jungle that surrounded their open-aired mess hall.

It was a nice gesture, Will supposed, even though Baker had turned thumbs down on the suggestion earlier. But Baker and Roul were both present and nodded their approval, Baker telling Tillie, "One day. You wear it one day, only. Then the little Jap flag comes off. Deal?"

Tillie nodded in the affirmative, then smiled at Baker.

What amazed Will more than anything else was how tactfully the swab-jockeys handled death and strife and disorder such as they'd gone through that afternoon. It was as if nothing had occurred. He wondered if he, too, would become as callused and tempered to the blues that accompany the chaos of war as the sailors appeared to be. Will scooped up a spam sandwich from the serving table in his one hand and held a steaming cup of coffee in the other, then made his way to the end of the row of tables. He threw Farmer a glance. The country boy had no appetite problem. He was shoveling the food down like a condemned prisoner eats a final meal. But he glanced up and saw Will looking at him, so he picked up his grub and moved over near to where Will was seated, saying, "C'mon, Will. Eat up. It's a long time 'til breakfast. That's what my mama would say if'n I didn't clean my plate at suppertime."

Will gingerly nibbled on the corner of the sandwich, swished the bland-tasting morsels down into his gullet with a swig of coffee and confessed to Farmer, "Eating is an occupational hazard when blood and guts finally make an appearance, isn't it? I have a weak stomach and my appetite went AWOL, I guess."

And then he grinned, recalling Baker chewing out his ass when he confronted the sergeant with the responsibility of Duffy's death.

"Whatcha smiling about?" Farmer asked.

"Oh, I was just thinking," Will replied between bites, "that if Sergeant Baker ground off as much porcelain from his teeth as he nipped skin off of my precious, pampered little ass this afternoon, I'd say we're about even."

Farmer laughed and reached accross the table to pat Will on the back, trying to encourage him, "Look at the bright side. That's the way to do. My mama used to say, when I was down in the dumps, 'Gloom is the Devil's doom.'"

"You're right, like always, Farmer."

"You know, Will, you kinda put me in mind of a colt I once't had back home on the farm," Farmer recalled.

"Me? A colt?" Will asked.

"Yup. But this here animal wasn't just an ordinary colt. He was special, a birthday gift from my pappy on my seventh," Farmer explained.

"Hm-m-m, nice gift. So, how do I remind you of him?"

"Wal, Will, he was a mav'rick of sorts. Had a mind of his own. Wouldn't toe the mark. Temperamental cuss if'n ever I saw one. All the time going off half-cocked. Wal, my daddy was as strong willed as that there colt, you see, and there was a couple'a times I thought they was gonna kill one another. But my daddy's persistence paid off. One day after the colt kicked a hole the size of a watermelon through the barn door my daddy just came around and looked him square in the eye. He took a firm grip on them reins and jerked that colt's head down and informed that obstinate rebel, 'Wal, is it going to be you or me?' It was like some kinda magic, I guess, 'cause from that day on that colt was as fine a pony as a guy could want."

"Okay," Will responded, asking, "What's that got to do with me?"

"Lotsa things," Farmer told him. "Don'cha see? You're the colt and Sergeant Baker is my daddy. Now, you two are gonna be sharing the same corral for a spell and Sergeant Baker's done told you, in so many words, 'Is it gonna be you or me?' So, from where I sit, it looks like the next move's up to you."

Will mulled Farmer's advice over in his mind for a moment, then said, "Perhaps you're right. So ... let's talk about something a little more pleasing, like for instance, did Gambler pay off yet on the bet you guys made this morning?"

"Nope. Not yet. But everthing's been in a turmoil, so..." Farmer replied.

Gambler overheard the comment from a distance and countered with, "I don't need you to remind me about the bet, Munday." He was visibly upset over Will's intervention; an inquiry that might be interpreted to mean Gambler didn't pay his debts. He jerked a wad of bills from his side pocket, peeled off a ten-spot, and handed it down the table to Farmer, asking, "How's about going double or nothing on tomorrow? It's a real chance to double your money. It's really foolish of me to make the offer, but I'm a pushover for foolish bets."

It was a good try, but Farmer wasn't buying. He waved off the offer, telling Gambler, "You're too generous. I'll pass."

Will watched Farmer stuff the ten dollars into his pocket, then began to have misgivings about weather being the terms of the wager. While it was true that Farmer would have lost his bet had it rained, the odds that Duffy would still be alive would have also improved tremendously. Will didn't figure the Japs would have been out searching for targets during a downpour. Then again, if they hadn't come gunning for Americans, Tillie wouldn't have that little Jap flag pasted on his helmet. Will glanced one more time at the tiny Jap flag decal, jumped up onto his feet, and lumbered away toward the bivouac area, trudging along with an easy gait, recapping the events of the past two days. In his own mind he wasn't overly pleased with his comportment. The infiltrator who slipped up behind him his first night on guard duty was one of the unpleasant events that grated him. The encroacher's identity still piqued Will's curiosity. And then his coming totally unglued as he did when first viewing Duffy's corpse was inexcusable. With so much to rue he had doubts over whether or not he'd get a good night's rest. He was, to put it mildly, totally unnerved by his own unconscionable conduct.

The fluffy clouds had parted, giving way to moonbeams that flooded the entire valley. A hot, stiff breeze blew in from the ocean, swishing the tall, gangly palm trees in its wake. Will paused, glanced in every direction, then determined there was no one within fifty yards of where he stood. He liked that. Being a loner was his bag. He chuckled over the thought. Unlike his comrades, he did at least have his thoughts to collaborate with. He knew that comfort was out of the question, because their sleeping bags were in shreds and their cots were twisted into pretzels. But he figured his thoughts would be a sedative that would relieve his anxieties and discomforts. He resumed his journey toward the tent, mumbling to himself, "Thanks, Farmer."

Chapter Seven

Corporal Schuster had every man on his feet at the crack of dawn. The captain had ordered the early rising to get the interrupted routines back on schedule. His thoughts were centered on keeping his men busy to discourage any acute cases of *morning-after blues* that oftentimes afflicted men after their initial encounter with actual warfare. And he obviously decided that the least said about it the better for everyone concerned, because when he took command from Schuster his only mention of the previous day's assault was, "With two exceptions, gentlemen, we owe the Imperial Japanese fighter pilots a 'thank you' for providing us, firsthand, some realism that simulated training sessions cannot offer. The first and most important exception is, of course, Duffy's untimely death. The second is your show of courage in the face of danger, particularly to one member of this unit, who made sure the Japs paid a price for their daring daylight raid by bringing down one of their aircraft. For whatever it might be worth as well as to satisfy your curiosity, Duffy's remains were removed during the night by Grave's Registration personnel and will be laid to rest in the military cemetery here on the island. It was Catherall, I believe, who once said that the three most important foundations to learning are; *seeing much, suffering much and studying much.* I don't think I need to say, in light of yesterday's attack, that you already have seen much and as a result have suffered much. Now, we must study much so that we can retaliate for yesterday's attack." With those words of wisdom he turned the formation over to Sergeant Baker.

During the short span of time that elapsed during the change in command, Will managed to steal a fleeting moment to analyze Roul's message. He halfway guessed that Roul accepted death as a factor that could not be changed in times of war, and he wondered just how many deaths the captain had witnessed. Will didn't think he could ever become so hardened. Death might've been a factor that Baker was referring to when he suggested Will get his head screwed on in the right direction. Will was not apathetic. He believed that apathy was like a cancerous growth that, left unchecked, could

115

eat its way through the veneer of war's glory. It was difficult for Will to foresee a day when the man he saw each morning when he looked in the mirror to shave might become a different person; a Will F. Munday who finally evolved into one of them. Was it possible, he asked himself, to follow in the footsteps of Dorian Gray, allowing the blights of war to desecrate his inner soul, while his outer shell appeared quite normal? He wondered precisely how deep the degrading pit of wickedness was, and if he might eventually tumble to its bottom because of his own indolence. This, among other thoughts, was on his mind that morning while he waited for Baker to take charge.

One apparent plus for Will was the fact that Sergeant Baker apparently hadn't retained any ill feelings toward him over his previous day's insolence. He just went about business as usual, telling his men, "As soon as a suitable replacement for Duffy can be found we'll be back to full strength. Until that time, Gooch will serve a dual purpose by filling his slot along with his scouting duties." He did suggest that, since this group was specially selected, it would be possible to end up training still one man short.

"Today, we're beginning to train in earnest. Stragglers, such as we encountered yesterday, are not acceptable," Baker informed them. "I am going to lead you boys, with a heavy emphasis on boys, into that jungle this morning, and when we come out I intend to be leading a group of men." That said, he instructed Schuster to "Move them out. I'll take the point. Captain Roul informs me he will bring up the rear, a vantage point from which he can observe everyone's progress. Let's go." And the corporal took command to accompany the unit on its maiden trek into the wildwood.

Baker set a grueling pace, ragging anyone who lagged behind, threatening to "leave your goddamn carcasses out here alone as hors d'oeuvres for the crocodiles" if they didn't keep the pace. And he further warned them, "I will not backtrack to look for anyone, so let your conscience be your guide." As a result of Baker's threats Will was left with no options but to put forth his best effort; an effort that dictated to Will that he had to keep abreast of Gooch's accomplishments, as he vowed he would do the previous day. To his surprise he did manage to keep up, which inwardly pleased him and no doubt delighted Sergeant Baker. It was beginning to appear as though Will's and Baker's strained relationship might course along smoothly for a change. Will credited Farmer, as much as anyone, for his change in attitude, recalling the farm boy's fond recollections about the contrary colt he'd been given on his seventh birthday.

Then the training grind began. Day one was followed by day two, then day three, and four, in a seemingly unending, repetitious torture chamber, wherein Baker and Schuster did their best to push the men beyond the brink of endurance. They traipsed through the formidable jungle, attacking imaginary villages, invisible compounds and transparent enemies. Of the eve of the fifth day in the field, Will hit the sack prior to *lights out.* He was exhausted. Farmer wasn't far behind him. He, too, was bushed, telling Will he felt like "a horse that's been run half to death, then was put in the barn still foaming in his own sweat."

Will chuckled. He was always delighted with Farmer's way of wending the subject of any conversation back to his roots. He agreed, though, asking Farmer, "Do you know what this past week reminds me of?"

"Nope!"

"Well ... it's kind of like chasing the little man who wasn't there."

"What little man?"

"You don't know? The *little man* who wasn't there from the poem by the same name," Will explained.

"What poem? Never heard of it."

"Well, I should've known," Will fired back, finally asking, "Don't tell me that you have never heard that poem about the little man who wasn't there."

"Can't say I have."

"Farmer, Farmer, Farmer," Will chided him, "You're admitting I know something that you don't. Amazing. But, not to worry. I owe you one."

"Owe me one what?"

"A return favor. You taught me how to hunt squirrels, so I'm going to teach you the poem about The Little Man Who Wasn't There," Will vowed.

"Will, I had a hunch you were going to do that, but ... that's the dumbest thing I ever heard you say. How can a little man be somethin' if'n he's not there?"

Will cringed. He could see this was not going to be easy. "Okay. You be the judge. Listen up. It goes like this: "Last night I saw upon the stair, the little man who wasn't there. He wasn't there again today. Oh, how I wish he'd go away."

"HU-U-U-U?" Farmer screeched.

"It's a play on words. It's literature."

"It sounds more like some hocus-pocus to me. You know what, Will? I've finally gotcha figured out. Your problem is that your mind's cluttered up with a lot of nonsense," Farmer reproved him.

"Maybe so, maybe not, but I can see you don't get the connection. Our training schedule is like the words in that poem. The compounds we assault are like the little man on the stair, a figment of our imaginations. And like the enemy soldiers we pretend to kill. None of it is real, yet we're supposed to see it," Will countered.

"Wal, if'n you put it that way, I guess it sorta makes sense. Come to think about it, the other morning, they loaded us up again on the LCI, then took us out a mile or so into the ocean, dumped our butts back into those rubber rafts, told us to keep our heads down, and cut us loose. They said we was establishing a beachhead. How could I tell? I had my head down so I couldn't see a thing," Farmer reluctantly agreed.

"Yeah. And d'ya want to know what really burns my ass? It's the captain. He stands off at a safe distance all of the time just waiting for one of us to screw up so's he can chew some ass. First I see him, then I don't, and when I do he's peering through his binoculars like a, well, kinda like a poltergeist," Will complained.

"What's a poltergeist?"

"A ghost!"

"Knock it off, Will. I don't like talking about ghosts," Farmer protested.

"Oh-h-h-h ... you don't, huh? Well, I'll be damned. I didn't figure you had a squeamish bone in your body, but you do. You're afraid of ghosts," Will wrangled him.

"I am not," Farmer yelped, sitting straight up in bed.

"Sure you are. And here you had me believing farmers didn't fear anything."

"I don't, 'ceptin' unnatural things. I ain't scared of any people."

"Ghosts are people ... they're just dead people."

"Knock it off, Will. You're giving me the willies," Farmer insisted, shaking a clenched fist a Will.

"YEAH! Knock it off, both of you. You're keeping me awake and I'm due on sentry duty at 0200. Settle your argument in the morning," Gambler yelled, trying to separate the two so they would shut up and let him catch some shuteye.

Will grinned; a self-satisfied, Cheshire cat sort of smirk that might've irked Farmer if he'd seen it. But Will said nothing. He was gloating, thinking, *Farmer, you sly old fox, you REALLY are afraid of ghosts.*

The following two weeks, Baker's dozen continued their hot pursuit of the little man who wasn't there. Will, however, was undergoing a radical change in both his actions as well as his attitude. Early one morning, during the third week of training, Will's attitude adjustment hit a snag just as he was coming off of sentry duty at 0600 hours. He had just rounded the rear corner of his tent and was about to swing around front to enter, when he overheard his name being bantered about in a conversation. He paused for a moment, wondering what it was all about and was also reluctant to just go inside on a pretense he'd heard nothing. Common sense told him to ignore it and get inside, but his curiosity won out and he stopped short of the front tent flap and listened.

"I don't get it, you dumb hick. What the hell do you see in Munday that no one else sees?" Gambler asked of Farmer, adding that "not a single guy in the outfit really likes him. Hell, man, it's like you worship the ground he walks on."

"So?" Farmer tried to minimize Gambler's view of Will.

"The way you stick by that asshole, even when he's wrong, is a crying shame," Gambler continued his tirade.

Will could sense by Farmer's tone of voice that Gambler had miffed him with the inquiry. "Wal, first off, he ain't an asshole, so don't be calling him one around me," Farmer fielded Gambler's opinionated remark. "And secondly, you don't give the guy an even break. If'n you'd lighten up a little you might even end up liking Will. He's an okay guy. Smart, too."

Gambler laughed, informing Farmer, "Me like Munday? That'll be the day. Baker's got him figured, all right. He's a whiner."

Farmer sounded perplexed. "Wal, you know," he suggested, "maybe the reason I get along with Will is because I understand him. He reminds me of Flicker."

"What the fuck's a flicker?"

"It ain't a what. It's a horse I once had," Farmer tried to explain, recalling his conversation with Will that evening concerning the colt he'd gotten on his seventh birthday.

"Horse? Horse's ass is more like it," Gambler cut him short.

Will thought it was time to make his entrance so he cleared his throat, shuffled his feet in the loose dirt, then lifted the tent flap and went inside pretending he'd heard nothing. His entry was greeted by an awkward silence, but he said, "Good morning," in a cheerful tone of voice, then asked, "What's on tap for today?" while he peeled off his web equipment and tossed it onto his cot.

He was actually quite disappointed after hearing the argument between Farmer and Gambler. Will had believed his relationship with the cardsharp was on the mend, since they'd had no hostile interchanges for quite a spell. Now, it appeared, he needed to reassess his affiliation with Gambler. In fact, he even considered giving up on his effort to cultivate a friendly atmosphere with the shyster. Gambler friendship, it seemed to Will, wasn't worth the hassle. The bright side, of course, was Farmer's reliant defense of Will's obstinate shortcomings. He regretted he'd paused long enough to listen, but he was happy to know that his faithful friend, Farmer, was still loyal and steadfast in his defense.

Will didn't yet know what the day's training schedule consisted of. The dispute between Farmer and Gambler, as things promised to turn out, was kid stuff. Will was in for a profound setback that day.

As soon as chow was finished and the unit was formed, Baker led his beleaguered troops up the steep ridges that formed the range of mountains south of the campsite. They climbed higher and higher, wiggling their way through obstinate undergrowth at times. Will's obsession with the flatlands was about to be compromised. Right at the moment Will was the only member of Stopwatch to suspect that he would customarily walk a mile out of his way to avoid skirting a precipice on the trail. He wasn't even comfortable looking out of a second-story window of the college dorm back home. Will was an acrophobic, but he'd deliberately neglected to confide those fears to anyone, including his best friend, Farmer. The deception was about to end. He'd managed to bluff his way through a lot of things since his induction, but this appeared to be an obstacle he couldn't fathom. Even his descent down the rope nets from the ship into a Higgins boat when they went ashore on New Guinea, while a traumatic venture, was bearable. At that time he hated to appear *chicken* in front of everyone with enough moxy to disembark from the ship like a man. But he knew that eventually a day would dawn when his pretense would be stripped bare naked. This was beginning to look like that day.

Corporal Schuster took charge of the unit when it was given one of the Army's infamous *"smoke if you've got 'em"* rest periods just after the unit climbed to the summit of a towering mountain peak. It was already mid-morning. Will silently wished the day was over. And when Schuster informed them that the subject of the day's class would be their "Introduction to an M-1, A-2 elevator,"—which, as things turned out, was simply a long coil of rope that Schuster was waving back and forth, clenched in the a fist, above his head—Will's heart skipped a beat. He was momentarily stunned. The palms of his hands began to sweat, his chest was palpitating and his tongue withered up like a piece of dry sponge in his throat.

Will's worst fears had been realized. The suspicions that pestered his thoughts while they climbed the hills all morning had materialized. Sir Isaac Newton's theory of *what goes up must eventually come down* was about to be tested for its accuracy. This was the moment of truth; the truth being that Will would be labeled a coward by this comrades if he refused to repel a rope down the sheer side of a precipice. And refusing any such order was exactly what he had in mind. Will just stood there, caught up in a barrage of memories of the indignities he'd tolerated during his stint in the Army, recalling the needle brigade at Camp Hood's dispensary and the degenerate major at Camp Dodge who inquired into his fascination with masturbating. Still fresh on his mind were the illiterate corporals like Hackmore at the replacement depot, whose projection of the enemy's nearness led Will into an ambush with Baker, which resulted in him being called, among other things, a "jurblowf," and even more recently a "whiner" and a "crybaby." Adding insult to injury, he recalled how he'd been subjected to the rigorous task of taking a twenty-five-mile forced march and the very next day was ordered to crawl on his belly like reptile through the infiltration course while some lamebrain fired a machine gun just inches above his head. All too often he was made to stand guard hour after hour in a downpour of rain. He felt as though he had been deprived of adequate nourishment when they handed him a packet of rations just big enough to tease his taste buds but small enough to leave him to suffer pangs of hunger. On the whole, he could remember nothing in the Army except countless disparaging assignments that withered his enthusiasm. But this assignment was the last straw. Will F. Munday, who'd really never tried to hide the fact that he was a reluctant warrior, decided it was *put up or shut up time.* He had every intention of drawing a line in the sand. Enough was enough. He would not repel a rope or scale a cliff or even get near enough to the edge of this perpendicular passageway to purgatory to look down. Compromise was not an option.

Unfortunately, while encompassed with thought, Will had already missed a considerable part the Schuster's presentation. The first words he could recall hearing were, "A guy never knows what's in store for him."

Will knew what was in store for him. He was on the verge of disobeying orders, which would earn him a court-martial, and he'd probably end up spending the rest of his life in a stockade for refusing to repel a cliff. In his way of thinking he should be pitied as a casualty of the war; the victim, the oppressed, the loser. He knew better, however. Sympathy was next to nonexistent in the military dictionary.

"A cliff is merely another obstacle to overcome," Schuster was explaining when he finally garnered Will's undivided attention. "Before we reach our final objective of this mission it's hard to say what we might encounter. Now, I've seen a day when we were forced to use a vine ... yes, a vine ... instead of a rope and, worse yet, we had to bare-knuckle our way down the face of a cliff because we were not properly prepared to tackle an unexpected obstacle. See, you lucky stiffs, the Army is pampering you. This is rope, not a vine," Schuster explained, shaking the coil aloft for a second time, "in keeping with the theme that nothing's too good for the troops." The comment drew a round of laughter from his pupils.

"Now, pay attention," Schuster cautioned them as he hooked a strand of rope about his waist, then tied a half-knot across his stomach. Bending forward, he reached behind his thighs, grabbed the rope's loose end, drew it taut up onto his shoulders, and squatted like a duck, explaining, "This is the position you attain to take the slack up in the rope." Jumping up onto his feet, he brought the loose ends around to his front side, tucked them underneath the waist band of the rope, and informed them, "And d'ya know what I've got? Well, gents, it's a crude version of a Swiss seat. Like I said in the beginning, this is your M-1, A-2 elevator; a handy tool to take you safely down a cliff side."

Will gulped, so loud in fact that several of his buddies turned and stared at him, Gambler sounding off as usual with a bright remark, "Bring that up again, Munday, so we can vote on it."

Will was actually beginning to regret his disparaging image of corporals, because Schuster did seem to be an adroit man for a two-striper. He was, at least in Will's estimation, above average, which was a contradiction to his opinion about those he'd met on previous occasions.

Schuster broke out several coils of rope and began to toss them to different individuals, suggesting, "Now, we're going to find out if you paid attention to the guidelines I gave you. If you make a suitable copy of my rope seat you should be able to repel down the cliff without any problems. That will indicate that I am a good teacher. If you screw up the seat and break your neck, that will suggest that you are a poor student. So, get busy and make me proud of you. I wanta see some Swiss seats."

"Are you kidding?" Perkins questioned Schuster, suggesting to him, "That's a stacked deck. Either way, you come out smelling like a rose."

"Yeah," Schuster replied with a grin. "Rank does have its privileges, doesn't it? Now, get to cracking."

Having had the final word, the corporal began to weave in, through and around the group, all of whom had busied themselves trying to copy Schuster's example. He would pause to make a suggestion, turn around to help someone else, then make another inspection tour. Finally, satisfied they'd done their best, he examined each rope harness carefully, pulled and tugged to check the knots, and assured himself that no one would meet their maker as a result of using a faulty harness. "NOW," he informed them, "it's that time. I'll bet you guys are really anxious to try these on for size, aren't you? So, let's get with it."

Will wasn't anywhere near ready to take the plunge. In fact, it disturbed him to no end when the others ribbed each other with barbs Will didn't think were cute; classics such as, "Watch yourself going over of the edge. The first step's a long one." And when someone else wisecracked, "Don't fret. It ain't the fall that hurts. It's the sudden stop at the bottom," Will almost fainted.

Schuster led them to the jumping-off point, where Sergeant Baker took charge and told them, "The corporal will now demonstrate the correct way to take a ride on his Toonerville trolley." He pulled his backpack off and tossed it onto the ground, then fished his hand inside and came out with a fistful of gloves. "These," he explained, "will protect your hands against rope burns. You will be issued a pair here today and you'd best have them if the need ever arises." He began to toss gloves to each and every man, including Schuster, then took the last pair himself. "We have enough seats for about half of you to take the first plunge," he observed.

Upon hearing that remark Will was elated. Perhaps, he thought to himself, he would be one of those who didn't have to repel the cliff side. Baker squelched that idea. "As soon as the first group has descended, we will haul the harnesses back up for the others," Baker informed them. That was definitely disturbing news.

Everyone else, however, was engaged watching Schuster snap the ring onto a rope, then slowly backstep toward the edge of the precipice. Captain Roul, who'd remained behind the scenes until now, stepped up to steady the rope, which was tethered to a towering palm tree. Will had to force himself to look. He was actually fearful for the corporal and once again his hands dripped with sweat and a cold chill darted up his spine, then came to rest like an ice cube on the nape of his neck. His knees were trembling. He tried to steady them, lest someone else take notice. Will was totally terrified. In fact, he didn't recall being this rattled during the strafing raid on the first day of training. And even worse, he realized that no one else would understand his agony unless they, too, were acrophobia afflicted. The odds were a million to one against the possibility. He was, he formulated in his thoughts, actually *fucked by the fickle finer of fate,* just like the Army adage claimed.

Schuster tugged at the rope, took up the slack, leaned his hind end out over the cliff's edge, then promptly jumped backwards and vanished from view, his voice echoing back up the hillside as he descended, "Take it. And follow me."

"Who's next?" Baker asked, dangling a rope harness in his outstretched hand. He glanced from man to man.

"Cheezus," Tillie exclaimed, "I'll go next if'n it's okay by you, Sarge, er, I mean Sergeant."

Baker nodded and pitched him a harness. "You know," Tillie jabbered while stepping into the rope contraption, "this here kinda reminds me of traipsing through the woods chasing coon. I coulda used one'a these here gadgets a time or two back home." He cinched the harness tight, snapped onto the rope with the ring, pivoted on his toe, then ever so slowly inched his way back until his heels were hanging over the brink. He appeared to be a trifle nervous, but not frightened half to death as was Will. He tugged on the rope just as Schuster had, then leaped backwards and out of sight, to a chorus of "ohs" and "ahs" from the others.

"Did he make it?" Gambler shouted.

"I didn't hear anything splatter," Slycord wised off. "Seeing as how it's Tillie, do you realize what a racket a guy as full of shit as he is would make when they hit the ground?"

"Funne-e-e-e-e!" Gambler reprooved Sly's pun.

"The way to find out, Gambler," Baker suggested, "is to go down yourself and take a look." He helped Roul tie off a second rope to a tree and flung the loose end over the side, then suggested, "This'll go twice as fast with two men going at a time." He ferreted out O'Hare and told him, "Gambler requests the presence of your company for the trip down. Would you oblige?"

O'Hare forced a grin, glanced at the other men, then reached out to garner his harness. Quickly stepping into it, then pulling it up and about his torso and rump, he took hold of the other rope and stepped closer to Gambler, asking, "Well, you betting fool, what's the odds we'll make it?"

Gambler chuckled. "I've said it before and I'll say it again. A good gambler never bets against himself," he yelped just as he leaped backwards from the cliff's abrupt edge. O'Hare was just a step behind him.

And so it went, two by two, until they paused to hoist the harnesses back up the grade for the others to use. Will had not yet been singled out. It puzzled him. Of course, he had no intention of making such a leap, so it really didn't matter. But after everyone else had disappeared over the rim of the canyon wall a short time later, Baker and Will were both left standing, arms akimbo, starting at each other. Roul had even disappeared. And Will could not recall seeing the captain take the Toonerville trolley down, so he did wonder where he'd vanished to.

"What're you waiting for, Munday? An engraved invitation?" Baker asked, informing Will, "It'll do you no good to put off what must be done. It's not the Army's way."

"Sergeant, sir?" Will finally managed to utter. He figured he might as well have the showdown now as later. He decided to tell Baker the truth, that he was terrified of heights, but before I could speak a solitary word the wily, old soldier beat him to the punch.

"I know. You've got a problem with heights. I've known it for some time. But you can't run away from your phobia any longer. If you want your diploma from Breakneck University you've got to take this plunge," Baker explained in a calm yet understanding voice.

"Sergeant, I ... I just ... I just can't—" Will managed to mutter before Baker cut him off with a sweep of his hand across the face.

"You can. And you will. I waited to go last just because I anticipated your reaction," Baker surprised him. "We're going down together. You on one rope, me on the other, side by side. I'll talk you down. I'll do whatever it takes. So grab that harness and get hitched up."

Will's hands were noticeably trembling when he plucked the harness from Baker's hand. He was also tongue-tied. He was just going through the motions as directed by Baker to don the harness and clip the ring onto the rope. Finally, Baker paused a moment after checking Will's gear out and said, "If it'll make you feel any better, you're not the first acrophobic I've encountered in this man's army. Not by a damned sight. But you will rise to the task."

Will was taken aback a bit by Baker's compromising attitude. Here was the sergeant who just three weeks earlier had called him a whiner and a pampered ass, suddenly catering to him. Was it, he wondered, just a con job or was Baker sincere? The sergeant gave him little time to consider the question.

"Let's go, Munday," Baker prodded him to begin pussyfooting backwards toward the rim. As they neared the crumbling edge Baker threw down the gauntlet. "You had me worried for a minute there, soldier. I thought you were considering taking up residence on this hilltop. Or, even worse, was tempted to refuse orders. Don't tell me that you've been busting your ass for three weeks to make me eat my words all for nothing? One more step, Munday, then kick off and let yourself swing back, so you can kick off of the bank, repeating the task to drop a few feet each time. I'll be right beside you. GO-O-O," Baker barked in summation and flung himself over the side.

A sudden surge of courage overwhelmed Will and he leaped back out into space and found himself dropping like a lead pipe. He recalled Schuster's mention of using the gloved hand as a brake. He grasped the rope underneath his thigh, and slowed his pace, then slammed against the wall, floundering, trying to kick himself free to avoid being laced by the crumbs of dirt that were spraying his face. That was when he glanced to the side and discovered that Baker was nowhere in sight. The sergeant had taken the quick route down and was already on the ground, shouting to Will, "C'mon. You're doing fine."

"That sonofabitch," Will mumbled. "He screwed me." Nevertheless, Will finally managed to reach the bottom, where he was rewarded with a big round of applause from his comrades, all of who'd been told while they watched Will struggling to join them that he suffered from acute acrophobia.

Although Will was tickled pink over mastering the task, he was taken aback when he saw Captain Roul standing there looking at him. He glanced back up at the top of the ledge, then back at Roul, and finally asked, "Permission to speak, sir?"

"Yes, Munday. Permission granted," Roul replied.

"Well, sir ... you were up there. You never repelled. But now you are standing here," Will inquired.

Captain Roul grinned and pointed over yonder, saying, "Oh, that. Yes, Munday. I walked down. Right over there at the end of the bluff. It's a trail the natives use."

"What?" Will exclaimed. Will had to admit to himself that the day hadn't been a banner day for him.

With the repelling exercise behind them, Baker took his men on a leisurely hike through the jungle that afternoon, pointing out various traps to avoid. Will needed the pause in his rigorous training schedule to recover his wits. The cross-country trek did require them to wade through a waist-deep swamp, and to take turns hacking their way through a canebrake, but they finally topped a hill just south of their campsite, a vantage point from which they could see their tents in the valley below. The view didn't come any too soon for the vanquished troops, all of whom were dragging their asses back into camp.

Will was totally exhausted. He headed straight into his tent when they were dismissed and began to peel off his gear, then fell face down on his cot and asked Farmer to "Wake me up when this goddamn war is over."

"It's chow time, Will. Aren't you going to eat?" Farmer asked.

"Are you kidding?" Will retorted. "Remember when Captain Roul told us that come nightfall we'd be glad to cuddle up to our bedrolls like they were a sensuous female? It was something like that, anyway."

"Yeah," Farmer replied.

"Well," Will said, as he hugged, then planted a big kiss on his pillow, "Goodnight, my dear."

He was already sound asleep when his head hit the bed. Farmer knelt down and unlaced Will's leggings, removed them from the calves of his legs, then jerked off his shoes and after he tossed them onto the ground stood up, towering over his friend, popped him on the rump with an open hand, and murmured in a caring tone of voice, "Sleep tight, Will. Don't let the bedbugs bite." Laughing softly to himself, he tiptoed through the tent flap and headed for the beach, because he was subject to a long-standing practice of eating his meals on schedule. Running faster with each step he took, Farmer charged into the seaside diner, waving his messkit in the air, shouting, "Hold everything. Shore sorry I'm late, but I'm hungry enough to eat a horse."

"We're fresh outta horse meat," the mess steward informed Farmer, then asked, "and where's goody two-shoes?"

"Goody who?" Farmer asked.

"Motormouth. Your friend who has a champagne taste on a private's pay."

"Oh, you mean Will."

"Yeah!"

"He's fast asleep."

"Thank you. You just made my day, mate. What's your pleasure? Caviar?"

Chapter Eight

Will estimated at the end of the third week of training that he'd explored the better half of the secluded reaches in New Guinea's rain forests while in reality he'd barely scratched the surface of the humungous island. Baker said they were "being acclimatized" for the hardships that lay ahead, using a word that very few of them knew meaning of. In fact, Will was a trifle surprised to hear Baker use a four-syllable word like it was an everyday habit. But the sergeant evidently knew its meaning, because he followed up with a caveat, advising them all, "We're prepping you for the austere lifestyles you're about to encounter." The upcoming mission, he warned them, "will offer frightful hardships. And your body and mind must be callused to endure the adversity of the situation." Adversity, he promised them, would definitely be on the menu in coming weeks.

The island's interior was savage. Will's analysis of New Guinea, when Farmer asked his opinion, was, "It's an unpleasant, primeval sanctum of contradictory extremes."

"A what?" Farmer exclaimed.

Will waved him off, saying, "Scratch that, Farmer. I'm so depressed over it I don't feel like taking time to explain. Just forget I said that."

But Will's observation was on target. The sunlight was all too often eclipsed by dense overhead foliage that hung like a shroud above the jungle's floor. A web of helter-skelter vines intertwined in, around and through the coppice, reminding Will of the lace curtains that draped his grandmother's window sills back home. Other times he discovered large open areas, sparse of either brush, bush or tree, but too frequently clogged with shoulder-high grass that obstructed his view and hindered his progress. Occasionally, they encountered canebrakes that were impossible to penetrate, a solid wall of bamboo that forced them to either detour to circumvent it or chop their way through it. One moment they could navigate freely, using distant landmarks as guides, only to discover a short time later that they could see no further than a few yards, and without the aid of Baker's compass, they might've all been smothered to death inside of nature's labyrinth.

It was then that Sergeant Baker introduced them to the machete; a crude, old-fashioned weapon in use since the bronze age. Still effective, although primitive, it was the logical tool for castrating obstinate terrain. He and Schuster taught them how to hold the long, razor-sharp knife and how to swing the blade, sweep left, then right, so as to open a swath through the cantankerous hinterland. So, each and everyone of the men would soon have another piece of equipment to lug around, as though they didn't already have a surplus. It was, Baker explained, "Standard gear from here on in. You'll be issued a machete when we return to camp."

That set Will's mind to wondering exactly what did lie in store. Were the jungles they were scheduled to conquer even more foreboding than those of New Guinea? He did, however, conclude it was a positive step. Someone was thinking ahead. He had been plagued with doubts over whether anyone did know what direction they were headed since the first day of training. What he had encountered so far consisted of a sea of new faces in the ranks, imperious swamplands, ferocious crocodiles, nasty little leaches, ugly centipedes, poisonous snakes, snakes not so poisonous but equally as ill tempered who, as Baker described them, "might not kill you but can make you mighty sick because they do not brush their teeth," and the worst enemy of all, swarms of malaria-infected mosquitoes. The jungle was an everlasting hothouse; a breeding ground for almost anything and everything obnoxious.

The previous day Schuster pointed out a flock of bats hanging from the upper limbs of the trees, dozing until nightfall, at which time, as the corporal warned them, "they can swoop down and put a hurt on you. They are often diseased. Watch out for bats." Will feared the crocodiles most of all, he thought. There was something awfully menacing about them. They thrived in the stifling, muggy air that caressed the swampland. "I've seen 'em close to fifteen feet long," Schuster advised them the first time they encountered one of the creatures. That had been a week earlier. "Crocs," he said, "move gracefully through the water, exposing only their snoot and eyes. You might not see them until they're on top of you, and that's a tad late. If you do see one, head for dry land ... pronto. The lion might be the king of the jungle in darkest Africa, but the croc is the master here."

Snakes, such as one elongated reptile Baker had called their attention to one day, also gave Will a creepy feeling. "Give them plenty of room. Take a detour if need be. Don't aggravate pythons. Unlike some smaller species, they become aggressors if provoked. They customarily dine on small game but are known to go after humans." There were many other species, some quite small, but just as deadly, Baker cautioned them. And mosquitoes, while no bigger than a speck sometimes, could be the most prolific predator of all.

They carried the Malaria germ. "Don"t forget to take your dose of Atabrine every day," the sergeant reminded them. Atabrine was a miracle drug that, while it was not a cure for Malaria, or even a preventative, would suppress the symptoms indefinitely. "We need well bodies. Malaria can knock you out for weeks, even kill you," he added, again mentioning, "Atabrine. Every day. Without fail."

As things were turning out, Will reevaluated Baker's claim that the jungle was an ally and decided it was an adversary as well. He thought he had seen every possible species of reptile that inhabited the earth, along with a zillion varieties of strange birds, bats, bugs and worms, all of which could make life miserable. The common leach was one of the worst. He shuddered just thinking about leaches, how they would latch on to a man's body, then cop a blood transfusion from their veins, and lastly refuse to part company until someone lit a cigarette and singed their keister with the smoldering embers. "Don't jerk them off. Encourage them to withdraw gracefully," Schuster suggested.

The overall outlook for the Stopwatch team was encouraging, though. It was gradually melding into a confederation of sorts after three weeks in the bush. Will could tell by just watching Roul that the captain was pleased with what he saw. That night when they convened for their customary critique, the captain took notice of the camaraderie. He was overly pleased with how they began to participate in discussions, and their willingness to offer ideas of their own to supplant regimented practices that all too often didn't measure up in their surroundings. O'Hare was one of the first to admit that he could fully understand why the natives rarely ventured into the forests on a lark. He asked the others if they'd even seen a New Guinea native. He hadn't, he confessed. "Where are they?" he wondered.

"Around," Baker assured them. "They're out there. They see us but don't want us to see them."

"Cheezus," Tillie exclaimed. "D'ya mean we're being stalked by a bunch of headhunters?" A shiver tickled his spine.

"No. Not headhunters. Natives. They're friendly, but are also skeptical. They prefer to keep to themselves. They mean you no harm," Baker said. "After their treatment at the hands of the Japs they look on us with a much higher esteem."

Roul's ears rejoiced when he eavesdropped on the meeting. He finally strode into the circle, dropped down onto his haunches, then his buttocks, and said, "You men have done yourself proud so far. We still have a ways to go, but I'm confident we will be ready when the call comes to move out." He paused a moment, then glanced around from man to man, adding,

"Remember this. Even the bravest of brave men have faltered when their stomachs turned into a bowl full of jelly over something frightening. It is a natural instinct. As I listen here tonight I can see that you are all wondering how you will respond when it comes time to face off against the enemy. That is a good sign, not a bad sign. I'm confident you will do well. And now, we should call it a night."

Will's mind wandered back a few days to the evening that Sergeant Baker had instructed Tillie and Gambler to "Take all of the canteens down to the swamp and fill them. And remember two things. No! Remember three things. First off, brush the moss away from the surface of the water. Second, make damn sure you add a purification tablet to each canteen. And third, keep an eye peeled for the crocs."

Neither Tillie nor Gambler moved a muscle. "Well?" Baker barked. "What're you waiting for ... an armed escort?"

Still they dilly-dallied, stalling for time, until they riled Baker's ire a second time. "Have you guys got a hook up your ass?" he inquired in a sarcastic tone of voice.

"Wal ... no, sir ... Sergeant, but ... how's come everybody just don't go down there and fill their own canteen?" Tillie grumbled.

The exchange caught Will's ear. He listened intently, wondering how Baker would handle this minor rebellion. Finally, Gambler offered his two cents' worth. "Well, Sergeant, we was wondering why we get singled out to go down to the swamp and stick our hands in that crocodile-infested fish bowl. What I'm asking is ... how's come we get stuck with the shit details?"

"Oh ... I see," Baker responded. "CROCODILES! Is that what this delay is all about? You guys are scared of a few crocs?"

Tillie and Gambler eyeballed each other, exchanging timorous glances, but said nothing.

"Is your silence a *yes* or a *no*?" Baker asked.

Still, Baker's inquiry went unanswered. Finally, he exploded. "I'll be a sad sack of shit. Soldiers, huh? You guys take the cake. It really frosts my ass. If you haven't got the guts to fetch some water because of a few crocs, we're going to be in a hurt when we get into action. Has it occurred to you that they might be sleeping and that if you are very quiet and don't disturb them, as did occur once, there'll be no danger? And have you considered the possibility that they are as afraid of you as you are of them?"

"Ah-haw!" Tillie yelped, explaining that fear was part of the problem.

"Problem? How so?"

"Yup! The problem is about them crocs being afraid of us, not us being afraid of them," Tillie claimed.

132

"Try to make me understand. Please, Tillie. And this'd better be good because if it isn't I'll consider your reluctance to fetch water from the swamp as disobeying orders," Baker told the both of them with a dour expression of disgust twisting his face.

"Wal … Cheezus, Sarge … er, I mean Sergeant … them crocs being scared of us IS the reason," Tillie. "We're just thinking about everyone's health."

"Everyone's health? How so?"

"Wal … if'n, like you say, them crocks is even half as scared of us as we are of them, then that water won't be fit to drink on account'a we mighta scared the peewadden out'a them," Tillie replied.

"Peewadden? What the hell is peewadden?" Baker inquired, realizing that it was some confounded hillbilly term that meant piss. But Sergeant Baker found it difficult to conceal his amusement. He joined the whole group in a belly laugh which, for a fleeting moment, raised the possibility that he might change his orders. Tillie was elated. It appeared to him that he'd knocked the wind out of Baker's sails and by so doing got himself and Gambler off the hook.

He was mistaken on both counts. "Very funny, soldier. Just what we need in this outfit. A comedian. So, if that's the finale of your performance, you can make your curtain call by trotting your asses down to the swamp so's you two can fill all of the canteens—just like I ordered you to do to begin with."

The pair of disgruntled soldiers collected everyone's canteen and turned tail toward the swamp, grumbling to each other as they vanished into the gloom of night that they were being picked on by Sergeant Baker, and each one trying to place the blame on the other one.

Actually, there might've been some truth to the accusation, because Tillie had caused quite a stir that same morning when he deliberately aggravated several crocodiles who, prior to his intervention, were satisfied to snooze a spell on the bank of the swamp the troops were scheduled to wade through. Tillie came close to being eaten by one of the crocs because of a childish stunt he pulled and was probably still alive thanks to Williams, who squeezed off a burst of bullets from the business end of his BAR into the approaching reptiles, to divert their attention away from the hillbilly. But there was more to the story. Tillie's feet got mired down in the swamp floor when he tried to make a quick turn to head for shore, and down he went into the murky water. It was Baker's and Schuster's instant response that saved him. Tillie was flaying around with his arms, trying to keep his head above the water, while Baker and Schuster were pulling him loose from the muck in a effort to get him out of harm's way. Although Williams did deter the menace for a

133

moment, the commotion Tillie provoked only made matters worse, because the rankled crocs turned back in his direction as soon as Williams suspended his fire. The way Will saw it, the only thing that actually saved Tillie, Baker and Schuster from certain death was when half the men brought their sights to bear on the creepy crocs and cut loose with a hail of gunfire that hit several of the predators. The water was churning and was also turning red, stained from the blood the crew drew with their volley of gunfire, and the crocs lost interest in Tillie and began to fight among themselves over the bullet-riddled remains of the crocs who'd been hit. During the impasse, Baker and Schuster managed to make land with Tillie. Baker was furious, as well he should've been. It was an encore of the day when Will challenged the sergeant over Duffy's death, if not worse.

"What the fuck's the matter with you ... you dumb bastard," Baker shrieked. "Do you see what you've just done? You put the whole damned outfit in harm's way over a stupid prank." He paused, glanced down at his soiled uniform, took a quick gander at Schuster's attire as well, then lit into Tillie again, asking, "Whatever possessed you to provoke those crocs, anyway? Listen up! If you ever pull a stunt like that again I'm personally going to feed you to those goddamn crocs. Is that clear?"

Tillie was totally subdued, which was rare for him. He offered no response, no silly grin, no wise cracks, as he customarily did when Baker got on his butt. So, Will sort of figured that Baker might be seeking some recompense in retribution for his bath in the murky swamp that morning when he assigned the shit detail to the pair. As for Gambler, Will supposed that Baker figured Gambler had done something wrong during the course of the day to deserve the canteen-filling chore. Besides, Tillie and Gambler were bosom buddies. The assignment made sense, to Will anyway.

The team returned to their base Saturday evening after a final exercise in deployment. It was nearing chow time when they marched back into the company street. Baker dismissed them with a cheerful thought. "The captain," he informed them, "has given you tomorrow off. He believes you have earned it. We are slightly ahead of projection in the training schedule."

The chow was another surprise. Will dined on a three-course meal for a change; the first one in weeks. They were served meatloaf, instant mashed potatoes swimming in brown gravy, whole kernel corn, and some freshly baked bread with a generous portion of some spread that resembled butter. The robust mess attendant even suppressed his customary urge to lace Will's meal with a ladle of fruit cocktail, inquiring instead while he waved the utensil above Will's mess kit, "D'ya wanta pass the laxative tonight?" Will nodded in the affirmative.

So, it appeared to Will that things were finally taking a turn for the better. Just having a day off to rest was a treat. It would give everyone adequate opportunity to catch up on their letter writing to the folks back home, or to sleep in awhile Sunday morning without Schuster's raucous awakening, even some time to make some minor adjustments and repairs on their personal gear. Gambler could break out the Bicycles and skim a few bucks from his friends, because they were to be paid that evening following chow. And the rumor mill could grind out dozens of inconceivable possibilities about their future. It figured to be tough, because Roul authorized a beer ration along with the back pay. In the Army, Will had learned long before, something bad customarily followed something good.

For Will F. Munday the words *day off* were a misnomer. It really had little significance for him. He wrote few letters, had no major flaws to repair on his gear, and a pass off base for recreation was out of the question. There was no place to go if he had a pass. And even if there was, he couldn't imagine having a jolly good time in a grass-hut community in the middle of nowhere.

A bag of incoming mail arrived on board a Jeep that rolled into camp before they had finished their meal. Everyone ran to get their mail; everyone except Will. As usual, Will came up empty-handed. It was his own doing. He just couldn't seem to justify writing to anyone back home, even to his mother, whom he dearly missed. There was, he decided, nothing to say. Anything he might want to say would be censored out of his letter, and anything that wouldn't be censored out wouldn't be worth writing about. He visualized a letter home as a cut-up piece of paper that began, "Dear Mom," was slashed to ribbons, then ended, "With love, Will."

Will did take his share of beer, then sulked off to drink by himself, where he could have a relationship with someone equally as intelligent as he; himself.

But Sunday morning ushered in a few surprises. A batch of unexpected visitors arrived at their remote campsite; a Jeep-load of brass hats who parleyed with Roul for most of the morning aboard the LCI. There was a lot of speculation among the men concerning their immediate futures. The rumor mill was in high gear because of the unexpected visitation. One rumor was, "The war's over." Everyone turned thumbs down on that. Another was, "I think we're moving out."

They knew no more when the guests departed than when they had arrived, except to notice the dour expressions that daunted their faces as the visitors climbed aboard the Jeep and bid Roul goodbye. Roul kept a tight lip throughout the day, letting his men speculate to their heart's content. Will's speculation wasn't rosy. He calculated that the unexpected visit spawned a message of bad tidings. That was how the Army operated. No news, contrary to the customary rule, was bad news.

Will made sure he had his affairs in order and his gear ready for Monday morning formation prior to noontime. He then slinked away into the jungle for a much need rally with his roily thoughts. It had been several days since he'd commiserated with his mind, and he no sooner plunked his carcass down beside a clump of bushes than he took the helm for his intellectual voyage back into reverie; reverie in this particular case being a few moments alone with a mental vision of MaryLou.

His thoughts drifted back to the last Valentine's Day Sweetheart Hop on campus. He'd calculated that the affair would be the perfect time to make his pitch for MaryLou. She would be there. He would be there. The strains of love ballads would make a perfect backdrop. Cheek-to-cheek dancing would give him his first opportunity to hold MaryLou in his arms and whisper sweet nothings into her ear. And the champagne would bolster his courage to finally make a play to melt the iceberg that separated them.

He had it figured that, owing to the fact that so many guys had joined the ranks of the military, the odds swung in his favor this year. There just weren't enough guys to go around. The war had seen to that. Looking back at last year's Valentine Day's dance, and using it as a barometer to gauge his chances, he believed he was on the threshold of opportunity for the first time. He was confident that MaryLou would have no escort. It was a sign of the times. She would come in the company of her sorority sisters and would sit with them throughout the evening, casually condescending to dance with certain guys she liked, and turning a cold shoulder to those she abhorred.

He was hoping against hope that if he showed up attired in his best bib and tucker, each lock of his wavy auburn hair neatly combed into place, and did work up the courage to ask her to dance, things just might naturally happen. He'd watched the lovers on the silver screen and figured to use them as tutors. It worked in Hollywood, why not in college? He needed to take the initiative and adopt a Charles Boyer approach to romance. Boyer always got his woman.

Two obstacles stood between him and his plan. First, and probably the most important, Will had no *best bib and tucker* to don. Secondly, and probably equally as important, Will had never learned to dance. He figured that if he asked the boss man at the soda fountain for some overtime he'd get it. The place was always short of help. Then, he'd have some extra bucks to buy some duds and, perhaps, enough left over to take a crash course in ballroom dancing at the local dance studio. One more obstacle did come to mind. Finding new clothes might be a difficult task because of wartime shortages. But this was a now-or-never proposition, so he decided to forge ahead with the plan; a trek into the no man's land that separated him from MaryLou.

As he could best recall the occasion that was always held at the Rambling Rose Tea Room, a rooftop banquet facility that sat atop of Rose's Department Store, it was almost overly decorated with a gaudy olio of hearts and flowers in any direction a person looked. The university's jazz band was busy knocking out a few of their renditions when Will entered. The melancholy strains of "I'll be seeing you" were almost synonymous with Will's motive for being there; he intended on seeing MaryLou in an entirely new light. The lyrics that proclaimed "I'll be seeing you in all the old familiar places, that this heart of mine embraces, all day through," gave his courage a much needed boost.

Actually, he'd arrived a tad tardy for the event, because he'd squandered too much time primping and preening in front of his mirror. But he was determined to look like he'd just stepped out of *Esquire* magazine when he made his entrance. And he did. He timorously tiptoed across the crowded dance floor, elbowing his way through a throng of revelers, so he could step up onto the refreshment balcony at the far end of the room. And when he did finally manage to mount the perch, he twisted his head back and forth, squinting his eyes to stare at each and every solitary face in the place, only to discover that MaryLou was not there. He was momentarily devastated. But he recaptured his composure after bumping into a fellow student, named Harvey Marks, who gingerly asked him, "What are you craning your neck to see?"

Meeting up with Harvey was actually an unexpected bonus. Harvey was one of the few students who owned an automobile and was a doer of sorts who somehow managed to cabbage on to more than one man's share of gasoline rationing coupons. Will was suddenly struck with the most unique idea. He doubted Harvey would go for it, but he was between a rock and a hard spot, so he gave it his best shot. "Harvey," he asked, "what's chances of borrowing your car a little later on tonight?"

Harvey scoffed at the question, laughing heartily, chiding Will with, "Hey! Do I look like one of these rent-a-car agencies?"

But Will refused to be deterred by the negative reply. "Listen," he quickly added, in a last ditch effort to borrow the car, "I've got a chance to date MaryLou later tonight … if I can somehow come up with a set of wheels."

Once again Harvey burst out laughing. "YOU?" he exclaimed, almost overcome with glee. "YOU? And MARYLOU? Don't make me laugh,

Munday. She wouldn't give you the time of day, let alone a tumble."

Will realized how foolish his proposition must've sounded, but he also knew he needed Harvey's car if he hoped to escort MaryLou back to her sorority house. He put on a bold front, informing Harvey, "Yeah! That's how much you know. It might shock you to learn that me and MaryLou have something going. I need the car, Harvey."

Harvey was no longer laughing. He began to see how desperate Will was. "Munday," he tried to explain his reluctance, suggesting to Will, "every guy in the class will hit on MaryLou tonight. And you are about as close to being Casanova as I am to being the college dean. D'ya really know who this chick is? I mean. Really know? She's one'a them chicks that gets you so hot that you damn near smother and then goes home to sleep with her mother."

Will was furious. "Knock it off. She's not like that," he shouted, then glanced around to see if anyone was paying attention to his and Harvey's dispute. Discovering they weren't, he continued, "I know she wants me. I can just feel it. It's my last chance, Harvey. It's tonight or it's never."

"Okay, Munday," Harvey finally conceded. "Here's my proposition. If you do hit on MaryLou and she takes you up on the offer, well, I guess I'd be a real butthole to turn you down. You can use the car if she leaves with you. But … I wouldn't dash right back to the dorm for a pair of driving gloves if I was you, because it ain't going ta happen."

In the middle of the New Guinea wilds Will continued to relive the past, totally oblivious to his surroundings. He recalled how, after getting Harvey's permission to use the car, he'd set the stage for his big finale with MaryLou—assuming she wouldn't end up being a no-show. Although he was walking on air, he was also depressed because he'd not caught sight of the beautiful vixen and the dance was well underway. He already had visions of him and MaryLou parked along the roadside in the lover's lane at Coyote Den Overlook a few miles outside of town. So, when the buxom beauty did finally walk through the door, flanked to either side by her sorority sisters, his heart was wound up like the mainspring of an eight-day watch.

Will just stood there, stage struck, almost paralyzed over the vision. She was even more beautiful than he'd ever seen her. His heart was throbbing, pumping rapidly within his bosom, while he stood there like a bronze statue, awkwardly staring at MaryLou's long, flowing tresses of flaxen hair; golden waterfalls that limply cascaded down across her bare shoulders. "Oh, God," he muttered to himself. He was a prisoner of his own lust. He had to have that woman.

The lacy party dress MaryLou wore hugged her resplendent body, accentuating her supple breasts, adding to the mystique that was already driving Will out of his mind. And that comely peek-a-boo bang that pretentiously waltzed from side to side, first hiding MaryLou's ruby-red lips from view, then swaying aside so he could catch a full-face glimpse of his obsession, was the finale to his fantasy. She was squirming, wiggling, sashaying her way between a dozen or so suitors who were making a play for her affections before she took her seat at a table across the room from where Will was standing on the elevated stage. His hopes were buoyed as he watched her curtly give a cold shoulder to the entire mob; a group of jocks that Will customarily believed he was inferior to. He'd never tried to compete with them. The odds, he always calculated, were stacked in their favor because of their popularity. And then a sudden realization swamped him. What were his chances, he asked himself, if she had her pick of the litter and was turning away the prize packages on campus? Zilch! Not a chance. She'd do the same to him. All of his preparation—the overtime he'd worked, the clothing he'd bought, the dance lessons he'd struggled through—was for naught.

The courage that Will had labored so hard to build for the previous two weeks began to sag. He desperately needed an assurance of some kind to recharge his ebbing ego. He ventured over to the serving table, figuring to fetch a glass of bubbly as an aphrodisiac. Recalling the previous year's dance, while he dipped a ladle of champagne to fill his glass, he remembered how he had struck out in his quest for MaryLou. In fact, being honest with himself, he didn't strike out at all, because of his timidity he failed to take his turn at bat to capture MaryLou's affection. Then, he remembered, there'd been the annual Sadie Hawkins Day dance—an affair that reversed everyone's roles. The occasion, taken from the Li'l Abner comic strip, made the girl's role that of the aggressor. Anything was fair. The gal snatched the guy she wanted and dragged him onto the dance floor. Will thought he'd planned that event carefully, too, but as it turned out, he flopped. Wearing a Li'l Abner costume—a pair of bibbed overalls, one shoulder strap dangling loose, he did resemble the cartoon character to some degree. He was confident the getup he wore would catch her eye. It didn't. So, here he was again, self-destructing this year.

Will just stood there casually sipping, refilling his glass, and sipping some more, while he stared down at the glossy surface of the bubbly in the cut glass champagne vessel when, much to his surprise, he discovered a reflection of MaryLou glistening like a mirage on the slick surface of the punch in the bowl. He slowly raised his eyes. Yes, it was she. MaryLou was standing directly across the table from him. He was speechless. The luminous locks of golden hair that framed her peaches-and-cream complexion; her ruby-red, so kissable lips, her profound, yet alluring, beryl-blue eyes held him captive for a moment, and she, like him, stared back at him as if wanting to speak, but intimidated. "Oh ... hi there, Will," she finally managed to murmur. She smiled, then asked, "Where's your date? Who is the lucky girl?"

She had broke the ice. She had spoken to him, but he was momentarily dumbfounded for a response. It took a minute to recover his poise but he did come back with, "Well ... I ... didn't..." letting his voice trail off in silence.

"Oh, dear. Me neither. I know exactly what you're saying. I came alone. Don't you think it is much more fun to go stag ... you know ... sort of play the field, if you get my meaning," MaryLou confided to Will. "I'm not planning on getting pinned like so many of my sisters have."

The truth was Will fervently disagreed with her but didn't admit it. She'd put him on the spot, so he lied, saying, "Yes. I suppose you are right."

Just as suddenly as she had appeared, MaryLou vanished back into the throng of hoofers that mingled on the crowed dance floor, leaving her reluctant suitor hanging out to dry like the wet blanket he'd turned out to be. He had to admit that Harvey was right. Will had made a fool of himself again in his quest to get the hand of the woman he cherished.

When the band finally played the last song, "Goodnight, Sweetheart," Will moseyed toward the doorway, glancing back to discover MaryLou in the arms of a handsome lieutenant, who was home on leave from the Air Corps. But it inspired Will to quit his objection to serving in the military. Being a civilian was hardly as glamorous as being decked out in a uniform glistening with brass buttons and shiny emblems of rank.

It was he, himself, Will decided, who was the misfit. And, recalling his last real encounter with MaryLou at the Saint Valentine's Day dance, Will leaned back against a huge rock, glanced around at the pristine surroundings of the jungle paradise that hemmed him in, and dozed off to sleep, scolding himself as he began to doze, "Munday. You're a dumb shit. You blew it like you blow everything. She was yours for the taking."

·

140

Chapter Nine

"Phase II," Baker shouted, pacing back and forth in front of the ranks Monday morning. "You'd best pucker up and suck it in. It isn't going to get any easier."

Schuster had routed them all out of the sack bright and early, and they were already formed and ready to move out at 0700 hours. But prior to launching the second phase of training, Captain Roul took charge long enough to offer a minute explanation of things in store. First, he thanked them, saying, "I am pleased with our progress to date," adding a verbal pat on the back with, "Your steadfast determination is a factor that complements that success."

Will couldn't help but notice that the captain appeared to be a lot more comfortable in his role of commandant than he was the day their training all began. He seemed relaxed, almost elated, with the group of misfits he inherited on day one. "The initial phase of training," he told them, "was your introduction to the natural enemies we will encounter in days to come, mainly the jungle itself. You were being conditioned. We told you in the beginning about how the Japs use the jungle as an aid. Even they could not conquer the high mountains of New Guinea. The hills beat them. You've seen but a tiny portion of New Guinea. The island is separated right down the center by the vast Owens-Stanley mountain range; a formidable foe, but not all that unique. Although the mountians of New Guinea might be higher than the mountain peaks in the Philippines, the terrain is quite similar; not overly friendly."

Was that a slip of the tongue? Will pondered Roul's announcement. *Hmm-m-m-m, the Philippines ... again bob to the surface.* Had yesterday's confab with his superiors prompted Roul's remark? Would Stopwatch's eventual terminus be the Philippine Islands? Or was it only wishful thinking on Roul's part? Perhaps the captain was just homesick. These were questions that dwelled in Will's thoughts while he tried to second-guess his commanding officer.

"This phase of training," Roul continued, "will be channeled toward the ways and means to pull off a clandestine operation behind enemy lines. I'm quite sure I do not have to tell you that our unexpected visit yesterday by the brass from GHQ weighs heavy on our immediate future. Colonel Gage, from G-2 intelligence, along with several of his staff, made the trip out here to confirm that our mission, Stopwatch, is definitely a go."

A grumble of undertones sifted through the ranks, which prompted Baker to intervene, reminding them to "Stand at ease in formation. Quiet in the ranks."

"Unfortunately, gents," Roul continued, "the Colonel didn't pinpoint our eventual objective, or even set a time frame as a guideline. He did, however, at my insistence authorize a change in weaponry. A radical change, I must say. But a necessity."

Will couldn't pass up an opportunity to be sarcastic. It was his nature. He nudged Farmer in the ribs, suggesting, "Bows and arrows?"

Farmer chuckled until Baker reminded them again, "Quiet in the ranks."

Roul pointed at the crude roadway that the Corps of Engineers had carved out of the wilderness to keep a supply line open between the main depot and the remote campsite they all called home. "They appear to be late. The arms were to have been here by now. But as soon as they do arrive you'll get a glimpse of your newest plaything." He glanced at his wristwatch, then added, "They should be here soon." He instructed Baker to put the men at rest while they waited, making sure to add, "And don't anyone wander very far away."

Will wasted no time dropping onto his rump near the closest tree. He wriggled around until he had his backpack against the tree's trunk, then scrunched down, to take the weight off of the straps looped across his shoulders. Farmer was quick to join him. "Wal, Will, what d'ya think we're in for? And don't say bows and arrows. Not that I couldn't use them if'n you're right."

"Awe, go on," Will chastised him, asking, "You can shoot an arrow with a bow? Awe, go on. Peddle your papers on some other corner."

"Wal ... I most certainly can shoot arrows with a bow," Farmer fired back. "When I was a boy my daddy made me a bow out of a willow limb. Yeah, a real bow just like the Indians used way back when. And he made me some arrows, too. The truth is ... I was a fair hand after I got the hang of it. I could hit a bale of hay dead center at twenty paces."

"Okay. My mistake. We definitely won't get bows and arrows then, because the Army never tries to make it easy on anyone. Maybe they'll issue sling shots," Will changed his strategy.

"Still no problem with them gadgets either. I can shoot one'a them things just about as good," Farmer boasted. "My daddy cut me a sling shot out of a fork of willow branch that he fetched from the same tree where he got my bow stock. He carved it and made a rubber sling out of a piece of an old inner tube. And he made a little cup outta a piece of harness leather, tied it off to the rubbers, tied the loose ends of the rubber on the prongs of the sling shot and he picked up a pebble. Then he taught me how to use it. And I got pretty good at that, too, 'ceptin' I once killed a bird with it. And I felt kinda bad about that on account'a that bird wasn't doing me no harm."

"Back when you were a kid you killed a bird and it bothered you. And it sounds like it's still festering in your craw. Now, you're being poised to kill people. That's an ambiguous twist of fate, isn't it?" Will commented.

Gambler had been quietly listening to Will's and Farmer's exchange. "Well, maybe," he cut in to the exchange, "that Mexican will get his wish. You remember? He wanted to be a machine-gun-toting commando."

"Yeah, I recall," Will replied with a chuckle. "We should be so lucky. But if I've learned nothing else in the Army, anything is possible, right down to and including them issuing each one of us our personal Howitzer. I can see it now. A cannon in every foxhole."

"Cheezus," Tillie exclaimed, after hearing Will's foolish forecast, "really? I'd like that. My own cannon."

"Don't hold your breath," Will cautioned him. "No one in their right mind would issue you a Howitzer. Tillie, I hate to rain on your parade all the time, but do you know what you are?"

"Yeah. I'm a soldier."

"No. You're an accident waiting to happen. After seeing you standing out in that clearing with your BAR back during the air raid, I'd hate to think what you might do with a cannon," Will needled him.

No one came to Tillie's defense. It was almost an accepted fact that Tillie was probably the outfit's one and only trigger-happy hooligan. The truck from the depot came lumbering into camp about then and the conversation ended with Will having the final word for a change.

As soon as the truck rolled to a stop, Captain Roul darted to the vehicle's rear and furiously began to tug at the chains that secured the tailgate. When the metal gate dropped, Will spotted two wooden packing crates in the truck. Roul, with Baker's assistance, pulled them to the rear, then lifted them out onto the ground. A dozen very curious GIs huddled in a circle, all trying to catch a glimpse of their new weapons. Schuster, using his bayonet as a pry bar, popped the lids loose, and when the tops were flipped over the guns everyone spawned a chorus of *Oh*'s and *Ah*'s. One of the crates was packed with two dozen new Thompson sub-machine guns, the other with the

143

RICHARD BEOUGHER

appropriate ammunition.

"Hey. Santa's coming early this year," Gambler shouted with glee. Roul shushed him, ordering everyone to step back so he and Baker had enough room to inventory the shipment. Satisfied with what he saw and that the correct number of weapons had been received, the captain informed them, "I'm going to have Corporal Schuster give you a demonstration. Everyone stand aside, in a row, over there." He pointed to a spot just short of the forest's edge.

Roul came to the front, Schuster just a step behind, both of them brandishing the new weapons. But what caught Will's eye was the fact that all of the weapons had been stripped clean of the cosmoline coating that customarily protected new weapons from rust and corrosion while in storage. "No cosmoline to clean, sir?" Will asked the captain.

"Ordnance took care of that for us. These weapons are ready to be fired," Roul quickly responded. It was good news. Normally they'd have spent half a day cleaning the weapons. "Anyone recognize this weapon?" he asked.

"Oh, sí, Capitán," Barrentos shouted. "Zee Ranger gun."

"Yes, it is often associated with Rangers, but not for their exclusive use. The Thompson is an awesome weapon. A deadly weapon. But I'm afraid I'm going to disappoint you, Barrentos, because we will keep the BARs," Roul broke the disappointing news.

"Awe, chingawa," Barrentos complained. "You mean Juan, he still gotta lug around zee big gun?"

"I know. Your heart was set on one of these the minute you spotted them. But," Roul consoled him, "the BARs will be needed. They have the range and fire power that Thompsons do not have and there will be certain tasks you BARmen will be called upon to perform."

"Cheesuz," Tillie protested. "You mean me and Barrentos and Williams hav'ta keep our blunderbusses while everyone else gets one'a them neat little Thompsons?"

"Yes. I'm afraid so. Yesterday I saw photos of a diorama that depicts our target area. It was small and it was blurry, as photos can oftentimes be, but as the land lays now we'll need no less than two BARs to take out the enemy strong points that circumvent the compound. You'll be much safer than your comrades, because you'll be deployed on the ridge overlooking the target well out of range of some weapons, whereas the other men will be much closer in proximity to the target area, where the Thompsons will give them an edge but where they'll be subject to return fire. You three BARmen will try to keep the Nips pinned down long enough for the demolitions men to plant the explosives, have enough time to detonate them, and then withdraw

144

from the area. Firepower. That's what we'll need. Lots of firepower does tend to keep a man from taking a peek."

"Sir?" Williams inquired. "You mentioned two BARs. We have three.'

Roul nodded, lowered his head to avoid eye contact with his men for a moment, and finally agreed, saying, "Quite true. I did say two and we do have three. That was to illustrate a possibility we haven't discussed prior to this. What are the odds we will all make it safely to the objective? There again.To be perfectly honest with you, this mission is a crapshoot. So, might I suggest that, if you have any questions about the meaning of crapshoot, pick Gambler's brain. He knows what it means."

The captain, although he tried to divert their fears by joking with the cardsharp, did touch upon a nerve. He was right. They hadn't addressed the possibilities surrounding the unexpected; the chances of the mission being a failure. Exactly what were the odds of them all completing the mission without any one of them being killed? They all exchanged curious glances, Seiverson finally bluntly inquiring of Roul, "It's going to be that bad, huh? What I mean, sir, is there any way to predict the odds pertaining to our getting in and back out in one.piece?"

Roul glanced back up, shook his head from side to side, and remorsefully advised them, "It's liable to get real hairy. We will be far behind enemy lines in a countryside that, more than likely, will be crawling with Jap patrols. It's like I said. This is a real crapshoot. There are no guarantees. We knew this going in. That was the main purpose for initially splitting the unit into three distinct squads."

Again, the inquisitive GI's exchanged glances, wondering what Roul knew that they did not. And, as usual, he anticipated their concern and didn't give them much time to think about it. "Okay. I was not given a precise target area yesterday, but I was told it will be in the Philippines. We do know we will be approaching the target from higher ground, which should give you BARmen a better vantage point from which to cover the assault. We also know the compound is well defended, that there are at least two lookout towers manned by men armed with Nambus, or I guess for your benefit I should say machine guns. We'll have to deal with that. That's openers, gents. And it is about all that I know at this time," he begged off, sharing the details he'd learned the previous day from the high command. He saw fit to abruptly add an afterthought, "Staying alive to see our mission through so that we can tell our grandkids about the experience should become the object of our affection beginning today. Our next phase of training will be devoted to the premise that we can destroy an enemy installation in an orderly fashion without getting our balls shot off."

Sergeant Baker passed through the ranks and, with Schuster's help, collected all of the M-1 rifles and replaced them with Thompsons, scurrying to complete the task in short order. The two truck drivers toted the old weapons back to the truck, tossed them into the truck bed, threw the empty crates on top of them, and quickly took their leave.

Roul stood quietly for a change, glancing left, then right at his men. Recalling the rowdy roustabouts he'd first encountered on the beach on the initial day of training, he nodded in the affirmative, and said, "Now ... you look like guerillas. So, it's time to learn to fight like guerillas. Corporal Schuster will give you a demonstration of the Thompson's proficiency so that you'll understand just how devastating such a weapon can be."

Schuster raised the barrel end of the weapon, popped a clip of ammunition into the receiver, chambered a round, pointed the muzzle at the grove of trees just west of camp, and proceeded to rip the leaves and limbs from the bough of a tree. "There," he barked when he released the trigger and let the weapon fall silent, "is an example of just how awesome the Thompson is. Its only drawback is that it can spit lead faster than the Transportation Corps can deliver it to the front line ... which means you must practice constraint and never waste a single round. On a mission such as this you are your own ammunition bearer. Your fire power is limited to the number of fully loaded clips you can tote on your person."

With the demonstration finished, Baker formed up the troops and marched them to the company street that fronted the tents. Once there, he brought them to a halt, put them at ease, then joined Captain Roul and Corporal Schuster for a short confab, maintaining a distance that put him out of earshot. They talked while they glanced at the curious onlookers in the ranks, which really puzzled Will. This wasn't Baker's style. There was a delay. The brass had already complained about delays holding up the training session, and here Will and his friends were anxiously shifting their body weight from one foot to the other, waiting for the brass to make a move. Finally, Baker returned to the front of the unit and shouted, "Belton. Belton. Front and center."

Each and every man glanced at one another, wondering why the sergeant was paging Gambler to take center ring. "That means you, Gambler," Baker announced, showing a tad of anxiety over Gambler's reluctance to respond to the command. "Front and center," Baker repeated himself.

There was, Will decided, something amiss. He slowly turned his head to observe Gambler reluctantly break ranks and report to Sergeant Baker. "Off with the backpack," Baker instructed him.

Oh, so that was it, Will concluded. One of Gambler's little scams had finally caught up with him. Somehow, Will wasn't all that surprised. Gambler was famous for taking short cuts. Just the previous evening he had boasted about "lightening" his backpack. His plan was to wrap his shelter half around two empty juice cans he'd scrounged up from one of the ship's crew. That would reduce the weight several few pounds. And, as he pointed out to the others, the pack was much neater in appearance. Tillie had warned him at the time that he'd be in a batch of trouble if he was caught, but he only laughed the advisory off, informing Tillie, "Look. If you're stupid enough to tote that pack around every day, carrying a bunch of gear you aren't going to use, be my guest, but I'm cutting down on my load beginning tomorrow." He insisted the plan was "a piece of cake" and didn't figure anyone would be the wiser. Now, it appeared, Sergeant Baker had somehow cabbaged on to Gambler's plan. The two stood toe to toe, staring at one another for a brief spell, while Baker was deciding how to deal with the flustered subordinate, at the same moment Gambler was trying to guess what Baker's game was.

"What were the orders for the day, Belton?" Baker asked.

"Which orders, sir? You mean the orders for our duty assignment, right?" Gambler retorted.

"Yes. Those orders. What was the prescribed uniform and equipment requirements posted for today?" Baker clarified his inquiry, wearing a smirk on his face.

"Well, sir ... formation was at 0700, Class C uniforms, with full field pack, all web gear, and weapons, full combat regalia, sir," Gambler replied.

Baker repeated his previous instructions for Gambler to remove his backpack. So, Gambler followed orders and wiggled free of the harness and let the pack fall onto the ground in front of his feet. Baker knelt down and examined the pack, carefully lifting it up, then letting it fall back down, gently shaking it back and forth each time while he played a game of cat and mouse with Gambler. "Hm-m-m-m, seventeen years of soldiering and I do not believe I have ever encountered such a tidy bedroll. Nary a wrinkle. A mighty tight roll, I must admit. Would this be the backpack you were boasting about to you comrades? The ... 'piece of cake,' as you called it?"

Roul had advanced to join Baker. He, too, examined the backpack, then handed it to Schuster, who stepped forward for a closer look. "Almost too perfect ... wouldn't you agree, Corporal?"

Will was joyfully mesmerized by the sarcastic insinuations Baker offered, although he would've denied how overjoyed he was to see Gambler finally being taken to task had anyone asked. Gambler was a testy guy who'd rankled Will's temper more than once and was, in fact, second only to Will as the most disliked man in camp. Will had created his own misery back in the beginning of their training session, so he'd tried ever so hard to earn a cordial acceptance from the other guys since that day. But Gambler had made other enemies. It was his incessant urge to scam everyone he could scam when payday rolled around. No one had ever caught him cheating, but he did win more than one man's share of pots, enough so as to arouse suspicions, anyway.

Baker's caustic censure was almost as though he'd rehearsed it. Perhaps he had, Will mused. He knew something was a breech in regulations because Baker had singled out Gambler, then asked to see his backpack. The sergeant had to have known something in advance. Had he, or perhaps Schuster, maybe even Roul, overheard Gambler's boast to *lighten* his load? Someone must have, Will suspected. How else could he have repeated Gambler's "piece of cake" twist? That had been Gambler's precise words. Of course the appearance of the backpack by itself should've been a caveat. In a sense, Gambler had betrayed himself. He was hardly a dandy when it came to grooming. His customary unkempt image and the perfectly rolled pack that Schuster held in his hand were definitely antonyms.

Gambler's face was flushed crimson red. He shifted his weight from one foot to the other, nervously trying to convey the appearance of surprise over being called to the front.

Baker took the pack from Schuster, tossed in onto the ground in front of Gambler's feet, then shouted, "Strip it out, Gambler."

Gambler knew that when he stripped the shelter half from the pack that the jig was up. He begrudgingly dropped onto his knees and began to dismantle the counterfeit bedroll, a routine that had every man in the ranks doing their best to refrain from laughing at the huckster. When the pair of empty juice cans rolled out onto the ground no one in the formation could contain their merriment. A cackle of laughter echoed across the glen.

"At ease. As you were," Baker shouted to quell the outbreak. He reached one foot forward and kicked one of the cans gently with his toe, sending it rolling across the ground. Will could see that Baker was far from amused. In fact, he suspected that Gambler had roused Baker's ire every bit as much as he, himself, had when he lost his cool on the day Duffy was killed.

Captain Roul knelt down and eyed the cans himself, finally suggesting, "I'd wager they were a gift from the galley on the LCI. Un-huh! Grapefruit juice cans. Mighty tasty stuff."

"I believe you're right, sir," Baker chimed in

"Now, Sergeant," Roul inquired, "how do you suppose those cans ended up in this unfortunate soldier's backpack … gift-wrapped to look like a bedroll?"

The sergeant and captain glanced at one another, then at Gambler, and back at each other, obviously weighing their options over how to punish Gambler. After a short hesitation, Roul observed, "It does seem a shame to waste all of that space, would you agree, Sergeant?"

"Yes, sir. It does, indeed," Baker agreed.

"After being a soldier as long as this man has been, he should understand the importance of utilizing every square inch of space on his person," Roul continued, dredging up an old cliché to illustrate a sort of "waste not, want not" theme to drive his point home.

"Yes, sir. I was thinking, sir, that with your permission, we might fill that void with something we have a surplus of, such as some rocks, perhaps?" Baker suggested.

"Rocks? An excellent suggestion," Roul concurred, turning to make a visual survey of those who remained in the ranks. After reaching a conclusion, he ordered three of the men, Tillie, Farmer and Will, to "take the two cans over to the hillside and fill them with rocks. When you're finished, return them to Gambler who, in turn, can then reassemble his pack. Let's go. On the double. Move it. We're wasting valuable time."

Will felt as though he and his soul mates were also being punished by being assigned the task to, in turn, punish Gambler. In his way of thinking they could, at their pleasure, lighten his load or put a double whammy on him by cramming the cans chuck-full of rocks. Roul was observant from a distance, but Will knew he was mentally noting every rock they picked up, then shoved into the pair of juice cans. When Will and the others were satisfied they'd completed the assignment, they returned to the ranks and handed the cans, one to Baker, one to Roul, then returned to their place in the ranks. They all watched Gambler re-roll his pack, and then, with a boost from Baker, swing it across his shoulders and onto his back. He cringed under the weight but managed to go through the motions as though it was no big deal. That was Gambler's way of doing things.

Without further ado, Baker instructed Gambler to return to the ranks, casually mentioning to him as he pivoted on his toe to face the front, "A smart gambler never tips off his hand, such as you carelessly did last evening when you were overheard boasting to your tent mates that you were going to lighten you load today." The sergeant then brought the formation to attention, commanded them to make a "Column, right," and hearded them into the thicket, asking Gambler as he passed by, "How's that backpack for a piece of cake?"

Baker broke tradition during the hike. He didn't put them at *route step* so they could bat the breeze with one another while they walked. Will was probably the only man who wasn't bothered by the intentional oversight. He could just stroll along and let his thoughts rove wherever they pleased, concentrating on the finer things in life, such as MaryLou. But again Baker surprised him. He pulled them to a halt a short time later, instructed the men to "Take ten. Smoke if you've got 'em," and moseyed off to one side for a confab with Roul. Will plopped down into a heap of flesh, leaned his backpack against a boulder, shinneyed down to take some weight off of the shoulder straps, and finally got around to pulling out his cigarettes. He fished a smoke from the pack, struck the flint on his Zippo lighter, and lit the fag.

"Hey, guys. The pack's out," Slycord shouted when he spotted Will's newly opened pack of cigarettes. He reached across and snatched them out of Will's hand. "Hey," Will protested, asking Sly, "What do you think I am, a Red Cross girl or one of those Salvation Sallys doing the Lord's work?" It was true that the gals from the Red Cross and the Salvation Army quite often served up snacks and smokes to troops that were delayed at their local railroad stations, but hardly apt to occur so out in the far reaches of the jungle.

"You've gotta be kidding us, Munday," Sly fired back, informing Will, "You ain't built right. Fact is, you're too ugly to be a chick."

"Goddamn, Sly," Perkins cut in. "Did you go and leave your smokes back in the tent again, accidentally on purpose, so's you could mooch butts all day?"

Sly raised his hand and hoisted his middle finger into the air, giving Perk the brush-off, inquiring of him, "When did bumming a smoke become a felony? You know goddamn well Munday only paid a nickel for that whole pack at the PX. Big deal. Anyone else want a smoke on Munday?" He pushed the pack toward the other men, all of whom respectfully declined the offer.

"Knock it off," Baker cut them short. Evidently their racket was overriding his and Roul's voices. A moment later, though, the sergeant garnered their attention, advising them, "No need to butt your smokes. We're going to have a short critique."

To a man they exchanged glances. Baker was definitely out of character. But they soon learned what his intentions were. "It's pretend time again, gents."

"OH NO!" came a chorus of voices.

"What, some more little men who aren't there stuff?" Will inquired.

"OH YES, it's that time again, and yes, you'll need your imaginations," Baker mocked them, directing his attention on Will, which came as a surprise. "You, Munday. You're the pretend expert, aren't you, so what's the problem with little men who aren't there? As a whole you're a bunch of ungrateful guys. Old Sergeant Baker burns the midnight oil trying to make preparations for the next day's field problem, while you jurblowfs are cutting Z's, and what do I hear, 'OH NO!'"

Will softly chuckled under his breath. It was a typical snow job, he figured, because training exercises such as this were prearranged by some clown in GHQ, not by a non-com in the field.

"Try to imagine,"Baker suggested, "that there is an enemy communications complex in that small clearing down in the draw." He paused and pointed down into a glade that separated two hills. "Take note. See the tallest tree over there, on the far righthand side? Using your imagination, try to visualize that as a radio transmitting tower," he said.

Tillie craned his neck, twisted his head from side to side, then responded with his usual causticity, "All I can see is a tree, Sarge, oops, I mean Sergeant."

Baker ignored him, leaving Tillie to hang his head in shame for being the only one of Baker's men to be out of step with the group. "Now, let's all try to enhance our vision by converting that large clump of underbrush just to the left of the radio tower into a shack that houses the transmitters." He quicky glanced in Tillie's direction and, seeing the hillbilly carefully scanning the area he'd pinpointed, asked, "Do you see the shack, Tillie?"

From Tillie's silent response to his question, he assumed that the rambunctious BARman had come on board, so he continued, telling them, "Now, if you can really stretch your imagination, picture that shack and tower surrounded by a bamboo wall, which has two observation towers, one to each end. Each tower has a search light and a Nambu." He paused long enough to remind them, "Nambu, in case you don't recall, is Japanese for machine gun." He then went on to expand a mental sketch of the towers.

"Now," he enhanced the visual, saying, "we'll thicken the plot a tad by surrounding the entire enclosure with trees, bushes and every other conceivable sort of growth you can imagine, and we have been forewarned that the entire area is cluttered with explosive devices, booby traps and flares so that, should anyone of you trip one of the devices, the sky will light up like a Fourth of July fireworks display back home. So, what happens then? Right! You'll get your asses shot off. Do you get the picture?"

A shudder raced up Will's spine. All of his prior training came down to this, an introduction to the real thing. It looked to Will as though Stopwatch was finally going to get down to brass tacks. The imaginary village that Baker had just envisioned in the middle of nowhere would one day translate into a cataclysm of momentous proportions, because this was the dry run for the real assault that would all too soon become a reality.

"So, how do we approach, then assault such a well-defended complex?" Baker inquired.

His question was greeted by silence. Will, for one, didn't want to stick out his neck with some outlandish proposal, then look like a fool if Baker didn't approve. And he halfway figured the other guys felt much the same. The sergeant, however, was neither disappointed nor surprised when no one offered a plan. "Okay," he finally said, when it was apparent he needed to prime them, "Williams. First things first. On the approach. Where would you station your BARmen? Look around. Study the terrain. Take your time. Then give me an answer, because you're the man in charge. Captain Roul came down with a hypothetical case of dysentery and I have a hypothetical compound fracture of my left leg. To make matters worse, Corporal Schuster went on furlough. You just inherited the command. Take charge."

That brought out a few snickers. Everyone glanced at Schuster, who was grinning like a Cheshire cat. But Baker bugged Williams, saying, "Come on, mastermind. It's time to move out. Give us the straight skinny. What would you do?"

The sergeant couldn't have been more delighted with William's response. The acting CO deployed his BARmen along the rim of the canyon, where they commanded an excellent view of the complex, then suggested, "We'll need to probe the outlying jungle for booby traps before it gets dark. The BARmen will maintain the high ground as a vantage point to provide a backup in case we are spotted and the Japs open fire on our pickets. If all goes well, and we're not seen, I would advance the demolitions squad to the wall, where they could set their charges, light the fuses, then pull back into a safe zone." He paused a moment, threw a glance at Schuster, then tacked on, "Have a good time in the States, Corporal." Everyone, including Captain Roul, cracked up when Schuster bid them farewell and turned away on a pretense of taking his leave. The laugh evolved into a deafening roar when Baker informed Schuster, "Not so fast, Corporal. It was a hypothetical case. Your leave is canceled."

"VERY GOOD, soldier," Baker then complimented Williams. He quickly pointed at Seiverson, informing him, "It's your turn in the barrel. Give us your two cents' worth. Is Williams' plan good enough? Would you make any changes?"

Seiverson wasn't the least bit bashful. "Well, sir, Williams' plan to reconnoiter while it's still daylight is perfect. I was wondering if he intended to follow through with the assault as soon as the area was cleared of booby traps, or wait until dark to move in," he responded, complimenting Williams by approving his placement of the BARs, admitting "Those BARmen would have a field day. It would be like shooting ducks in a pond."

Unfortunately, and as was usually the case, Will had temporarily lost touch with reality. He was off in another world, trying to analyze his comrades instead of evaluating their input. Williams, he decided, was probably the sharpest guy in the outfit, but he credited the intellect to the former preacher's age. While it was true that Williams wasn't nearly as old as Baker, who'd been clad in khaki since most of his charges were born, he did have an edge over the other men with his worldly knowledge surrounding the facts of life. Will hadn't actually given Williams' age a thought prior to this, but he guessed that he might be in his late twenties, perhaps even his early thirties. As usual, Baker shattered Will's self-induced cocoon—his security blanket—shouting out, "BINGO!" Will pried his eyes open to discover Baker staring directly at him.

"I hope, Munday, that I'm not interfering with your delusions, or is it illusions? Whatever, I suggest you join the rest of your comrades in plotting our strategy," Baker informed the moonstruck soldier.

With those words of advice, Baker gave some direction to Stopwatch, launching the second phase of training, which was the actual assault they were expected to perform at a future time in an undisclosed location. The redundancy they had suffered in the beginning made a radical change. Although they repeatedly surrounded, reconnoitered, assaulted, then captured a mystical compound that Baker had managed to sculpture from a tangled web of flora, there was no time for boredom. It was physical, it was testy, it was unpredictable. Squad by squad, they alternated positions, one group defending the imaginary fortress, the others attempting to overpower it. It was all part of the war game. Unless there were observers to point out mistakes being made by the invaders, Baker cautioned them, how would they know if they'd been seen, or heard, or otherwise detected by the defenders? Will actually understood Baker's motives, but Tillie evidently did not. He objected when it came his turn to observe. "Y'all tellin' me I'm a Jap, now?" he argued. It was, he insisted, "un-American." But like the others, he took his turn, under protest of course, to man an apparitional observation tower located on the corner of a phantasmal communications compound which, in reality, amounted to shinnying up the rough bark of a palm tree, then hanging on to the fronds for dear life on the chance he'd eyeball one of his comrades sneaking up on the hallucinatory structure he could not even see.

Will recalled his exchange with Farmer back a few days when he taunted him with the tale of the Little Man Who Wasn't There. He didn't pass up an opportunity to remind the country boy, telling him with a nudge to the ribs, "See? The little man who wasn't there. He's back! That's who we're chasing.

153

We can't see him, but he's right there in that imaginary compound that we cannot see, watching every move we make. We can't kill him because we can't see him, but it wouldn't make any difference, anyway, because they've got us firing blank cartridges that have no lethal significance." Farmer only wagged his head and rolled his eyes around in their sockets, insinuating Will had finally lost his marbles.

Phase II, however, was hardly a stroll through the park. And it wasn't a one-day outing to commune with their creator. Mother Nature decided to complicate the maneuvers. On the third day out it began to rain, and to rain, and to rain, much to Will's chagrin. Will's loathing for being soaked to the skin hadn't been tested in recent weeks. His feelings hadn't changed. He was pissed. Tillie told him, "Cool it. It might just rain for forty days and forty nights like the Bible says it once't did. We might oughta be building ourselves one'a them ark boats."

Williams informed Tillie that the Scriptures didn't forecast another flood, but that the end would come with a shower of fire and brimstone, not raindrops, prompting Baker to add, "When we get into a fire fight you'll think fire and brimstone."

By the first week's end they were oftentimes wading in ankle-deep sludge, striving to keep their footing on the slippery slopes of the mountainside. Trails through the wilderness that were parched pathways a few days before evolved into bogs. Silt surged down the hillsides, pushed by torrential walls of water, inundating the stream beds—transforming tiny brooks into roaring rivers that they were compelled to navigate in order to meet the criteria of the training schedule. They were obliged to catch what little sleep they could in the out-of-doors, huddled underneath hastily pitched tents composed of two soldiers' shelter halves buttoned together. The custom of digging a shallow trench around the perimeter to keep water out was impossible because the torrential rain flooded the tiny moats, letting the water run at will across the floor of their accommodations. They fell asleep soaked and wet and discovered upon awaking that they had been snoozing in a puddle of water most of the night. And Baker did not ease the burden. He pushed them to the limits, then beyond, trying to meet deadlines prescribed in their itinerary. The only ray of sunshine they encountered came, not as a beam of light from the sun, but with Baker's vow that "If you jurblowfs pick up the pace and we finish training on schedule, there's a surprise in store for all of you." He didn't elaborate, so Will was a trifle skeptical. He rued how he'd been busting his butt to please Baker and could not imagine any surprise that would reward him for the effort. When he complained to Farmer, the country boy reassured him, saying, "Baker's always been a man of his word,

Will. So, just maybe, there is something positive coming our way."

The rains finally abated on the third Wednesday of Phase two, just as abruptly as they had begun. The sun broke through the clouds at daybreak. As far as Will was concern, though, it was too late. He felt as though his hide was withered like a dried prune. That was, of course, the only agony he suffered. Seiverson did come down with an acute case of dysentery that knocked him out of commission for a day, and everyone of them, except for Barrentos, was scratching to overcome an itchy case of jungle rot, Barrentos being the exception. Baker explained to the others that it was Barrentos' heritage, being born a dark skinned person, that gave him an edge. The penetrating rays of sunshine transformed the dense, saturated jungle into a steam bath. Breathing the heavy air was a chore to itself, more like drinking than inhaling.

As Phase II drew to its conclusion, with but two days remaining, Baker's surprise had not materialized. The final hours were focused on more redundant dry runs to destroy Baker's conceptual compound. There was, some of the men admitted, a visible trace of the structure if a person eyeballed the terrain that their shoes had pounded until most every living plant was ground into pulp. Tillie even admitted he could vision it. "Yup," he said, staring at the barren trails they'd blazed during their dry runs, "I can see her." He glanced around, everyone waiting, because they knew Tillie well enough to understand that he wouldn't let the topic end on a high note. "Yup. I see her. And if'n I never see her again, it'll be too damned soon."

But he was to see her again. The only predominant sign that had withstood the brutal ground-pounding was the stately palm tree that towered above a tattered clump of brush which had been designated as the shack back in the beginning. And its days were numbered, because Roul finally got around to instructing Baker to "Issue live ammunition for our next assault. You powder men will have to settle for Nitro Starch, in place of dynamite, because we'd like to leave some of this pristine valley to replenish itself. The Nitro Starch will add some realism. For God's sake, gents, don't use each other for target practice, and you demolition men take every precaution to cut long enough fuses so you'll have time to reach safety prior to the explosion. I don't want any casualties. Understood?"

Having issued his final warnings, Roul invited Baker to add his two cents' worth. He was brief. "Okay. Here it is. I'm gone. You're on you own. Everyone hike back up the hillside for a short critique; a critique without my input. A plan concocted by you and you and you. We'll assume the position of observers. We're going to decide just how much you jurblowfs have learned. Bear this in mind. This exercise is as close as you're going to get to reality in preparation for the real McCoy. Do your stuff. Make a good showing and you'll be rewarded, just like I promised sometime back."

Will was in shock. For the first time in his military career he actually felt stimulated. Here he was finally going to get a crack at that little man who wasn't there. He discovered, much to his dismay, that he was anticipating a thrill, an emotion he'd never before sensed as a soldier. The adrenalin was pumping through his veins when he fell into line and hightailed it back up the hillside along with his comrades, each one trying to outdo the others by reaching the crest first. They were more like kids playing tag than warriors in training. Shouting, "Last man up is'a warthog," Tillie challenged them to overtake him. The big, lanky hillbilly, taking strides that only a long-legged man like he could manage, topped the summit several yards ahead of his closest competitor.

When the last man came dragging in and they assembled for their meeting the mirth evaporated. They looked toward Baker, who positioned himself a good fifty yards away and just stood there, ignoring them, arms folded across his chest, waiting to see if he'd accomplished the task he set out to do that day on the beach when he dressed them down for their less than acceptable performance coming ashore. Finally, Gooch broke the silence. "Well, you guys ... I guess we're on our own," he observed. "Are we going to blow that complex down there or stand here with our fingers in our butts to embarrass Sergeant Baker?"

The dead came to life. "Someone has to be in charge," Williams suggested.

No one protested the idea.

"How about you, Gooch?" O'Hare asked.

"Yeah," Gambler agreed, pointing out that Gooch was the only real combat veteran in the group. "Hell, none of us really knows anything about the real thing compared to Gooch."

"Any arguments?" Perkins cut in. "I vote for Gooch."

No one disagreed. He was elected unanimously by his peers to lead the way. Shrugging, he knelt down and snatched a broken tree limb from the ground, then smoothed out the dirt near his feet and began to sketch a crude map of the area they were poised to attack. The others all gathered around in a circle, studying his artistic flair. When he had finished the grid, he asked them, "Does anyone here have anything specific to suggest, I mean concerning our strategy?"

"Yeah," Seive replied. "What's wrong with the plan we used a couple of days ago? You know the one ... where we assign one BAR right over here," he continued, pointing to a spot several yards away that was located on the rim of the slope overlooking the compound. "Then … remember? The other BARmen circled the compound and took up positions on either flank."

"Yeah, I remember," Will cut in. "They covered the rest of us while we fanned out into the thicket to defuse booby traps."

"Un-huh," O'Hare recalled, "and then we took up positions to cover the powder men while they infiltrated the perimeter to set the charges."

They glanced at one another. "Not bad," Gooch approved. "I remember it. It came off pretty smooth that day. Foreman, you were one of the guys guarding the complex if I remember right. Do you recall if you spotted anyone on their approach?"

"I was a Jap that day. Come to think of it, I didn't see a soul until you clowns moved in for the kill," Foreman recalled.

"But you did spot someone?" Gooch asked.

"Yeah. But not until the charges were planted," Foreman replied.

"Sounds like a plan," Farmer approved.

"Okay. Let's implement it," Gooch countered. "Now, everyone listen up. Keep out of each other's line of fire. We've got live ammo today. And you powder men remember what you were told. Give yourself some breathing room."

So, the die was cast. The stopwatch team, their umbilical cord severed for the first time from the mother who'd nurtured them through the gauntlet, set out to prove their worth. Gooch directed them like a champion, moving his men methodically around, one stationed here, another positioned there, others creeping along through what was left of the underbrush they mutilated, until the moment of truth finally arrived. The cackle of BARs echoed across the valley, punctuated with volleys of bursts from the Thompsons, while the powder men crept forward, tediously lodging the explosive charges in and around the majestic, towering palm tree that Baker had designated a radio transmitter. Nitro Starch charges in place, they gingerly lit the fuses and hauled ass for the rear, with one exception; Gambler. He jumped to his feet, cupped his hands about his mouth and screamed at the top of his lungs, "Fire in the hole," before he took off on a dead run and dove headfirst into the bushes for cover so as to escape the concussion of the explosion. It was a doozey. The charges splintered the palm tree, splitting the trunk into three separate spears, and it literally fell apart and dropped onto the ground in a cloud of smoke and dust, its swan song applauded by a chorus of hurrahs from every last member of the Stopwatch team.

Sergeant Baker was ecstatic. As were Roul and Schuster. Baker's dozen had passed their final exams with flying colors. Schuster regrouped them on the hilltop for a critique, at which time Baker smiled at them, saying, "My compliments, gents. You whupped their asses good and proper."

Roul intervened, praising Baker and Schuster. "My compliments to both of you," he told them. "When I first laid eyes on this bunch of rednecks that day we washed ashore I had some doubts. Due to your more than able leadership and the determination of these soldiers we have a gold medal team."

With the mutual admiration affairs handled, Baker turned his attention to Gambler and inquired, "You, soldier. One question. Just what in the hell did you think you were doing with that grandstand play. Fire in the hole? Whatever made you do such a foolish thing?"

Gambler's face was twisted with his customary shit-eating grin, his cocky way of boasting whenever he pulled some stupid stunt. "Well, Sergeant, it was sorta like this. I've been wanting to do that since my first day of training in demolitions and ... well, today just seemed like the right time in the right place if I ever intended to go through with it," he confessed.

"Gambler," Baker countered, "I'm going to buy that alibi. NOW! You've had your moment of glory. Don't even think about doing something that stupid again."

Kudos given, ass chewing finished, Baker ordered them to "Fall in." Everyone scampered to take their rightful place in line. He motioned to Schuster, telling him, "Take them back to camp for a good night's rest, Corporal. I can't speak for everyone, but a clean, dry bunk sure sounds inviting to me."

Schuster moved them out, advising them they could talk or smoke in the ranks on the return trip to camp. However small it might've seemed, that was a reward to the dowdy dogfaces who'd just spent three weeks honing their talents so they could make a good showing when they finally joined the fray somewhere in the Philippines.

Will walked in silence. He didn't even light-up a smoke. He communicated with his subconscious every step of the way. He'd been so occupied chasing, then eliminating, the little man who wasn't there that he'd neglected his world of make-believe. He just knew MaryLou was waiting for him to pop into her life again. Sharing the five-mile hike back to the base with the woman he loved was, he figured, an equivalent to Gambler's scam to tote an empty backpack; his burdens now weighed little or nothing. The long walk to the campground was "a piece of cake."

Chapter Ten

When the unit arrived at the hilltop overlooking the campsite, Schuster halted the procession and curtly informed them, one and all, "We're not returning home looking like a bunch of misfits. We're going to double-time down that hillside and into the company street like soldiers."

"WHAT?" Tillie exclaimed.

"After all we've been through, you're going to make us run, not walk, into camp?" Foreman moaned.

"Yes, indeed," Schuster informed them. "We're soldiers. We're Stopwatch! We're good at what we do. And we're going to give those swab jockeys on that LCI cause to look in our direction. And how are we going to do that? We're also going to sing all the way down the slope. You know the song. When I say, 'Move out,' I wanta see you looking sharp, running fast, and hear you chanting like the Mormon choir."

The corporal brought them to attention, then sent them on their way, shouting, "Forward, march. Double-time, march. Chant those cadence, loud and clear."

And so, the weary warriors took off on a run, singing an old refrain they'd voiced many times before.

We're the raiders from Stopwatch.
We're the riders of the night.
We're those dirty sonsabitches
who would rather fuck than fight.
We're heading to the front lines.
Kiss the girls and hold 'em tight.
All you've got to take with you
is a memory of this night.
We're off to circumcise old Tojo
with a broken piece of glass.
And then we'll shove our bayonets

159

up that dirty bastard's ass.
When this war is over
and the killing's all been done
the world will know that Stopwatch
was the reason that we won.

They heaved a sigh of relief when Schuster brought them to a halt in front of their tents. They were just plain tuckered out.

"Do you see what I see?" the corporal barked, pointing at a Jeep parked on the beach. "It's mail call. Dismissed."

Mail call it was. The mail clerk from the replacement depot was standing on the backseat of the Jeep, a fistful of letters hoisted high above his head, shouting, "Mail call. Mail Call. Come and get 'em or they're going back."

Baker's dozen had a resurgence of energy. They darted to the beach to get the letters from their loved ones; with one exception. Will F. Munday did not join the throng.

Will stood motionless, watching everyone run their butts off in hopes of getting some mail. He finally wheeled about, strolled over to the tent, pushed the flaps open, and pitched his rifle onto his bunk, followed by his backpack and web equipment. Being certain he would get no mail, he opted to spend his evening in the remote sanctuary of jungle west of camp, where he'd not be disturbed by all of the guys trying to read excerpts from their letter to other guys who were trying to read excerpts of their own letters to other guys.

Will had exhausted his excuses for never getting mail. In the beginning he condemned his "constant displacement" from one unit to another, suggesting that the mail just hadn't "caught up with me yet." His last communication from home had been a brief letter from his mother that limped in at the replacement depot. He did, however, realize that the prominent reason he received no mail was his own doing. He never wrote letters to anyone, so why would he receive any replies? So, here he was again, sitting alone rather than to suffer the indignity he faced each time the mail clerk said, "I guess there's nothing for you, Munday." It was simply a matter of banishing himself to save face.

Will slinked down into his favorite spot, a small nook behind a fallen tree, where he could bury his face between his upraised knees, and regress his thoughts to grandiose illusions of things as they might've been, rather than how they actually were. He had a good three weeks of catching up to do, so he wasted no time transporting his thought train to his own mystic dimension, where there were no Rouls, no Bakers, no Schusters, no nothing that

160

reminded him of the military. It was just a matter of allowing himself to jump on board of his magic carpet and journey from this untamed corner of New Guinea to the marble halls of learning at the university back home. And so he did.

"Ah-haw," Mister Edmundson chided Will. Shaking a crooked finger in his face, he asked, "Where has my star pupil been keeping himself? Busy, I hope. But not in the classroom, I see."

Didn't he know, a curious Will Munday wondered. Oh, he'd done it now; conjured up some sort of nightmare to complicate his journey. Everyone knew Will was in the Army. He'd become a soldier and was no longer that naïve lad who worshipped his educators with a passion, especially Mister Edmundson, who'd been his mentor as far back as junior high school. Perhaps, Will reasoned, he'd made a wrong turn on his journey back in time. He set his sights on the soda fountain in the drugstore near the campus, where he hoped to catch a glimpse of MaryLou. What was wrong? He was back in a junior high school setting. And the vision of Mister Edmundson would not evaporate, as Will had wished. "Sir," he finally explained to the distraught teacher, "didn't you know about me? I'm halfway across the world from you in a faraway place called New Guinea."

"Oh, yes. Indeed. Now that you mention it, I recall hearing something about you being called to serve your country. Pray tell me, Master Munday, what have you learned in those faraway places?"

"Learned, sir? What have I learned?"

"Yes, Master Munday. Learned. Don't tell me the war has dulled your keen desire to learn; has dampened your aspirations of becoming a renowned scientist."

"Oh, NO!" Will insisted. "Not me. Never. Not on your life. But this confounded war has sidetracked those ambitions."

"Come, come, my boy. Nothing should stand between a man and his convictions. Especially such a promising student, Master Munday. Remember! I have told you this again and again and again AND AGAIN! A scientist must be dedicated ... dedicated ... DEDICATED ... DEDICATED...."

"STOP! STOP THAT INFERNAL SHOUTING! STOP," Will screamed aloud, so loud in fact that his own voice summoned him back to reality. He shook his head vigorously, trying to blot out the irrational vision he'd just concocted in his subconscious, then gingerly glanced around in all four directions to reassure himself no one had heard his outburst. But he was still very much alone. He was bored. He was stymied over his silly reflection of Mister Edmundson. So, he paused to get his bearings by studying the surrounding terrain. A curious lizard scrambled up onto a rock, stopped short when he spotted Will, then craned his neck and silently studied this alien intruder on his turf. Will craned his neck and bowed down to stare straight into the eyes of a grotesque creature that he suspected had even fewer friends than he, himself, did. To Will's surprise, the varmint seemed to acknowledge his stare by flipping his tongue swiftly in, then out, then into his mouth cavern. Will grinned, then responded in kind, sticking his tongue out, and finally shouting, "SHOO, you repugnant critter." If he was frightened it did not show. The reptile just sat there staring at Will.

How utterly interesting, Will mused. *Just think. A mere month or so ago this horny reptile would've frightened me out of my wits.* Now, Will seemed almost at home sharing the jungle with him. Perhaps he had finally blended in to become part his surroundings, as Baker suggested he learn to do back in the beginning.

"Okay, wise guy," Will curtly informed the monster. "So, you wanta play games, huh? All right. You be Mister Edmundson. I'll play myself, Will F. Munday. Sure. I know. You're happy to make my acquaintance. So, let's get started." Will paused to catch his breath, then continued the debate. "Remember me? I'm Will. Don't tell me you've forgotten in such a short time. I was your student. Now, do you recall?"

The lizard cocked his head, fluttered his eyes, and flipped his tongue once again, appearing to understand every word Will had said. "Oh, you've nothing to say in rebuttal, huh? I'm not surprised, Mister Edmundson. You've always been a sly old fox. Well. Okay. So, the cat's got your tongue. The least you could do is tell me what you think of your prize student. I was your prize, wasn't I? Oh, not going to talk, huh? Okay. Then I shall. As you can readily see, I have changed vocations. Yes, indeed. I remember how you always harped about dedication. About following one's dreams. But do you know what? I've discovered any number of new aspects in life that your precious text books didn't mention."

Will paused and glanced at the lizard again, only to discover a second creepy cousin had joined him on the boulder. Now there were two to debate. "Oh, you had to call in the reserves, huh? I'm not surprised, sir," Will continued, asking the pair, "Are my questions too difficult to answer? Surely that is the case. But I can relate to your indifference. You are being indifferent. It shows on your face. I was indifferent until I arrived at this godforsaken place. Where am I? Well, sir, I'm enrolled in Abolition University. It's the antonym to any stateside college you'd recommend. Yes, indeed. I'm majoring in murder. A-haw! Shocked, huh? It's true. They're teaching me numerous methods for snuffing out a human life. I'll bet you didn't know that a tiny projectile from a rifle's barrel can split open a man's head like a ripe watermelon at fifty paces distance, now did you? It's a fact. And I can do it quicker than you can slip a slide under the lens of your microscope. Remember? You taught us about options and applications. I'll wager you never once considered that both options and applications apply to abolition. My options? To kill or not to kill. My applications? Rifle, machine gun, bazooka, bayonet, dagger, oh, there's too many to itemize. It's almost an unending list, some of the methods too ruthless to even consider." Will threw his arms into the air, gazed up at the last rays of sunshine creeping between the trees and finally resurfaced in the real world. "SHOO, I TOLD YOU. GIT!" The frightened lizards darted out of sight. In a way he was sorry to see them leave, almost as sorry as he was for having again secluded himself in the jungle to brood.

He'd been proud over the fact that, for the past three weeks, he'd taken control of his life. He was rowing with the flow, accepting things as they actually were for a change. Now, here he was again sitting in his solitary solace trying to recapture precious memories of the past. When the visions didn't materialize in a manner that was acceptable he turned his thoughts toward the clear and present danger he faced as a dogface. It was comforting to realize that the training cycle was nearing its end. He recalled a similar period back at Camp Hood when that cycle came to a close. At that particular time, as he could best remember, he'd felt a twinge of pride, and now, when looking back, he was almost melancholy. The highlight, he thought, was the final dress parade. It was crystal clear in his memory. He could almost hear the *tr'um, tr'um, tr'um* of the drums and the *Taw-taw-ta-taw* of the horns when they passed in review across the neatly manicured lawn of the parade field; guidons fluttering in a brisk breeze preceding a sea of khaki strutting in a coordinated lock step to pass final muster. Yes. He had felt some pride that day, probably because he'd finished something he'd started for a change. "Un-huh," he grunted after recalling the event, "I do have some grit, after all. Baker was wrong. I can make the grade. I did it at Hood and I'm doing it again, right here, right now."

Those thoughts only prompted him to ponder the immediate future. Tomorrow, he guessed, would be another graduation day. He didn't anticipate being rewarded with some sort of certificate that verified his academic excellence; his steadfast determination to keep both feet moving on the treadmill that was, in actuality, Roul's Institute for Hired Killers. So, he contemplated, was this another ending that only led to another beginning? "NO!" he barked. "I've got to quit this brooding. I must purge the morbid thoughts," he mused, recalling, "I came out here to commiserate with the pleasures of life, not to hone in on the gloomy prospects that lie ahead. It'll soon be dark. MaryLou. Yes. I must switch my efforts toward MaryLou. Now. Before it's too late." And he did.

MaryLou, Will's taunter; his sensual, salacious sweetheart, swung her rear up onto a stool at the soda fountain. Will caught his breath. His heart began to pound and he could feel the blood coursing through his veins. *Yes,* he considered the odds, *it's tonight or it's never. I must condition my mind against rejection.* His thoughts wafted into tomorrow. *No! Tomorrow would be better. Wouldn't Professor Boon's classroom be the perfect place? It would.*

There was something comforting about his teacher, Professor Boon. He could be amusing, a droll-faced wag, when the necessity arose, or he could dissect a man's brain by simply staring through his skull bone. He was a strange duck for a university professor; not the tidiest of men. 'Unkempt' best described him; always attired in a redundant, threadbare double-breasted suit; a remnant of the depression era. A plump belly overhung his belt line, making him leave the suit coat unbuttoned. The shirts he wore were almost passé; stiffly starched collars held together at the front of his neckline by a gaudy red bow tie that bobbled up and down on his Adam's apple when he lectured the class. This foggy vision began to clear and Will could see Boon, pacing back and forth, to and fro, at the head of the classroom. "The assignments, please," he was reminding them. "May I have them?"

It was fate, indeed. The homework assignment had been an essay explaining "Rejection Syndrome; the cause, the cure." Right up Will F. Munday's alley. He'd pored over the document the previous evening until far into the night, trying to make it letter perfect. While he studied the learned professor, he couldn't help but wonder if it would be his paper Boon would opt to read aloud to the entire class. He did such things with regularity. Will needed a boost in confidence. Boon could provide that by simply reading Will's submission. Will was an expert on rejection. He'd suffered the cryptic symptoms for the past two years; always striving to get the courage to ask MaryLou for a date and backing out when the opportunity came. His greatest fear was that Boon would, as he often did, select Terrance Farnsworth's essay to read aloud. Will was second only to Terrance as Boon's favorite. He was tired of taking the backseat to his classmate, whom he actually abhorred for the simple reason that his name had a feministic tone to match his demeanor.

Professor Boon moseyed up and down the aisles, collecting the papers, leafing through the stack while he returned to his desk. He plucked one essay from the pile and pitched the rest onto his desktop, slowly turning while he scanned the assignment. "Hm-m-m-m," he mumbled as he retraced his steps to begin his ritual; an almost uncanny ability to tread between the rows of desks while his eyes were glued to the document he held, but somehow managing to avoid stumbling across the corner of a desk, or tripping over someone's feet that had been deliberately posed to trip him. It was as though he had a built-in radar system. He paused. "Very interesting," he commented. "Shall we share what Mister Munday has to say about rejection syndrome?"

"Oh, God," Will uttered under his breath. *It's mine. He's actually going to read my testimonial to MaryLou.* She would know the discontent he suffered over longing for her, but being too timid to ask her out. Now that reality had struck it didn't seem like such a great idea. The entire class would know. *No,* he retreated. *They won't. MaryLou might if she listens intently enough to read between the lines. I didn't mention her by name.*

"The world," the professor began, "is peopled by many unfortunate mortals who suffer rejection syndrome. They are often ne'er-do-wells whose accomplishments in the sprint for success fell short and they were classified as 'also-rans' by their peers. Why do they fail while others succeed? Was it simply lack of courage? Reluctance to claim the prize when it is within their grasp? The answer appears to be elementary and the cure is all too obvious. Putting it in plain language, they are afraid to take what is rightfully theirs out of fear they'll be criticized or otherwise berated. That is rejection. Rejection syndrome separates winners from losers in the run for the roses, because those who come in last didn't apply their desires strongly enough to claim the rewards at the finish line. This is contrary to the Scriptures that claim 'The meek shall inherit the earth.'"

Boon paused, reached up and scratched his chin while he shook forth the paper he held in his other hand and said, "Interesting indeed, Mister Munday. I shall finish reading this and will grade it in the privacy of my study this evening."

Will was disappointed. Had Boon read enough for MaryLou to pick up on the theme? If so, how would she respond? He swiveled in his seat and turned his head in her direction. His faced flushed. He felt the heat scorching his skin. She was staring directly at him, a puzzled expression dimming her usually radiant face. She smiled, a kittenish snicker that enhanced the dimple on her cheek. It was just too much anxiety for Will. He turned away and stared at the wall.

Will might've daydreamt his way into the night had a voice not summoned him. It sounded like Farmer. "WILL! WHERE ARE YOU?"

165

"Over here," Will replied, hoping the sound of his voice would guide Farmer into his lair. "How'd you know where to find me? What's up? Don't tell me there's another confounded meeting."

"Will, Will, Will. How could you doubt old Farmer's loyalty? I keep an eye open for you every time you venture out into the wilds alone. Betcha you didn't know that, didja?" Farmer exclaimed with a giggle.

"What so funny?" Will asked.

"You. That's what," he replied, after fishing a letter from his breast pocket which he slid underneath his nostrils, inhaled the odor of perfume, then explained, "Some stinkum, you rascal, you. You done went and got yourself a sweet patootie and never even told old Farmer a thing about it." He tossed the letter across to Will's outstretched hands with a "Tsk, tsk, tsk."

"No. Not me, Farmer. I have no idea who this is from, but it sure ain't from any sweetie," Will countered.

Farmer disappeared as quickly as he'd come, leaving Will to sit by the downed tree, his heart overjoyed at receiving a letter. He lifted it up underneath his nose and sniffed the fragrance of stale perfume; stale but not so faint that he didn't recognize the odor as MaryLou's customary essence. *How could this be?* he wondered in silence. It took his breath away, leaving him almost gasping for air. He wanted it to be a love letter but somehow knew it couldn't be. He gingerly flipped the envelope over to see the return address, then cautiously peered at the flap. Eureka! There it was, bigger than life; MaryLou's name, her dorm address, and the letters S.W.A.K. He was momentarily dumbfounded and, as a result, was actually too faint-hearted to rip the envelope open, lest it be nothing more than a friendly greeting from an old school chum. *Hnm-m-m, might be a joke,* he fretted. Sorority sisters had a way of idling away the hours pulling stunts on other people. It was part of campus life. He'd heard them boast about insensitive pranks they'd pulled, then listened to them laugh and giggle over the joke. There was no use delaying the inevitable any longer, he reasoned. Carefully, he slit the envelope open and withdrew the folded sheets of paper from within. It said:

My Dear Willie,

Will paused after reading the letter's salutation and chucked to himself. "Willie," she'd called him. It had been quite some time since anyone identified him by that nickname. In fact, only those who knew him well at the college used Willie on a regular basis. He glanced back down and continued to read.

Surprise! And I hope you are. It's me. MaryLou. I think that I'm as surprised to be penning this letter as you will be to receive it. I guess I needed to satisfy my curiosity. We, here at home, are constantly reminded to write letters to our service people. They tell us that "mail call" is the highlight of every soldier's day. I want you to know that I am proud of you.

You're probably wondering how I managed to get your address. It did take some doing on my part. One evening a few days ago one of my sorority sisters asked me, "Whatever happened to the handsome auburn-haired boy in Boon's class?" I didn't know how to respond. You had just vanished with the end of the last semester. So, I stopped off at the attendance office the following afternoon to see if they had a record of your whereabouts. I was disappointed when they didn't. I guess the receptionist noticed my reaction, so she suggested we might check last year's records for your home address. It was there. So, I took the liberty of sending a note to your mother, whose name was registered on the records along with your address, inquiring about your welfare. She responded, writing in her return letter that you had gone into the Army and went on to explain it had been some time since she's heard from you, which was troubling. But she did give me your last known address after I told her I wanted to write to you. So, here I am. I do hope this letter gets to where you are, and that you are well and safe.

I'm disappointed that I never told you goodbye, but I had no way of knowing you were leaving school. When your name came up the other night I suddenly sensed a feeling of loss that I couldn't explain. It pestered me far into the night. So, here I sit, alone in the dorm room, trying to find the right words to express myself without being presumptuous. I must confess, I miss your happy-go-lucky grin and the warm glow of your shy glances at me every day in Professor Boon's classroom.

Looking back, I can see that I held myself aloof, which I'm sure was a factor that scared you away. My friends tell me that I am pretty. Still, when I look in the mirror I cannot agree. Then I consider how I seem to influence young men to date me, so there must be something different about me. That is, perhaps, why we were never able to form a relationship. And after two days, and nights, of self-analysis I've concluded it was me, not you, who is to blame. I should hate myself for telling you this now that you're so far away, but I was always hoping you would just walk up to me and ask me for a date. Darn you, Willie.

And then it occurred to me that it might not be too late after all.

If I sound embarrassed, I am. I would be pleased if you would respond to this letter. I would like very much to have that relationship with you. Although we will be separated by a great distance, is it not possible to share our lives? I would like that very, very much. My mother taught me to follow my female intuitions. They tell me that you really did care for me. Hopefully your feelings haven't changed. Please forgive me for playing hard to get. I will be on pins and needles awaiting your reply.

My prayers are with you. And, my love. Yes. I really believe that I do love you, however bold the word might seem. Please be careful and may God bless you and all of your comrades.

With love,
MaryLou

P.S. My lips will kiss the flap of this envelope after it is sealed in the very spot marked, S.W.A.K. How strange, I thought when I considered doing it, that our first kiss would be much like a long-distance telephone call.

Luv ya. ML

Will was astonished, more so than if he'd been decorated with a Congressional Medal of Honor. He was, in fact, dumbfounded. He just sat there, staring first at the envelope, then the letter, then pressing his lips to the flap, and repeating the process over and over again. A passionate ripple coursed through his entire body. He was amazed that, while holed up in his lair surrounded by a sea of trees thousands of miles apart from MaryLou, he could sense the intensity of ecstasy as though she was cuddled snuggly in his arms.

Twilight was gloaming when he finally surfaced from his stupor. He squinted to read the letter once again, then carefully folded the sheets and placed them inside of the envelope. He could not resist kissing the flap again before he shoved the letter into his breast pocket. The dark of night inundated the jungle, so he had to grope his way between the trees to reach the perimeter of the campsite. When he hotfooted it toward his tent he realized he'd missed out on evening mess. But it really didn't matter, he guessed, because he was sated with satisfaction, having dined on the fruits of love.

The tent row was abuzz with chatter on his approach. Gambler was bickering with Tillie over their customary card game. When Will rounded the corner of his tent he spotted several of the guys huddled around some of the others, most of whom were planted on their knees around the outside hem of a blanket, feverously engrossed with a game of five-card draw. Will had no intention of getting himself involved, but he did elect to observe from a safe distance. He advanced just close enough to peer over the other observers' shoulders. It was quite dark, and Will wondered how the players could manage to read their cards. As it turned out, they were passing around a GI flashlight, each man illuminating his hand of cards when it came his turn to either bet or call or fold.

There appeared to be yet another commotion behind the row of tents. He heard O'Hare exclaim, "Well, if you ask me I think it's the royal shits."

Then he overheard Foreman agree with O'Hare, saying he was "really shocked. I mean, I was as shocked over the news as I was over his reaction to receiving the news."

As Will drew closer to the confab, Foreman continued, suggesting, "You know, there's must've been a ... oh, a strange relationship ... wouldn't you agree? What I mean is, when you consider how it all began."

"You mean you don't think he loved her?" O'Hare asked.

Will couldn't stem his curiosity any longer. "What happened?" he intervened when he sauntered into their midst.

"Where the hell have you been?" O'Hare asked.

"Where d'ya think?" Foreman cut in. "He's been out communing with nature, as usual." He gave his head a disgusted shake.

"Well, what's all of the commotion?" Will asked. "What's all this stuff about being shocked over the news.? What news?"

"You shoulda been here when this shit hit the fan," O'Hare replied.

"Yeah. Instead of vanishing like you do," Foreman chided Will again.

"Knock it off," Will retorted. "Skip it. Sorry I asked," he muttered in an angry tone of voice.

"It's Williams," O'Hare explained.

"What happened to Williams?" Will barked, quite obviously concerned that something terrible might've happened to one of the men.

"He went off of the deep end, that's what," Foreman offered.

"The preacher? Went off the deep end? That's hard to believe," Will replied.

"Yeah. The preacher. He got a *Dear John* letter from Peg." O'Hare began to fill him in on the events that unfolded while he was in La-la Land.

"You're shitting me. Preacher? Deep-sixed by Peg? Over what?" Will wanted to know.

"I guess she's found another man," Foreman added, "leastways, that's what he said was in the letter. And it turned into a free-for-all. Perkins had to give him an uppercut to the jaw just to get his attention."

"Damn," Will asked, shaking his head in disbelief. "A fist fight? Perk smacked him? That's awful."

"Not really," O'Hare disagreed with Will's assessment. "You should've been here. He went berserk. He was running to and fro, back and forth, waving the letter over his head, screaming at the top of his lungs. He said, 'I'm going to go get that sonofabitch that's screwing Peg,' and he took off for the beach and just waded out into the tide, like he was going to swim clean across the ocean to get his revenge. Perk, he waded in after him and tried to coax him back, but Williams just pulled free of Perk's grasp and headed out to sea. So, Perk went after him, cold-cocked him, and drug him back onto the shore."

Will just stood there in shock. Williams, always the laidback individual, just didn't seem the type to lose his cool. "So, then what happened? And where is Williams now?" Will demanded to know, angry at himself, more than anyone else, for missing out on the exhibition by slinking off in the jungle. He was having a great deal of trouble trying to fathom Williams complete change in character.

"He's on the LCI with Baker and Roul ... at least we hope he is," Farmer finally intruded. He'd been standing off to one side, so Will hadn't even noticed him until he spoke.

"Me, too," Will admitted, then asked, "Are you sure he's on board the ship?"

"Roul and Baker took over," Foreman explained, telling Will, "They escorted him in that direction. No one has seen him since, nor has anyone seen the captain and sergeant, so he must be with them."

Will was almost overwhelmed after hearing the news. He wanted to tell Williams how sorry he was, although he actually couldn't relate to the problem, having never received a *Dear John* letter himself. He guessed anything concerning affairs of the heart could lead to heartbreak. "Man," Will finally chimed in, "it is the shits. I kinda liked Peg.... I mean, I didn't know her, but the way Williams described her, and spilled his guts about their relationship, made me feel like I did. My first impression was obviously wrong. Any woman who would crap over a guy when he's incarcerated over here isn't worth the powder it would take to blow her all the way to hell and back."

Will stepped back, figuring on going into his tent, when he heard Gambler's raucous voice split the night air. "C'mon," he shouted, giving Tillie a hard time like always. "It's a buck raise to you, clodhopper. So, either bet 'em or fold 'em and quit screwing around."

Will was a little surprised that Schuster hadn't put a damper on the card game when darkness fell. Normally, he'd have made his rounds, telling everyone to "Hit the sack. Lights out in ten minutes." Will wondered if he was just cutting them a little slack as a goodwill gesture. They hadn't had much time for leisure since the outset of training.

Tillie, as usual, was hassling Gambler in return. "Cheezus, Gambler! You'd make a jug of shine nervous. I'm thinking," he stalled.

"With what? You haven't got any brains," Gambler verbally spanked Tillie. "In? Or out?"

"Wal ... I'm ... gonna fold, I reckon, seeing as how I'm just holdin' a pair'a tens," Tillie finally complied, throwing his cards on top of the pot that was piled center way on the blanket.

Will chuckled. He'd grown accustomed to their constant bickering. They were, he thought, like two children, especially when they got tangled up in a game of poker. They were noisy, inconsiderate of each other and anyone else within hearing range, constantly wrangling one another with uncomplimentary barbs, insults and profanity. But Gambler was definitely the wealthiest man in camp. Tillie was runner-up. They'd gleaned every last dollar from every last man who still had enough pocket money to sit in on the games. If Will's calculation was right, Gambler was siphoning the loose change that remained in the camp from Barrentos and Slycord this very minute. Will and Farmer were the only two who never played cards; also the only two who weren't constantly reduced to the role of moochers when funds ran short long before the days of the month had expired.

Will hated to admit the truth, that Gambler was good at something. He was a sloven soldier without a lick of sensitivity for guys he claimed to count as friends. But when it came to fondling a deck of cards, he was a pro. Tillie was a rank amateur if compared to Gambler. Lady Luck did appear to look after him, though. He tolerated Gambler's constant harping, absorbing insults that most anyone else would not have overlooked. It was, Will thought, the nature of the brute.

Gambler once verbally flayed Tillie during a dispute over cards, telling him in a boisterous manner that the hillbilly didn't have the foggiest notion of what poker was all about. He said, "You're so goddamn dumb, ridge runner, you probably believe that a one-eyed Jack is a half-blind mule."

Tillie ignored it with a grin, sluffing it off with, "You're just sore on account'a I won a pot. You're a poor loser."

And Gambler countered with, "Loser, my ass! Does this pile of money lying in front of me suggest I am a loser? I'm the big winner." Will sort of figured it was Tillie's obsession with Gambler that made the relationship flourish in spite of the barbs. Tillie made no excuses for his devotion to his friend. It was evident he did idolize the huckster.

All things considered, Baker squad was a unique assembly of opposites. Gambler was the addicted speculator, Tillie the obedient valet, of sorts, who bowed to Gambler's wishes, Farmer a puritan who frowned on worldly pastimes, and Will an overeducated nonconformist surrounded by ordinary people. To the man, they all stayed the course throughout the training cycle. So when Will nonchalantly approached the circle of gamblers crouched about the blanket, and then dropped onto his knees beside Barrentos, Gambler could hardly ignore him, so he said, "Make room for a player, spectator," and dealt another round of cards, leaving Will empty-handed.

The letter from MaryLou had somehow converted Will into a romanticist of sorts and, buoyed by a surge of confidence resulting from bagging the prize he'd sought for so long, he informed Gambler, "What about me? I don't see any cards."

Gambler paused, swiped the sweat from his brow with the sleeve of his shirt, and grimaced. "YOU?" he barked. "You? The loner ... having visions of grandeur? Well, I'll be dipped in shit."

"You are shit, Gambler. Just quit flapping you lips and deal me in.... Or isn't my fresh money welcomed in your game?" Will sarcastically replied, shaking a fistful of folding money in his outstretch hand.

Gambler gleamed with delight when he saw Will's bankroll. "Well, lookie here, guys, old Gambler's got a new lamb to shear," he badgered Will, ignoring Will's reference to his loose tongue. "What's your pleasure, loser? Five-card peek, Spit in the Ocean, maybe we'd better stick with something simple, like five-card draw?" he asked, giving Will his option to pick his own poison.

"Dealer's choice," Will replied in a calm voice. "Make it easy on yourself."

"Okay, wise ass. High-stake game. Can you handle the action? A buck limit, three raises now that you've sat in, and nothing wild. Five-card stud, last card down and dirty," Gambler explained his house rules.

"I know," Will responded. If he was nervous, it didn't show. Gambler's forehead was again laced with sweat, Will's was dry. "Deal, hotshot."

Gambler was totally perplexed by Will's calm demeanor. He shuffled the cards, offering a few snide innuendos to goad Will; verbal sucker punches such as, "Does Missus Munday know her precious little boy is out so late ... playing with the big boys?" before he dealt a solitary card.

"Leave my mother outta this and deal or ... are you scared?" Will fired back.

Will glanced over his shoulder. It seemed like almost every man in camp, with the exception of Williams, had elbowed his way to a spot from which they could watch this spectacle. It pleased Will, while it added to Gambler's discomfort. Gambler, trying desperately to retain his image as a cocksure champion, finally forced a grin. He cocked his head, reached up to shove his cap back onto the crown of his skull, and nervously fingered the deck of cards, glancing first left, then right, to scan all of the participants, and finally snapped his fingernail against the edge of the cards and began to toss them, one at a time, around the circle. He called the face value of each card as it dropped in front of its recipient, offering his opinion over whether it was good, or bad, then muttered, "Ace high bets, Munday," after he discovered Will had the best card.

From that point on things unraveled for the entire group of players, including the cardsharp from Reno. They played, or folded, until Barrentos yelped, "I'm busto," and called it a night, complimenting Will with, "Señor Munday. He is very lucky guy. Barrentos, he's not so lucky, huh? Barrentos, he lose all of his dinero." The game continued, but Will was on a roll the likes of which no one had ever witnessed. He could do nothing wrong. Gambler and Tillie and Slycord could do nothing right. Slycord dropped out when he bet the farm on three Queens, only to be aced out by Will's four tens. Tillie lost his bankroll. "Hey, Munday," he suggested as he folded his last hand of cards and pitched them onto the pile of money in the pot, "you'd better save some of the shithouse luck for the fighting. I ain't never seen anything like this in all my born days."

So there they sat, Will F. Munday staring at the gambler, waiting for him to either go head to head or quit. Gambler's bank was starving for a transfusion. The surplus of money that Will had accumulated came predominantly from the Reno racketeer's stash. Will's good fortune was as much a result of Gambler's reckless wagering, in an attempt to recuperate his losses, as it was Will's sudden run of luck. Time and again he tried to bluff Will out, or to buy the pot, only to end up with a hand of cards that was no match for the pasteboards Will held. Gambler was striving to hide his discontent, because, as a true gambler, he knew a man's luck could change in an instant's notice. He probably would've given the game one more shot if Tillie hadn't interrupted, suggesting to Gambler, "Why don'cha quit? Munday's cleaned your plow ... good and proper."

"Shut the fuck up, you hook-nosed, ugly hedgehopper," he yelped, then pulled his money back, shoved the deck of cards into his breast pocket, and informed Will, "Game's over. I'll be wanting a return engagement. You're not good, Munday. You're just lucky. I'm good. I will win it all back, plus."

Unbeknownst to the group, Sergeant Baker had been observing from a distance. He sauntered up to where they were all assembled and informed them, "Yeah, Gambler's right. The game's over. Lights out in ten minutes."

Will, however, just could not resist the temptation to take one more dig at Gambler. "How'd you like that piece of cake?" he asked.

"Fuck you," Gambler replied, then folded up his blanket and pivoted on his toe to take refuge in the tent.

Farmer, who had been an observer as soon as the first card had been dealt, jumped into the fracas. He didn't try to hide his glee over Will's triumph. "Man," he remarked as he fell into step at Will's side when they headed for their tent, "you shore gave him a lesson."

Will chuckled. "Me?" he asked. "I gave Gambler a lesson in playing cards? Hardly!"

"No, I didn't say in cards," Farmer teased him. "You done give him a lesson in humility. Anyway, I've been waiting to hear about that there letter you got. Ain't you going to tell old Farmer about that sweet patootie what wrote to you?" He'd been dying of curiosity all evening.

"Huh?" Will asked.

"I done said I wanted to hear about the letter. Man, she must be some gal to give a man so much spunk," Farmer suggested.

"Yeah ... she is indeed, Farmer," Will agreed, augmenting Farmer's words of praise by informing him, "She's not some gal. She's *the* gal, if you get my drift."

"Wal, I'll be darned," Farmer mumbled. His diagnosis of Will's sudden surge of energy was, "The love bug's gotcha, Will."

After they crawled into their bunks, Will raved on and on about MaryLou, keeping Farmer awake indefinitely. It was Gambler who, as usual, finally drew a line in the sand. "Hey, Munday. Shut up! I need some shuteye. What do you know about women, anyway? Let me tell you a thing or two. There ain't no woman, even your precious MaryLou, that's worth getting all lathered up over. They're all alike. Stand every women in the world on their head, then spread their legs, and they all look alike."

Will was not swayed by Gambler's opinion. He ignored the remark, rolled over on his side, and stared outside through the open tent flap into the darkness of night.

Gambler fell asleep with a frown on his face, bemoaning the dough he'd forfeited. Farmer was snoring as soon as Will closed his mouth. Tillie was first to get to sleep because nothing bothered him, not even Will's big mouth. He was grunting, snorting, and pitching and tossing while cutting Z's the minute he lay down. Will lay awake for the longest time. He was wound up like an eight-day watch in spite of the troubling news he'd received regarding Williams and Peg. Will had heard of *Dear John* letters but had never seen one. He mused over the fact that a single mail call brought him a joyous letter of acceptance from his lady love, whereas Williams had gotten a note of rejection from his woman. The letters, he decided, were an antithesis to one another; the *Dear John* and *Dear Willie* letters bearing opposite messages.

He reached over to where he'd draped his clothing after he'd stripped to the buff for bed and touched the letter in the pocket of his fatigue jacket, then smiled, heaved a big sigh of relief, and silently congratulated himself for finally winning the "run for the roses." It was much too late to even think about writing a response to MaryLou's letter, so he decided to wait until daybreak to pen a reply. He figured it wouldn't take too long to compose such a letter. How long, he asked himself, would it take him to tell MaryLou, "I love you, too. And I want you."

Chapter Eleven

Will had oftentimes deplored the fact that his military education was laced with surprises. Every time he began to feel comfortable someone pitched a knuckle ball and caught him napping. The previous evening he anticipated there was but one more field problem left on the training schedule, after which they'd graduate to another level; guerrilla. The morning brought with it an abrupt change in plans. The timetable had been moved up. The surprise announcement came right after they'd eaten their breakfast. During the meal something occurred that should have been a warning. A caravan of vehicles came thundering into camp from the replacement depot. They carried a bunch of officers who didn't stay long. They departed immediately after having a brief confab with Captain Roul. Will figured there'd be a change in the wind.

Schuster didn't call them to formation at the customary 0700 hours. The entire group just sat on their duffs, entertaining themselves as best they could, waiting for something to happen. Noontime was nearing when Corporal Schuster came jogging in and announced, "Okay. Fall in." After they were assembled, Schuster put them "At ease," then told them to stand by until the captain arrived. "I think he wants to have a word with you," Schuster explained.

Another half hour passed. They were growing weary of standing in the ranks. Shortly thereafter, Baker and Roul emerged from the LCI and sauntered over to where the Stopwatch team was impatiently waiting. Baker waved a hand on his approach and shouted, "Stay at ease in the ranks. Knock off the small talk."

Captain Roul ventured to the front, paused to eyeball the troops, then announced, "We're moving out this afternoon."

Silence reigned in the ranks. Not a man uttered a word, not even a sound. They just glanced back and forth, then stared at their commanding officer, who'd just dropped a bomb in their midst.

"Unfortunately," Roul continued after a short pause, "the training cycle is ended. To set the record straight, the promise Sergeant Baker made some time back about a surprise if we all excelled—and we did—has to be broken, not by his choice, but by those in the high command. Unbeknownst to you, the Corps of Engineers has spent the past two weeks constructing a replica of our target. It was our intention to make the assault on the structure our final assignment. That was the surprise, a ˙ surprise that might've been beneficial in preparing us for the real thing. However, the chiefs of staff have instructed me to transport this unit to the replacement depot, where we will await further orders. Our intended objective, I've been told, will have to be destroyed much earlier than originally planned. Subsequently, it has created a domino effect. We do know, and are permitted to pass on to you, that one of the changes in plans squelched the original idea to transport us by submarine to our destination. There is no time for that, now. We will be flown by seaplane to a rendezvous point and take refuge on an uninhabited island, where we will be intercepted by the Philippine underground, then guided to our objective. That, gents, is what I know at this time."

It was enough information for Will F. Munday to comprehend that the beginning of the end was about to start. It was also a big kick in the ass to the reluctant acrophobic who had never considered in his wildest expectations that he'd be airborne. His stomach was too squeamish for that. He had trouble looking out of a third-story window without experiencing a traumatic case of the heebie-jeebies.

The captain then left them to stew among themselves. He immediately departed in a Jeep, leaving Sergeant Baker and his aide, Corporal Schuster, to supervise the evacuation of their rustic quarters. Will was inquisitive. How much did Roul actually know? And was Baker informed? Will figured that Schuster, holding the lowly rank of Corporal, probably knew very little. But one thing was certain. Captain Roul had brewed up a zesty morsel for his subordinates to munch on while they busied themselves striking the tents and packing up to bug out.

Soon after their gear was packed up and readied for transport, three 6x6 cargo trucks rolled into the clearing. Baker wasted no time getting the equipment loaded on one truck, then divided his men, assigning half of them to ride in one vehicle, half in another. The journey was not pleasant. The roadway was corrugated with ruts, and it was a bumpy ride. As luck would have it the truck driver of the vehicle Will rode in was a huge cowboy who answered to the name Barney. He turned a deaf ear to complaints when the truck pitched and tossed, bouncing Will and his friends around like yoyos doing rock the cradle. When they did finally reach the depot, Will informed his chauffeur, "I chipped half the porcelain off of my teeth during that buggy ride," but his only response was a grin from the big lug who'd delivered them in one piece. The unexpected bright spot of the event was Will's good fortune to run into the cigar-smoking captain who'd originally dispatched him on the journey by handing him an envelope containing sealed orders and offering some advice about body bags being the only mode of transportation available for returning to the depot. He saluted when he encountered the old CO, then asked, "Remember me, sir? Private Munday."

"Yeah. I guess. Why?" the captain asked, taking pause to stuff the smelly cigar in between his lips.

"You said I wouldn't be back, except in a body bag," Will reminded him, calling attention to his well-being, then smugly advising him, "Look. No body bag. I'm back." The captain pivoted and walked away, shaking his head in disbelief or, perhaps in disgust. Will didn't know which.

The stay at the replacement depot was, as they'd been forewarned, brief. It seemed as though they'd no more than caught their breaths than they were once again loaded onto trucks and whisked away, finally coming to a stop on the beach. The first thing Will spotted was a large airplane, parked beside a wooden dock, bouncing on the surface of the water. "What's that contraption called?" he asked Baker.

"It's a PBY," Baker replied.

"That's our next mode of travel?" Will protested.

"Un-huh." Baker muttered in response.

Will was already ailing with a giddy stomach that was brought on by being hustled from one point to another so quickly. The past couple of days reminded him of his childhood, when his mother once sat him atop of a plaster horse on the merry-go-round at the County Fair, then stepped off just as the carousel began to sway, leaving him to fend for himself. He was frightened rather than overjoyed as his mother had anticipated. He hung on to the plaster steed for dear life, wanting so bad to jump down, then off of the whirligig, but he was too scared to get off and too afraid to stay on. His mother, sensing his fear as he whirled past where she stood, remounted the merry-go-round and rescued him, patting his little back to reassure him as she carried him away from the ride, whispering, "There, there," into his little ear to calm his childish anxiety. However, that was then and this was now. His mother was nowhere near to "there, there" him, or to pat his little back, or stroke his tiny brow to make everything better. Will F. Munday was on his own.

The plane's cabin floor, or deck as sailors called it, was butt-numbing; so cold that Will felt as though he was seated on a cake of ice. He wiggled around trying to find some degree of comfort. Nothing helped. Comfort, he guessed, wasn't in the plans. As soon as the plane was aloft they were told the flight would take several hours. That meant Will had a lot of idle time on his hands, which wasn't always in his best interest. He didn't want to regress into the past by dwelling on college days, and he wasn't wild about having a wrestling match with a series of what-ifs regarding his future. He was momentarily caught in limbo, about halfway between the two options. He finally decided to analyze his fear of flying. Actually, he was surprised that the ride was fairly smooth, nothing like the journey by truck from their old base to the replacement depot. A smooth flight was a plus. But it was the only plus he could muster up on such short notice. He felt compromised. He'd never flown and had never seriously considered he might. He was hesitant to glance out through the portholes, but temptation kept nagging him to take a gander. So he finally succumbed to the inquisitive urge and peeked out, first seeing only blue sky decorated with white, puffy clouds. It didn't unnerve him like he'd anticipated it might, so he leaned a tad closer to the window and let his line of vision drop. His courage dropped with it. He reared back, his entire body quivering, the palms of his hands sweating. *Damn,* he scolded himself. *It's okay,* he added, trying to calm his nerves with a pep talk. *So, you're soaring through the cloud several thousand feet above terra firma, destined for some mystic terminus where a promising future is a long shot, and you're worried? Over what? Cool it, self!*

Will slumped back onto his rear and let his backside lean against the bulkhead. It was time, he informed himself, to deal with his phobias once and for all. He had thought of himself as the only member of Stopwatch with a phobia affliction. Venturing back through the pages of his life, he tried to match some occurrence to his torment over high spots. There had been, he recalled, the air show his mother took him to see in a nearby town. Perhaps that was the event that triggered it. He did remember he was frightened, not for himself that day, but for the barnstormers who took a zillion chances to amuse their customers. They loop-de-looped the fragile planes, took turns climbing out of the cockpits to walk out onto the wings, portraying daredevils with nerves of steel for the fans down on the ground, while Will chewed his fingernails to the bone fretting because they might fall. And he did recall how he'd dreamt about the stunts for weeks thereafter.

What irked him even more were people who didn't understand that acrophobia was not the case of a man being a coward. It wasn't an option. It was, in reality, an accepted adversity that, while unexplainable, was also incurable in medical circles. For example, prior to boarding the plane, Baker's "C'mon, jurblowfs. We're going for a kite ride," unnerved him no end. That was when a strange twist of fate intervened. It was the first time that Will actually suspected he was not a loner in his fears. Seiverson almost panicked when it came his time to walk the plank into the cabin. This was quite a shock to Will, because in recalling the day they all descended the cliff side during training, Seive didn't balk. He did, however, pause on this occasion. Baker, taking notice, told him to get his ass on board, and when Seiverson still stalled, he informed him that he would pitch him on, then added a few additional threats to encourage him. Seive, knowing Baker wasn't a man to be trifled with, dutifully pussyfooted his way across the gangplank onto the plane, but Will sensed Seive was terrified equally as much as he figured to be when it came his turn to climb on board.

He let his mind wander back to the replacement depot, where their short stay was kept under surveillance from moment one. They were, it seemed to Will, prisoners—not soldiers. That prompted him to wonder why. The secrecy routine didn't bode too well with Will's skepticism over the future. He recalled that from the moment his military career began he was constantly under a shroud of secrecy. It began at Camp Dodge, when he and his fellow conscripts were ushered to the waiting train to ship out to training camp. They were not even permitted to tell their immediate families they were leaving. He kept his lip zipped, but it didn't matter, because most of the local folks who had kids leaving town knew that the only train scheduled out was the one they were put aboard. Naturally, a few dozen concerned parents and relatives came to bid them farewell, which had the MPs in a dither. But their hands were tied. They could not maintain a wedge between the draftees and their loved ones; a crowd of people who broke through the human barricade and kissed the boys goodbye in spite of orders to the contrary. That, however, was just the beginning. Will suffered through two additional *secret* moves prior to boarding the ship to sail overseas. First, his delay en route furlough, that gave him time to stop off at home a few days, was supposed to be kept strictly confidential. As it turned out, half the town came to greet them when the train pulled into the station. And the second time his move was wrapped in secrecy was when they were trucked from Fort Ord under cover of darkness to embark on their voyage. At the time he'd thought that only he and those with him knew about their transfer. He was wrong. While he was on board the ship on the high seas Tokyo Rose broadcast a special message to the boys on his ship, wishing them luck, but predicting they'd be killed by Japanese soldiers. If Tokyo Rose knew where he was he figured the entire world also knew. So much for secrecy.

He shook himself back to reality. For some unexplainable reason he was not enjoying his subconscious journey back in time. When he raised his head he noticed Tillie staring directly at him with a hollow-eyed glare that made it appear he was looking through, not at, him. He swiveled his head to the side and caught sight of Gambler slumped down, catching some Z's. Farmer was also in the land of nod. So, Will struck up a verbal exchange with Tillie for lack of something better to do. "What d'ya think?" he asked the hillbilly.

"Me? Awe, nuthin' much. I'll shore say one thing. This here aeroplane is shore an ugly bird, ain't she?" Tillie responded.

"Yes. It is that,"Will agreed.

"She kinda resembles a pregnant pigeon," Tillie added.

Will nodded in agreement. He had to admit that Tillie's description was appropriate. While he'd never seen a pregnant pigeon, mainly because there was no such thing, he thought such a bird and this plane might resemble one another.

Being uncomfortable flying, Will had suspicions about many things that the ordinary passenger wouldn't. He wondered how far such a plane could fly on one fueling. He did recall overhearing one of the PBY's crew mention something about "jettisoning" all the excess baggage to accommodate additional fuel, so he shrugged off that problem. Up until this point in time most of Will's experience involving aircraft was negative; first as a child at the air show and second when the Nips laced their camp with a hail of machine fire. This being his third encounter with planes, he found it difficult to believe he was actually sitting inside of such a contraption, winging his way to an unknown goal. He would have preferred a round-trip ticket, but that issue was settled before they ever boarded the plane when O'Hare asked Baker about it and was told, "The travel agent didn't mention a return trip."

Sergeant Baker wasn't exactly making things any easier for Will. He was nervous, a trait he'd never exhibited before, which in turn filtered down to his men, tending to undermine their morale. But Will delved back into Baker's past and recalled how he'd been both wounded and decorated at the Battle of Buna, so he allowed Baker the benefit of the doubt. Baker, Schuster, Roul and Gooch already had been in the thick of things, while all of the others were green horned rookies. Perhaps their overseers had every right to be a trifle edgy.

Will glanced around to discover almost everyone but him was either asleep, or were in a half-dazed stupor, most of them wearing blank expressions on their kissers. Having no one to jaw with, he let his thoughts slide back to the depot. His recollection of the great meal that was prepared for them was an upper. After the beachside café's bill of fare, along with K-rations in the field, the whole gang hit the chow line like a pack of rabid wolves. It was the first time in months that Will had tasted real potatoes, smothered under brown gravy, along with an actual cut of beef that the mess sergeant insisted was "steak." Will guessed he was finally getting the hang of soldiering. The bad points about the military seemed to bother him less and the good things looked even better than they actually were. Remembering a joke Baker had once told them while taking a chow break during training, Will recalled that Baker claimed he could tell how long a man had been in the Army by his table manners. Will chuckled to himself. "Table manners," he mumbled, as if any such thing existed in the Army. Anyway, Baker said, "During a man's first year, if he finds a bug crawling in his mess kit, he dumps the food and all into the garbage. On his second year, finding a bug, he takes the bug out, then eats the grub. When he's got three years service he eats the bug along with the grub and after four years, if the bug tries to get out, he grabs him and puts him back into the food, then eats." At the time Will had looked on the tale as far-fetched. He wasn't so sure anymore. He knew he had finally begun to deal with the harsh lifestyle. Will's acceptance factor had risen. That was, in his mind, what the Army was all about; acceptance. He had concluded that if the Army was to coop any man up in some far-flung outpost for an extended period of time, he would comply with any outlandish request made of him.

While his recollections were centered on the depot, he thought about the sizzling letter he had penned to MaryLou, along with one to his mother, as well. The letter to MaryLou was a different thing entirely than the one to Mom. About all he told his mother was that he was fine, eating regularly, and that he loved her. The MaryLou letter was something else. He'd scrapped a half-dozen sheets of paper at the Red Cross Club before he even managed to decide on a worthy salutation. He tried, *My Dear MaryLou,* just plain *MaryLou,* and *My darling,* and *MaryLou, Dearest, and* finally *Beloved,* which he scratched because it reminded him of a funeral. He then settled on, *Dearest Sweetheart.* He wasn't overjoyed with it because he thought it sounded a tad corny, but having had no previous experience writing love letters made it a challenge. He shared the blame with her, admitting they'd suffered from a breakdown in communications. And he admitted that his shyness was a factor, writing, *I was just too timid to ask you out.* He assured her, *Every glance I aimed your way was sincere,* and he closed by claiming, *You will always be in my heart, as you've been since my freshman days.* He ended by vowing, *My Love forever. Your slave. Willie.*

Will's legs began to cramp. He opened his eyes, glanced over at Farmer, who was fast asleep. Will shifted his stance, deliberately kicking Farmer's leg, hoping it would disturb him enough to awaken him. It did. Farmer rubbed his eyes, stretched his arms above his head, then stared directly at Will, asking, "How's your acro stuff doing?" As was customary, Farmer's thoughts were on Will's welfare, not his own.

"Acro stuff?" Will asked, having no idea what Farmer was talking about.

"Oh, you know, Will. That there two-dollar word for you being skittish about high places," Farmer explained.

"Oh, that," Will replied, shrugging. "You mean acrophobia. Well, to be real honest about it, while I'm penned up inside, not looking out, it really isn't so bad."

Their relationship had become so entwined during the past few weeks that Farmer considered Will totally predictable. And he had learned to live with Will's compulsions to just drift off into one of his trances, ignoring everyone and everything around him. So, he too, had picked up on Seive's reluctance to get on board. "It must be kinda nice knowin' you ain't alone, huh?" he asked Will.

"Alone?" Will asked with a chuckle, glancing at those who surrounded him in the plane cabin. "Hardly! I don't see anyone who is alone."

"Naw, I don't mean alone that way," Farmer clarified himself. "I was talkin' about Seive. He's scared of high places, too, ain't he?"

"Well, if he was intimidated he must've made a quick recovery," Will assessed the situation, taking notice that Seive was sawing logs at the present time. "But you're right. He was pretty edgy. I imagine I was the only one who felt sorry for him."

He recalled that during Seive's and Baker's exchange Seive had informed the sergeant, "I'm not a bird, not a paratrooper. I'm in the ground forces, not the air corps. If God had intended for me to fly, he'd have given me wings."

And he recalled how Baker had responded in a less than sympathetic manner, asking Seive, "Is that a refusal to obey orders?" That was when things turned a tad hairy.

Seive abruptly informed Baker, "Whatever! If refusing to get on that plane and then to be taken on a flight is a refusal to obey orders, I'll have to plead guilty."

Baker had managed to survive testy subordinates before, Will being one such example, and he wasn't the type to change his tactics this late in the game. "Just on the chance I didn't make myself clear," he gave Seive a chance to renege, "and considering the probability that you wouldn't like to face a court-martial, I'm going to give you another opportunity to board the plane and quit holding up the procession. Be forewarned, soldier, that should you pass this only opportunity to clean the slate, I will personally pick you up and will pitch you headfirst into that goddamn PBY." The pair stood nose to nose for what seemed like a lifetime to Will but was probably no more than a few seconds, when Seive cautiously pivoted on the narrow, wooden catwalk and tiptoed his way onto the plane. Once again, Sergeant Baker rose to the occasion, leaving no doubts in anyone's mind over who was the top soldier.

The plane suddenly lurched, then wig-wagged from side to side, jarring Will back to reality. He'd been totally comatose for some time and hadn't even noticed most of the guys were awake and stirring. Gambler's voice sounded above everyone else's, which was nothing unusual. He was rehashing redundant, old tales of his adventures back in Reno, reciting for the umpteenth time about the episode when he was caught in bed with a married woman, whose hubby came home early from work, requiring him to make a half-naked retreat through the kitchen in an effort to avoid coming face to face with her man. Will had it memorized as well as Gambler. But someone invariably urged him to retell the tale. This time is was O'Hare, egging him on, asking, "Yeah. Then … what was it happened?"

"Well, it's like I've told you guys before, this clown waltzes in unannounced, me with my pants down around my ankles. The wife didn't seem to care, because she was on the verge of having a climax, so instead of turning loose of me, she threw a hammer lock around my shoulders and started pumping her ass up and down like a jackhammer. I told her, 'Someone's here,' but she paid that a never-mind.

"She yelped, 'I don't care. Kiss my tit, honey, I'm coming.'

"And I said, 'You kiss my ass, I'm going.'"

Things never changed. One of the guys, Will wasn't even sure who it was, barked, "Go on. Go on, What didja do then?" Hell, they knew the story backwards and forwards. Will thought they just liked to hear Gambler admit he got the short end of the stick one time in his life.

But being the dupe he actually was, Gambler went on with the exposé. "Well, I headed through a door I thought would lead to the hallway. Instead, it went directly into the kitchen, where this guy was standing, holding on to an empty glass and a quart of milk. Man, you shoulda seen the look on his kisser. He up and drops both the glass and bottle on the floor, then heads for me. Here I am, trying to pull my pants up with one hand and trying to turn the doorknob with my other one, when the damned knob came loose and fell on the floor. I'm down there groping to get a hold of it while this guy is pounding the hell out of my backside, but I finally got the knob shaft back into the hole, twisted it, and the door flew open. Man, I was gone like a striped-assed ape."

Foreman finally shut Gambler up. "Gambler, you hot shot," he scoffed at the story. "Truth be known, you're probably still a virgin. I'll bet a cold shower and a change of undershorts would kill you. You never get the story the same. Last time you said the knob came loose in your hand and you were down on your hands and knees, trying to find the hole, while this guy was flogging your ass."

"So-o-o-o?" Gambler retorted. "I was coming to that part."

"You already passed it. You just said you took off like a striped-assed ape," Foreman reminded him.

The plane pitched again, giving everyone a start, but Baker was quick to reassure them, "Just some turbulence, gents. Nothing to sweat over. Relax."

Will turned his attention to Captain Roul, who heretofore on the journey had maintained a low profile. Now, he was on his feet, groping his way between a web of outstretched legs that blocked the aisle. He had ventured to pay a visit to the pilots a short time earlier, and Will wondered what he'd learned; if they were closing in on their objective. But he only commented on his return, "Enjoy. This is the easy part of our assignment. Things will get tough soon enough."

That set Will to thinking. He'd never considered what an impact the weight of command dealt men like Roul. Perhaps, Will allowed, the captain was bearing a heavy cross. He was responsible for everything that might befall them in coming days. Win, lose, or draw, he'd be held accountable for the good and the bad, the victories, the failures. Will entering a new phase of adjustment, where he took other people's problems into consideration, was a radical change in attitude for the reluctant warrior. Prior to this, showing compassion for his superiors was never a consideration. He glanced over to check on Farmer and, finding him awake for a change, nudged him with an elbow and asked, "D'ya know what?"

"Nope. What?"

"Oh, it's really nothing, I guess," Will sheepishly replied. He'd reconsidered. It bothered him that Farmer might say something like, "I told you so."

"Awe, c'mon, Will," Farmer coaxed him. "Don't give me that 'oh, nothing' stuff."

"You'd only laugh."

"I would not."

"You sure?"

"Yeah. I'm sure."

"Well, something odd just occurred to me," Will confessed, telling his friend, "I might've been wrong about a few things."

Farmer cackled like a Rhode Island Red on a roost, razzing Will, even though he promised to not laugh. "YOU?" he asked in a a skeptical tone of

186

voice. "Will Munday? Wrong? Awe, go on. Perish that thought."

"See? You lied. You said you wouldn't laugh."

"I ain't laughing at you. I'm laughing with you."

"It's still laughing."

"Okay. I'm sorry. Get on with your story. I promise, cross my heart, I won't laugh."

Will was hesitant, but he finally continued, explaining to Farmer, "What I was going to say was … I wouldn't trade places with the captain for all of the tea in China."

"You wouldn't?"

"Well, I wouldn't trade worries with him, anyway."

"Oh, me neither," Farmer agreed. "He's in a torment right now, for sure. Can't you see it? He's really edgy."

It pleased Will to see that he and Farmer were on the same wavelength. Whatever communication barriers stood between them in the beginning had mostly evaporated. He even believed that he'd influenced Farmer to improve his vocabulary. Farmer didn't talk in riddles like he did when the two first met. After weeks of tutoring, that subliminally interjected proper grammer in their chats, the country boy appeared to comprehend Will's palavering a lot better. This was good. However, along with Farmer's enhanced vocabulary came the knack for expressing his views a tad more forcefully, too. So, Will wasn't the least bit shocked when Farmer noted, "Is this the same Will Munday what once said that we got the worst of both ends with a captain like Roul?"

It was the same Will Munday. "Okay. Rub it in." Will mournfully regretted that he'd been unfair with Roul, admitting to Farmer, "I guess I had to grow up some day. This was quite a learning process, tucked away in the jungle, segregated from the rest of the world, wasn't it? I feel like I really got to know you well, Farmer, and it was my good fortune to be assigned to the same unit as you."

Farmer grinned. He wasn't much on words at a time like that. "Un-huh," he finally managed to mutter, adding a curt, "Me too."

The crew chief, who'd been overseeing things in the cabin since they'd lifted off of the water, took to his feet and tiptoed his way down the center aisle to where Baker was perched on his haunches. They conferred for a moment or two, talking in whispers, but loud enough for Will to pick up on bits and pieces of their exchange. He listened quite carefully and was able to hear the chief say, "We're fairly safe after dark," before the sound of his voice trailed off. A moment later he added something about them being "vulnerable," and even later another phrase that ended using the word "intercepted." Baker then asked something that Will couldn't decipher, but he did manage to hone in on part of the chief's response that sounded like a caveat. It sounded as though he was warning Baker, saying, "The closer we get to our objective," after which his tone of voice faded away and didn't rebound again until he closed his sentence with, "prepared for the unexpected." Trying to put the isolated pieces of the exchange into context, Will decided that the worst was yet to come, based primarily on the tone of the chief's voice, which seemed to carry an ominous pitch.

Roul came stumbling along, making his way forward again to confer with the pilot, but paused en route to comment, "Listen up! Everything is going according to plan so far. We are, however, still flying in friendly skies, where we're less apt to be intercepted by Jap planes. With the coming of sunset, that will change, leaving us without an umbrella of escorts. From that point on we'll be, technically, behind enemy lines, traveling to keep our date with destiny in the Philippines."

Will was not overwhelmed with the news. He'd figured their terminus long before. The subject had been given adequate exposure during training. Now, the fact that Roul was a Filipino by birth, his appointment to lead the charge made sense. As was customary, Will tuned Roul's voice out and tried to analyze the puzzling scenario. Roul, the Filipino, made sense, as did both Baker and Schuster, who were combat veterans. And he didn't ignore Gooch's heritage, either. Will was, after all they'd been through, most impressed with Baker and his credentials. In fact, whether or not he dared to admit it, he'd grown fond of his sergeant; a father figure of a man who was the obverse of his flesh and blood father. He also suspected that Baker was a fraud of sorts by pretending to have no sympathy for anyone. Will knew different. More than once Baker had betrayed the image he tried so hard to reflect by casually complimenting someone for a job well done. Will was sure he'd even detected a "that's my boy" gleam in Baker's eyes on certain occasions when he, himself, had excelled.

"Depending on weather conditions," Roul's voice stirred Will's subconscious to recapture his attention, "our E.T.A. is 2300 hours." He smiled then for the first time ever; a genuine smile of satisfaction, even though a cunning gleam of anticipation in his hard-set eyes contradicted the whimsical nature of his grin. He was, Will decided, definitely a man on a mission. "All too soon, gents, we will discover if you have truly adapted your hearts, your souls and your beings to the task at hand. Did our training meet its expectations? It's almost impossible to realize that only six weeks ago this motley mob of misfits washed ashore on a beach in New Guinea, somewhat disorganized, totally disoriented and having assumed a disheveled appearance that was frightening. Look at you now. Professionals, one and all. It seems like it was a year ago, doesn't it? Be that as it may be, our objective is one of the Philippines' seven thousand islands, many of which are uninhabited. G-2 believes we'll be landing on one of those deserted mounds that rise out of the sea. We're hoping it's a safe haven. If this flight is not detected on its approach, we should make landfall before midnight. I urge each and everyone of you to catch some shuteye.

"Prior to debarking we will dine on K-rations. Being unable to predict what might occur, we should have full bellies. And, some good news. Shaving will not be required until further notice," Roul informed them. That was a break from tradition for the captain. He'd been adamant about a daily shave throughout training. And following those welcomed words, Roul vanished into the cockpit area.

The meeting, however, didn't end with the captain's departure. The crew chief seized the opportunity to have his say while everyone was still focused on Roul's message. "Before you guys all turn in for a nap, we should cover the emergency procedures for abandoning ship," he announced.

A murmur spread through the cabin, followed by a multi-voice inquiry, "Abandon ship?"

"Yes," the chief assured them. "It's a possibility, not a probability, but you need to know the procedures for an orderly evacuation."

"You're telling me I might have to bail out of this crate?" Will protested.

"Yes, it's like I said, a possibility," the chief replied.

"I don't do parachutes and stuff," Will informed him.

"There's nothing to it, soldier," the chief tried to ease his apparent anxiety, explaining that jumping out of the craft was "as easy as falling off a log."

"No," Will disagreed. "Falling off of a log is kid stuff. This is falling out of an airplane several thousand feet above the sea."

"Un-huh!" the chief agreed.

"Well ... with all due respect, sir, I'll just take my chances and go down with the ship if it comes to that," Will insisted.

The chief was quite obviously nettled. "Uh-hem," he cleared his throat with an exasperated shrug of the shoulders, trying once again to outline the proper procedures for abandoning ship. He stared directly at Will and said, "Shut up and listen. If I say abandon ship, you will get into line just forward of the escape door and on the given signal will bail out, one person following the other until everyone has jumped. Do not, I repeat, DO NOT pull the rip cord until you feel the wind hit your face. By that time you will have cleared the ship enough to open your chute. You also have a Mae West life preserver.

It will keep you afloat for hours on end once you're down, but, there again, procedure. Do not inflate the Mae West until you feel your feet touch the water. Reason? If you inflate it in advance you will break your goddamned neck when you touch down. Understand?" He glanced around, being careful to make eye contact with Will in the process, then continued. "When you inflate the Mae West, after ... remember I said *after* you touch down, you'll be ten feet underneath the water's surface by the time the life preserver opens. It will bring you back to the surface like a cork. So, once through again. Line up at that door," he pointed at the exit, adding, "Follow one another through the hatch until everyone is out. Do not pull the rip cord until you feel the wind hit your face. When your feet touch down on the water, inflate your Mae West. Like I said," he summed up the routine, "it's like falling off a log." He gave Will another stare, paused a moment, then added an afterthought, "Procedure. The crew chief is the last man to abandon ship. Everyone bails out ahead of me. It is not my intention to go down with the plane. Should it become necessary to bail out, everyone goes ... including you."

"Damn," Will muttered, complaining to everyone within earshot, "this war's going to be the death of me yet."

Everyone laughed, not an outlandish guffaw such as they had back in training when someone popped a funny, but a more subdued chuckle over what Will said. He had, in fact, said a mouthful. Anxiety was choking everyone's nerves. Will didn't think that anyone of the others was overly wild about jumping from a moving plane, either. He was right, of course. They weren't.

After everything settled back to normal, with the meetings apparently finished, Will tried to catch some Z's, but his sleeping mechanism balked. He just sat there, wondering if they had already crossed that imaginary line that divided friendly skies from those belonging to the enemy. A cold shiver tiptoed up his spine, then settled like a chunk of ice in the nape of his neck. He shuddered, recalling the strafing raid back at camp. He had, somehow, survived that encounter, so he tried to convince himself that he could just as easily make it through the next confrontation. Luck of the draw, he'd begun to think, was the deciding factor. Thinking back to the trek across the clearing where he was an easy target for that trigger-happy Jap, he marveled how every bullet the pilot fired in his direction somehow missed him. Duffy got riddled, Will didn't have a scratch. How did the Grim Reaper decide on who goes and who stays, he wondered. Were the lucky charms some of the guys carried a factor? "Hm-m-m-m," he hummed, trying to remember who among them relied on a token of luck. Farmer, he recalled, had once shown him a rabbit's foot that he claimed would get a man through near any scrape unscathed. Barrentos depended on his beads, or "Rosary", as he called it. He was definitely a god-fearing man. He, in fact, chided Will regularly because he never went to services when the chaplain came to the camp on Sunday to offer some words of encouragement and to share communion for those who believed. He would always return to the tent area, advising Will, "Oh, Señor Munday. She's okay. I pray that zee gods watch over you." Will also recollected that Gambler carried a two-dollar bill, which he said was lucky, while the other guys insisted two-spots were bad luck. Seiverson kept a four-leafed clover tucked away in his wallet. Beyond that, Will had no idea if any of the others believed in charms. He knew that he definitely didn't. He was sure he'd made it through that hail of fire in the clearing strictly due to the luck of the draw.

Gambler shifted his legs, brushing one up against Will's foot. When Will glanced in his direction he noticed the gambling man's eyes focused on him. "Hey, Munday. Let's pick up where we left off the other night. I'll bet your luck has run out by now," he challenged Will to an encore.

"No. Not on your life," Will refused, using as an alibi, "Playing cards isn't really my bag."

Gambler pretended not to hear Will and amused himself by cutting, then shuffling, then re-cutting the deck of cards he was holding in his hands as an enticement to induce Will to play. When Will continued to ignore Gambler, he flushed the cards in a sweeping arc through the air from one hand to the other and tried a different approach. "Not your bag, huh?" he inquired, giving Will a left-handed compliment to wear his resistance down. "You couldn't prove it by me. That was quite a spectacle the other night. You surprised me. You do know cards. You've been sandbagging. Where'd you learn your strategy?"

"Oh, you'd like to know, wouldn't you," Will came back, rejecting Gambler's attempt to lull him into a game by telling him, "If you're trying to con me into another hand of showdown, forget it. Why don't you try a game you can play all by yourself, like … say, Solitaire? Now, if you are insistent on playing cards with me, we might try Crazy Eights, or Old Maids, or perhaps a face-off in War. I like that game."

Gambler knew Will was taunting him, but he couldn't wait forever to recover his losses. All too soon they'd be up to their necks in the war and there'd be no time for card playing. He cautiously mulled over Will's suggestion, finally responding with, "We could do that. Crazy Eights, you say? I haven't played that since I was a kid. Yeah. That could work. Let's say, the loser pays the winner a buck a point."

191

Will laughed aloud. "Please," he came back, explaining to Gambler, "My point was, in case you didn't catch on, I don't want to play cards, not even Crazy Eights. First off, I'm next to broke."

"WHAT?" Gambler exclaimed.

"Broke. B -R - O - K - E," Will reiterated, spelling the word to clarify its meaning.

"Like hell, you say. You cleaned me out, along with the other guys, and you're broke? Knock it off, Munday. Don't try to BULLSHIT the troops," Gambler shouted.

"I'm broke. I don't care if you believe me, or not. Back at the depot I got to thinking about where we were going and, well ... I figured I might not live through it ... so I up and sent all of my money home to Mom for safekeeping," Will revealed.

Gambler was obviously devastated by the news. He was hopelessly broke for the first time since he'd entered the Army, and his only means of getting the money back vanished with Will's decision to send his windfall home. "I'll be dipped in shit," he moaned, then turned away and closed his eyes on a pretense of sleeping, leaving Will to himself again.

Will tried to sleep. Again, it didn't work. So, he figured if he let his thoughts slide back to happier times he might dose off. As he rolled over onto his side and propped his head up with his hand, his dog tags tumbled out through the neck opening of his jacket. He started to shove them back in place, then paused, and peered at them for a moment. "Odd," he thought to himself, "I've never really gave them a close examination." He hadn't. They'd been dangling from a chain around his neck for almost a half a year. So, he figured it was time to see if everything punched into the metal disc correctly ID'ed him. It was quite dark. He could barely make out the images. The information suddenly took on a vital purpose. What if there was an error? He'd heard that when a man was killed, his sergeant jerked the tags from around his neck, put one of them into the victim's mouth, and kept the other to turn in with his casualty list. An error would not be acceptable. His thoughts wandered back to the day Duffy was killed. He'd not seen Baker place one of Duffy's dog tags into his mouth. He wondered if he took care of the repulsive task later to spare his men a bad memory. Squinting, he wiggled the tags back and forth to make a reflection glisten on the metal surface, which enhanced the lettering. He read, "MUNDAY, WILL F.," and his serial number, "37756079," then his blood type, "A," and finally his religious preference which erroneously listed him as "P," which meant Protestant. He couldn't recall if they'd even asked him. They must've. Maybe they didn't have a symbol for agnostics and just arbitrarily lumped everyone but Jews and Catholics into one category. Whatever, he decided, the tags looked okay as best he could determine in the dark of the night. He wondered if it even mattered. Soldiers were, he just naturally assumed, more statistics than flesh and blood. The dog tag merely verified the stats. A casualty's name must pass through a hundred hands without being even examined. There had to be something indifferent about wartime deaths. There were so many, he calculated, that he was afraid they just became another acceptable part of war. The people who handled the paperwork had to be complacent, lest they go nuts. He didn't figure there was any feeling of remorse attached to a casualty's notification to next of kin until it was finally delivered to the heartbroken mother. He shoved the tags back down the front of his chest, rolled over onto his back, and closed his eyes. He was actually quite sleepy. The hum of the plane's engines served as a sedative of sorts; an almost pleasant hum to his ears. His arm was still sore from another inoculation he'd received prior to departing from the replacement depot. It had something to do with Oriental sleeping sickness, they were told. Will guess it worked. He was having one helluva time getting to sleep. Before long he caved in to necessity and slipped into euphoria; the sleep he needed in preparation for what lay ahead.

He was still sleeping soundly when a racket erupted to arouse him. The cabin echoed with voices, each one trying to outtalk the others. He tried to ignore the interruption, figuring he'd just dozed awhile, not realizing he had slept the rest of the way to their destination. He wanted to catch a few more winks, but Sergeant Baker put the kibosh on that. He kicked Will's shinbone with his toe and barked, "C'mon, Munday. Hit the deck a'running." Will acknowledged his command, but no sooner had Baker turned his back on him than he dozed off into La-la Land again. His numbed mind spawned a vision of the Rialto Theater, back home, where an imaginary world crammed with excitement always thrilled him. He saw once again the twinkling lights—a never-ending aurora of synchronized bulbs flashing on and off, playing a game of tag—that dazzled the marquee on the front of the building. And he found himself seated once more in the very front row of the auditorium, where he could hone in on another chapter in the never-ending saga of Flash Gordon doing battle with Ming, the Merciless.

"C'mon, Munday. Last call," Baker aroused him again, this time poking his booted toe into Will's thigh. "We've got a war to fight, soldier, in case you've forgotten."

Will shook his head to jar loose the cobwebs that had a stranglehold on his thoughts. He guessed he'd never know if Flash did eventually overpower his nemesis. He figured it didn't really matter. That was fantasy. This was reality. The moment of truth had arrived. But it was very dark in the confines of the cabin. His eyes were still filled with sand. He rubbed them, trying to dislodge the remnants of his nap away. When he opened his eyes again he saw everyone, except himself, up on their feet, milling around in a mass state of confusion, Baker trying to restore order, instructing them to, "Get your gear in order. Leave nothing behind."

Will reached up and grabbed a truss on the bulkhead, then pulled himself up onto his feet. The plane felt as though it had a case of heebie-jeebies. It was vibrating. The chief explained the sensation, telling them, "We're at a thousand feet, and slowly descending. The air is turbulent, which tends to shake this bird. And we have to skim the water, more or less, from this point on. The lower we fly, the less apt we are to be detected. Hang on to your hats. The ride'll be rough until we sit down."

Farmer reached over and tugged at Will's wrist, asking in an uncertain tone of voice, "Are you doing okay, Will?"

Will sensed the anxiety his friend was undergoing. *Why,* he wondered, *is he fretting over me when he's going through the same trauma as I?* But he dismissed the question and insisted he was doing fine.

"Okay," Farmer curtly replied, but Will doubted his sincerity. As usual he was trying to bolster Will's courage, ignoring his own welfare. It was his way.

Time continued to creep, the hands of the clock moving ever so steadily toward zero hour. Will was actually afraid. And some of the other men on board didn't help his apprehension. Barrentos was fumbling his beads, muttering Latin prayers. O'Hare was softly humming to himself. Gambler fondled his deck of cards, cutting them with one hand, while nervously tapping his toe against the bulkhead. Tillie didn't appear to be troubled. It figured. Will always believed he was comfortable with a vocation like the Army. Of course, Will recalled, he had already made a kill when he shot down the Jap plane, which might explain his cavalier attitude. Will took a glance at Corporal Schuster, who was just kneeling on the deck, staring at Sergeant Baker. The scene was almost abstract, no one moving now, everyone staring off into space. He took notice that Baker was staring at Roul, as if anxiously awaiting the command to "Go." And Roul, much to Will's surprise, did appear to be unnerved. He was pacing up and down the aisle, hands clasped behind his back.

"I've gotta piss." O'Hare announced.

"Just like a goddamn kid," Baker scolded him. "Wait until almost the last damned minute to take a leak."

"HERE!" the crew chief shouted, handing an empty tin can to O'Hare.

194

"That'll have to do. We're set to disembark. Try to hit the can, too. I don't want to slip on a puddle of piss after you're gone and break my damned neck." ·

O'Hare relieved himself, let out a big sigh of relief, and handed the can back to the crew chief, offering a timid "thanks" in appreciation. But Gambler was moved to comment, "Yeah, don't take any chances, O'Hare. I've heard tell a guy can get the piss scared outta him," obviously referring to Will's accident during the strafing raid. He had hoped that was ancient history. It wasn't. Gambler wasn't the sort of guy to let sleeping dogs lie.

Will wasn't feeling very good. His stomach was queasy and the palms of his hands were sweating. He could feel his body trembling, and an urge to cry almost overwhelmed him, but he shook it off by remembering his mother's words when he was a lad; *big boys don't cry.* Actually, Will wanted to run away from this assignment. But there was nowhere to run. He was hopelessly trapped just like the other guys who surrounded him, and he wondered if they were also plagued with doubts. Within a short time Baker would be ordering them to debark and, like the others, Will knew he would obediently leave the safety of the PBY and take to the rubber rafts like the puppet he had become. To a man, they'd been indoctrinated to dance to Roul's cadence, where there was no room for self-pity and no time to squander grieving over what-if syndrome. And thoughts of *what if* did have a choke hold on Will at this particular time. *What if,* he silently asked himself, *someone in command screwed up and, instead of landing on an uninhabited island, there is a platoon, maybe even a regiment, of Japs just waiting for us to set foot on land?* Thoughts of Tokyo Rose, who'd been so well informed about his voyage across the ocean, crept into his thoughts. *Could she know this plane is already behind Japanese lines? If so, has she informed the Japanese defenders of the Americans' encroachment?*

The crew chief put an end to Will's antagonism. "It's party time," he barked in a routine, matter-of-fact voice that offered little solace to the Stopwatch detachment he was about to evict from his craft.

"I ... I ... can't believe it," Tillie muttered.

"Believe what?" Perkins asked.

"H-m-m-m, I didn't think I'd be scared when the time came."

"But you are?" Baker asked.

"Yup. Well, maybe not exactly scared, but I've got the jitters." Tillie conceded.

"Good," Baker complimented him. "That's good news. You might make it through this war in one piece after all. Being scared could keep a hot-dogger like you alive."

"LISTEN UP!" Captain Roul yelled. "We'll be touching down very soon. We must make haste to evacuate this plane. The chief will inflate the rafts as he pitches them through the hatch. Baker squad will be first off. The others will relay the supplies to them. As soon as they're loaded, they will push off, and Able squad will debark into the next raft. We'll repeat the procedure, relaying the rest of the gear to them. When they shove off, Charlie squad will take the final raft, along with Corporal Schuster, Sergeant Baker and me. Our raft will guide you to shore. Put your backs into those oars and get clear of this plane, because these lads want to lift off and head for home before some Jap intercepts them. Any questions?"

Roul was greeted with silence, so Baker took command, telling them to "Lock and load those pieces. Keep the muzzles pointed at the sky."

Will pulled a clip from his pouch and shoved it into the receiver of his weapon. His hands were trembling. He wasn't surprised. As he glanced around he encountered a circle of dour faces staring at Baker. He guessed they were all apprehensive.

"Brace yourselves," the chief shouted just as the huge craft let its belly skim the choppy water. Will could hear Barrentos mumbling to himself, repeating his "Father, forgive me, for I have sinned" routine. He calculated that the Mexican had pled for a thousand Hail Marys during the course of their friendship. He hoped his pleas hadn't been a waste of time. Will kinda liked Barrentos, and he doubted that Juan had so many sins blighting his soul at such a young age that he needed to fret over his fate. But Will also knew that the tally of sins would grow by leaps and bounds from this time forward, considering that their assignment was to waste as many Japs as humanly possible in order to accomplish their mission. Somehow, in his way of thinking, killing was killing. He doubted there'd be any allowances to justify killing in the hereafter, if such a place did exist.

The plane bounced a time or two, still skimming the white caps, then lurched and finally waddled down into the water and ground to a stop. When the hatch was thrown open, the waning roar of the engines was still audible. The big craft was bouncing like a gigantic cork, and the ocean was slapping the exterior of the plane's fuselage. "Let's go, you landlubbers," the chief barked just as he pitched the first raft through the opening. It was an awesome spectacle. The raft self-inflated as it tumbled down onto the surface of the water. The chief jerked the raft back against the side of the ship, then temporarily moored it, tying off a single rope attached to the raft to a bracket just inside of the doorway. "GO, GO, GO," the chief urged his charges to evacuate, and Will stepped in line behind Gambler, who elected to be the first man into the raft. One by one they jumped into the rubber boat, then began the task of grabbing the gear from the men still in the plane, stowing it in the bottom confines of the raft. From that point on everything seemed to be in a mass state of confusion, punctuated by the chorus of voices, shouting such things as, "Get moving."

"This goes next."

"What the hell's in this box?"

"Ammo, nitwit."

"Here, Tillie, catch."

"Cheezus! Take it easy, you damned near knocked me into the drink."

"Shove off, Baker squad. Make room for another raft." And Will suddenly found himself floating away from the plane in a raft that seemed so small, so insignificant, so utterly overwhelmed by the huge body of water surrounding it. He grabbed an oar, dipped the blade into the water, and began to bring the raft around. It was very dark. Still, he could see the silhouette of a land mass in the distance. Glancing side to side, front to back, it was the only island he could see, so he asked Farmer, "What're we supposed to do? Start rowing toward shore?"

"Nope. Don't think so. I'ma thinking that the captain is leading the way, or did I hear him right?" Farmer yelled back.

"Yeah. Just hold our position," Gambler offered. "Here comes another raft right now. See?" He pointed back toward the plane. Will copped a visual on what appeared to be the second raft floating away from the plane, on a collision course with their own craft. A moment later the two rafts collided, but there was no cause for alarm. A swell just as quickly pulled them apart, and the two rafts danced on the water, their occupants on hold, waiting for Roul and his men to clear the plane to join them.

A moment later, the small flotilla came together. The captain waved his hand at the chief, who, seeing they were clear of the aircraft, slammed the hatch shut.

It was actually very noisy. Between the ocean's roar and the rumble of the plane's engines revving up to take off, Will could not hear much of anything else. When the craft began to pull away from them, he thought he heard Sergeant Baker scream, "Thanks for the lift," to the crew chief, who had taken up a position by a porthole where he could eyeball the rafts as they taxied away.

A shroud of darkness enveloped the rafts, which Will considered a good omen. If he could see nothing, it was reasonable, he figured, that no one else could see anything, including them. His eyes were acclimating themselves to the night, though, and he could make out the mountainous mound he'd spotted earlier clearly enough to determine it was, indeed, an island. As he glanced around he also spotted several other such silhouettes at a distance; bleak memorials testifying to Roul's earlier statement that the Philippines was, indeed, a mass of many islands both big and small. And then he heard Baker shout, "OKAY. PUT YOUR ARMS AND BACK INTO THOSE GODDAMN OARS, JURBLOWFS." With that, the Stopwatch was activated, and the crew of soldiers turned sailors set a heading across the churning water, urging their clumsy crafts toward what appeared to be their destination.

The PBYs' engines soon faded from earshot, finally little more than an echo. The plane was gone. Stopwatch had severed their last and final link with the civilized world as they knew it. They were drifting on rubber rafts somewhere behind Japanese lines in a place known only to God and GHQ.

Before long, the rolling swells took the rafts in tow, washing them across the tops of the breakers, and finally onto the beach. Will's night vision had kicked in quite handily. He could see most everything, including a long strip of sand that separated the jungle from the sea. Will clutched his weapon, then leaped over the side of the raft and lunged ahead several yards before bellying down to take up a prone position. The surf surged ashore far enough to drench his feet every time it rolled in, then dissipated into foam as the sandy beach inhaled it. However much he detested being wet, he opted to stay put until such a time as he was told to advance. Overhead, the palm fronds were rustling in the stiff onshore breeze. The billowing surf still percolated, wave following wave, coming ashore with a splash. Other than that, they were greeted by silence; a tomblike silence that again sent a shiver up Will's spine. Nature's symphonic overture was their welcome mat, not the rattle of Japanese gunfire as many of them had feared. While Will lay there for what seemed hours but was actually only a matter of minutes, he recalled they'd been told that G-2 Intelligence had determined that the island was uninhabited. They were obviously right. And he remembered Corporal Hackmore from the replacement depot, who had once assured Will there were no Japs within forty miles. Will guessed that he, too, was right, at least for the time being.

Baker scampered to his feet, barking orders left and right, "On your feet. Let's go. That means you, jurblowfs. Corporal Schuster! I want a head count. Is everyone accounted for?"

The count was right on target. They'd all made it to shore without a mishap. Captain Roul came to the front, exclaiming, "Good show, gents," then spun on his toe and faced the sea, waving his hand aloft, thanking the flyboys who'd delivered them safely to their destination. "Godspeed!" he wished them, asking his God to guide them safely back to their base.

Chapter Twelve

Will noted a drastic change in Roul's comportment soon after they landed. The confident image he had always projected was suddenly supplanted by a stand-offish posture. If there was ever a time when the neophytes who'd just landed on a hostile island needed strong leadership, this was that moment. So, it was natural for Will to be concerned. Taking a wild guess over what spawned Roul's unexpected change in dispositions, Will suspected it was only a temporary seizure resulting from the pressures of command, and that it would pass quickly. Baker, however, noticed Roul's reluctance to take command by promptly securing and vacating the beach, so he captured everyone's attention, shouting, "C'mon. Let's clear this beachhead. Grab the gear out of the rafts and get it all back into the jungle, out of sight. On the double. Move it."

While the men busied themselves with their assigned tasks, Baker also instructed Corporal Schuster to "Post some sentries. I want four men on watch at all times. I want them out of sight from the sea. And I want one stationary post at each end of this sector and the other two roving the intermediate area."

Will momentarily dismissed Roul from his thoughts and concentrated on Baker's performance. It was, without a doubt, outstanding. If Roul elected to withdraw from the limelight and turn the duties over to his capable next-in-command, it seemed appropriate. As things were turning out, this landing on a hostile beach was nothing more than another routine exercise, not too different from similar maneuvers he'd participated in during basic training. Will also got a lesson concerning the brass in the high command who'd projected that the island would be deserted. To all outward appearances it was uninhabited. He did have to wonder how they could know. Then, Roul resurfaced in his thoughts. He decided to take a laidback stance concerning Roul's conduct and not let it bug him. It was, he realized, nothing like it had been during the regimented training schedule back on Guinea, where Roul rode herd like a shepherd tending a flock of sheep. But with Baker to cover for Roul, Will was comfortable with his command. He'd wait and see what morning brought.

Schuster wasted no time complying with Baker's orders. He culled out Baker squad to take the first watch. Sentry duty was, in a manner of speaking, Will's nemesis. He hated walking a post. And he halfway suspected that Schuster knew it. When he weighed the pros and cons of drawing the first watch, however, he realized that by doing his chore early on he might catch some sleep before morning, whereas the guys relieving him wouldn't fare so well. They were all busting their balls to stash everything out of sight, which figured to take the better part of an hour. Then, they'd be mustered to relieve Will. The real plus was, of course, the fact that the island was apparently a safe haven, which would make sentry duty a snap. And without fretting over some Jap sneaking up on him, he could let his thoughts wonder aimlessly back in time to the better things in life; college, freedom of movement, and MaryLou. He needed that.

Will was assigned to watch over a designated but isolated strip of beach some fifty yards down the shoreline from the main body of men. "This is post number two. Keep your ass outta sight," Schuster warned him. "Back in the trees. Keep your eyes focused on the sea. Any hostile forces we might encounter will most likely come from that direction. There sure as hell ain't any Nips on this island, or they'd have given us some flak already. Jap patrol boats, we're told, do patrol these waters." And with that encouraging bit of advice, Schuster disappeared into the jungle, trailed by Gambler, Tillie and Farmer, who were yet to be assigned to a post.

Will slithered back into the edge of the jungle, cautiously glancing left, then right, then ahead, making sure that Schuster was right when he projected there were no Nips on the strand. There was an abundance of forestry. Some twenty yards from the beach, he discovered a clump of bushes sprawled out underneath a towering palm tree. It appeared to be a suitable hiding place, because he could slink down out of sight into the shrubs and still catch a good glimpse of the ocean. Thoughts of G-2 being wrong did creep back across his mind, but he dismissed them, figuring Schuster was right. Had there been any Japs the landing wouldn't have been such a pushover.

It wasn't long before he actually felt comfortable with his new surroundings. He would have much preferred to be up the beach with the rest of the group catching some shuteye. Rather than dwell on the thought, he planted his posterior on the sand in the midst of the patch of shrubs, heaved a big sigh of relief and put his mind and body to rest. One thought did surface for a fleeting moment; his first night on sentry duty back on Guinea, when someone stole up behind him and stifled his breath with a half nelson around the neck, then muttered into his ear, "If I was Tojo, you'd be dead." That might've been ancient history, but it still bugged him no end that he did not know who pulled off the stunt. He long ago decided it was one of his superiors, but which one still was a mystery. He guessed it no longer mattered. What did matter was the goings-on right here, on this spot, at this time. And he didn't figure anyone of his command had any spare time to play games with the men on this occasion. The serious side of war had finally begun to dictate policy.

A sound of rustling palm fronds perked up his ear. A cold shiver skulked up his backside again, sending a bone-chilling shiver into the nape of his neck. His wet attire aided and abetted the chill. "Why me?" he lamented, wishing he hadn't been soaked with sea water when they hit the beach. He ushered his thoughts away from the present predicament by taking to his feet, then cautiously meandered back a short ways into the reaches of the jungle for a look-see. Except for nature's sounds all was quiet. Returning to the clump of bushes, he scanned the sea's surface as far as the dark of night would permit and, seeing nothing, once more sat down. Every now and then he'd repeat the process, first checking the jungle around him, then eyeballing the rolling surf that gracefully rose, then ebbed, along the beach.

Just when he decided he could not handle the boredom any longer, he saw a shadowy figure approaching along the edge of the tree line. Startled, he jumped to his feet and peered relentlessly into the dark of night, trying to decide if his eyes were playing tricks on him or if there was actually someone closing in on his position. A short moment later he realized it was another person, and since they were making no pretense to hide their approach, it must be a friend, not a foe. He pulled his weapon up to a port position and barked, "HALT!" That was the standing procedure in such cases.

A friendly voice called out from a distance, informing Will, "Gooch coming in." Will was ecstatic. The Tom Thumb of Stopwatch had arrived to relieve him of his post.

"You spooked me for a minute, Gooch," Will cautioned him, adding, "I might've shot you."

Gooch only laughed. "Time for you to catch some sleep, Munday. Sorry. I didn't mean to frighten you, that's why I came straight up the beach in plain sight," he explained, then chuckled.

"What's so funny?"

"I was just thinking ... that ... if I intended to slip up on you, I could have and then, if I was Tojo, you'd be dead," Gooch replied.

Will was stunned. It was Gooch who'd done a number on him that first night in Guinea, not Schuster, or Baker, or Roul as he suspected. "YOU!" he exclaimed. "It was you!"

"Yeah. It was me," Gooch confessed, defending his actions by explaining that it was Schuster's cunning plot to give the greenhorns a rude awakening. "Don't feel betrayed, Munday," he continued, trying to quell Will's torment. "You weren't the only victim. You were but one of three men I caught napping that first night. And I'll bet you haven't dozed on guard duty since then ... have you?"

"No. I haven't," Will admitted. "I suppose you do understand that you scared me out of ten years' growth with that stunt, don't you? And then you left me to suffer with my guilt all of this time, causing me to think I was the only one who screwed up." He paused a moment, then inquired, "Who else did you get?"

Gooch wagged his head from left to right and back, parrying Will's inquiry with, "No way. That's for me to know. Besides, if I told you that would remove the anxiety you'll suffer while you're wondering who, besides you, was derelict in their duties." He paused a moment, then added, "You should consider that incident as a reward. Together we learned a lot in Guinea, didn't we? From this point on in our journey you aren't apt to repeat your error, which can save your life as well as mine."

Will was saddened because Gooch refused to tell him, but he was just as anxious to get some sleep, so he bid the Nisei lad farewell. "She's all yours," he said, turning over the responsibility of maintaining the watch to Gooch with an admission and a warning, "I'm totally spent. Need some sleep. Take care, d'ya hear?"

Will trotted down the beach to their temporary domicile. When he arrived in camp he discovered that everyone was sound asleep—everyone, that was, except for Captain Roul, who was seated on a stack of supply crates, his chin resting on an upraised hand supported by an elbow on his knee. He was just staring out across the broad expanse of ocean. At first glimpse it appeared to Will that the captain was just momentarily mesmerized by the sea and Roul probably would never have known Will was nearby had he not stumbled across someone's outstretched feet. When Roul heard the shuffle of Will's feet he tried to regain his posture as an officer, acknowledging Will's arrival with a nod, but saying nothing.

Realizing he had intruded on the captain's privacy, Will figured he at least owed his CO an explanation. "Sir," he inquired, "are you have difficulty sleeping?"

Roul hung his head for a moment, appearing to be surprised over the interruption, but he nodded, denying he was having trouble sleeping, but admitting he was "a little apprehensive. I find it difficult to reconcile things at this particular moment. After such a long absence from my native land, sleep, it seems, is secondary to just sitting here in silent celebration."

Will was taken aback by his captain's reply. He had never given Roul's homecoming a thought and now, after watching the pensive Filipino wrestle with his personal feelings, he could understand its importance. "Well, sir," Will sympathized with the captain's honesty, "it's like the poet said; *Breathes there a man with soul so dead, who ne'er to himself has said, this is my own, my native land.*"

The captain was evidently surprised with Will's response as much as Will had been on seeing the captain sitting alone in the middle of night. *"Whose heart has ne'er within him burned as footsteps he has homeward turned, from wandering on a foreign strand,"* Roul finished the stanza of the classic poem. Tears of joy, yet remorse, glistened in his eyes and he lifted his arm to blot them away with the sleeve of his shirt. "How pleasant to once more hear the profound verse of Sir Walter's elegant works," he complimented Will, admitting, "I am impressed, Private Munday. After I scanned your 201 file I couldn't help but notice that you were a third-year college student who majored in science. But didn't realize you were also a literary buff."

"My minor, sir. I have a love affair with the English language, particularly its literature," Will explained, suggesting that he thought "Scott's words seemed appropriate under the circumstances; almost as though they were penned for this precise moment in time."

"So it would seem," Roul agreed, calming Will's apprehensions about being away from home by promising him, "Just as I am standing on my native soil tonight, so shall you be when this awful war has ended." He turned away to avoid eye contact with Will, adding in a way of explanation, "It's been some thirty months since ... well, since we tucked our tails between our legs, which I hate to admit, and went to Australia, leaving our countrymen to the mercy of the Japs. It wasn't, I hope people do understand, the proudest moment in our lives. We carried out our orders. That's what's expected of a soldier."

Roul's surprise confession caught Will off guard. He dredged his mind to come up with an appropriate response, finally blurting out, "Well, sir, the General was right. He did promise your countrymen he would return and, well, I guess he has in a manner of speaking."

"So he has, soldier. So he has. We are the vanguard to honor his pledge," Roul agreed.

Baker came calling before daybreak. He shook everyone out of the sack, barking, "OKAY, you jurblowfs. Let's go. Up and at 'em."

Will chose to ignore the page. He was still tired, having had but two or three hours of rest. Still half asleep, he rolled over and dozed off again, picking up on a dream he'd been having prior to the brief interruption. He was once again back home. He had been picnicking with MaryLou when Baker tried to rouse him. Now, they were together again; sitting atop of a blanket on the well-manicured lawn in the city park back a short distance from the campus. MaryLou looked up at Will and smiled, enhancing that darling dimple that sparked Will's lust, then reached her hand into the picnic basket and tried to remove a wrapped sandwich. Seeing her dainty hand, he could not calm the urge to hold her hand within his own. He reached out and tenderly slipped his fingers about her fingers. She glanced up at him again. then let the sandwich fall onto the blanket. Brushing aside her peekaboo bang with the other hand, she leaned forward, offering her lips to Will. He leaned forward. His lips were just inches away from hers when she abruptly pulled back, jumped to her feet, and ran into the surrounding forest. In the flash of a single second she had vanished from view. Will glanced back down at the blanket. The sandwich she had held was gone, as was the picnic basket. He reared back when he discovered what had displaced them; a deck of playing cards. Then the sound of someone laughing perked his ear, and he saw Gambler sitting across from him on the blanket. The cardsharp pitched a fistful of crumpled currency down beside the deck of cards and challenged Will, suggesting that they play "One hand. Showdown. Winner takes all ... including the chick." He punctuated the offer with a brazen, gloating snigger that infuriated Will, but there was more to come. Looking up, he saw Tillie standing on the grass directly behind Gambler. He, too, was laughing and shouting, "Gambler'll whup your ass, Gambler'll whup your ass, Gambler'll whup your ass," over and over again.

"NEVER," Will disagreed, vowing he "would NEVER stake MaryLou! NEVER!"

"Okay," Gambler changed his tone, "let's see some spending cash."

"I have no cash," Will responded.

"Oh, yes. You lie. You won my bankroll the other night. Get it up on the table."

"I've told you. It's gone. I sent it home."

"Okay. Then you've gotta throw the doll into the pot," Gambler insisted. He carefully fondled the deck of cards, again insisting, "Either she's in or you're out, Munday. And remember. It's winner take all. Winner take all. Winner take all."

Without further ado Gambler dealt the cards, sarcastically remarking as each one fell face-up on the blanket, "She loves me, she loves me not, she loves me, she loves me not," until the fifth and final card was next to be dealt. He paused, scanned both hands that were fanned out face-up on the blanket, informing Will, "She's mine, sucker. D'ya see that? I've got two tens showing. You have nothing and here comes the final card. You've gotta beat a pair of tens, at the least." And then a sudden summer downpour drowned them. Lightning and thunder accompanied a torrential downpour of rain that soaked Will to the skin. He stared at the cards he'd been dealt. The rainwater was gradually erasing the spots. He could no longer read the cards' face values. How could he win MaryLou's hand with five blank playing cards?

A distant voice called Will, shouting, "C'mon, Munday. Wake up. Hit the deck." Will squirmed. He rolled over. He was shivering. And very wet. These raindrops were real, not those of his dream, and he shivered in his saturated clothing. It seemed as though he was lying in a puddle of water. He was. Because he'd opted to catch some sleep on an overturned life raft, his weight had formed a recess, which was gradually filling with water.

"C'mon, Will," he heard Farmer's voice calling out above the others, "You're gonna drown. It's raining cats and dogs."

Will was very cold. Raindrops slapped against his face like tiny pellets. He was lying in at least a half inch of water. He glanced up to discover a half dozen guys gathered in a semi-circle about the raft, all of them clad in their ponchos and all of them laughing at Will's imbroglio.

"What's wrong, Munday?" Gambler needled him, asking, "Are you having a wet dream?"

Baker was standing near Will's feet, hands on hips, arms akimbo, just shaking his head back and forth. "Rule number one, Munday," he explained to Will, "is never sleep on an overturned raft. They make a dandy bathtub if it rains. But I guess you already know that."

Will was miserable. He could've gotten along nicely without the barbs. Being wet was punishment enough. "Thanks for the advice ... SERGEANT," he shouted, "although it's a little late."

"C'mon. Get 'em while you can," Schuster was shouting from somewhere back in the trees. "Grab some chow. K-rations on tap. Don't know when we'll get our next meal, so eat up. We'll be fading into the jungle shortly." It was only a carton of K-rations, but Will was famished. He almost savored the thought of the scrambled-egg concoction the ration consisted of. And he figured they were in for a steady diet of K's for the next few days, perhaps even longer.

The dark of night was giving way to dawn. It was a gloomy morning, almost depressing. The skies were steel gray in color. The heavy downpour that drenched Will had finally dissipated to a fine drizzle. It definitely was

205

RICHARD BEOUGHER

an ill omen for a man like Will F. Munday, who so detested wet clothing. He hated days that began on a downer. This promised to be such a day. A stiff on-shore breeze chilled Will to the bone. Will stood up after climbing out of the raft, water trickling down his legs and into his shoes. He slogged his way back to where Schuster was issuing rations, reluctantly accepted his meal, glanced around to locate Farmer, who was sitting on a supply box, and shuffled over to join him. Farmer was gulping down his meager ration of grub like a ravenous hound. "What's on the menu?" Will asked as he plunked his posterior down on another box closeby. "I suppose we've got some more of that goo from a dead Chinaman's ear, huh? That scrambled stuff?"

"Yep," Farmer replied between bites. "You sure know how to spoil a man's appetite. I'll give you credit for that."

Captain Roul intervened, calling for their attention. He was, Will took notice, back to his old self; a take-charge individual. "Here's a few facts regarding this mission. We are to sit tight on this island until we are contacted. That shouldn't be long. Our target date is such that we're pressed for time. Throughout this war there has been a well-structured guerrilla force operating behind enemy lines. Our contact is codenamed Cebu. I do not know at this time how or when Cebu will come. Our final objective is, however, on a different island, some distance north of here. We have been aware that several complexes were constructed by the Japs in the Philippines. Our target is one of those. The Philippine underground, via means of passing along information to submarine crews who slipped in and out of these waters on a regular basis, has kept in touch with GHQ throughout the war. They know the precise location of our target."

Will was almost astonished to learn that he and his unit had been preceded several times to the Philippines. The news tended to deflate his ego as being the vanguard of MacArthur's return. Gambler, on the other hand, wasn't the least bit upset with what had already transpired. Prior to this Will had thought Gambler had no hangups. He was wrong. Gambler admitted, "I'm glad things changed. I never told your guys this, but I was really tickled when I learned we were flying instead of traveling by submarine. I don't think I could've handled even getting aboard one of those floating coffins." So, Gambler was and had been a claustrophobic. Now there were three of them with a phobia that could be tested by military standards at any given time. Will wondered to himself just how many others had a mania over some uncontrollable situation that they hadn't confessed to.

The captain, overhearing Gambler's confession, chuckled and remarked, "You can thank your lucky star that our mission was moved ahead, or a sentimental journey on a submarine would've been your fate. Flying was the

206

only option with time running out."

The captain had shared this confidential knowledge with his men, which surprised Will. That was a first. And learning that the United States wasn't a second stringer when it came to subversive dealings pleased him, because he'd long suspected that the Japs had an edge. Now, it appeared that the Filipinos working underground, and right under the noses of the occupation forces, had not only located a target but had been successful in relaying the information to GHQ. Roul did go on to say, "This is a communications complex in the middle of nowhere, but its purpose is to serve as an early warning station to alert the Imperial Air Force and the Japanese batteries along the coastal areas of any approaching ships." He admitted that, should it be operational when the Allied fleet sailed in, it could spell the difference between a successful beachhead landing and a dismal failure. It would be, he went on to say, Stopwatch's job to knock the transmitters out of commission just prior to the projected invasion, which would provide the Navy with an open window to slip through undetected. He summed up his critique by first praising them, saying, "You have come a long way. You've conditioned yourselves for this date with destiny. And I must say, you did a fine job," then adding on a more serious note, "but zero hour for completing our task is set for 2400 hours on October nineteenth, when we will manage to do our duty so that when daylight breaks the morning of October twentieth our troops will be put ashore in the initial phase of recapturing the Philippine Islands."

Although they had all known for quite some time that the moment of truth would come, the news sent emotional shock waves seething through the ranks. There was a mixture of emotions ranging from excitement to anxiety to fear. They appeared to be relieved to finally know their eventual purpose in the scheme of things. But Roul, as was customary, didn't let them dawdle very long. He suggested, "We should take cover up on the hillside where we can see the landscape and the sea without being seen ourselves. After we find suitable cover we can then begin our wait for our contact, Cebu." He instructed Corporal Schuster to take Baker squad up the hillside to reconnoiter the area for an observation site, then assigned Charlie squad to relieve Able squad from sentry duty so that they could grab a bite to eat. After that, he noted, everyone would pitch in to stash the gear out of sight in the depths of the jungle on the chance that a Jap patrol boat might venture along the coastline.

There were skeptics, however, like Slycord, who asked, "Sir, do you think we landed here last night without being detected, or could we be looking at some Nips coming ashore anytime soon?"

Baker answered for Roul. "It's not likely," he assured Sly, explaining, "If they had a fix on us we'd already be on the receiving end of their hardware." But he did concede that the plane might've been detected at some point or other during the trip, and as a result the Japs could be out poking around as a precaution.

Baker signaled Schuster to proceed on his assignment, then began to bark orders right and left to those who remained behind. Schuster merely yelped, "OKAY! Let's go, Baker. Keep the ranks closed up so no one gets separated." And they departed.

The drizzle finally ended. A few hazy rays of morning sunshine began to penetrate the clouds, which was a good omen to Will. He figured with any kind of luck at all his soggy uniform would dry in a short time, which would improve his disposition. He could still hear faint traces of Baker's voice as he penetrated the wooded hillside, but they finally diminished to faint sounds, then into silence. Baker squad was swallowed up in a dense jungle thicket, the closeness of which tended to smother Will's breath. His introduction to the Philippine jungle proved little different than the terrain of the island he left behind. The climb was steep and the going was strenuous. Will was puffing to catch some fresh air; a stark reminder of Camp Hood, when he and his buddies were ordered to make a simulated assault on an imaginary machine gun bunker. He had run uphill with such an effort that he really feared his lungs would explode. That exercise was, they were told, a way of preparing them for the unexpected in a combat area. But the gentle hills of Texas were no match for this Alp-like arena. This was a pristine woodland that, he halfway guessed, had never before been trod by men's feet. There were no trails because of that. There were vines aplenty entwined around limbs that impeded their passage time and again. Schuster detoured whenever possible to avert the natural obstructions. The humid air stifled Will's lungs. He compared it to drinking, not breathing. And the quietude was a stark reality. Except for the customary sounds of the jungle, this arboretum was void of noise. The terrain was slippery underfoot. Will kept his Thompson slung across his shoulder, because he needed both hands to grapple his way over several outcroppings of moss-coated rock.

Leading the way, Schuster was first to reach a plateau, which, he exclaimed before his charges caught up to him, was, "Perfect. Perfect vantage point." When the others finally overtook him they all agreed, Gambler asking, "Now, is this a great lookout, or what?"

It was precisely what they needed; an outcropping that hung out over a recession in the hillside, forming a roof to protect them from the.elements and a natural rock ledge along the lower outer rim to give them cover. Will took notice of the hanging vines that dangled down across the front opening, like a curtain which would provide some privacy from the outside world. To a science buff like Will, it was a breathtaking sight to behold. The mountainside was smothered under flowering plant life, some that he suspected were survivors of ancient forerunners. He spotted some gigantic blooms that he thought might have evolved from an orchid of prehistoric origin. A waterfall trickled down the mountainside and splashed into a small hollowed-out cistern that formed a refreshing pool from which they could obtain an adequate supply of drinking water. Will never shared his feelings with his comrades but he was taken in by the untamed, primitive landscape so much that, for a moment, he confessed that there might be a God after all; what else but a deity could have spawned such a threshold to a heavenly penthouse?

Schuster stood on the edge of the precipice and surveyed the view; a grand one-hundred-and-eighty-degree view from where they could observe the approaches to the island and not be observed doing so. "Yeah," Schuster approved, telling Will and Farmer to "Get back down that hillside and fetch the others. We've found a home."

Both Farmer and Will were surprised how well they'd memorized the terrain while making their ascent. They had no trouble finding their way back to the beach. And seeing that everyone was sitting on their cans, waiting for some news from Schuster, they led the way back up, Roul right behind them, followed by Baker and the other two squads of men. When they reached the spot that Schuster had staked as their claim, they all cheered. It was an inviting panorama, and they showed their approval by breaking out in a loud chorus of cheers. Baker quickly stifled their celebration. "Shut the fuck up," he barked, warning them, "The goddamn Japs could hear that clean up in Tokyo."

"JAPS?" Will asked, twisting his head to stare at Baker. "There ain't no Japs here, Sergeant. In fact, I'll bet there ain'ta Jap within forty miles of here."

Baker paused, then glared at Will for a moment, and finally grinned. "Munday," he warned Will, "don't ever bring up that subject again. I think we can make this trek without any advice from rear echelon Hackmore."

The two studied one another for what seemed an eternity, then Will returned the grin. *There it is again,* he silently mused. *It's that there's-my-boy gleam in his eye.*

Baker pivoted, whirled about, and shouted, "Okay, jurblowfs. This is home … probably for a very short stay. Let's all take ten to catch our breaths. I think we've earned a few minutes of R&R."

Chapter Thirteen

"Eight men on and four men off." That was Sergeant Baker's duty roster until further notice. Will caught the first shift being off duty, which he welcomed, but at the same time he couldn't see what difference it made. Eight men were assigned to keep the watch, leaving four to catch some sleep, or just sit there and watch the other eight men pulling guard duty. Sleep was out of the question. Gambler and Tillie were already squared off playing cards. It was the customary noisy hullabaloo, Gambler badmouthing Tillie, and Tillie replying in kind. Baker reminded them to "Keep the noise down," which they ignored, so Will just naturally assumed that there were no Japs within forty miles of there, or Baker would've come unglued.

With nothing else to do, Will busied himself taking a visual of their new quarters. It was, he reaffirmed his original opinion, a natural fortress. He actually felt kinda safe within its confines. Everything was at combat readiness, should a frontal assault materialize. Baker had positioned the three BARs so that they commanded a full sweep of the approach. Perkins and Slycord were alternating, first one of them manning the weapon while the other one assumed the job of lookout with Captain Roul's binoculars, then switching roles for a spell to break the monotony. O'Hare was slumped down against a huge boulder, his head resting on one elbow, winking and blinking his eyes in an almost vain attempt to stay awake. He'd nod, his head would drop, he'd jerk it back up, shake it back and forth, then nod again. Will found it amusing just to watch him. Gooch finally caved in. He was supposed to be on watch but his get-up-and-go obviously had-got-up-and-gone, because Will could hear him snoring. Will didn't figure it mattered much. He didn't anticipate a visit from enemy forces anytime soon.

Will discovered that boredom had as many drawbacks as being active. He'd always adored boredom, or so he thought. But this was a test of real endurance. Having nothing in particular to do after maintaining such a grueling pace back in New Guinea was a radical change. So, he decided to play a game with Baker by being a pest. "Hey, Sergeant," Will paged him,

211

asking, "how long are we supposed to just sit here in limbo?"

"As long as it takes," Baker replied.

"How long is that? I mean, an hour, a day, a week?"

"You heard the captain just like I did. We wait for our contact with Cebu."

"Okay. But," Will added to his sarcastic inquiry, "let's suppose this Cebu person doesn't show?"

"I imagine that could happen."

"What do we do then? Sit on this island and rot?"

Baker shook a crooked finger in Will's face, asking him, "What's this third-degree crap? You're asking questions I cannot answer. What're you up to, anyway? Are you just putting me on or are you seriously concerned?"

"Both, I guess," Will admitted. "It just occurred to me that something might've happened to Cebu and I was wondering what our contingency plan was if he didn't show."

"Okay. First off, Munday, if you'd stay awake during our critiques instead of letting your mind stray off to the Land of Oz, you'd know that Cebu is a hardcore guerrilla who's been dodging the Japs for over three years. So, he isn't apt to be caught at this stage of the game. We just have to sit here and wait and believe that Cebu will show," Baker reaffirmed his confidence in the war department's expertise. Pausing for a moment, he reconsidered his reply and added, "In answer to the final part of your question, there is no contingency plan that I know about. The plane that brought us is gone. We're behind Japanese lines. Did you have something in mind?"

Will gave his head a negative wag, admitting it was curiosity, nothing more.

Gambler couldn't resist an opportunity to slight Will. "Yeah," he agreed with Baker, suggesting, "Cebu won't have any trouble finding us. Munday's constant yakking should guide him in."

Will ignored the card player's remark until he could dredge up a suitable reply, all the while weighing his odds of beating Baker in their game of cat and mouse. But he figured he'd run the gauntlet, so he backed off to pester Tillie instead. "Hey, Tillie," he yelped, turning his attention to the poker party in progress, "did you check to see if that's a marked deck?"

Gambler, hearing Will's barb, cocked his head to one side and peered through the corner of one eye at him, asking, "Marked cards? You really think I used a marked deck? You've gotta be shitting me, Munday. If I'd been using a marked deck the last night in camp it would've been you, not me, who lost his ass." He paused a moment, then grinned, offering to let Will in the game. "C'mon, Munday. Do you want'a try your luck again? I'll even let you examine the deck with a fine-toothed comb. I'd love to pick your pocket."

Will laughed, declining to play by claiming, "Can't. I'm broke."

"Your ass," Gambler argued with a simpering chuckle, pretending he wasn't bothered by the drubbing he'd suffered at Will's hand. "You're the richest guy in this unit. You stole me blind the other night."

"Stole? Stole you blind? I won. Fair and square," Will disagreed. "But," he went on to reiterate, "I already told you the money's gone. I sent it home when we were back at the depot."

"Sure. Un-huh!" Gambler offered as a rejoinder. Turning away, he diverted his attention to the task at hand. "Your bet, dummy," he lashed out at Tillie, hustling him to "shit or get off the pot."

Will turned his attention away from the card game and took stock of the other guys lounging around in the confines of their quarters. His eyes came to rest on Williams, who was kneeling behind his weapon, turning his head from side to side, going through the motions of reconnoitering the sea that stretched away from the beach below. Will sensed that he was just biding his time, trying to heal up from the shock of being dumped by Peg, and that he was not actually the least bit concerned about the Japs or anything else. He was still suffering an acute case of rejection. He stopped shooting the breeze with the other guys, like he had prior to his personal setback. Slycord had mentioned to several of the men during a bull session back at the replacement depot that he didn't think Williams gave a damn whether or not he lived or died. At the time, Will had disagreed with him, insisting, "He's a man of the cloth. Parsons don't customarily let their spirits sag like this. He's a strong person. I don't think he'll do anything foolish."

Slycord disagreed. "Naw, he's got it bad. He's helpless. Don't you see? He's over here, she's over there, and there's nothing he can do to salvage his marriage. I wouldn't doubt he's considered suicide," he suggested.

Farmer agreed with Will. He had a lot of confidence in Williams. "Naw, Will's right," he chimed in to support Will, preferring to believe, "He'll get over it by putting his trust in God. You'll see! God does work in strange ways."

Gambler, who hadn't offered an opinion up until that time, conceded, "Hell, he's more apt to get killed by a Jap than to kill himself."

No one argued over whether that was a possibility. But Farmer did have another thought to inject into the discussion, being the pious man that he was. "Well, Williams is the same guy that he was before that letter came. I liked him from the git go. I admired his honesty that night when he spilled his guts to everyone of us. So, I feel sorry for him. I don't have a girlfriend but I think that if I did, and she brushed me off, I'd be … well, you know, I'd be feeling down in the dumps. But I don't think I'd consider suicide."

No one disputed Farmer's opinion.

Will's thoughts were rescued from the quicksand that so often held him captive when Gambler and Tillie got into a heated argument about the pot being short-changed. Baker evidently had had his fill with their bickering. "SHUT UP!" he shouted, calling them "Damned kids, anyway."

Will couldn't have agreed more with Baker's assessment of the Stopwatch team. They were kids. He'd noticed that back in New Guinea. Just a year or two earlier most of them were still playing kickball on the cinder lot behind the schoolhouse. He credited Baker with transforming the oddballs he'd inherited into first stringers, though. He felt confident that Baker could rely on each and every man when push came to shove—a moment in time that was closer than Will could have imagined, because he'd no more than purged the thought from mind than Perk jumped to his feet, tapped Sly on the shoulder, and shouted, "Take a gander out there."

Sly jerked the binoculars from Perk's hand, raised them up to his eyes, and stared long and hard out at the object Sly spotted. "Damn," he finally announced. "Did you think you saw what I think I saw?"

"Yeah. A patrol boat of some sort," Perk replied.

"Yes indeed. And it's cruising right at us," Sly announced.

That brought everyone to their feet except for Barrentos, who bellied down behind his BAR and shoved the butt plate against his shoulder, then stared down the barrel, taking aim at a target he could not even see.

Captain Roul scurried to the front and took the glasses from Sly. Gazing through the lenses, he brought his eyes to bear on a small object that appeared to be at least a half mile off shore. Will strained his eyes trying to see what the commotion was all about, but without the aid of binoculars he couldn't make out exactly what Sly and Perk had spotted. Roul had no difficulty identifying the craft, however.

"A damned Jap patrol," he mourned. "Just what we didn't need. And unless I miss my guess, they've set a course directly at this island. We'll not take any risks, Sergeant. There can't be but a half dozen men on such a small craft. Take Baker squad down the hill and get a close-up look at these guys if they get close to or come ashore. Don't compromise your positions unless it's an absolute necessity."

Baker motioned to Will and the others to follow his lead, but Roul detained them another moment to offer some advice. "Do not, under any circumstances, fire the first shot if they do come ashore. If they do land and then see you they'll take the initiative. Should that happen, oblige them with

214

enough fire power to kill every damned one of them."

"Yes, sir," Baker replied, and he led Will, Farmer, Gambler and Tillie into the thicket. He advised them all to "maintain your cover as much as you can while making the descent. We don't want some lookout spotting us."

The slope was still quite slippery underfoot as a result of the early-morning downpour. Underneath the umbrella of trees the sun could rarely penetrate deep enough to dry things out. But they did make pretty good time and were brought to a halt as the terrain leveled off near to the beach. Baker assigned each of them to a precise spot to occupy during the waiting game. Will's nerves were on edge. He figured he was on the verge of meeting the enemy face to face for the first time and he wondered how he would perform. He was hardly a celebrity, surrounded as he was by comrades who were just as concerned. It was customary for first-timers to question their courage, and except for Baker, they were all beginners.

Will heard the engines of the approaching Japanese launch before he actually saw it. When it came into view, less than a hundred yards off shore, his heart skipped a beat. As far as he could ascertain there were, as Roul had predicted, about a half dozen men on the patrol boat, unless there were others crouched down out of sight. The Japanese crew was actually lackadaisical, making them easy targets to pick off, so Will halfway suspected that their curiosity was a routine reconnaissance as opposed to a search and destroy mission. That being the case, he hoped they'd confine their exploration to making a visual scan of the coastline and, assuming they saw nothing suspicious, head back out to sea.

Baker moved over beside Will and took up a position behind a generous growth of brush, motioning Will to move slightly to his right and a tad further ahead to where another clump of leafy ferns grew. Baker glanced around, taking note of each man's position, then pressed his fingertip against his lips as a gesture demanding silence.

The patrol boat more resembled a barge, Will thought, than a warship. As it slowly slid its bow onto the sandy beach, Will inhaled a deep breath, then brought his Thompson up to a ready position, and took aim at the intruders. Four of the group jumped over the bow of the craft onto the sand. They were jabbering like chipmunks, but Will had no idea of what they were saying. They also were laughing as they began to make a probe into the forest. Still, in Will's estimation, they had no idea they were being surveyed, which gave him a chance to breathe easy for a moment.

Baker raised his open hand and slowly wig-wagged it, indicating he wanted everyone to hold their position and their fire. But to Will's surprise, the interlopers paused, then returned to the beach, where they appeared to be examining the sand in almost the same spot where Stopwatch had landed just hours earlier. Evidently, Roul's insistence that they leave no traces, no telltale signs behind to betray themselves, paid off, because they seemed satisfied nothing was amiss. A short time later one of the Japanese soldiers, who'd remained on the launch, shouted to the others. Will had no idea what the man said, but it obviously seemed more important than continuing their excursion on the beach. They held a confab, taking turns pointing back out toward the open sea, then all returned to the vessel to cast off, turning their backs on Baker and his men. It was the break Will was hoping for. He and his chums had managed to circumvent a premature showdown that might've compromised their actual mission of destroying the radio complex on a different island.

Relieved, Baker withdrew his men as soon as the barge backed off of the strand and led them back up the hillside, satisfied the Jap patrol had humbled their curiosity. When he came trudging into the outcropping Roul gave him the high sign and said, "Good show, men. We should have no more incursions from inquisitive Japs today."

Will sat down on his haunches beside Farmer and noted, "It was kinda scary, wasn't it?"

"Yup. I thought for a minute or two we was going to have ourselves a scrap, but like my mama used to say, 'all's well that ends well.'"

Roul, however, continued his vigil. He must've had some suspicions that everything was not quite as simple as it had appeared to be. "That patrol boat, Sergeant Baker, left kind of abruptly, didn't you think?" he asked the sergeant.

Baker agreed but told Roul he thought they'd just satisfied their curiosity, so there was no reason to continue their probe of the island's interior.

Roul raised his arm and pointed a finger out to sea. "Maybe. Maybe not," he said, suggesting everyone take a gander at what he'd spotted.

Will jumped to his feet and scrambled to the edge of the precipice at the front of their cavern. Glancing out to sea, much like Roul, he saw a magnificent sight some distance away. It was a fishing trawler, its mainsail fully billowed, cruising on a parallel to the island. But the Japanese barge that had just left their neck of the woods was making a beeline to intercept it.

"Un-huh," Roul commented. "My guess is that we are about to make contact with Cebu." He squinted to carefully examine the trawler. "YES! It's the *Señora Rosita*," he exclaimed.

"And?" Baker asked.

"I know the ship. I know Cebu's identity," Roul announced.

"You do, sir?" O'Hare asked.

"I do, indeed. At least I'm relatively certain that I do. Now, our fate hangs in the balance. That Jap patrol is headed out to intercept them. That is why they left in such a hurry. Although you couldn't see the trawler from where you were posted, they evidently could. They will board her. They will search her from stem to stern. Hopefully, they'll find nothing distracting and will give Cebu a clean bill of health," Roul explained.

Will wondered if the Japs would be so generous. He had a sneaking hunch they were on a mission that was an outgrowth of their previous night's arrival. "Sir, do you think the Nips detected our plane last night and that's the reason they're patrolling this area?" Will asked the captain.

"Anything is possible. It is odd that they centered their reconnaissance on this particular spot," Roul halfway agreed with Will. "Still, there is nothing we can do but wait."

"We could've blown them away down there," Gambler claimed. "I had them in my sights. They'd never have known what hit them."

"Probably," Baker agreed, "but there were a couple of men still on the barge. They'd have backed off of the beach and hightailed it, leaving us with four dead Japs on our hands and the whole Japanese navy headed our direction. You can bet they had radio contact with other surface ships."

Roul nodded, agreeing with Baker's assessment. "Yes, and our weapons are worthless at this range," he lamented, reminding them, "It's like I said, men, we have to sit this out. And don't get so mesmerized with what you're watching that you ignore what you're not watching, mainly the entire frontage out there. Keep a sharp eye peeled. For all we know those Nips might've already radioed for reinforcements."

Will was on the samewave length as the captain and had been for some time. He even complimented himself, silently of course, that he might be "officer material" someday. He watched the two water crafts finally come together and noticed how the Jap helmsman swung the barge abreast of the trawler so they could board the suspicious ship. The distance was such that he couldn't make out everything that was taking place, but he thought he saw a couple of Japs clamber up onto the trawler, where they were greeted by one of the trawler's crew. The three men then vanished from sight. Will supposed they'd gone below to search the inner confines of the ship.

"You mentioned that you were certain you knew the identity of Cebu," Baker said. "What makes you so certain?"

The captain whirled around, telling Baker, "It is the ship that tattles. I know, or am reasonably certain, that it is Miguel's ship, the *Señora Rosita*."

"Who is Miguel?" Baker asked.

217

"We go back a long ways, Miguel and I. He is a fisherman by trade and his wife, Rosita, is of Spanish origin, a direct descendent of the early Spanish explorers who came to these islands. A fine lady," Roul replied.

"You would know, sir, I'm sure," Schuster cut into the conversation. "I take it that you have good reason to believe that this Miguel fellow is Cebu. Why? You've been out of the region for years."

"Times change," Roul responded, "but people rarely do. Miguel's loyalty would be beyond doubt. He would be one of the first to join a resistance movement. Most likely, he is one of their leaders. I know the man well enough to say he would never succumb to treacherous people like the Japanese, at least, not without a fight. His wife, Rosita, the ship's namesake, would mirror those feelings."

Will heaved a sigh of relief, right along with most everyone else. He knew that Roul was not the sort of man who'd hang his reputation on a wild guess. If Roul believed Miguel was Cebu, that was good enough for Will. Now, they had made a visual contact with their intended host, but the obstacles that prevailed at the moment raised a question over whether they'd make a physical contact. This was one of the variables that few strategists could forecast with much accuracy. It was another fly in the ointment. And all of the research that could be attributed to man's intellect couldn't correct the problem. This was not, as Will had been taught back during his school-days, a situation with a solution. Stopwatch was hopelessly trapped on a hillside of an uninhabited Philippine island with but one solitary hope of survival; Roul's friend Miguel, secretly known as Cebu, had to pass muster without a glitch. And so they passed the time away, each one of them silently searching their souls, doing nothing, because there was nothing they could do.

Finally, the frustration dictated Will to speak. The silence, he thought, made things worse. "How long do inspections like this normally take?" he asked of Roul.

Roul confessed he did not know but observed, "They are searching Miguel's ship. When they are finished they will either give him a clearance or they will take him under tow and escort him to the closest port. I do trust Miguel. So should you, because he is your passport."

Will could hardly dispute that point. He was a hostage, just like everyone else in the group, without a single bargaining chip. Baker suggested to them that they "Keep a low profile. Remember, if we can see them, they also could see us. It isn't likely, but one of them could glance at the right moment and spot some activity on this hillside, which would give them a reason to return to this island for another look-see."

The interim period did offer Will a chance to probe a tad deeper into his soul; much deeper than he had done previously. He was pleased to discover a new Will F. Munday. He had learned so much from so many different people in the past few months. He considered the fact that prior to two months earlier, he'd never met any one of the men who presently surrounded him and upon who his well-being relied. Perhaps he was evolving into a more caring individual, because his concern for Miguel, a man he'd never met, was deep-seated. He wondered what drove men like him to sacrifice everything for someone else, people in particular like Will, whom he didn't even know. That was, he calculated, what Miguel was doing this very minute. He could only second-guess but he had a vision of the man standing nose to nose with the Japs, being firm but ever so polite, trying to usher them through the bowels of the ship without revealing his purpose for being there. He was, Will imagined, walking a tightrope, where a single slip would spell disaster, not just for him and his crew, but for Roul and his crew as well. He recalled that shortly after he'd taken his pledge to become a soldier someone had said to him, "Welcome to the brotherhood." At the time this had little or no meaning. Now it was taking on a new light. When he took pause to glance about himself and look at each and every man in the unit, he realized they were a brotherhood, not out of choice, but through the benevolence of one of the Army's redundant scapegoats; the Fickle Finger of Fate. They were "fucked" if anything went wrong on board the ship that was momentarily anchored a half mile off shore.

Will had, up until that time, been the only man who'd not been offered a turn to peer through the field glasses. He was elated when Roul offered them to him and suggested, "Take a good look. What's going on out there might be history in the making."

Will gingerly grasped the binoculars, raised them up to his eyes, and took his first close-up look at the goings-on aboard Miguel's ship. He could see several men on deck, two of whom appeared to be in uniform, all waving their arms to emphasize their point of view. The two he'd assumed were the Jap inspectors abruptly turned away from the sailors and moseyed back over to the ship's railing. Will suspected it was time to return Roul's glasses, since he would be more apt to know what was transpiring. "Thanks, sir. Best take a look. It might all be over," Will suggested, handing back the binoculars.

Roul stood motionless, glasses pressed against his eye sockets, studying the events unfolding aboard the ship. "Yes, Munday, I think you're right. It would appear they are returning to the patrol boat, evidently satisfied with their findings," he agreed.

The news was received with a great deal of zeal. It had been a long afternoon, more of a "hairy crapshoot," as Gambler described the long wait, than anything else. But Roul warned them not to get overanxious, suggesting, "We know nothing for sure. When the barge has pulled away and heads out to sea, we'll know. And ... even then, we will have to wait to see if this is who I suspect, our contact codenamed Cebu. The waiting game just takes on a new dimension, now."

For the most part everyone treated Roul's suspicions as a caution light. Now they had to wait for a green light to proceed. But the pressure was relieved. Will was second-guessing Roul. He had been all day. He figured, much like the captain, that if anything was wrong they'd have impounded the vessel already. For all Will knew Miguel might've shared his personal stock of liquor with his guests, which would account for the delay. But whatever he did, Will conceded, he'd evidently made all of the right moves. The patrol barge pulled away from the trawler, made a wide swing around the ship, then sped off in the direction of a different, distant island that was barely visible on the horizon.

"Evidently, gents, Miguel got a clean bill of health. He'll stall awhile, I'm sure, before trying to make contact. I don't think he'll try to come ashore until after dark. So, we've still got awhile to wait," Roul surmised, telling Baker, "We'd best have some chow. There's nothing we can do yet. We'll hold our positions until the sun sets."

Will was famished. He'd not eaten since daybreak. It was late afternoon. Baker and Schuster broke out some K's and distributed them to everyone. Will was about to park his carcass and feast awhile when Roul brought things to a sudden halt. "Tell you what, gents. I think a little celebration is in order. Corporal, if you reach into my pack I think you'll find a small canister of wine. Get it out here. It'll only be a taste teaser, understand, so don't spill a drop. Everyone get your mess cups over here," he suggested.

A sip of wine did sound refreshing. Roul carefully dribbled a small portion into each man's metal cup, poured himself a shot, then said, "To Miguel. Our benefactor." Each and every man raised his cup and repeated Roul's toast, "To Miguel," then downed the precious liquid.

Will crashed beside Farmer and began the tedious task of cutting open the small tin of food with his GI-issue opener; a small device, hinged in the center, with a cutting edge along one side. When the top peeled off, Will began to spoon the contents of the can into his mouth, commenting to Farmer, "It beats the eggs. What is it? Could it be hash?"

"Beats me," Farmer fired back, "but I was hungry enough to eat the ass end out of a dead skunk.'

Will reared back his shoulders, gulped to swallow the morsels in his mouth, spun his head around and shouted, "Farmer, you bigot. Just a few hours ago you gave me hell for ruining your appetite, and now you're doing the same thing to me."

"I know," Farmer replied with a wide grin. "See how you are? It ain't so much fun when you're on the getting end, is it? Anyway, my mama always says that turnabout is fair play."

"Checkmate." Will settled for a draw.

Everyone was doing their best to unjangle their nerves; nerves that had been stressed out most of the day. They were jabbering with one another, rehashing the events that had occurred up until then. It was the first bull session they, as a group, had shared in quite a while. Baker actually kicked things off when he stared at Tillie and said, "I'll be switched. You've got your store teeth in you mouth."

"Yup," Tillie replied, confessing the close call with the Japs had a bearing on his decision to keep his teeth in his mouth. "I don't know about you guys, but I got to thinking about them Japs coming after us and, well … I thought how it would be if'n I got myself killed without my teeth in my mouth. Kinda silly notion, ain't it?"

"No. Not at all," Roul assured him. "Being on death's doorstep can set a man's mind to wondering all sorts of things."

"Yeah," Will agreed, admitting, "I was on pins and needles. I felt so helpless. I've always had this hangup about not being in control of my own destiny … you know?"

"Yup. You said it right. Pins and needles. That's exactly how I felt," Tillie agreed. "You know, my mama used to tease me about that. Whenever she'd see me with a long face, she'd ask me, 'What's got you on pins and needles?' Sounds sorta silly too, doesn't it?"

Will didn't think it was the least bit silly and he told Tillie as much. "I'll just bet that every one of us was on pins and needles this afternoon, if we'd all fess up and tell the truth," he noted.

Roul cut him short before he could poll the troops. The captain, who had been concentrating his efforts on observating his surroundings while the other men shot the bull, alerted them, saying, "It'll soon be getting dark. And I see that Miguel has drifted closer to the island. In fact, he's but a couple of hundred yards off shore." He handed the binoculars to Baker, suggesting he take a look, then asked, "Did you take notice that his crewmen are going through the motions of preparing nets on deck?" Roul asked Baker.

"Un-huh! I know very little about commercial fishing. But if it fools me it probably fools the Japs, too," Baker replied, then asked, "So what's our next move, Captain?"

"We'll continue to wait until the sun goes down. I do not think he will attempt to make land until dark. We should be in position to intercept him at that time," Roul answered, quickly adding after taking a look at his wristwatch, "I'd say … we'd better plan on moving out in about forty-five minutes. So, let's tidy this place up and leave no clues behind. Police the area. Make sure there's not so much as a single cigarette butt lying around."

Will finished his meal, tossed the empty can and outside wrapper in a hole that Barrentos had dug to be used as a burial place for the garbage, then pitched in with the others to erase the blight they'd created by just occupying the spot. It took the better part of a half hour to complete the task. Twilight was slowly descending across the treetops, and Will knew from past experience that it grew dark much quicker in the coppice than out in the open. It always seemed to him that the jungle was more intimidating after dark, too. But Baker took his feet, slung his Thompson over his shoulder and informed the boys from Baker squad, "It's time to move out. Keep a low profile so we aren't spotted. Keep a visual on one another so no one strays. Let's go."

Captain Roul wished them well and informed Baker, "We'll be fifteen or so minutes behind you. Secure the beach, check out our cache of supplies, and standby. Should Miguel come ashore before I get down there, maintain your positions. Do not expose yourselves."

Leading the way down the hillside, Baker set a grueling pace, cutting left, then right, then around an outcropping, making haste with each stop. Will had been up that hill twice before, and once made the journey down, so he didn't think he'd have any problems. However, in his careless pursuit to keep pace with the sergeant he stubbed a toe on an exposed tree root and he went tumbling down the hillside, floundering through leaf and limb like a rag doll. When he did finally slide to a stop he was in agony. Baker, hearing the commotion, turned back and dashed to Will's aid, asking, "Are you okay, Munday?"

Farmer was next on the scene, then Gambler, and finally Tillie. "Give him a quick once-over," Baker instructed Farmer.

Farmer checked him for broken bones, spinal and neck injuries, and finally pulled up the backside of Will's jacket to discover he'd done a real number on his hide. "I need to clean and dress those abrasions," Farmer informed Baker. "It'll take a while. Why don't you keep moving? We'll catch up just as soon as I treat Will's injuries," Farmer suggested.

"How bad is it?" Baker asked. "I mean, will he be able to keep pace?"

"Oh yeah," Farmer assured him. "He's gonna hurt for a while, but I don't think he has any broken bones, so he'll be able to keep up with the rest of us."

"I think it's best if we all stay together. Get to patching him up, so we can move out," Baker decided.

Farmer dug into his medical kit and came out with a fistful of paraphernalia he'd need. Taking a piece of gauze in one hand, he doused it with some liquid from a bottle he held in his other hand, carefully recapped the glass vial and began to gently rub Will's scratched backside. Will moaned, and Farmer told him, "Yeah. I know it hurts. But I've gotta clean up those scrapes." When he had finished the clean-up task, he doused Will skin with a purple solution, then warned him, "This crap will stain your uniform. But it'll help to heal and keep out infection." Farmer carefully slid Will's fatigue jacket back over his shoulders and let it slide down every so slowly over his beltline. "There," he said when he was finished, "you'll be hurtin' for a day or so, but you'll be fit as a fiddle after that."

Will took to his feet, being very careful not to stretch the twill fabric of his uniform against his back. "Didn't mean to hold us up, Sergeant," he apologized to Baker, "but I can make it on my own now that young Doctor Kildare has treated me." Actually, he was suffering from the pain but wouldn't have admitted it to the others if it killed him.

"Okay, let's move out," Baker suggested, again taking the lead. "You, Munday, take your time. And Farmer, you tag along with him. If you fall behind don't fret. We're not that far from the beach."

When Will and Farmer finally reached the base of the hill, Baker and the others were busy checking over the supplies they'd stashed in the jungle prior to going aloft. Darkness was settling across the island, but the open sky above the seaside offered a trace of daylight yet. Baker paused, then arose to his feet, telling them, "It looks like the captain's theory was right. I think there's a longboat headed toward shore from that ship."

Everyone broke through the cover that had concealed them to catch a glimpse. Gambler confirmed Baker's observation, saying, "Yes. It's a boat all right."

"What if," Tillie interrupted, "it ain't Cebu? Could be a trap."

Baker chuckled, informing Tillie "It's him. It all figures. Don't expose yourselves. Get back into the trees and stay put. The captain should be coming in any minute."

Will heard leaves rustling and the slog of feet in the jungle behind where he stood, and not sure if it was friend or foe, he pulled his weapon up to port position as a precaution. However, it was just like Baker said it would be, the captain coming in with the rest of the team.

In the meantime the longboat had beached its bow on the sand. With everyone now present, Roul informed them, "It is our contact, of that I'm

223

certain. I'm going out on the beach to intercept him. I am the only one in our group who knows the proper password."

Will could've kicked himself. He should've known there'd be precautions, such as a password. It was the Army's way of doing business. He watched with a great deal of interest when Roul broke his cover and moseyed out onto the strand, taking brisk steps directly toward the boat. And when he came within a few yards of the craft two men came over the side, jumped onto the beach and scurried across the beach to intercept Roul.

"Checkered," Roul barked.

A cold chill danced up Will's spine. What if, he wondered, Tillie was right. Roul had offered the sign. Will turned his head and listened carefully, hoping to hear someone from the boat offer the countersign, but it didn't come until the interlopers had come abreast of Roul.

"Flag," one of the men gave the countersign.

That was all it took. Will marveled that two words, checkered and flag, could be so important. It was his first encounter with using passwords in a combat area, which was a far cry from those dry runs back in basic training. He then took notice that Roul darted a few steps ahead and embraced the man who'd come ashore last. "Miguel, Miguel, Miguel," Roul shouted, "it is so good to see you."

But the celebration was short lived. Stopwatch, their courage bolstered by a string of positive events, charged out onto the beach to greet their contact. Roul didn't waste time making introductions. He told his men, "We must make haste. Time is wasting and Miguel has taken a great gamble to come ashore for us."

But everyone insisted that they be told if Miguel had been cleared by the Japanese, so Roul backed down, asking his Filipino friend, "Of course. We were watching from up on the hillside. How did you manage to get a clearance?"

Miguel laughed, as did one of his confederates. "We fooled them. They believe we are but a harmless crew of fishermen making a run. But they are not to be trusted, either. They are treacherous people. They can look you in the eye and smile while plunging a dagger into your back."

"Did they ask about the plane that brought us in?" Baker asked.

"Indeed. They questioned us at length about it, asking if we'd seen any floating debris during the morning's voyage," Miguel explained, but he informed them, "From what they ask I think they are looking for wreckage of a downed plane."

Roul didn't pussyfoot around. Time was precious. He instructed the men to get busy hauling the supplies from the jungle to the waiting longboat and to fetch their rafts, which was their only means of boarding the *Señora Rosita.*

They all set to work retrieving the gear and supplies they'd cached the previous night and hauled them to the boat. Will felt good about things for the first time since their journey began, when the PBY departed from New Guinea. For one thing, he was impressed with the Filipino underground, who'd come to guide them in. Everything, so far anyway, was proceeding according to plan. He didn't particularly like it when Miguel and Roul sometimes reverted to their native tongue to exchange notes because it left him wondering what they were discussing. But he guessed Stopwatch was in capable hands even though he couldn't comprehend a word they were saying at times.

Stopwatch were at sea again, reversing the procedure of the night before, this time going from shore to ship. It was, Will learned, a lot harder to paddle crafts against a breaking surf than to row with the tow, as they had on their arrival. But as they finally broke free of the tides and set their heading for the *Señora Rosita,* Will couldn't resist swiveling his head for a final glance at the nameless island; a peaceful sanctuary that had him wondering if, indeed, they were the first human beings to step foot on its topography. *Surely,* he told himself, *it must have a name. But not knowing for sure, I christen it 'Utopia.'"* It was a fitting name for a remote garden of Eden, he thought. And he vowed that should he pass this way again he would post a sign on the beach proclaiming the island to be "OFF LIMITS TO MANKIND." It was, he believed, the least he could do to repay the pristine landmark for allowing him the pleasure of its company. He turned around, dipped the oar into the water, and put his sore back muscles to work, propelling the raft toward their next phase of the operation.

Chapter Fourteen

After they'd all boarded the *Señora Rosita* and had dutifully stowed their supplies and gear into an empty cargo hold underneath the forward deck, Baker's dozen was a sad-looking bunch of misfits. Each of them sported a two-day growth of beard and their uniforms, after only two days in the field, were a sorry mess. With but one chore left to perform before they could take a break, that of stashing the rafts in the rear cargo hold, they followed the directions dictated to them by one of the crew members; they lifted the hatch's lid, pitched it aside onto the deck, and dropped the rafts down into the depths of the boat. To a man, though, they were nauseated by the stench that emanated from the compartment; a cargo half filled with fish that the crew had amassed as evidence they were fishermen, not members of the Phillipine underground network. Will figured they all should've realize there would be fish; without it, Miguel and his crew would never have passed muster with the Japanese inspectors.

"It stinks," Farmer complained, wondering, "Just how'n the heck do these people stand it? The smell almost turns my stomach."

"They're acclimatized to it," Will told him, explaining, "It just goes with the territory. Dead fish stink."

"It's awful," Farmer added to his objection, informing Will that if his livelihood depended on inhaling such an odor all day, he'd find a different line of work.

"You're putting me on, huh?" Will asked.

"Nope," Farmer insisted.

"You live on a smelly old farm and then complain about a smelly old trawler," Will reproved him.

"Smelly farm? Did you say smelly farm? Are you sayin' my daddy's farm smells?" Farmer objected.

"Yeah … that's what I'm saying. I've visited farms. They reek to high heaven," Will fired back.

"Wal, is that so? Betcha ain't never seen a farm up close, let alone sniffed one. Farms have some wonderful smells. Now ... take for instance at harvest time. Didja ever get a whiff of new-mown hay?" Farmer asked him.

"Yeah. I have. I'll admit that new-mown hay does smell pleasant," Will agreed, but he went on to agitate Farmer some more, claiming that he'd "once stood not fifty feet from a hog wallow and it stunk ... believe me, it stunk. And when I went into the barn I stepped in manure, which also stunk, and I almost puked when I tried to clean the sole of my shoe with a stick."

Farmer burst out laughing. "Really?" he asked, still giggling. "I can't even imagine you cleaning up your shoe with a stick. You're kidding me."

"No. It's true. And I never went back to visit another farm all my born days," Will informed him.

"Knock it off," Baker intervened between Will and Farmer, advising them, "I'll settle the argument. Farms stink. This trawler stinks. This whole goddamn war stinks. Life in general stinks. So, knock off your stinking chatter and catch some shuteye." He whirled around and strutted across the deck, leaving the pair to munch on his message of discontent. "Why me?" he asked as he walked away. "What did I do wrong to deserve this bunch of jurblowfs?"

Baker pretty well settled the issue, although both men were a tad surprised he'd taken time to mediate the dispute. "He's pissed," Farmer suggested.

"No. I don't think he's pissed. He's got a lot on his mind and we were probably disturbing his train of thought or something," Will defended Baker. He raised up and craned his neck as though he were searching for something or somebody.

"Whatcha lookin' for?" Farmer asked.

"Well, I can't speak for everybody, but I'm getting hungry," Will complained.

"So? Whatcha lookin' for? A hamburger stand?" Farmer teased him with a laugh.

"I'm hungry. I wish there was a hamburger stand. Right there," he said, pointing his finger at a funnel on deck.

"Me, too," Farmer agreed. "I'll buy, Will. My treat. What's your pleasure?"

"You're nuts, you know," he badgered the country boy. "I'll bet if we were stateside right now and standing right in front of a hamburger stand you wouldn't be so generous."

"I would so," he disagreed. "And ... I'd get myself two hamburgers smothered with catsup and a thick slice'a onions. And if'n they had any ice cream I'd order a double chocolate malt."

"Damn," Will moaned. "Stop it. I told you I'm hungry. Boy, I could go for that double chocolate malt myself."

Will's hunger pangs were doing a number on his innards. "Hey, Sergeant Baker!" he shouted.

Baker peeked around the corner of the ship's cabin and asked, "What do you want now, Munday?"

"I'm hungry. A soldier needs nourishment," he complained.

"We just ate … a couple of hours ago," Baker reminded him.

"I know. But that was a late dinner. It's past suppertime," Will jogged Baker's memory.

Baker scratched his chin, hung his head, then agreed, admitting to Will, "I guess we did only eat twice today. Okay. Gooch. Break out some K's before we have a mutiny on our hands." Again, Baker gave his head a disgusted bob and moaned as he disappeared behind the cabin, "And historians rave about the trials of Captain Bligh. I should be so lucky as he and just have a crew of mutinous swab-jockeys to contend with."

Gooch dropped himself through the hatch atop of the cargo hold, then began to pitch cartons of rations over the top, letting them fall on deck. Everyone scrambled to get their share.

Will wasted little time ripping the carton of grub open. It was a treat; a can of some sort of cheese substitute which was one of his preferable entrees. There was also a chunk of wrapped chocolate, a small package of biscuits that tasted like pasteboard, a four-pack of cigarettes and a packet of instant coffee mix, which was of no value, since there was no hot water with which to brew the drink. Will dipped the cheesy mixture from the tin using the biscuits as a spoon. It wasn't like dining at the Ritz but the small portion of food did satisfy his pangs of hunger. He pocketed the chocolate treat for later, then leaned back against the outside of the cabin wall, and asked Baker, "Can we smoke?"

Sergeant Baker glanced in Miguel's direction, seeking his approval, to which the Filipino suggested, "Cup the embers inside of your hands. It's better if we do not attract any unnecessary attention. It's doubtful we'd be spotted."

With the smoking lamp lit Will and the others who smoked pulled out their packs and lit up. Will, however, taking notice that the Filipino crewmen didn't join them, inquired, "Doesn't any of your crew smoke, Miguel?"

"Oh, yes. But we have no cigarettes," he lamented.

Will tossed his four-pack to Miguel, inviting him to join them in a smoke, but that was not enough to go around, so every one of them gave their sample packs of cigarettes to the Filipino crewmen. They, too, lit up, and they showed their appreciation with deep-throated moans of approval. "We have not had American cigarettes for so long," Miguel bemoaned, explaining that, "We can get Japanese cigarettes now and then, but they taste awful."

Will crawled across the deck on his hands and knees to deposit his garbage into a bag provided by Miguel, who warned them, "We must be ever so careful not to pitch anything over the side., especially anything made in America."

Returning to his spot beside the cabin, Will leaned back against the bulkhead and heaved a big sigh. The wooden surface of the wall was cool, a soothing treatment for his aching back. He just sat there, taking an occasional drag on his cigarette, and let his thoughts wander. His hands were trembling. He did not know why but suspected it was a result of the nerve-wracking day, which was capped off with the hustle-bustle to get on board of the *Señora Rosita*. He was also tired. Thinking back over the activities of the past few days, he didn't think he'd had a total of more than ten hours sleep. He tipped his head back against the bulkhead, closed his eyes, and listened to the monotonous throb of the ships old engine going *whu-u-u-ump, whu-u-u-ump* as it labored to propel the craft across the choppy sea. Miguel had opted to forego the sail. The engine, he said, would be much faster. Listening to the tiring power plant, Will thought about the little train that could. The *whu-u-u-ump* almost sounded like *I think I can*. He hoped it was the antiquated vessel's way of promising Will, *I'll getcha there, I'll getcha there*. It was a soothing melody of sorts.

He recalled MaryLou's letter, which he'd been carrying in his breast pocket since it first arrived. He knew he couldn't read the endearing lines she'd written in the darkness of the night, but just holding it was reward enough. He raised it close to his nostrils and inhaled the stale fragrance of MaryLou's perfume. He envisioned himself holding her body close to his own and gently kissing her delectable lips, wondering if the sensation of actually caressing and kissing was anything like he imagined. He wanted to hold her, to squeeze her breasts against his chest, to snuggle up to her just one time. One time. He needed that. She could rescue him from the throes of anxiety, tenderly stroke his brow, whisper into his ear, "I love you." And with that thought in mind his weary body gave way to his wandering thoughts and he drifted off to sleep, sitting straight up, the cabin wall sustaining his body. Sleep was possible. MaryLou's company was not.

"WAKE UP!" The harsh words shattered the silence, rousing Will from his slumber. It was Baker voice. "C'MON! Let's go! Hit the deck!"

Will opened his eyes and glanced up to see Baker staring down on him. He reached out his fist and pounded on the deck. "Okay, wise guy," Baker said, "what's that supposed to mean?"

"I'm hitting the deck," Will replied with a chuckle.

"Now, get on your feet. That's what I want to see on deck, your feet," Baker informed him.

It was still very dark, probably the middle of night, Will figured. The Army had a way of getting a man up early so he wouldn't be late for an engagement; an engagement that never seemed to begin on schedule, so they normally played a waiting game after busting their balls to get there. Then, he remembered he'd fallen asleep with MaryLou's letter in his hand. He groped around, sliding his fingertips on the surface of the deck, until he finally located his precious message of love. He snatched it up, stuffed it back into his breast pocket, and jumped to his feet. The air was crisp for the tropics. And the sky was a never-ending ocean of stars twinkling above an ocean that glistened under a shower of moombeams. Will peeled his ear to listen. The old engine was still *Whu-u-u-ump*-ing somewhere down in the lower depths of the hull. That was good. He thought for a minute that this might well be the *Señora Rosita*'s last voyage and that was why she was laboring to make port one final time. And he considered how odd it was that the warship leading the initial assault for MacArthur's triumphant return to the Philippines was a rotten old fishing trawler with no gun turrets, no radar, not even a decent coat of paint.

Baker summoned his men to gather on the afterdeck, where Schuster and Roul stood waiting. There was a ghostly silence, except for the ship's engine and the flapping of a solitary sail that was not too well secured to the mast. Will glanced from Baker to Schuster, then to Roul. Baker, he noticed, was shivering in the brisk breeze, and Schuster's always too tidy mustache appeared to be etched on the upper lip of his expressionless face. Then, Will came down with a traumatic case of shivers. He'd been sweating in his sleep and was abruptly awakened with perspiration soaking the underarms of his fatigues. All in all, the whole affair was a rude awakening for the lot of them. The trauma of just thinking about the next phase, that of setting foot on an island occupied by the Japs, added to all of their woes. Aside from the strafing raid back on Guinea he'd never known the torment of fear. Now he was beginning to wonder what loomed just ahead. He recalled when he'd encountered several combat veterans back in the depot how they'd told him, "Waiting is the worst part. You wait. And you wait. Then, out of the clear blue sky all hell breaks loose and things are happening so fast that you have no time to think. And that is where your training pays off. You'll do what you were trained to do just like a puppet on strings." But this mission promised to be a different story; the shoe was on the other foot. It was Stopwatch who was poised to deliver the surprise blow. This would be nothing like the day those aviators swooped down out of the sky and blistered them with volleys of lead. Will F. Munday and his friends were going to swoop down on the Japanese much the same. And he recalled how President Roosevelt had said the only fear he needed to fear was fear itself. Fear was, he guessed, at the root of his problem. His anxieties were all spawned by the long wait, he suspected.

Roul called for their undivided attention. He glanced from man to man, finally informing them, "Gentlemen ... the time has come to earn our pay. We are the vanguard, MacArthur's envoys. It is we who will thrust the dagger into the dragon's heart, and someday many years hence, when you look back on this mission, you'll feel a great deal of pride for having helped to slay that dragon. You are writing history; the history of America's return to the Philippines. Right now I know without being told that a fleet of ships is plowing through the sea to keep a rendezvous. There is no turning back, as we discovered while sitting up on the hillside, all of us wondering what we'd do if we were caught by the Japs. Today is October 18 and the time is 0430 hours. We have less than forty-four hours to reach our final destination. Miguel will put us ashore on a delta where a river empties into the sea. He will leave and set sail for home so as to return from his fishing run without raising any suspicions. We will conceal ourselves, once again, in the jungle and wait for him and his men to trek overland to join us. Hopefully, we'll be ready by 0900 hours to begin our journey to our target area."

Roul glanced at his wristwatch, turned to take his leave, then paused for a moment and pivoted to add an afterthought. "I should add that I suggest you don't be deceived by the Filipinos' austere appearance. It is true they have no uniforms, such as we, but they are first-rate soldiers nonetheless. Consider for a moment that they have more at stake in the outcome of our mission than we do. They've been waiting three years, while enduring inhumane cruelty, to seek their revenge, and the very fact that they stand here today alongside of our unit, willing to sacrifice everything, is proof of their mettle. I can assure you that they are dependable, and I have assured them we shall respond in kind." He scanned his men again, glancing into each one of their faces, then instructed Baker, "Prepare to disembark, Sergeant."

Disembarking from a vessel into rafts was hardly a new adventure. They'd repeated the routine time and again, first back in Guinea from the LCI for their ill-fated voyage to the beach, and lastly from the PBY to make the landing on the uninhabited island. So, what could go wrong? If there had been some outside pressure, such as enemy fire, most everyone would've overlooked the snafu that unraveled. But there was nothing negative that might've spawned a misfire of such proportions. The problem began when one of the mooring ropes affixed to a raft down in the hold came untied. Baker immediately dispatched Tillie to "shinny down there, retie that knot, and give that raft a lift." That was the beginning of the end. Tillie slipped while crawling over the side of the top rail leading down into the hold and tumbled head over heels down into a heap of slimy fish. He screamed, "Get me outta here," at the top of his lungs, while Baker stood above him repeating his order, "Tie the goddamn rope and quitchur whining." Somehow, Tillie did manage to accomplish the task and then to shove the end of the raft up where some of those on deck could get a grip on it and hoist it out of the hold. Tillie was then given a boost by two of Miguel's men, who leaned over the side and pulled him out of the smelly compartment by his outstretched hands.

Meanwhile, several guys were pulling the cargo they'd stowed in the front hold out onto the deck, while Miguel's men busied themselves pitching the rafts over the side, then tying them to the ship's deck railing. Tillie continued to voice his disgust over coming out of the hold "smellin' like a swamp rat" while Roul just stood there, hands on hips, arms akimbo, a puzzled expression twisting his face. It was evident he could not believe what was happening, particularly a moment later when someone dropped a wooden case of cartridges; a whole bunch of cartridges that slid every which way across the deck.

Baker finally lost his cool. It was a first in Will's memory. He dropped to his knees and frantically began to scoop up the loose cartridges and toss them back into the wood crate, shouting, "Jesus Christ on a crutch. What the fuck got into you jurblowfs? C'mon. Get these goddamn shells picked up and let's get to cracking."

"HALT! AS YOU WERE!" Roul shouted at the top of his lungs. "Hold the fort. Stop and listen."

Motionless could best describe the reaction to Roul's outburst. This, too, was a first. Will could not recall ever seeing Roul raise his voice in such a manner. Frozen like statues in varied patterns of posture, it was as though everyone was caught up in a time warp. They stood, or they knelt, or they paused from whatever project they were pursuing and stared at the captain with expressions of disbelief etched on their faces.

"You are professionals! You've been through this procedure numerous times, each time improving over the previous attempt. Very deliberately, now, gents ... slow down ... and take your time ... and get it right. You're responding like raw recruits. You are trained soldiers. Carry on," he said.

Roul's reprimand seemed to be the magic potion they needed. Everyone painstakingly picked up where they'd left off when Roul took charge and, in an orderly fashion, finished their chores, making an orderly exodus from the *Señora Rosita* into the rafts without any further ado. However, they'd managed to humiliate their leaders in front of the Filipino hosts, which, needless to say, made fools out of Roul, Baker and Schuster, all of whom had been bragging up their subordinates to Miguel's deck hands; a motley crew of deckhands who could not believe their eyes when Roul's raiders melted down in such a manner.

Once they shoved off and turned their rafts toward an island that loomed on the horizon, they put their arms and backs against the oars and, like the regimented soldiers they actually were, atoned for their sins. But Will was curious over what he imagined Miguel and his men were thinking when their debarkation went astray. *Surely,* he mused, *they must question our competence and even be a tad skeptical over joining forces for the upcoming mission.* He knew that he, and all of the others, had not performed up to their customary standards. Was this, he asked himself, a caveat? Were they really ready to tackle the monumental task of destroying an entire enemy complex when they couldn't even disembark from a ship in an orderly manner? It was a scary thought.

Owing to calm waters and accommodating swells with a low surf they made up some of the time they'd squandered while evacuating the ship, and Roul led his tiny flotilla into the mouth of a river, where they went ashore like the professionals they were supposed to be. The landing was not much different than the previous night, when they bellied down on the beach of the uninhabited island; they were greeted with a tomblike silence that almost defied logic. Sooner, or later, Will mused when he went ashore, their run of luck would end and they'd be met, head to head, by an enemy force. That would be the appropriate time for him to decide whether he was more afraid of the foe than of fear itself.

Chapter Fifteen

There was no pause from duty to catch their breaths after they crossed over the wide sandbar that formed a delta between the jungle and the sea. Baker immediately put them on alert. He dispatched Schuster, along with Able squad, to make a probe into the jungle, while he deployed Baker and Charlie squads in a skirmish line just inside of the tree line so they were facing the sea; far enough back in the depths of the jungle so as to blend in with the terrain and close enough to the beach to keep a watchful eye on the delta. Will stood for a moment watching Schuster deploy his men, ordering two of them to survey the jungle while the other two covered their advance from a secluded spot. They played hopscotch, two-by-two, half of the squad advancing, and half of the squad observing, until they all vanished from sight. Since they obviously hadn't been detected Will supposed they had successfully made another entry without being observed, and subsequently intercepted by Japs, which was a big relief. So, once more the powers in command at GHQ did know what lay in store for Stopwatch.

This was, Will mused, just a curtain call from the last island. The same stiff breeze wafted onshore to rustle the palm fronds overhead. The breeze was often the prelude to dawn, so he figured daylight would be breaking soon. Schuster returned just long enough to update Baker. "Nothing doing," he reported, "no resistance." Feeling secure with Schuster's report, Baker put the others to work, pulling the rafts onto the beach, unloading their contents, then dragging everything back underneath the cover of trees. He snatched up a fallen frond and handed it to Will, telling him to sweep away all of the footprints that they'd left on the sandbar. It was actually more of a "better safe than sorry" assignment than a vital necessity, Will figured, but he hustled out on the sandbar and complied with Bakers orders. It was nearing "0600 hours," Baker informed them when their tasks were finished, so he instructed them to keep a low profile and get some rest. Will needed some rest. His backside was beginning to itch. He thought that was a good sign; a sign of healing. The salt water that had sprayed across the raft while coming ashore did dampen his shirt, soaking through the cloth, so that the salt contributed to his discomfort, he believed. So, he slipped out of his jacket and hung it on a branch to dry, even though he felt a chill from the early-morning draft that penetrated the jungle's interior. It was time, he decided, to park his carcass and spend some time with MaryLou. He dropped down beside a tree trunk, gently leaned his shoulder against the rough bark, and closed his eyes, figuring to troll the depths of his subconscious for a spell. But he was wearier than he'd thought. Rather than conjure up visions of his lady love, he fell sound asleep almost as soon as he closed his eyelids.

Will awoke with a jerk, glanced around at the terrain, then up at the sky. There was, he discovered, a parting of the branches overhead that had let the sun shine down on him and he was well done. He wiped the sweat from his brow with his sleeve, then noticed that Farmer had taken up residence just a few yards away and was also snoozing. "Hey, country boy," Will paged him, saying, "It's morning. Rise and shine and enjoy another shitty day in this tropical paradise."

Farmer moaned, then rolled over onto his side and propped his head on an upraised fist. He looked different. Will couldn't say exactly what was different. It was the expression he wore on his face that bothered Will. "What's wrong?" Will asked.

"Nothin'," Farmer replied, adding that it had been "a fitful nap."

"Fitful? How so?" Will asked.

"It ain't nothin'. Just a crazy dream. No big deal," he downplayed whatever was bothering him.

"Okay," Will said with a shrug, pretending he didn't care if Farmer shared his problems or not. "Forget I ask. Just trying to repay you for all of the times you've boosted my morale," he added, looking out across the river delta as though it didn't matter.

"Well ... it was just a dumb dream, Will. I'd be ashamed to tell you about it," Farmer tried to beg off, when actually Will sensed he did want to be encouraged.

"That's what friends are for, you know. But ... if you aren't comfortable confiding in your best friend ... so be it," Will continued his pretense of not caring, which was not true. He was very concerned over Farmer's change in character.

"You're jiving me, aren't you, Will?" Farmer suggested. "You're pretending you don't want to know what I dreamt, but I can tell you're dying to know."

"Okay. I'm dying. What did you dream?"

"D'ya promise not to laugh? I told you it was a dumb dream."

"I won't laugh."

"Promise?"

"Yes, yes, yes. I promise."

"Well ... I dreamt there was this here loaf of bread and jug of wine lying on the trail right in front of me," Farmer replied.

Will snickered.

"I knew better. I shouldn't have trusted you. You promised you wouldn't laugh."

"I'm not laughing at you, Farmer. Honest. But just telling me out of the clear blue sky about a loaf of bread and a jug of wine on the trail is kinda ... well, kinda ... different."

"Forget I mentioned it."

"No. I won't. Tell me what's fitful about it."

"Well, back home it would be an omen."

"A bad omen or a good omen?"

"BAD! Why d'ya think I woke up frettin' over it?"

"You've got me. Why did you?"

"Because whenever there's a vision of a loaf of bread and a jug of wine a death is sure to follow," Farmer finally leveled with Will.

"Awe, go on," Will chided Farmer.

"Oh, I knew you'd make fun of it. But it's true. There was this here neighbor man ... he farmed the quarter section right north of my daddy's place ... and he had a vision of a loaf of bread and a jug of wine lying there on the barn door sill."

"Yeah? So what happened?"

"He didn't believe in such nonsense, either. He thought someone was pulling a prank on him."

"Yeah?"

"Well, he just went ahead doing his chores. He milked the cows, toted the buckets of milk to the separator shed, and went back to clean the horse shit out of the stable."

"Yeah? So?" Will was suddenly all ears.

"Well, he was pitching that horse hockey outta the barn when one'a his horses up and kicked him right in the head."

"So, did he die?"

"Well, not right then. He crawled all the way to the house to fetch some help from his woman and when she seen him she almost fainted. But she drags him inside of the house, and while she was tendin' to a big gash on the side of his head, he told her about the bread and the wine."

"Yeah? So? What did she do?"

"That's when she fainted on account'a she knew what to expect. And while she was out cold, that poor old guy up and died. Yup! Poor fellow." Farmer concluded his tale of woe

Will just sat there staring in dismay at his friend. It was, he thought, a thought-provoking argument if ever he'd heard one. And he suspected that Farmer truly believed in omens and curses and such, which accounted for his concern over the dream. The best approach, Will decided, was to change the subject, and he had the perfect switch. His stomach had been turning flip-flops ever since he awoke. "Farmer," he advised his friend, "look at it this way. It was a dream. Besides, I need your medical expertise."

"What's the problem?"

"Bellyache. Man, have I got a bellyache," Will complained, poking his index finger against his groin.

"Are you crappin' regular?"

"No. I've always had constipation problems when I'm in the field," Will related his problem.

"Hm-m-m-m, ain't never heard you mention that before."

"Well, a guy doesn't customarily talk about such things."

"Yeah, you're right. I wouldn't."

"Well, things have a way of coming out ... sooner or later. But I'm sure miserable today."

"I've got the cure, Will. Right here in this bag. They're called 'brown bombers.' Actually, they've got one'a them highfalutin medical names, but they work," Farmer assured him.

He fished into his medical haversack and come out with a small brown-colored glass vial, screwed the cap loose, shook a couple of pills out into the palm of his hand and offered them to Will. "Here. Take these," he suggested, promising Will, "You'll get some relief before very long. I promise."

Will responded with a dour expression and asked Farmer, "Now, these pills won't give me the trots ... will they?"

Farmer grinned, admitting the possibility did exist, but assured Will, "I've got some stuff here that'll cure the trots, too."

"Yeah? What's it called?"

"Oh, para ... something. It's another one'a them medical terms I wrestle with."

"You mean paregoric?"

"Yeah. That's it. How's come you know that?"

"My mom uses it."

"Oh," Farmer replied, mumbling under his breath, "College folks. They know everything."

But he was genuinely concerned about Will's well-being, so much, in fact, that he sought some advice from the captain. Diarrhea or constipation had a history in the military; a bad reputation for being as much of an enemy as the foe toting a weapon. It could, if left unchecked, render an army incapable of performing its functions. So, the captain in turn mentioned Will's discomfort to Baker, and he hunted Will down to satisfy his curiosity of whether or not Will would be up to pulling his duties. But Will assured Baker, insisting, "I'm okay. Just bound up. It'll pass. Farmer gave me some little brown pills."

"Brown bombers?"

"Yeah. That's what he called them."

Baker chuckled and told Will, "Stand by for action. If you feel it coming on, get your pants down … pronto!"

Schuster's voice cut Baker's and Will's exchange short, shouting, "Chow time," but Will decided to forego breakfast. He didn't want to add any fuel to the fire that was churning around in his gut.

A short time later Will drew his tour of perimeter duty and was escorted to the inner reaches of the jungle, where he was told to "Hunker down. Keep your eyes and ears open."

Being left alone, he figured it would be a good time to try to relieve himself, so he sought refuge behind a clump of shrubbery. Farmer's prediction was right on target. The pills didn't tarry long until they tunneled through his bowels. When Perkins showed up to relieve him Will was feeling much better. He returned to the beachhead and found a shady spot underneath a towering palm tree and planted his posterior on the ground.

Farmer caught a glimpse of Will returning and darted over to where he was sitting. "Well?" he asked.

"They worked. I do feel better. The fact is, if your daddy had that load of shit back on the farm it would fertilize eighty acres," Will boasted.

Farmer cackled like a setting hen again. He said, "Man. That's must'a been a chore. That's a heap'a manure. Now, if'n you need some of that para … something, let me know."

"I'll be fine. No thanks," Will refused the offer, but he did take time to ask Farmer, "What're you going to do when this damned war is over and you go home?"

Farmer was puzzled by the query. "I ain't gave it any thought, why?" he asked. "Whatcha asking about that for?"

"I've been giving your future some thought, Farmer," Will explained, suggesting, "You're kinda handy with the medical stuff. You took care of my backside and it's healing … I think … and now you cured my constipation.

You should consider a medical career when you get outta the Army."

"Awe, go on," Farmer sluffed off Will's suggestion, reminding him. "I'm a farmer."

Will shook his head in disgust, informing his friend, "And ... you're willing to settle for that ... for the rest of your life?"

"Why not? It's an honest man's profession."

"I'll tell you why not, honesty aside. You should be everything you can be. Not that there's anything wrong with farming, but there's a whole different world out there, Farmer," Will exclaimed. "You're a pretty cool guy, really. You're laid back and that would mean everything for your bedside manner."

"What's a bedside manner?"

"You know. How you deal with people. Like ... earlier today, when I told you I was constipated ... you made me feel at ease about it. That's bedside manner," Will explained.

"Oh," Farmer humored Will, "and you're saying that having a bedside manner would make me a good sawbones."

"That, and some other things," Will went on, describing some of the studies required of doctors. "You'd have to finish high school, then go to college, and then you have to serve what's called an internship. It takes several years to become a full-fledged physician. But the rewards are worth it."

"Naw. Never happen. Us country boys who got our learnin' in a one-roomed schoolhouse can't compete with you city boys," Farmer hedged.

"Bull! That's a cop-out. Lots of famous men came from the sticks. Why, take Abe Lincoln as an example. He got most of his education in the backwoods just from reading books. Now, Farmer, look how far he went in the world. You, too, can do it. I just know you can."

Farmer sat in silence mulling over everything Will had said. He wanted to believe Will in the worst way, but had some doubts. Finally he asked, "How will I get all'a that schoolin'?"

"The Army's already taking care of that. There's this new GI Bill thing. Veterans can go to school for free and, according to what I've heard, even get a stipend to help out," Will encouraged him.

"Stipend? What's a stipend?"

"Money, Farmer. Moolah! They're going to pay you to go to school in appreciation for what you've done."

"Fat chance. Look! I didn't even know what that there word *stipend* meant ... and you think I can go to college? You're putting me on."

"No. I'm not. You can do it. It just takes a heap of determination, that's all. I'll tell you what I'm going to do when we get outta this army. I'm going to come and see you and I'm going to get you aimed in the right direction so's you can become a doctor," Will vowed.

Gambler's voice intruded on their conversation, but Will guessed he'd said about all he could to influence Farmer to make something of his life. And Gambler was rejoicing, retelling his infamous escapade back in Reno when the husband caught him making love to his wife.

"D'ya really think old Gambler did all'a them things?" Farmer asked Will.

"Probably. Well, it's probably half truths with a little wishful thinking tossed in. I've never been in Reno, just heard about it from him, so it's anyone's guess," Will replied, giving Gambler the benefit of the doubt.

Captain Roul, who'd been mysteriously missing for quite some time, suddenly loomed up, walking out of the trees followed by several Filipinos. They were jabbering in a native tongue. Roul had once mentioned there was a language called Tagalog that was sometimes spoken in the Philippines, so Will guessed that's what they used to communicate. Evidently, the captain had gone to meet the Filipino hosts, some of which, Will noticed, were the crewmen from Miguel's trawler. Since Will couldn't understand their conversation he could only surmise that it focused on the trek they were about to take.

Schuster was busy opening a crate of weapons; several new Tompsons, which he issued to the islanders. And Roul, calling his men into a huddle, explained, "These men will be our guides. There will be one guide assigned to each squad." Will took notice of how frail they all appeared. He wondered if it was due to limited rations over a long period of time. And their clothing was so tacky that he almost felt sorry for them. Evidently, he assumed from what he'd seen, life under the Japanese occupation forces must've been dreadful.

Roul instructed Schuster to pull in the sentries. While they all stood around waiting for the guys on perimeter guard to return to the site, Roul began to make assignments. Baker squad drew a Filipino named Fidel as their guide. After taking stock of the man Will was a trifle suspect. Somehow he didn't measure up as an avant-garde pathfinder. He might've weighed in at a hundred pounds. His tattered clothing needed a laundering, and the half-worn-out sandals on his feet didn't appear to be much protection from the elements. To Will he looked more like a war refugee than a scout. A dirty canvas hat was slouched down across one eye, which made his physical appearance all the more sinister. But when he was introduced to the four members of Baker squad, he spread his arms wide apart and smiled from ear to ear, saying, "Welcome to our country." Will was astonished that he spoke English but found it even more remarkable that Fidel was quite fluent with the tongue. The whole scenario sent Will on a guilt trip. He should've believed Roul when he warned them about the Filipinos' dowdy appearance while further suggesting they not interpret that as a sign of weakness. Will had every right to be remorseful. Here he was, a member of the best-dressed, best-fed, best-equipped, best-trained army ever assembled, but not so efficient that they didn't need to rely on the shabby remnants of a once proud Philippine army to chart their course through enemy territory. Will felt that he could and that he should admire men of spirit who survived the tyranny through three years of occupation just so that they would be on hand when MacArthur did return. There was obviously no doubt in their minds about MacArthur returning. It seemed that, to them, it was a matter of when MacArthur came, not if, so Will was gratified that he'd drawn Fidel to guide him through the gauntlet and deliver him to the designated target area.

While Roul conducted his final critique prior to moving out, Miguel and one of his men stashed the empty cargo cases and other trash so it couldn't be seen on first glance. Then came the moment of truth. Sergeant Baker called his men to formation, had them line up, dress off, and stand at attention for a moment. He nodded at Captain Roul, who responded in kind, then barked, "It's time to move out. All scouting chores will be performed by the Filipino guides, who know the territory. On the command 'Dismissed,' you will break ranks and follow your designated guide. Able squad will take the left flank, Charlie the right flank, while Baker squad advances directly forward. Be sure all of your pieces are locked and loaded and that you leave nothing behind." He paused, glanced to check the whereabouts of Miguel's scouts, then dismissed the formation.

Will was comfortable with Fidel leading the way. This was, he realized, Fidel's turf. He knew the pitfalls, the shortcuts, the trails and the taboos and wouldn't inadvertantly stumble across a roving Jap patrol; the routine patrols whose habits he and his friends had studied to a point that they knew almost precisely when and where the Japs would be at any given time. And the weather took a turn for the better. It was almost a cheerful day if a person could ignore the purpose of their goal and just enjoy the scenery. The sky was clear and blue, all of the clouds having evaporated under the torrid heat of the sun. The terrain was such that the going wasn't all that difficult. Toting his share of gear was the hardest part of the assignment. He felt like a two-legged arsenal. Baker had suggested they discard their gas masks and let Miguel dispose of them, keeping the empty bag for toting spare ammunition. Will didn't take a tally when he was issued the hardware but he knew he was carrying at least a dozen hand-grenades, several loaded clips for his Thompson, in addition to several more BAR clips as spares for Tillie.

The pleasant weather didn't endure, much to Will's chagrin. They had taken a pause for noon chow, and while Will sat, his back leaning against a tree trunk, he noticed the sun dimming. He said to Farmer, who was sitting just a couple of yards away, "What's this, huh? Don't tell me it's going to rain some more."

Farmer glanced up through the palm fronds and confirmed Will's suspicions, telling him, "Yup! You're right. It's clouding up. It looks like rain."

"I told you 'don't tell me', didn't I?"

"Wal, yeah, but I thought you just wanted my opinion."

"I did. But then … I really didn't, either. I knew it was going to rain. How did I know? Because a drop of rain about the size of a spitball just creased my nose," Will complained. "This is some shit, d'ya know? I hate rain. I hate wet clothes and I hate wet feet. And for all of the good it will do me, I'm launching a formal protest."

Captain Roul overhead Will. He, however, was tickled pink over the impending storm. "Be happy," he told Will, explaining that "rain can be an ally. It's not always negative. It'll make our hike a little easier, because the Japs will hole up to stay dry, while we move freely around their playground."

"I should be so lucky," Will moaned as he slipped his poncho over his head.

"Lucky?" Roul asked.

"Yes, sir. Lucky. I'm so lucky to be an American soldier, instead of a Japanese soldier, because I get to waltz around in the rain while the Nip hunkers down in a nice, dry, warm bunker, or hut. To put it another way, perhaps I'm on the wrong side of this war."

"WILL!" Farmer called him down. "I can't believe you said that. That's almost blasphemy."

"So be it," Will ignored Farmer's lecture, taking his argument one step further. "Make a note," he suggested, "that you heard the captain say the Japs will hole up high and dry while I get drenched to the skin."

"But he didn't say that."

"In so many words, he did. So, who are the smartest; the Japs or us? You make the call," Will dared him. The discussion was over anyway. Baker yelled, "Okay. Let's move out and make tracks. We should have a clear passage."

Will and Farmer fell in behind Fidel, and in between Tillie and Gambler. But Farmer was curious. "Will?" he asked.

"Yeah?"

"How's come you can always find the right words to back up those silly notions of yours?" Farmer inquired.

"Book learning, Farmer. Good old-fashioned book learning. Something you're going to get a taste of when this damned war ends," Will replied with a grin. He hadn't forgotten his vow to encourage Farmer's educational pursuits after the war was over.

Chapter Sixteen

The abrasions on Will's backside continued to itch. The sensation was discomfiting because he could not scratch them. The misery of traipsing across the unpredictable countryside while wearing wet fatigues that clung to his legs and body was taking its toll. He did so abhor being a sponge. In many ways Will had come around to conform to the Army's way of doing things, but he had serious doubts over whether he'd ever cotton to suffering the elements without protesting.

Walking through the jungle with no anticipated threat from the enemy pending, or so Captain Roul had said, gave him ample time to study the pros and cons of military life. He imagined himself back in the college classroom, where'd he been delegated the task of writing a thesis about war. Actually, he even made the challenge tougher. The thesis would be centered on "War: its drawbacks versus its rewards." He sort of figured that would be a snap but when he began to weigh the cons against the pros he discovered the cons had a definite edge. In his estimation war was *A waste, pure and simple, not only of the human species, but of the world's resources. It pollutes the atmosphere, poisons the vegetation and eradicates endless numbers of man-made landmarks, such as antiquated cathedrals that have withstood the test of time for centuries on end.* He was confident he could challenge the prediction that this, like World War I, would be a final war to end all wars. The world being populated with an unbalanced society of have-nots over haves was partly to blame and that inequity predicted *a never-ending saga of survival that will trigger wars.* His summation came down to one simple fact; the common man would be subjugated to *tread the battlefield, attired in soggy, rain-soaked clothing,* while the world's society of the affluent would *sit high and dry up on Knob Hill sipping saké with the goddamn Japs, who hole up to stay dry.* These things, among others, were on his mind that afternoon while he elbowed his way between the tangled branches of tropical flora.

He recalled, while trudging along, Farmer's premonition over a loaf of bread and a jug of wine. For some unexplainable reason he regressed and found himself chewing his cud over Duffy's demise. He liked Duffy, even though they had just met one another. And he really adored Farmer for the simple, laidback rascal that he was. Perhaps that was why the two men came to mind. They were a lot alike, both rolling with the status quo, accepting things as they were instead of how they wished they were. Will had never actually given any thought to love of others, except his latest postal fling with MaryLou. He guessed there had to be many kinds of love, such as *motherly love and fraternal love*. The fraternal love thing was a new sensation for Will. He knew he loved Farmer and speculated it was because Farmer had catered to him from the beginning, overlooking his faults, defending his errors, and standing by him through thick and thin. His feelings had nothing whatsoever to do with hugging and kissing or passionate behavior. It had to do with a man's willingness to lay his life on the line for someone else of the same gender. And to put one's trust in another man to respond in kind.

Unfortunately, Will was so wrapped up in reverie that he inadvertently strayed away from his formation and suddenly realized he was separated from the other guys. He started to panic. There was no one within sight and he couldn't hear a familiar voice, or sound, except the customary noises of wildlife that inhabited the jungle. He paused to take a bearing, wondering how far off track he'd veered and how long he'd been off course. Surely, he rationalized, someone had missed him. Then again, he halfway hoped no one had. If he could find his way back to the squad without his absence being discovered it would probably save him from another reaming-out from the sergeant. He'd had a taste of that before and didn't care for a repeat performance. So, he stood quite still and listened carefully, hoping to hear any sound that might be manmade. Then, as he swung his head, his eyes caught a glimpse of someone passing through a gap in the trees; a someone who vanished, however, before he could verify whether it was animal, vegetable or mineral. Figuring he had estimated his heading nearly right, if the movement he saw was one of the guys, he should reappear in a clearing just ahead and to his left. Hopelessly alone, he had to rely on his training bout how to shoot an azimuth, and how to stay put, and to stand very still, and wait rather than panic. His patience was rewarded. A moment later Farmer loped into the glade, swinging his head back and forth, until his eyes came to rest on Will. He motioned to will, waving his hand furiously back and forth, shouting, "Where you been? I lost my visual on you."

Will shoved his index finger up across his lips and shushed Farmer, trying to keep him quiet until they could talk confidentially. "Had to take a leak," he lied, using that as his excuse for getting twisted up with his directions.

"Oh," Farmer replied, buying the story with no hesitation.

Will was so tickled to see Farmer that he swung his arm around his shoulder and said, "Farmer. I love you. You're the best thing that ever happened to me."

Farmer was shocked. He pulled away, telling Will, "Hey, man. The other guys will think we're a couple'a fruitcakes." He could not hide his embarrassment.

But Will wasn't bothered by Farmer's rejection. He guessed he shouldn't have shown affection for another male specimen, but he did really love Farmer, like the brother he'd never had in real life.

The terrain underwent a radical change. Will and Farmer both had to discontinue their discussion and concentrate on ambulating. They were descending now, down a steep hillside, and the footing was treacherous. Will's toes were pinched in the ends of his leather shoes. It was difficult to slow the pace. It brought back memories of the hill country in Texas, where he'd gone on ten-mile hikes that were uphill in either direction—away from camp, returning to camp. Common sense, of course, dictated otherwise, but it did seem to him that the Army had a knack for defying logic. Will was certain that he'd walked more miles uphill than downhill since his inauguration into the military. And he'd also walked *one helluva long ways* if all of the miles he'd marched and hiked were tallied together. They had been, he realized after he retraced their journey so far that morning, on either a level landscape, or a gradual rise, since they'd departed from the beachhead that morning. There again, he should have suspected that what goes uphill must eventually go back down the hill. His training back in Guinea popped into mind. They had gone to a great deal of trouble teaching him to repel ropes. Why? In the event they encountered such an obstacle they had to be trained to overcome it. That's what Schuster told them. He scoffed to himself when he recalled the corporal's *in the event* part of the warning. He and Baker must've known for a fact that the odds favored their chances of repelling a rope down a cliff side before this the mission was completed.

Will's socks were squishing inside of his shoes. He thought he could hear his feet protesting with *slurp, slurp* every step of the way. But there was an upside. Roul predicted they'd encounter no Japs, and they hadn't. Well, at least he hoped they hadn't. For all he knew some scout had spotted them and was, at this very minute, summoning help from the closest Japanese garrison to intercept and kill the American intruders. However odd it might've sounded, Will actually believed that the Japs wouldn't need to fire a single cartridge. They could conquer by just sitting tight in their dry quarters, while Will and his buddies came down with pneumonia and suffered a slow, agonizing death from consumption. That, he decided, made sense, and in Will's opinion is was hardly the proper way for a soldier to die. *No glory?* he silently protested. *No medals? Just gurgle, gurgle and you're dead?*

Roul relieved Will's antagonizing strife. He brought the column to a halt and suggested they eat chow at 1500 hours. Will was hungry. He'd eaten but once since the previous night. His distressed entrails were on the mend, thanks to Farmer's brown bombers, and even better, they hadn't triggered a case of the trots like Farmer predicted they might. That let Will off the hook for ingesting some of Farmer's "para … something."

Will planted his hind end on the soggy ground, not even bothering to look for a dry spot, and ripped open his ration carton. Farmer quickly joined him and, as he fell down beside Will, asked, "Would you like to dine with me?" He giggled at himself.

"Dine?" Will ask, hanging his head in disgust. "Dine? You did say dine. By gosh, Farmer, your vocabulary is reaching new heights. You've come a long way; from *'pigging out'* to *'chowin' down'* to *'dining.'*"

Farmer grinned in response and nodded.

"Well," Will continued, "I'd love to dine with you." He turned, waved his hand as though summoning someone, then said, "Maître d', escort this gentleman to my table … and bring us a bottle of your finest champagne, I mean imported. Nothing domestic."

"Maître d'?" Farmer inquired with another giggle. "What's that?"

"It's a high-toned title for a host, dummy. The head honcho in one'a them New York dining establishments," Will explained, "if'n you know what I mean."

Farmer burst out laughing. "SEE?" he barked. "You've got me sayin' *'dine'* and I've got you sayin' *'if'n.'*"

Will saw the humor. "So you have, so I have," he agreed, then asked, after watching Farmer wolf down his meager ration of food, "Hungry?"

"Yup! Hungrier than a bear, but d'ya know what? I'd trade a week's worth of these here vittles for one big platter of mama's flapjacks and a rasher of side pork," Farmer recalled his mama's cooking.

"I'll bet you would, at that."

"Yup! And … so long as I'm wishin', I'd take a heap of scrambled eggs and … a big wad of mama's home-churned butter right on top of them griddle cakes," Farmer padded his wish list, asking Will, "Don't that just make your mouth water?"

Will grinned, telling Farmer, "Close your eyes, listen, and concentrate."

Farmer went along with his game.

"Now … Maître d', my guest wants a stack of his mama's flapjacks, smothered in his mama's home-churned butter, with a side of bacon and some scrambled eggs. And make it snappy. We cannot tarry for long. We're on our way to the front," Will drummed up a mental mirage for his friend, adding, "Now, Farmer ... just inhale that scrumptious aroma. C'mon. Breathe in, very slowly, and savor that smell."

Farmer sat there, his eyes closed, and sniffed, then smiled, admitting to Will, "That pretend stuff sorta works, huh? I can almost smell Mama's breakfast. You're all the time daydreaming, aren't you? Maybe it does have some advantages ... like takin' a guy's mind off'a the war ... but I ne'er had a hankerin' to pretend, like you do."

"Well, you oughta," Will suggested, telling his friend that "pretending can turn a crappy day into a bounty."

"Yeah, maybe. I kinda think I was daydreaming a tad back there on the trail this morning," Farmer confessed.

"You were? How so?"

"Oh, it weren't nothin' in particular."

"Well, it musta been important or you wouldn't have mentioned it," Will coaxed him, "so ... come clean, Farmer. Tell me what you were daydreaming."

"You won't laugh."

"NO! How come you always think I'm going to laugh?"

"Because you do laugh. You always say you won't and then you do."

"Well, I won't this time. Promise," Will vowed, holding his right hand aloft as though being sworn in for jury duty.

"Well, I was just thinking about Sunday School and about my cradle."

"Sunday School? Cradle?"

"Yeah ... thinking more about the cradle roll, I guess."

"Cradle roll? A rolling cradle?"

"No, silly," Farmer fired back explaining how, in his church, they kept records of births and honored the new arrivals by displaying a small paper cradle that someone had cut out of purple construction paper. Then, he explained, they hung them along the lower fringe of a much larger picture of a cradle. The child's name was printed on the small cradle. It hung on the wall in the church's vestibule, he claimed.

Farmer had Will by the short hair when it came to religious-related things, because Will never attended Sunday School. "And you're telling me," Will inquired, "that you had a little purple cradle with your name on it."

"No. Not had. Do. At least, that's what I was wondering, if my cradle was still hanging there."

"Is it that important?" Will asked, adding that he supposed they took them down at some point in time. "Maybe, now that you're in the Army and don't attend church regularly anymore, they took it down."

"No," Farmer argued. "I ain't ne'er saw one taken down in all'a my born days. And yes, it is important … to me, anyway. I know you don't believe in God, but I do, and that cradle is one of my links with God. You just ain't much on churchgoin', are you?"

That was fact, Will admitted, explaining to Farmer, "Religion around my house was a hit-or-miss proposition, mostly miss." Now that he'd encountered a pious man like Farmer his curiosity had been piqued a time or two about Sunday worship services. He almost envied Farmer his absolute faith in a god that he could not see and a utopian hereafter for which there was no guarantee. "You know," Will continued after the pause to reflect, "I did tell you that I was coming to visit you after the war and … when I do, I was wondering if you'd go to the trouble of taking me to see that church and … that cradle?"

"Trouble? You're kidding me, aren't you?" Farmer replied, boasting, "I'd be tickled pink to take you there, but you wouldn't need me to get you inside, because it's a house of God and it's there for everybody. The preacher, he calls it a 'safe haven'. But I'll go you one better than that. You come to my house on Sunday morning, like early on, and Mama'll fix you some vittles like you ain't never ate. She'll nag you 'til you clean your plate and then offer you one of her home-baked cinnamon rolls for dessert."

"You wouldn't have to worry about me cleaning my plate. I'd love to have one'a your mama's big country breakfasts right now, thank you," Will told him.

Farmer grinned, an almost childish smile of innocence as he so often did when Will embarrassed him, then hung his head and asked Will, "Is that kinda dumb of me to fret over a little purple paper cradle?"

Will reached out and patted Farmer's shoulder with his hand, reassuring him, "Farmer, if there's one thing I'm sure of in this whole fucked-up world it is that you're anything but dumb. In fact, I wouldn't be at all surprised if you're famous one day. I can see it and hear it now. You're attending an opera at the Metropolitan. There's a scream and people are shouting, 'Help!' And someone cries out, 'Is there a doctor in the house?' And you rise to your feet and modestly acknowledge you are a doctor, at which time they usher you to the main auditorium floor to tend a lovely young lady who has fainted. All eyes are on you, not the performers on stage as it should be, while you labor to save this young maiden's life, and when she opens her eyes and sees your handsome face, she reaches up and caresses you and tenderly kisses your lips. You lift her into your arms and carry her up the aisle toward the exit, to a thunderous ovation from the audience, then place her limp body into your awaiting carriage, crack the whip over the backs of the steeds in harness and take your true love to your castle on the mountaintop, where you live happily ever after."

It might've been a tad corny, but Farmer's eyes glistened. He just sat there dumbfounded for a moment, tears welling up in his eyes, staring at nothing in particular, mulling over in his mind a fairyland forecast for a country boy. "Aw-w-w-w-w-we, go on, Will," he finally moaned in his laidback manner. "You shore got a way with words."

"We'd best be moving out again," Roul shouted, which squelched their exchange. The captain suggested that the odds would change when the sun came out from behind the clouds. "The Japs," he warned, "will definitely come out to play now that the rain has stopped."

Will got to his feet and moseyed over to fall into line behind Fidel, which placed him beside Tillie for a change. After they moved out Will noticed that Tillie slipped an envelope from his breast pocket, glanced at it, then placed it back inside of the pocket. That struck Will as strange, so he asked the hillbilly, "Is that a letter from home?"

Tillie just nodded and replied with his customary "Yup."

"Not bad news, is it? You appeared upset when you glanced at it," Will remarked.

"Naw, nothin' wrong, I hope," Tillie declared, explaining he didn't actually know what the letter said.

Will was stunned. It had been several days since they'd gotten any mail, so he figured Tillie had been toting it around that long and, now that he thought about it, he did notice the envelope appeared to still be sealed. "How's come you haven't read it?" Will asked.

"Can't," Tillie replied in a remorseful tone of voice. "I can't read, Munday," he confessed.

"What?" Will exclaimed.

"Sh-h-h-h," Tillie shushed Will, imploring of him, "I don't want the other guys to know."

Will had never suspected that one of his teammates couldn't read, which prompted him to inquire, "How'd you get into the goddamn Army? I thought everyone had to be able to read."

"Naw. Mighta once't been like that, but it ain't no more. There's more guys than you think what can't read, or write. They've got a special place for them down at Fort Sam."

"Fort Sam?"

"Yup. It's down by Houston. They've got a school. It's called STU, which stands for Special Training Unit, and they teach guys like me how to read the duty roster. You know, just enough English to get by," Tillie shocked Will. He'd never heard of it.

"Well, didn't Gambler ever offer to read your letters or to help you write a letter home?" Will asked.

"Nope! No way. But it ain't necessarily his fault on account'a I never told him I couldn't read. He's a good guy, all right, but he can be a real asshole, too. He'd needle me about it night and day," Tillie rather accurately described how Gambler would've treated the news.

"So, you ain't read your letters from home. I mean, all of this time, just because you were afraid to ask Gambler to help?" Will asked.

"Naw, it ain't like that, either. This is the only letter I got. I don't know for sure who wrote it on account'a my kinfolks can't read or write. But it's got my name on the envelope bigger'n you please, so somebody wrote it by hand for them," Tillie explained with a grimace.

Will was about ready to kick himself in the ass. He was as much to blame for never getting to know Tillie as anyone. And had he realized Tillie couldn't read or write he'd have made an offer to help him long ago. He wanted to make amends, so he suggested, "I'll be glad to read the letter to you, Tillie. Anytime. Just give me the word. And I'll even write an answer to the folks back home for you." He figured he owed him that.

But Tillie begged off for the time being, saying, "Not just yet. Maybe later. Thanks, anyway, Munday. I always sorta figured you for a good egg."

Will might've been embarrassed if there'd been time, but Fidel threw his arm above his head, then sideways, in a motion to bring the entourage to a stop. "Down," he said. "Everyone down," while pushing an open palm toward the ground as a warning signal.

Will dropped to his knees, then lunged forward, breaking the fall with the butt end of his weapon. The grass was at least three feet high, so he could not see anything beyond the tip of his nose. He did recall they were about midway through a clearing in the trees when they were placed on alert, and he wondered who was close by, or if anyone was. He could hear the shuffle of someone moving through the grass and supposed someone in command was belly-crawling forward to confer with Fidel. Curiosity was killing him. He started to raise his head a tad, hoping to catch a glimpse of whatever Fidel had either heard or seen, but someone's hand came to rest on top of his helmet and pushed him face-first into the ground. "Sh-h-h-h," a voice whispered. "Keep your head down." He turned his head, facing to his right, and saw Gooch lying in the grass beside him. He was overjoyed to see him. And actually thankful that the little guy went to the trouble of keeping him from lifting his head too high. He listened carefully and, at first, heard nothing. Then a distant chatter of voices penetrated his ears. He thought that he overheard laughter mixed with idle conversation. And he just lay there rejoicing that whoever they were, they hadn't yet spotted Stopwatch violating their turf. In fact, he suspected that they had no idea they were within a few yards of an American patrol, or they'd stifle the chatter. He glanced at Gooch, asking in a whisper, "What is it? Who is it?"

"Jap patrol," Gooch replied in a hushed tone. "Very careless, huh? They suspect nothing, so we're probably okay ... unless they stumble over us."

Will was even more curious now. The Jap soldiers were making a lot of racket, jabbering among themselves, laughing, even shouting at one another. He reached out his hand and tapped Gooch on the elbow to garner his attention, then inquired, "What are they saying? You should be able to understand them."

Gooch nodded in the affirmative, advising Will, "It is soldier talk, much like we talk. They are boasting of their exploits, bragging about their women, talking about home, and about gambling, and about the war's end."

Will was momentarily awestruck. He'd never thought of them as being human beings. He had, he suddenly realized, been brainwashed to think the opposite. From the opening shot at Pearl Harbor until this very moment he'd been influenced to look upon them as barbarous demons capable of almost any gregarious atrocity. Now, Gooch raised a point to ponder. Did they, he silently asked himself, have a Gambler in their midst, or a trigger-happy Tillie, or a rice grower, which would be something akin to Farmer's rural background? Were they oftentimes homesick, and weary of the war, and did they have melancholy memories of loved ones back in Japan? It was just something else to boggle Will's already overtaxed gray matter. He yanked himself from the trance, then noticed Gooch had crawled away and was out of sight. Who else might've taken their leave, he wondered. Was there an order to pull back issued while he daydreamt?

The sound of voices neared. Will's breath caught in his throat and his hands began to sweat. That was a bad sign. Sweaty hands unnerved him. Gooch had mentioned they'd be okay unless the Japs walked right into them. From where Will lay in the grass it sounded to him like the whole patrol was about to step on his head. He pulled his Thompson up, checked the clip, made sure the safety was off, and cradled the butt plate against the ground. He was trembling, squinting his eyes upward, trying to catch the first glimpse of a Jap that might happen along his way. He had the edge. He would kill him without giving it a second thought. He raised the muzzle of the weapon slightly up, then held his breath. He waited. He continued to wait. He exhaled, then heaved a sigh of relief when he detected the voices at a distance once again. They'd obviously passed him by. They had, in fact, bypassed everyone. It seemed to Will that the odds defied such a dream, but it must've occurred.

Gooch came belly-crawling back to where Will was stretched out in the meadow. He smiled. "They missed," he said in a soft tone, then advised Will, "Hold your position for a few minutes until we get the word to proceed."

Will felt good about himself. His taut nerves unwound and his breathing returned to normal. The sound of voices was fading away, and he suspected the Jap patrol had vanished back into the hinterland. He also noticed that the weather had made a drastic change. Except for a few lingering raindrops dangling from the leaves, things were beginning to dry out. Being wet to the skin was once more his major crisis to deal with. The sun was trying to peek through the cloud cover, although he figured it was too late in the day to help dry him out. Fidel passed the word to move out again, and they all took to their feet and gave the surrounding area a once-over, trying to reassure themselves that the Japs were, indeed, out of the picture.

When they left the clearing and re-entered the jungle the sun was ablaze. Its powerful rays penetrated the tree cover enough to vaporize the water standing in puddles along the trail. The atmosphere evolved into a hothouse of sorts, making the air muggy and difficult to inhale. And to top things off, they were beginning to negotiate a gradual rise in the terrain, which seemed to become steeper with each step. The ground did level off, and it looked like they were atop of a huge plateau. Will stopped, then froze in his tracks. He listened. The sound of churning water filtered into his ears. It was, he thought, somewhere off in the distance, but a force to be reckoned with. That was about the time that Farmer finally overtook Will and slowed his cadence to walk beside him. He noticed Will was edgy and asked, "What's wrong?"

"Do you hear it?" Will inquired.

"You mean that sound of water running?" Farmer asked. "Yeah. I hear it. Sounds like a waterfall, or something like that."

Baker came from the rear, rushing past Will and Farmer, casually mentioning as he passed by, "Prepare yourself, Munday. We've got some rough going on the menu."

"Oh, God," Will moaned. "Oh, God. Not that."

"What?" Farmer quizzed him.

"It's one'a those hairy cliff-side deals, you know, like that one back in Guinea when we had to repel the ropes," Will complained.

"What makes you think so?"

"Did you hear Baker?"

"Yeah. I heard him. He said to prepare yourself."

"Why else would he say that? He knows I suffer with acrophobia. I can see it now. It's a big, deep crevice with a menacing waterfall."

"Hold on, Will. Relax. Don't fret over something we haven't yet seen. Heck, I'll bet it's not scary at all when we finally get there."

"Prepare? For something that isn't frightening? Farmer, you're my best friend, but don't try to con me. There is no such thing as a cliff, or a waterfall, or a combination of the two that can't be bad news," Will scolded him, serving notice that he wasn't going. "This is it. I'm drawing a line in the sand," he shouted, shaking a defiant fist in the air. "A man's gotta take a stand sooner or later. If I don't take one sooner, later might be too late, because I'll be lying at the foot of some cliff deader'n a doornail. This is as far as Private Will F. Munday's going. The war's over."

"Just like that?" Farmer asked with a bewildered expression of surprise before he broke out laughing.

"Just like that!" Will reiterated.

Chapter Seventeen

Baker's dozen finally partook a laidback reunion for the first time since they'd embarked on the journey that morning. Every man was visible to the eyes. Will was happy to see they were all fit as a fiddle. Miguel appeared to be calling the shots now that they'd probed so far inland. On his signal, Roul lined his men up in single file, then instructed them to follow Miguel. He led them to the jungle's edge; a very abrupt edge that ended just a few feet from a sheer precipice. Miguel veered to his right, then proceeded out onto a ledge overlooking a deep ravine. Will forced himself to look. The aperture was, perhaps, twenty-five yards across and, as best he could determine from where he stood, the only option for circumventing the chasm would require all of them to grope their way along a narrow ledge that skirted its rim. He knew the waterfall must be in close proximity to his present locale. He really needed to know what lay ahead, even though he dreaded the truth. He inched forward, squeezing past Gambler, and craned his neck. His suspicions were right. He could see but a portion of the waterfall but enough to understand that the gushing water spilling over its brim was cascading down between the walls of the gorge with a powerful thrust. However, that didn't settle his worries over what ensued the nerve-shattering trek to the waterfall. Was there a secret passageway that would take them across the ravine? It was just logical he'd be forced to cross over the ravine at some point. That was the scary part. So, he had a desperate need to satisfy his curiosity, even though common sense warned him against it, and he ventured another step or two ahead, then abruptly froze in his tracks. The tableau that unfolded in front of him was a worst-case scenario. The trail wound along the cliff for a hundred yards, or so, then vanished. But he could see something that appeared to be a cavern behind the streaming deluge of water and that, he prophesized, led to a passageway underneath the falls. Across the crevice he saw a barren shelf that might've been a trailhead leading into the jungle. That would be, he figured, the spot where they made their exit from the subterranean cave. Will was fit to be tied. He knew his limitations and they didn't include inching his way along a ledge barely three feet wide, then jeopardizing his welfare by creeping through a life-threatening maze that completely terrified him.

Will did get a reprieve in the form of a postponement of the inevitable. It was welcomed news to Will's ears just the same. Miguel suggested, "Best we bivouac here tonight and make the crossing just after sunup. The Japs will be sleeping, and this view is accessible for a great distance. We could be easily spotted this time of day."

Will, unlike some of his counterparts, was fighting a war on several fronts. While the others were focusing their attention on the Japs, he was wrestling with ledges, and waterfalls, and phobias as well.

Miguel's decision was only a stay of execution for Will. His knees trembled, the palms of his hands sweated profusely, and he was short of breath. He guessed he was suffering a panic attack but just couldn't help himself. Nothing, except the time frame, had changed. With the morrow's dawn he realized he'd be called upon to make another supreme sacrifice; to pussyfoot his way along a ledge that might tempt him to jump. He'd felt that sensation before, an urge to just leap out and drop. Now, he wished they'd moved on. If they had, he would either have made it safely across the ravine or be lying dead on the canyon's floor. Which way didn't matter that much to Will at the present time.

Captain Roul instructed them to "Make camp. Pitch your shelter halves for cover and let's keep the noise down to a whisper. We'll have chow shortly before turning in for the night." He beckoned to Baker and after getting his attention informed him, "I want one man from each squad on sentry duty all night. They can rotate so that everyone gets some sleep. I intend to hold a critique tonight after chow with everyone present. I'll ask Miguel to have his men keep the watch during that meeting." He glanced from man to man, then asked, "Any questions?" There were none.

Will withdrew back into the thicket, plunked his posterior down onto the ground, wiggled free of his backpack, then leaned his still tender backside against a tree trunk. Farmer wasn't long in joining him. He sensed Will's distress and wanted to console him. "Will," he offered his advice, "there ain't no use in fretting over something yet to come. Come morning, I'll be right there at your side when we cross over. I won't let anything happen to you."

Will weighed Farmer's thoughtful proposal carefully. He realized the country boy meant well, but he also realized that Farmer could not begin to comprehend his anguish. He just sat there, not bothering to respond to Farmer's comments. Farmer, however, was not the type to be pushed aside so easily. He asked Will, "Did I ever tell you about me and my uncle? About the time he left me dangling from a bough of a tree?"

Will finally broke his silence. "No," he mournfully replied, "not that I recall."

"Well, you see, I had this uncle who was a real piss-cutter. He was my dad's kid brother and he used to come up for the summer to help out with the planting and cultivating and that sorta stuff. He was also an ornery cuss. He come near to drivin' my mama nuts with his pranks. I wasn't very big but I do remember this happening and it scared the peewadden outta me. We had this here tar swing, see—"

Will cut him short at that point and asked, "Tar swing? What's a tar swing?"

"A tar swing, Will. Don't tell me you ain't never saw a tar swing."

"No. Don't recollect seeing one. What's it like?"

"I can't believe that. Almost every kid in the country's had a tar swing at one time or another. I just don't know what to think about you city boys. I can't believe they don't have tar swings in town. It's a tar. Just a plain, old, worn-out rubber tar. They loop a rope around one side of it, then tie the rope up around a high tree limb, and let the tar just dangle about two feet off'a the ground."

"Yeah ... but I still don't know what a tar is."

"It's a tar, Will. They're on every car; four of them and sometimes a spare tar," Farmer expatiated.

Will began to laugh. He punched Farmer on the upper arm with his fist, informing him, "You're going to be the death of me, yet, the way you decimate the English language."

"Decimate?"

"Forget it. Scratch that. I didn't say it. So, you had a tire swing."

"Yeah. That's what I've been telling you for five minutes."

"Okay. Go on with your story."

"Okay. Well, this here uncle of mine he ties a second rope on the tar, then he tells me to climb in. I did. And then he says he's going to crawl up the tree, hoist me way up there and cut me loose so's I can REALLY sail through the air like a man on the flying trapeze."

"Yeah? So what happened?" Will asked with chuckle.

"He did it, just like he said. Up the tree he shinnies and then he hoists me up and then he ties the loose end of the rope to a limb. Yep. And he left me hanging up there scared half to death. What d'ya suppose he did, then? Shinnied back down the tree trunk and hightails it outta there," Farmer recalled.

"No kidding. What did you do?"

"Nothing. I just hung up there yellin' my head off, that's what."

"You must've done something to get down. You're here, not still tied up in that tree."

"Well, my screamin' brought Mama runnin' and she started screaming just as loud as I was, 'ceptin' she was givin' my uncle a tongue-lashing. But she scampered up that tree, just like my uncle did, and untied the rope so's she could lower me back down to the ground," Farmer explained.

Will wasn't quite sure why Farmer shared the experience with him, but he halfway suspected it was a tool to calm the anxiety that was numbing his brain. Farmer had once been afraid when he was up high, so it was all right for Will to be scared. It didn't matter, anyway, because Roul broke up their confab.

The captain passed out the rations himself, scooting around from man to man, offering a word or two of encouragement. He informed them he was going to critique them and he didn't think it would hurt to "munch some lunch" while he was lecturing. He invited them to form a circle around him when he finally settled down onto his haunches, then carefully spread a large paper map out on the ground. When he was sure he had everyone's attention he pointed his finger at a spot on the diagram and stated, "We are here." He pointed toward the waterfall and pinpointed its location on the map, telling them, "We'll cross over that gorge first thing in the morning and regroup on the other side. At that time we will be splitting our force into separate units for the final leg of our journey."

Will, as was his custom, happened to be visually trolling the group, in place of paying attention to the lecture, when Roul revealed the plan to break up Stopwatch into smaller groups. He could sense that Baker was as shocked over the news as were all of the men. In fact, he even inquired of Roul, in an apparent surprised tone of voice, "You're splitting the force, sir?"

That proved Will's suspicions. Baker hadn't known prior to now. That, in turn, puzzled Will. He could understand why a private in the rear rank, such as he, wouldn't be told in advance, but he'd thought all along that Roul and Baker had a tight relationship. The captain, however, did have a knack for reading faces, and he perceived from the shocked expressions on everyone's kisser that a more thorough explanation was in order. "Well, Sergeant, there are times when secrecy overwhelms military protocol. GHQ made this decision days ago, but I was ordered to keep it under my hat until the proper time. This is that time. Until now, the less everyone knew, the better, because should anyone of you have been captured the enemy would know as much as we. They do have methods for prying information from the hardiest of men. So, taking a lesson from Gambler," he rambled on, pointing a finger at the cardsharp who was standing to Will's left side, "I'm putting my cards face up on the table."

The captain drew a laugh from his parallelism, Gambler chuckling the loudest. But Roul wasn't quite through using Baker squad's huckster for a tool. "It's time," he continued after the revelry died down, "to play the hand that Dame Fate dealt us. It's a favorable fistful. We might be facing the greatest odds an army unit ever encountered; perhaps thousands of Japs to each one of us. But by splitting our force and by advancing over alternate routes we stack the odds in our favor. In a scenario such as we are committed being little is better than being big. Three small groups might pull this off. It is apparent, after what we discovered today, that the Japs have numerous patrols prowling the countryside. Miguel tells me that they make regular visits to most every town and village. After we cross the ravine in the morning we'll split into three groups, maintaining the same squads we presently have. Corporal Schuster will be in command of Able squad. Sergeant Baker will be in charge of Baker squad and I will oversee Charlie squad. Now I want you all to listen up and pay attention to everything I say and do." He paused and glanced around, making sure he had everyone's eye, then pointed to the map again and, moving his pointer finger across the paper surface, said, "Able squad will take the left flank, following this approximate route to our point of bivouac." Sliding his hand to the right, he called their attention to a second pathway through the jungle, advising them, "Baker squad will take this center approach," and, jerking his hand a bit further to his right, he added, "and Charlie will take the right flank by following this route to our rendezvous." Pausing again, he lowered his head and peered at each and every man through the corner of one eye, then slammed his fist down on the map and matter-of-factly stated, "This is our objective. We will meet there tomorrow night and carry out our assignment. I recommend you try to get a good night's rest. It may be the last sleep you get until we have accomplished our mission and have regrouped and made our escape. Yes, this is a bold probe. Our fate will be in our own hands after we have destroyed the enemy communications compound." Having warned them that the future might be sketchy, he said, "I'll see you all at sunup."

The mood among the men was far from festive. Roul had obviously struck a nerve, because he'd no more than vanished into the night than they broke up into squads and shared a chin fest quite different from what they'd done in the past. Will sat down, crossed his feet in front of him, pulled out his pack of cigarettes and lit up a smoke. It would be the final fag until morning. This bull session hatched the first and only down-to-earth communion the foursome had shared. Gambler left his deck of cards tucked inside of his pocket and there wasn't the customary exchange of barbs that so often rankled one another. A strange mood settled across the campground like a shroud across a graveyard. They needed this opportunity to square things. Except for Farmer, they had grappled like children all too often over petty differences, and this get-together had all of the earmarks of a sequel to the gut-wrenching introduction session Roul had hosted the first night back in Guinea. They talked about memories of home and recollections of their childhood. They spoke of loved ones they wished they could see one more time before jumping off on their mission come morning. They pondered the possibility of death and asked one another if they were afraid and went so far as to isolate what kind of death each one of them feared the most. Gambler told them he feared drowning more than anything else, while Tillie harbored a dreadful fear of fire. Farmer suggested, "I can't think of any pleasurable way to die," but informed them, "I put my faith in God. He will, through His profound power, guide me safely through this battle. If, by chance, I do not survive, then I believe that was part of His divine plan."

Up to then Will had said little and when they asked him about his fears he said, "I envy you, Farmer. Your faith. I am not satisfied there is a God—I mean a God such as most people worship. Somehow, I've always found it difficult to believe that there is a mysterious deity sitting up yonder on cloud nine, keeping a score card on my runs, hits and errors in life." That closed the door to any further reference about religion in the exchange.

They did continue to chat, though. The subject came around to grub. They all missed home cooking, and Will recalled, "Every Thursday afternoon when I came home from school and walked into the house the aroma of fresh-baked bread teased my nostrils. I'd dart into the kitchen for a glimpse of my mama's cinnamon rolls. Yeah. Piping hot cinnamon rolls, just outta the oven. Damn...." he concluded, his eyes wet with tears.

Tillie yearned to go coon hunting again. He told of how he'd turn the dogs loose and then he'd "scamper down through the hollow like a striped-assed ape" to keep up but never could. And then, the mutts'd begin to bay and he'd know they'd tree'd a coon. It was a thrill beyond explanation. "You'd hav'ta go coon huntin' to grasp it," he insisted.

Farmer said that he missed so many things he'd taken for granted all of his life that he couldn't settle on one certain memory, but he asked them, "Did you ever just stand outside after sundown, when the daylight is fast fading, and listen to the lonesome call of a whippoorwill from off in the distance? I used to do that nearly every evening and never thought about it. Now, I find myself thinking about many things, like old Sport, my dog, barkin' in the cows, come milkin' time every night. And I don't know about you guys, but I get to wonderin' sometimes what I'm doing way over here, when my heart is way back there. I've gotta admit it. I'm a homesick son of a gun."

Gambler didn't bare his soul. He was a guarded individual in that respect. Admitting he was human would've been, Will suspected, a sign of weakness. He tried to joke about dying, but the others all knew it was just talk. He said, "The only fitting way for a REAL man to die is … to be shot by a jealous husband on his eighty-first birthday." That pretty well ended the session. They all laughed out of courtesy, then pitched their bedrolls out on the ground, ignoring Roul's suggestion to pitch tents with their shelter halves. Upon hitting the sack, Farmer offered a final observation. "That was kinda fun, guys, just shootin' the bull without a lot of bickering. Thanks. I needed that. See you all in the morning."

Will rolled over onto one side, his back turned to the others, and stared off into the darkness. He tried to pull up a vision of MaryLou without success. He was too keyed up to concentrate, he guessed. He was dog tired, but doubted he would sleep well, being depressed as he was about what lay in store come morning. He remembered that way back in the beginning Roul had warned them that they'd see many things in the coming days; things they'd take with them to the grave. He figured the pending mission fell in that category. He dwelt on Farmer for a few minutes, or rather, more about Farmer's God than Farmer himself. He couldn't help but wonder if that Creator actually knew what Farmer was facing just a few hours away and, if so, could He actually intervene on Farmer's behalf and change the outcome? Did Farmer's God have a hand in Farmer's premonition; the loaf of bread and the jug of wine? Will knew little about religious rites but had heard about communion. Wasn't bread and wine the sacramental offering, supplanting Christ's flesh and blood?

Will finally fell asleep, concluding that war was, indeed, hell, but the waiting was proving to be the harshest of the two options. The possibility of Will crossing the threshold into the hereafter was definitely looming on the horizon. He knew this. He was also exhausted. He would fall asleep in spite of the threat, because he'd reached a point where he really could've cared less. Will had his priorities. The Sandman had his. He would sleep, ignoring any of the consequences that might be a result of lowering his guard.

Chapter Eighteen

Sunrise the following morning was spectacular but all too soon gave way to a bank of seething clouds—dreary ground-level clouds that smothered the terrain like heavy fog. Captain Roul, unlike Will, rejoiced. The weather, he said, must be divine providence and he interpreted it as an omen; a good omen. But to Will the clouds were a prelude to misery. He had hoped, this possibly being his final day on earth, for something pleasant in the way of weather. His thoughts throughout the night had rankled him. He tossed and turned, wrestling with morbid apparitions of death. He wished that Farmer could snap his finger and appeal for protection from this all-powerful God; perhaps a miracle such as the Scriptures boast, like the parting of the Red Sea. Or, if nothing else, a day blessed with sunshine. But he suspected that the captain had already petitioned his God to render nasty weather, and it was becoming increasingly obvious to a doubter like Will that Roul did stand in better with his God than Will did with Farmer's God.

The atmosphere felt as though it had been electrically charged; not a climatic static, but a spark of uneasiness that penetrated each and every man to the core. Will's nerves were taut, stretched almost beyond their limits, much like the strings on a fiddle. He blamed his uneasiness on the long, restive night of catnaps alternating with weird dreams. In one such fantasy he'd seen MaryLou standing in front of an altar with another man. His protests went unheeded when he struggled to intervene. It was as though an invisible barrier separated him from the ritual. He awakened with a shudder, he recalled, only to doze off again to see his aging mother standing on the dilapidated porch of his house, one hand grasping an upright roof support, the other holding a yellow-colored envelope that could have but one meaning; Will's supreme sacrifice. Tears streamed down her wrinkled cheeks. She was crying out, "WILL. Come home, Will. Come to Mother, Will." He sat straight up and shook off the image. He was awake. There were no more dreams, because he barely slept the rest of the night. He tossed and turned until he was roused by Baker's voice, leaving the dreadful ordeal in its own wake. One of his first thoughts was to consult with Farmer about his dreams, but he opted to say nothing. He could hardly expect any sympathy from his friend, who, just hours earlier, had seen a jug of wine and a loaf of bread that forecast rough weather ahead. Farmer, he remembered, diagnosed his own dream's meaning as an ominous portent. Will didn't see the connection. He doubted Farmer would interpret the illusion of his mom and the cablegram as a negative vibe.

Baker called everyone to formation. Will suspected this might be the last formal roll call until after this dastardly deed was done. He doubted they'd stand another until after they reassembed at the rendezvous point. After Baker put them "at ease," he glanced around at the others, taking special note of the Filipinos. They were not as subdued as their American fellow travelers. They were, in fact, quite verbal, almost ecstatic over making the final leg of the journey. Will guessed their exuberance was understandable, because he could hardly comprehend what their lives had been like under the Japanese regime. Fidel seemed unusually spirited. He was dancing around like a child who needed to urinate, and he wore a cocky expression on his face. The new Thompson he'd been issued was slung across one shoulder, and he was juggling three hand-grenades like a circus performer, ignoring the lethal consequences of a miscue. Fidel, like the other Filipinos, had evidently bided their time awaiting this occasion. It was, Will imagined, payback time, and they acted more like they were headed for the annual turkey shoot than a deadly mission to kill Japanese. It was obviously a premature celebration of a gala event that had been a long time coming.

Roul was back in true form, emblazoned with a suave touch of class so unbecoming of a field grade officer. He paced to and fro, walking between the ranks, individually wishing each of his charges, "Good luck," as he passed. Then, he came to the front of the formation and reminded them for the umpteenth time of the importance of perfection in their duties. "You, gentlemen," he said, "have the distinction of being chosen as bearers of glad tidings. You are the vanguard of this invasion to free the Filipinos from the yoke of tyranny they've toted for three long years, not to forget you are also keeping General MacArthur's vow that he would return." Will's suspicions that they were actually pawns, not conquering heroes, came back to mind after listening a final time to Roul's rehearsed dissertation. It was questionable in his way of thinking to assign the dirty work to the peons. MacArthur, he felt, had made the vow; he should keep his rendezvous with destiny, not send youngsters from a fatherland that actually had no stake in the outcome of the struggle. The captain, however, didn't let Will dwell on his thoughts. When he shouted, "Move 'em out," Will reverted to the present tense and, after watching Roul pivot on his toe, spin sideways, then strut away, fell into a column behind him. Will could boast, he thought, something few soldiers could. It was his good fortune to serve under such a classy commanding officer.

Will swiveled his head back and forth to catch a final glimpse of the other guys who would all too soon go their way. It was a sad occasion. He caught Williams with a woebegone expression, slogging along as though he really didn't care if he went or stayed. The *Dear John* had inflicted a wound to Williams' heart that only time could mend, and there wasn't much time left for the cure. He didn't think the preacher cared one way or the other what happened when they assaulted the Japanese compound. He suspected he might even sacrifice himself. The official record would list his death as "killed in action," while down inside those who knew him feared he would expose himself to end it all. That would be suicide. In Will's estimation Williams deserved something better. This God he spoke of, probably the same God that Farmer worshipped, was said to be a forgiving deity. Could He not alter the outcome? This man who once served Him as an ordained minister of faith, the same man who had sinned and atoned, and was then defrocked, needed his God's intervention more than anyone else in the world. Obviously, it wasn't forthcoming. Williams was about to die to liberate a speck of dirt in the middle of the high seas. That speck of dirt was also one of Will's concerns. He couldn't help but question how such a small, innocent landscape in the middle of nowhere could qualify as a strategic region. It was only a jungle, still men were pledged to die defending it, or while trying to occupy it. Was it possible that he was caught in a crossfire, so to speak; Williams, a victim of his own lust being punished, dragging Will along out of chance? He settled for that version and turned his attention on Barrentos. The Mexican lad was clowning with Slycord and Foreman as they trudged along. He didn't appear to be the least bit concerned over his fate. He was, in fact, inadvertently aping the Filipinos, acting as though he was about to hit the big casino. Will halfway figured Barrentos relished the very thought of killing Japs. Like the Filipinos, he did have an axe to grind; his brother who died at Pearl Harbor. Vengeance was theirs to seek.

Will also noticed that Gooch was walking side by side with Miguel and that the pair were having a discussion of some kind. Roul pulled back from the point and engaged both Gooch and Miguel in a confab. He hoped it wasn't another change in strategy, but Gooch soon hustled ahead and took the point, relieving the captain of his job, and nothing came of it. That was a positive reward for Will. With so many things going on, Will had momentarily forgotten what lay ahead. His thoughts were on his comrades, and he continued to probe their identities. O'Hare caught his attention when he shouted to Roul as he trotted past, "Captain, sir. Question?"

Roul broke stride and fell into step beside O'Hare, acknowledging his interruption with "Yes? Go ahead."

"Begging the captain's pardon, but I want to lodge a complaint," O'Hare exclaimed.

Roul was obviously taken aback by O'Hare's interruption. "Lodge a complaint?" he asked. "Whatever for?"

"Your recent amnesty, sir."

"Amnesty?"

"Yes, sir. You rescinded your customary routine that required a daily shave, sir."

"Yes. I did."

"Well, sir, as you can see the other guys have a three or four day growth of whiskers. And I still look well groomed."

"Yes."

"Well, sir. My routine wasn't affected. I still only shave a time or two a week, while they have been pardoned from shaving on a regular basis, so I was wondering if that isn't discriminatory," O'Hare objected.

Roul grinned, then broke out laughing. He suspected O'Hare was pulling his leg. "I guess," he responded, "you have a valid point. Consider yourself eligible for a three-day pass as a reward."

"Pass? To where?"

"Where would you like to go?"

"Home."

"Impossible. It can't be done in three days."

"So?"

"You'll get that pass for three days R&R after we've accomplished our mission. You have my word on that."

"Thank you, sir," O'Hare obliged him. He was pleased that his peach fuzz beard finally got a deserving recognition.

Everyone laughed, but their festive mood was quickly stifled when Baker reminded them, "Quiet in the ranks. Remember where you're at."

Will shifted his observation toward Gambler. The card player was a tough case to diagnose. At the moment he appeared to be on edge, which was a departure from his customary "whatever" demeanor. But everyone was edgy. It went with the territory. Will knew what a difficult taskmaster anxiety could be. He figured Gambler was reminiscing about another one of his whore-hopping adventures back in Reno, which gave him cause to chuckle.

Farmer, overhearing Will's laugh, inquired, "What's so funny? You gonna let me in on it? I could use a laugh right now."

"Oh, it's really nothing," Will sidestepped the question. "Just amused, that's all." He didn't want to get into a chin fest with Farmer while he was picking through the bone pile of thoughts concerning his comrades. And that brought him to his analysis of Farmer. He wondered what the country boy would be doing now if he was back home. Knowing so little about the logistics of farming, he could only base his observation on things Farmer had told him. But he could visualize the lanky kid stumbling along behind a horse-drawn plow. Or he might be milking cows. Or slopping hogs. Will had lost track of his mental calendar. He really didn't know what day of the week it was. It could've been, for all he knew, Sunday. And if it was, Farmer might be sitting in church this very minute. Maybe he would be standing in the vestibule of the building, staring at the little purple paper cradle cutout that bore his name. He guessed it really didn't matter. A man who couldn't even keep track of what day it was could hardly be qualified to dissect the personality traits of anyone else. Now that he'd succumbed to being trapped in a time warp by not knowing the day of the week, his thoughts ricocheted from analyzing his friends to that of understanding himself. Somehow, knowing what day it was seemed important. He did know what day of the month it was, however, but only because Roul had told them the previous day that it was October 18th and that tomorrow would be the 19th, which the captain had pointed out would have some significance regarding the war's outcome. He took a mental pause, then, and asked himself, "Was it yesterday Roul said that? It seems like it was yesterday. I could be wrong, though, then today wouldn't be the 19th. Oh, hell. The year is nineteen-hundred-forty-four. I'm sure of that."

"Whatcha jabbering about now, Will?" Farmer asked.

Again, he dodged the question, telling Farmer, "I was just thinking out loud." But he knew Farmer wouldn't accept a half-assed explanation a second time, so he added, "I was thinking about Gambler in the buff, a doorknob in one hand, his trousers wrapped around his ankles, trying to outrun that irate husband back in Reno." He hated himself for lying to Farmer, but it was an easy way out.

"Yeah," Farmer agreed with a chuckle of his own. "That would be a sight to see, wouldn't it?"

Will might've daydreamt his way clear across the island had Roul not shouted, "Okay, Sergeant. Here's where the fun begins."

Staring straight ahead, having been oblivious of where he was during his trance, he discovered he was standing some six feet from the sheer drop-off where the trail abruptly evolved from a pleasant passageway through the trees into the frightful ledge he'd dreaded all through the preceding night. A cold chill darted up his spine and settled in the nape of his neck. Once again his hands were sweating profusely. The sound of water smashing against the rocks on the crater's floor was the proverbial straw that broke the camel's back. Will was almost paralyzed with fear. He inched ahead, forcing his feet to scoot along at a snail's pace.

And then the worst possibility arose. The voice coming from behind him said, "Okay, Munday. You going to stand there all fucking day holding up the parade?" It was Gambler, nudging Will in the backside with his finger, urging him, "Move out, chicken liver."

"Are you getting nervous in the service, Gambler," Will retorted, trying to keep his poise. He had a hunch that Gambler deliberately worked his way up in line to get behind him, just so he could be a pain in the ass. Gambler did thrive on such things. But Gambler was right when he said Will was holding-up the parade. Farmer, who was immediately in front of Will to begin with, was now at least ten yards ahead, leaving a gap in the column. He had paused to let Will catch up. Baker, however, anticipated the problem and worked his way from the rear of the column to a point just behind Gambler and as he approached he reached a hand out and shoved Gambler aside, saying, "Coming through." Will was so rattled by then, torn between his acrophobia and Gambler's harassment, that he had already started to scoot out onto the ledge and work his way toward Farmer. Baker was the incentive he needed to carry on, because he'd already sensed an urge to leap off of the cliff and end his misery.

When he felt Baker's hand grasp his upper arm and heard the sergeant's words of encouragement, his entire demeanor changed. "Munday? How's it going?" Baker asked, holding fast to Will's arm, lest he do decide to take the plunge.

"Im'a ... I'm ... okay, now, Sergeant," he declared in a less than convincing tone of voice.

"Sure you are!" Baker patronized him. "It's kinda spooky. But remember, Munday, you pulled it off back in Guinea. Remember? You repelled that cliff, when you thought you couldn't."

That had been one of those how-could-I-ever-forget assignments, but Will did recall that it was Baker who pulled his fat out of the fire that day, and it pleased him no end to see him standing tall again to talk him through this challenge.

Gambler was impatient. He couldn't control the urge to badger Will again. "C'mon, Munday. What the hell's the matter? Teacher gotta hold your hand?"

Baker didn't give Will an opportunity to respond. "AT EASE, GAMBLER," Baker barked. "We both know what's coming off here, and you don't help your comrade by needling him. He has a problem with heights, as you well know. So, shut up!"

Farmer started to return along the ledge and, as he'd promised Will he'd do, give him his support, but Baker motioned him to continue on his way, then said to Will, "Let's walk while we talk. Okay? You've got a girlfriend back home, huh? MaryLou?"

Will was surprised he knew and asked, "How'd you find that out?"

"Your mail, soldier. Your mail. Remember, your mail is censored," Baker reminded him that one of his superiors had to read and censor every homebound letter to cut out slips of the lip that might aid and abet the enemy.

"Yes, I do. MaryLou. Right," Will admitted.

"Keep moving, slowly. I've got a grip on you. I'd bet a month's pay that if MaryLou was standing right over there," he said to encourage Will, pointing across the ravine at the rock ledge near the waterfall, "you wouldn't have any trouble at all getting over there. Huh? Squint. Focus on the spot. Can you see her?"

Baker continued to urge Will along. When they reached the halfway point, Farmer had already gotten to the waterfall and had hesitated to duck underneath and out of sight. "Stand by there, Farmer," Baker shouted to him. "Wait for us. We'll pass under the falls together."

Farmer grinned from ear to ear. He was delighted Baker was going to let him be a part of this.

"By God, Munday, I'd swear there's two ladies over there. Who is the other one? She older, graying hair, kinda hunched over," Baker continued, inventing imaginary visions to keep Will moving.

"Oh, that would be my mother," Will replied in a more confident tone of voice.

"They're waiting for us," Baker suggested, "so we shouldn't tarry too long. Look, we're almost there. Farmer's waiting on us, too."

Baker paused, gently turned loose his grip on Will's arm, and turned his head to check on Gambler's progress. "Everything okay, Gambler?" he asked.

"Yes, sir. It is now," Gambler replied with a strange expression on his face. He smiled then, and threw Baker a curt hand salute. It was a compliment, one soldier to another, for a job well done. The event had served a twofold purpose; helping Will to master his own destiny while changing Gambler's outlook about other people with other problems.

Bowed by a surge of courage he never thought he had, Will stepped off the remaining distance to where Farmer was standing, Baker just a yard or two behind. Farmer was first to duck under the overhanging outcropping and enter the cavern that nature had carved out from underneath the falls. Will scampered in behind him, then glanced around at the underground aperture; a huge cave-like depression of moss-coated rocks forming a precarious bridge to the opposite side.

"It's greasy," Farmer warned Will. "Take care. Don't slip."

Farmer was moving along nicely. But he was the outdoor type of adventurer who actually enjoyed the challenge. Will, on the other hand, was quite timid about such a venture. That might've accounted for the fact that he lost his hold when his shoe slipped off of a huge boulder he'd selected to use as a toehold for boosting himself up and over the rock. He began to slide down the precipice into the roiling water below. He screamed. Farmer whirled around and, seeing Will gradually vanishing from view, threw himself prone and reached his long, lanky arm over the side just in time to catch hold of Will's fatigue jacket. Will was screaming and kicking while Farmer grunted and groaned to maintain his hold, but he knew he couldn't hold Will indefinitely.

Baker was the factor who could change the outcome. When he reached the point about midway through the cavern where Farmer was stretched to his limits trying to hold Will, he rolled sideways to the edge and reached out to take hold of Will's jacket too. "Okay," he yelled down to Will, "We've got you. Don't panic. Farmer, on the count of three, let's heave ho and pull him back over the brim."

Farmer was frantic. His eyes glistened and his teeth were grinding on one another. He nodded, then told Baker, "Better start counting. I can't hold on much longer. I just can't."

Will was floundering around like a fish on a lure, unable to do anything to help. Baker began to count, "One ... two ... three," then added, "Heave ho," and the pair began to gradually hoist Will up enough to pull his arms onto the rock facing where he could get a fingertip grip on a crevice. "Hold tight. We've got to make some adjustments. We'll have you back up here in a jiffy," Baker vowed.

Gambler came into view, and when he saw what was happening, he crawled in between Baker and Farmer and reached both hands out and filled his clenched fists with the fabric of Will's jacket, trying to keep him from sliding back over the edge, then told Baker, "Okay. I've got him. Make your move. Let's get him outta there."

And they did; pulled him right up onto the huge boulder, rolled his body behind theirs, and they all sprawled out in the prone to catch their breaths.

"Ga-a-a-a-a-wddamn," Will finally yelped, confessing, "I thought I was a goner." He turned and stared at his rescuers, taking note that Gambler was in the trio. "I owe you guys," he said in a trembling voice. "I'm beholden to all three of you."

"Yeah," Baker responded, as much as to say, 'you owe us nothing,' then informed them all, "Break's over. Let's go. Move out, Farmer. Take the point."

The last few yards were a breeze for conditioned solders such as these. They had proved themselves to one another. When they finally crawled out onto the ledge and slinked back into the edge of the trees, Will felt compelled to thank all of them again, but Farmer rejected his praise, telling Will, "You'd have done the same for us, so don't go embarrassing me like that."

Baker did have a few words to offer, though. He stuck his hand out and took Will's hand in his, saying, "Great job, soldier. I think I owe you an apology. I once said I didn't think you had the moxie to be a soldier."

Will nodded. He was back in control, after having the wits half-scared out of him. Now, it was he who was embarrassed, but not so much that he couldn't correct Baker. "It was backbone, sir, not moxie, if I recall correctly," Will informed him.

"It might've been, at that," Baker assented, "but whatever I said, I was wrong. You just had some growing up to do, young man, but I think down inside you were made of the right stuff all along."

The sergeant pivoted on his toe and whirled around, calling his squad to muster. "Over here, Baker squad," he said, pointing at a small clearing just inside of the forest's outer fringe. Schuster and Roul assembled their men, too, and when they were all gathered in one spot Roul cautioned them, "Exercise extreme caution on your trek, today. I will see all of you at our point of rendezvous tonight. This is the day, the hour, the moment we've been training for. Good luck."

Having given his final pep talk, Roul waved his hand, signaling them to move out, and Baker led his detachment along a well-beaten pathway through the jungle after he had designated Fidel as the point man. His only orders were, "Keep a visual on each other. I don't want anyone straying, because I haven't got time to play hide-and-seek to locate you. We're on a tight schedule if we intend to keep our appointment tonight."

They hadn't covered very much ground when Will realized they were descending a grade. He couldn't tell it by looking, because the jungle was a maze of tangled undergrowth with an umbrella of towering trees sheltering it. But his toes kept him informed. They were bunching up again, pressing against the toes of his shoes. He was actually glad they were going downhill, instead of climbing, because the hardware he was toting was dealing him fits. His backpack straps cut a deep furrow into his shoulders. The pain was almost unbearable, but something he'd learned to live with over a period of time.

A short time later Fidel appeared a few yards ahead on the trail. He held his open palm facing Baker and his men, a signal intended to stop the procession. "What's up?" Gambler asked.

"Sh-h-h-h," Fidel hissed through puckered lips. He pointed his finger toward the ground at a spot just ahead, then walked on his tiptoes, setting an example of what he wanted them to do. Will cautiously crept ahead, holding his weapon at high port, craning his neck to catch a glimpse of what Fidel had found that he considered to be a threat. When Fidel again raised his hand, signaling everyone to hold their position, Will had already seen the problem. A huge snake was lying in wait, completely drawn up into a coil, his upraised head teetering back and forth, his eyes focused on the interlopers who had invaded his playground. He was definitely displeased, which was good enough for Will. "Let's work our way around him," he meekly suggested, adding, "Waaaaay-y-y-y around him."

"Cheezus, Munday. Why should we detour? I ain't gonna walk a quarter mile outta my way because of a goddamn snake. I'll just squeeze off a burst or two with my BAR and cut him in half," Tillie volunteered. He pulled the cumbersome weapon off of his shoulder and swung the muzzle around, only to be stopped when Sergeant Baker grabbed the barrel end and informed him, "Not so fast. D'ya want to bring the goddamn Japs down on us? How do you know they aren't just a hundred yards away? Leave this chore to Fidel and knock off this trigger-happy bullshit, Tillie."

Tillie responded with his usual grin, saying, "Wal ... I never thought about them Japs being that close. Are they really?"

"Who knows?" Baker offered.

"Wal, all the same ... I'll betcha I could've cut him in half," Tillie insisted.

And Will had no doubt that he could've. In the meantime, while Will and the others stood idly by, biding their time, Fidel vanished into the thicket. Baker advised them, "Stand easy. Don't move. Stay quiet. Snakes aren't my specialty ... nor yours. Fidel will know how to handle this with a minimum of racket."

Fidel came slinking back, winding his way between trees and shrubs, to rejoin the group. He made a wide circle around the reptile, taking every precaution to keep a low profile so as not to disturb the wily creature while he made a thorough circumspect of the surroundings. Will was mesmerized

274

by Fidel's fleet-of-feet style; so deliberate, so cocksure of his every move. Finally, when he drew abreast of the snake he unsheathed a long machete, hoisted it above his head, swung it in an arc, then unleashed it. His aim was true. The hit was direct, but the big knife did flip over, then sail into the woods, leaving a bleeding, but still live, nemesis wreathing about, swirling, uncoiling, recoiling, and bleeding profusely. He'd evidently realized he'd met his match in Fidel, because he slithered away into the underbrush and tall grass.

When Fidel rejoined them he said he wasn't pleased over his performance. "I cut him up good, but he's not dead ... so ... unless he crawls off and dies somewhere he could remain a threat. Keep your eyes open," he warned them. He then scampered into the thicket again to retrieve his machete and, after locating it, returned, stroking the blade across his trouser leg to remove the blood while he walked.

Will was impressed. He recalled how the captain had vouched for the courage of his countrymen, and Fidel certainly did measure up to the billing. However sloven Fidel's appearance was, it made little difference, because his talents outweighed his shabby appearance. Now, Will was really comfortable with Fidel leading the way.

"Time's a'wasting," Baker reminded everyone. "We're falling behind schedule. Let's get to cracking." And he moved them out again, grumbling under his breath, "That damned snake cost us at least fifteen minutes; time we'll wish we had back later in the day, I'll wager."

Will tried his best to purge the snake from his mind. He realized they were a natural part of the territory but shuddered at the thought of sharing the jungle with then. It just wasn't his bag. In fact, he was busy glancing to the left, then to the right, then behind, making certain the reptile wasn't slipping up on him. As a result of the encounter a new phase was added to his already crowded itinerary; keeping a watchful eye trained in every direction for snakes. He already had his hands full maintaining a vigil for Jap patrols, but the incident spawned some therapeutic benefits. Instead of letting his mind wander around in his juvenile Land of Oz, as was his custom, Will concentrated his efforts on performing his duties as a soldier. As a result, he was wide awake when Baker halted the precession to keep them from inadvertently wading into a marshland that suddenly loomed up just a few feet ahead.

"Oh," Baker observed with a grin, "I see that your mind and body are functioning as one. It's nice to have you aboard for a change, Munday."

"Un-huh," Will acknowledged Baker's barb, then inquired, "What have we got here? A slough? Something to screw up my uniforms again? You do realize I detest wearing wet duds."

Baker grinned, then replied, "It does look that way, doesn't it? Suck it in, Munday. You oughta be used to soggy shorts by now."

Will did think he detected a tone of urgency in the sergeant's voice with his reply, so he wondered if Baker was distressed. His patience appeared to be wearing thin. He was responding with short, curt comments, which was not his style. Baker put them at rest and said they could smoke a cigarette during the impasse. Will's feet were aching, anyway, so he welcomed the break, however brief it might be. He plunked his posterior down onto the ground, shoved his backside against a small outcropping of rock, and slid down to relieve the pressure of his backpack's straps across his shoulders. The sun finally broke through the clouds, something Will hadn't even noticed until he sat down. His uniform was dry, for the moment anyway, a welcomed change but one he suspected wouldn't last after seeing the soggy slew just ahead. He pulled out his pack of cigarettes, lit one, left it dangling from between his lips, closed his eyes, and let himself tumble into another hypnotic trance. His attempt to mentally recapture the past was as short lived as the break, because the sound of Baker's voice roused him. "I don't like it," he was saying when Will opened his eyes. "Fidel's failed to report back to me for quite a while."

"Do you think he's encountered some Japs? Or what?" Will asked.

"I wish I knew. These are the coordinates he gave me when he took off to reconnoiter the area. He said to meet him at this swamp and that he would either be here waiting or join us shortly."

"What're you going to do?" Gambler inquired.

"Wait. He said to meet him here. I'll wait for fifteen minutes, anyway," Baker told him, glancing at his wristwatch to verify the time of day.

Will was pleased the break was extended. It would give him an opportunity to reminisce in reverie again, providing he could ignore the apprehensions of Fidel's disappearance long enough to concentrate on a voyage back through time. But again it didn't work. Fidel's absence intervened. Will had Fidel figured to be a punctual guy, and he couldn't erase his image from mind. And, he couldn't discount the possibility that Baker was screwed up on his interpretation of the coordinates Fidel dictated. He wondered if Fidel might be waiting at some other location. But he discarded that idea. His faith in Baker was steadfast.

"Fidel did make mention of a village that borders this slew when we last talked. He said we'd probably have to work our way around it, that Jap patrols often paid a visit to the place. So, maybe, he's just scouting it out, making sure the coast is clear," Baker informed them, adding that he thought it best to "hang tight a little while longer."

That came as a surprise of sorts, because the sergeant had already reminded them that time was precious. He'd complained that the time squandered because of the snake as a waste. Now, with Fidel's whereabouts a mystery, another delay couldn't be discounted. What effect would continuing on their trek without Fidel's expertise have on the timeframe? Will had hitched his wagon to Baker's star back in Guinea. Fidel was a comparative rookie compared to the sergeant. Still, Fidel had impressed Will so much with his dexterity and his graceful manner that he hated to think about continuing this venture without him in the lead. The way Fidel went about circumventing the reptile sometime earlier in the day was proof of his mettle. And he was, indeed, a perfectionist when it came to hurling a machete through the air and putting it right on target. Will decided he'd best quit fretting about something over which he had no control. He peeled off his helmet and dropped it with a thud onto the ground between his feet. The midday temperatures were soaring and sweat was rolling down his forehead, then into his eyes, causing them to smart. He blinked, then raised his sleeve to blot the perspiration away, leaned back and concentrated his thoughts on the bowery of leaf and limb that surrounded him. He hummed softly to himself while he eyeballed the diverse varieties of growth; dredging up a childhood ballad that suddenly popped into his mind.

"How about that?" Baker said to him.

"What?"

"That song, 'Billy Boy.' It's been a coon's age since I've heard that."

"Oh, I didn't think I was humming so loud."

"You were," Farmer cut in. "I heard it, too."

"Yeah ... I was having trouble recalling the words, so I hummed it."

"Shucks. I know them words," Tillie boasted.

"You do?" Gambler asked.

"Yup! Cheezus. I reckon most every kid knows 'em."

"Tillie, you're shitting me," Gambler chided him. "Why, you never went to school. Where'd you learn it?"

"My mama. That's where. My mama knew that song."

"Awe, go on. Okay. Let's hear it," Gambler dared him to prove he knew the song by giving a performance. "C'mon," he ragged Tillie, saying, "Sing a few bars."

"Okay. It went ... something like this ... 'Can she bake a cherry pie, Billy boy, Billy boy?'" Tillie complied, much to Gambler's chagrin. Actually they were all surprised that Tillie could even carry a tune, but he did quite handily.

"Keep your BARman's job, Tillie. You're not cut out for the stage," Gambler just had to badmouth him.

"I thought it was pretty nice, Tillie. Pay Gambler a never-mind," Farmer went to Tillie's rescue.

"Yeah. Cherry pie," Will cut in, while he kicked his helmet with his toe. "And speaking of cherry pie, I could bake one in that damned steel helmet that's been frying my brain."

No one disagreed. Wearing a steel helmet was an unbearable experience in the heat of the torrid tropics.

"Do you guys have any idea what's going to become of us?" Will polled his buddies.

The all responded with a negative wag of their heads.

"Well, I'm going to tell you. We're all going to melt, then ooze through the pores of our hide, and gradually evaporate from heat prostration ... leaving a stew-baked bag of bones that some future archaeologist is going to win the Nobel prize for discovering. Five sets of bones, the skulls hopelessly trapped in steel helmets, their bony fingers clutching their weapons. Now, d'ya get the picture?"

"Crude, Munday, crude," Gambler scolded him, but they all had a good laugh. They needed that. But Baker stifled them. Pointing his finger at each one of them individually, he said, "At ease. Knock off the noise."

"Party-pooper," Gambler muttered.

Baker glanced at Gambler, then grinned, explaining to Gambler, "That's one of the duties that go with positions of command, hotshot. Better I be a party-pooper than you push up daisies around your headstone."

Fidel, however, did not return. With Baker's deadline approaching, he said, "Something's wrong. He should've been back. We're going to have to move out and hope he hooks up with us later on."

Baker pulled a crumpled piece of paper from his breast pocket, explaining to them, "This is the map. Gather around and pay attention."

They all took their feet and flanked Baker while he pin-pointed their present position on the chart. "We're here," he said, "and this is the swamp. It appears to be a couple hundred yards wide ... but that's a seasonal thing, depending on rainfall. Over here ... is the village Fidel mentioned. It looks to be another couple hundred yards beyond the swamp. It would take half a day to circle around this bog, so pucker up, Munday, because we're going to take a bath."

It was Tillie who surprised everyone, not Will. "Cheezus, Sergeant," he protested, "are you figuring on just leaving poor Fidel behind?"

"Sh-h-h-h," Baker shushed him with a raised hand, asking him, "What would you have me do? It's time to move out. Can't stall any longer. We have no idea of where he is or how to find him, and even if we did there is no time for that. Hopefully, he'll find us. Remember, our rendezvous is the priority. So, let's saddle up."

Baker scanned the map one more time, then shoved it back into his pocket. Baker's reaction to Fidel's disappearance confirmed Will's observation that Baker was distressed. He suspected that advancing without Fidel added fuel to the sergeant's worries, but Will also understood that military protocol dictated what Baker must should do. The mission was first, everything else second. He hated it almost as much as Baker and was far from pleased about leaving Fidel to fend for himself. Still, he couldn't fault Baker for proceeding according to plan. This was a sequel to the 'party-pooper' label Gambler pinned on Baker after he shushed them awhile earlier; another unpopular decision that went hand in hand with a position of command. For the moment Will was satisfied being the buck-assed private in the rear rank.

Baker stepped off the bank into the ankle-deep slough of murky water, motioning everyone to follow in his footsteps. "Keep the noise down and visual on each other," he cautioned them.

It was tough going. The swamp bed was gooey and it adhered to Will's shoes like glue. He couldn't walk normally. He had to deliberately lift his foot, move it a few inches ahead, then repeat the process with the other. In addition, he found himself concentrating so much on his footwork that he momentarily lost his visual on Baker. A clump of leafy swamp grass was the culprit. The sergeant soon reappeared. The swamp was, however, a maze to negotiate. The further they ventured the more obstinate the twisted imbroglio of flora became, and Will had to weave left, then right, back and forth, to keep up the grueling pace Baker was setting. And the further they waded, the deeper the water became, finally reaching their waists. Will held his weapon at high port to keep it dry. He was half scared of what he might encounter swimming in the smelly pond. Anything was possible in the jungle. So, he was delighted when he saw some dry land just ahead. In fact, Baker had already reached the high ground and stood there, motioning Will and the others to hustle. Will made the shoreline, followed by Farmer, then Gambler and finally Tillie, all of them soaked to the skin from their chests to their toes. They were no longer a spit-and-polish unit representing the world's best-dressed army. They looked like ragamuffins and they felt even worse.

Baker pointed down at the ground and instructed them to "Belly down. Keep a low profile." He spoke in whispers to them, saying he was going to sneak into the jungle for an undisclosed distance to make sure they weren't being sucked into a trap. "Hang tough," he advised them as he vanished into the trees.

He was gone but for a short time, and when he returned he told them to "light up a smoke. Take ten." Will was satisfied that Baker was, in turn, satisfied they weren't in any immediate danger of being engaged by a Jap patrol.

"The coast looks clear," Baker critiqued them while they rested.

Will lit up his cigarette and inhaled a puff of smoke, quickly exhaled, coughed, then turned his attention to Baker, who had retrieved the map from his pocket for another look. The sergeant appeared to be satisfied with what he saw, because he replaced the map into his pocket almost immediately, knelt down close to his men, and pointed off into the jungle, telling them, "See those trees? They block the view, but I figure that village has to be right behind them. Now, we're not about to waltz into that jerkwater town like we're taking a Sunday stroll through the park. I'm hoping to locate Fidel there, but first we're going to advance through those trees to reconnoiter the lay of the land."

Baker told them to "Butt those smokes and let's go. This grove of trees doesn't provide much natural protection as you can probably see. There's lots of open spaces. Use the trees for cover and advance one man at a time, each one taking your turn to cover the other man's advance. Go."

Will jumped to his feet and was first to enter the woodland, Farmer close on his heels. The foursome dodged from tree to tree, one at a time, pausing to eyeball the surrounding area with each leg of the advance. It was smooth sailing. They suddenly found themselves without cover, standing on the brink of a lea; a grassland covered by waist-high grass. "Down," Baker barked when he came darting in to join them. He'd brought up the rear. "Shit," he cursed, telling them, "I sure as hell hope we weren't spotted."

"I don't think we were, Sergeant," Will tried to reassure him. "Hell, I can't see much of anything, so it ain't likey anyone else can."

"Everyone raise your heads, very slowly, and take a peek off to the left," he suggested.

Will guessed that what he saw was only one of many reasons men like Baker were promoted to the rank of Sergeant. There the village was, tucked in another span of trees, perhaps only a hundred yards away.

"Now, take a gander to your right, up on that hillside," Baker suggested.

Will swiveled his head and stared but saw nothing in particular to stimulate his curiosity. "What's there?" he asked Baker, claiming that he saw nothing.

"That outcropping. Up there," Baker again pointed.

There was an outcropping that formed a rim along the frontage of the hillside. "Yeah, I see it, Sergeant," Farmer concurred.

"Okay. Here's the deal. We're going to flank that town by working our way up on that hillside. From there we can get a good view of the village, hopefully without being seen. It'll be like looking in their hip pocket. Munday, I want you to move out to the right, staying in the trees until you reach a spot straight down the hillside from that rock formation," Baker informed them.

"ME?" Will protested. "Just me? Alone?"

"Stay calm, Munday. Don't get your shit hot. We'll be coming right behind you, one man at a time," Baker admonished him.

Will nodded to reply. He wasn't overwhelmed with joy, but he knew Baker would make no change in plan. He was, he mumbled under his breath, "finally dicked by the dangling dong of destiny," quoting an old cliché he heard many times.

"Lighten up, Munday. And listen up," Baker dressed him down, telling him, " No screw-ups. Take your time, Munday. Speed isn't as important as security. Stop, look and listen whenever you get the urge. When you reach the grassy area, belly-crawl up the hillside. Shit, if you stand up, or even crouch and run, you'd be spotted in a second. So, stay low, crawl, slide over the top of those rocks with as little fanfare as you possibly can and then go on standby. We'll be right behind you."

Will glanced from man to man. His friends all wore worried expressions on their faces. He jumped to his feet, reached a hand down, patted Farmer on the shoulder and said, "Don't keep me waiting too long up there, guys." And using that as his farewell, he darted into the trees for cover and was quickly swallowed up by the coppice. But he did overhear Gambler tell the others as he drew away, "Tell you what. I'll give two-to-one odds Munday makes it into the crag up there in one piece. Any takers?"

Will wasn't exactly bowled over with Gambler's offer. He'd seen the huckster offer better odds with a lot less at stake. But when he considered the ongoing feud he'd shared with the oddsmaker he guessed he shouldn't complain. If ever there had been an orange and an apple sharing the same crate, he and Gambler were that duo. If nothing else, Gambler's less-than-generous offer did buoy Will's courage. He was finally beginning to believe in himself.

Chapter Nineteen

Sojourning solo into the wilds was a transition period Will hadn't anticipated. For the first time he was all alone. There was no backup to save his bacon if anything went wrong. There'd be no reassurances from Farmer, the guy who was always there when Will needed encouragement. Will had never thought he'd see the day that he'd miss Baker, but it came. This was it. The men he'd left behind were his crutches, his security blanket. They'd helped to guide him safely through a minefield of trials and tribulations but now they were back there and he was here, standing on the threshold of accountability. He and he alone was charged with the task of carving out a toehold on a hillside. There would be no tolerance for bad judgment. He'd worked hard. It was, as Roul said, time for Will F. Munday, the reluctant warrior, to earn his keep. The possibility that Fidel might've gotten in over his head did give Will cause to pause. Fidel was a native. He knew the *ifs* and the *ands* about the jungle much better than Will. If he had been captured, would he have talked? That being a possibility, did the Japs already know there was a tiny American patrol on their doorstep?

Will decided to quit worrying about Fidel. And to concentrate on the job at hand. The more he dwelt on the negatives the worse he felt. It seemed like something was lodged in his throat, and he was agonizing with an air lock in his lungs. He was struggling to breathe, experiencing an entirely new strain of fear, not like the panic that took a stranglehold on him when he dodged bullets and bombs during the air raid back in Guinea. But an insecure feeling of inadequacy. He knew he had to measure up and climb to the top of the crest overlooking the village without screwing up.

As he neared the meadow a flock of birds took to their wings in a flippant, skyward migration, making enough racket to wake the dead. He'd obviously spooked them, which was bad news, because they might stir someone's curiosity; a Jap, perhaps. So, he dropped down onto his hands and knees and crawled into the grass lea that extended from the foot of the hill to the outcropping of the crest. From his present location he could barely see the rock formation straight up the slope. He was halfway there, beyond a point of no return; turning tail and running in an opposite direction having crossed his mind. But he knew the consequences for cowardice was probably certain death, so he opted to climb that hill if it was the last thing he ever did. He had finally made Baker's honor roll, and he didn't want to jeopardize their relationship. Baker assigned him the task of blazing a trail up the hill and to subsequently occupy the outcropping, and he wasn't going to let the sergeant or anyone else down. Dropping onto his elbows and belly, Will began the arduous undertaking. He pushed with his feet and pulled with his elbows and slid on his belly, managing to gradually grope his way up the grass-covered slope. He could not see how far he had come. The thicket blocked his view. As a result, he couldn't judge how far he was from his goal, but he figured if he kept a straight heading on his present course he'd locate the outcropping. He was panting, fighting again to inhale some air. Belly-crawling a hundred yards or so uphill was a formidable chore. When his helmet made contact with the rock ledge he was elated. Now, he needed only to scamper over the rocks and drop behind them without being spotted. He raised his weapon up and threw his arm across the ledge, then wriggled his body up until he could use his feet to propel himself headfirst over the escarpment. After he'd rolled free of the rocks and given the surrounding territory a brief visual to make sure he wasn't seen, he turned his body about and lifted his head just high enough to catch sight of the village in the vale below. It was awesome. Just like Baker predicted. He felt like he was looking into the valley's hip pocket.

A rustling sound caught his ear. He figured it was one of the other guys shuffling through the grass. It was. Farmer came sliding across the rim of the rock ledge to join him. The country boy was grinning, but Will figured he wasn't half as delighted to see him as he was to see the country boy. Farmer rolled over, then sat up and stared at Will, saying nothing.

"What's wrong?" Will asked him.

"City boy, don't you ever wash you face? We've got pigs back home on the farm that's cleaner'n you," Farmer poked fun at Will's dowdy appearance.

Will was not offended. "So?" he jived Farmer. "Surely your mama told you about the pot that called the kettle black. Too bad I don't have a mirror so's you could get a glimpse of your dirty kisser."

The country boy only laughed, admitting his mother had mentioned that, and then turned his attention to Gambler, who was slipping across the top of the rock ledge to join them. Tillie wasn't far behind, but Baker didn't show up for several tense minutes. When he did finally arrive he advised them,

"Keep that low profile. I'm going to hotfoot it back into the trees for a look-see. Stay put."

Sergeant Baker disappeared, leaving his charges to ponder their next move. Will did keep a vigil on the village, peeking several times to satisfy his curiosity. There was a break in the rock formation that offered a perfect view, and he told the others they should also take a gander.

"It's kinda like them Tarzan picture shows ... ain't it?" Farmer commented after getting his first clear image of the village in the draw. Will agreed. There were any number of huts, all but one of them on stilts, their roofs covered with thatch and the walls constructed of bamboo. Will noticed someone standing near the hut located closest to their observation post. He nudged Farmer. "Take a look. Is that a Jap soldier?"

The individual Will had spotted was clad in khaki-colored clothing and appeared to be wearing a billed cap on his head. A rifle was slung over one shoulder, and he would mosey back and forth as if walking a post, pause and give the hillside a once-over, then walk again. Gambler and Tillie, hearing Will mention a Jap soldier, had to see for themselves, too. It was the first actual enemy soldier they'd seen, if they discounted the aviators who raided their camp and the sailors on the beach a couple of days earlier.

"He's a midget," Gambler observed.

"Wal, he ain't very big. Are all of them varmints sawed-off runts?" Tillie asked, after he took a peek.

"I think it's a racial trait," Will told him.

"You know," Tillie brainstormed, "I could rip him to shreds. From here. Easy target."

"Forget it," Gambler warned him. "There might be an entire company of Nips down there. What're you thinking about? You're going to get all of us killed one of these days with your gung ho, trigger-happy hangup."

And Gambler's forecast of more Japs did materialize. Two more khaki-clad sons of Nippon came into view and paused to chat with the man. The three Jap soldiers disappeared behind the hut just about the time that Baker came waddling in like a duck. He was maintaining a low profile, too. "Damn it," he muttered, advising the others, "The goddamn Japs captured Fidel."

"You're shittin' us," Tillie exclaimed.

But he wasn't, he assured Tillie. "They're holding him center way of the main road that passes through the village. I didn't want to take any chances, so I backed off, but it appeared to me that Fidel was tethered to a post."

"Ga-a-a-wd," Gambler squawked. "What'll they do to him?"

"You really don't want to know. They're barbarians when it comes to interrogating prisoners. They could make a dead man talk," Baker said in a dour tone of voice.

"Cheezus!" Tillie chimed in. "Like how? What do they do?"

Baker shook his head, ignoring Tillie's inquiry. "There's not time now. It's our move. If they don't already know we're here they will before long. They'll get it out of Fidel," Baker warned them. The conditions were red. There was no time left to waste. "The road cuts the village in half, huts to either side. A small stream passes just north of the burg, but it provides us with some natural cover. It's overgrown with leafy plant life. We're going to back off, feel our way down the hill, retaining our tree cover, then cut back to that little stream and observe what's going on from there. Everyone try to get a head count on that Jap patrol. Is it squad strength, or bigger? Follow me. Let's go."

Baker led the way, once more crouched down on his haunches, duck-waddling to get back into the inner reaches of the jungle. The others followed his example, finally taking their feet when they thought they were obscure, and hustled down the hillside, where Baker stopped the advance. He figured to give them a few words of caution before they engaged an enemy force of unknown strength. Keeping his voice down to a whisper, he told them, "No noise. Follow directly behind me. Try to keep your heads down. And, Tillie … keep your fucking finger off of that fucking trigger until I tell you to put your fucking finger on that fucking trigger." Baker knew all too well that Tillie had to be throttled now and then, lest he try to be a hero. This was not the time nor the place for any one of them to court disaster for the sake of an award for valor, or as Baker recalled with an inner chuckle, a Japanese flag decal to paste on his helmet.

Tillie mumbled, "Un-huh," keeping his head bowed to avoid eye contact with Baker.

The sergeant led them to the ditch. Except for having to wade in ankle-deep water it was, as Baker had described it, a perfect observation post. Once they stepped down into the creek itself the foliage concealed them from prying eyes. The leaf and limb that thrived in the creek did, however, provide them with a gap here and there through which they could spy on the village. Will's thoughts regressed to their first day of training in New Guinea, when Baker had stressed the importance of utilizing the jungle as an ally and told them how the jungle provided an edge over their enemies. The picture Will couldn't quite comprehend that day was now coming into focus. The jungle was his friend and he now had the edge.

Will was, however, suffering pains of anxiety over Fidel. He needed to see Fidel in the flesh, to know he was okay, because his capture was a blow to Will's ego. He'd had been so confident having a learned man like Fidel as the scout that he overlooked the human element; error. Fidel had erred, or he wouldn't be a hostage. Will never considered the possibility of their Filipino pathfinder being captured on his own turf, but when he got his first glimpse down the roadway passing through the village his eyes came to rest on Fidel. He was, just like Baker said, standing in front of a hefty pole, his hands tethered behind him with a piece of cord. Fidel had, much to Will's surprise, obviously betrayed himself, in spite of his heritage and familiarity of the surrounding area.

Baker sashayed back and forth, between his men, checking on Fidel's welfare with redundant regularity. He constantly reminded them to "Stay calm, don't anticipate the command," the military meaning of which was "Don't go off half-cocked until you're told to."

Will had a problem with the reality of the situation. It was hard for him to comprehend that he was a mere fifty yards from a bunch of Jap soldiers, all of whom would've killed him instantly if he was spotted. And getting the head count Baker wanted wasn't easy. The enemy soldiers seemed to be in motion, moving from here to there and back to here, sometimes vanishing behind huts, only to resurface again in another location. They all looked pretty much alike to Will. They were, just as he suspected, rather short in stature, compared to Farmer, or Tillie, who were both string beans. Their uniforms were actually quite shabby compared to those issed to Americans He couldn't be sure because of the distance between them, but it looked to Will as though they wore wrap-style leggings over the calves of their legs. Their trousers were baggy. In fact, Will thought they looked pretty tacky. The Japs were armed with bolt-action rifles from another era, perhaps World War I. The rifles appeared to be longer than the American M-1, and for some unexplainable reason the Nips were parading around with bayonets affixed to the muzzles of the guns. That sent a chill up Will's backside. Being stuck through the middle with a bayonet wasn't an acceptable fate. In fact, it frightened him, and his hands began to tremble. The reality of stalking the enemy had finally come to its conclusion. There was no way they could avoid a fire fight, unless they abandoned Fidel and continued on the mission without his services. Will couldn't imagine a humanitarian like Baker turning his back on one of his own people. So, it was that time. The long wait was over. It was time for Will F. Munday to shed his reluctant image.

He continued to observe the goings-on with a great deal of interest. Fidel was being interrogated in an unmerciful manner. He was at the mercy of a Japanese officer—at least Will supposed he was an officer because of a long, narrow sword that hung from his belt. He dressed considerably spiffier than his men, strutting around in calf-high leather boots that gleamed of spit and

287

polish. He had the aura of an officer, standing erect, shoulders back, chin up. The face-off between Fidel and his captors was also being observed by any number of villagers, most of whom stood back, forming an intermittent circle around the center ring. The Jap officer was flanked to either side by one of his enlisted men, both of whom appeared amused by the entire scenario. The officer slapped Fidel across the face and began to shout at him, but even though Will could hear everything being said he had no idea what was being said, because the exchange was not in English. Evidently, he didn't frighten Fidel, who laughed at him. But the belligerent gesture only infuriated the man, so he slapped Fidel again and again until blood was oozing from the corner of Fidel's mouth. Still, Fidel was not moved. He was, just like Will suspected from the outset, a man with nerves of steel. He was even defiant, and when the officer approached him a third time, Fidel didn't wince. He boldly spat on the man's face, a response that changed the tactics of the interrogation.

One of the commandant's subordinates handed Fidel's shiny, new Thompson to the officer. He shook it in front of Fidel's face, shouting again at the top of his lungs. Fidel didn't flinch. Will did. Even he was smart enough to realize that this new weapon didn't just turn up in the middle of nowhere. Someone had to have provided it, which meant there was a strong possibility that the Americans had launched their long-awaited return to the Philippines. Fidel continued his obstinate response. A streak of blood coming from Fidel's left eye dribbled down across his cheek.

Baker had just paused by Will's side to catch another glimpse when Will asked him, "Is that what you mean about making a dead man talk?"

"It gets worse. Much worse," Baker opined, telling Will, "The Thompson will be our undoing. Damn. Why did he have to get caught? Those heathen sonsabitches, anyhow."

Tillie scooted over to where Will and Baker were conferring. He was troubled. "Sergeant," he murmured, "are we just gonna sit here? And do nothin'?"

Baker shushed him with a finger across his lips, then inquired if he'd taken a head count. Tillie said he'd tried, but "Those stand-eyed bastards don't stand still long enough. I think they've got ants in their pants. They're all over the place."

"How many did you count?" Baker pressed him.

"Wal ... I counted eleven, leastwise I think eleven, if'n I didn't count someone twice."

"And you?" he asked, turning to face Will.

"That's what I got. Eleven. But it's like Tillie says ... I can't be sure,"

Will more or less verified Tillie's count.

Baker motioned for Gambler to join them, and when he crawled into the circle the sergeant asked, "What's your head count?"

"Twelve ... I'm pretty sure. Yeah. Twelve ... counting that goddamn butcher with the sword dangling from his belt," Gambler replied.

"That's what I got. Twelve. Squad strength. An officer and eleven enlisted men," Baker agreed.

Will turned his attention back to the arena on the road near the center of the village. "What's this?" he asked, nodding from left to right and back, trying to coax everyone to take a look.

The inquisition had entered a new phase. The interrogating officer focused his attention on two of his subordinates. One of them was tying a leather thong around Fidel's forehead.

"What the hell are they doing to him?" Will asked.

"It's one of their favorite tricks. They'll keep tightening that strap until Fidel can no longer endure the pain, or until he passes out. I told you guys, they'll make a dead man talk," Baker explained it.

"Shit, man," Tillie muttered, then asked Baker, "Wal, are we gonna keep sitting here while they torture Fidel?"

"We are. It's too risky. We should be moving out right now if we intend to keep on schedule," Baker reminded them of what their mission actually was.

"Sergeant," Gambler challenged him, inquiring, "How can you? I mean, just turn your back on him?"

"He knew the odds when he took the job," Baker expounded his reasons. He tried to justify his decision, telling his surprised warriors, "I don't like it. But the mission comes ahead of everything. Thousands of guys' lives are riding on our success or failure, and I can't let the life of one man change the odds."

Fidel screamed; a bloodcurdling shriek that vibrated Will's inner ear. Will looked to see what they were doing and discovered they had done precisely what Baker predicted. Fidel's face was twisted in agony, and blood was streaming down his chin, but he twisted and squirmed, trying to fend off his attackers. "Damn," Will muttered. "Nerves of steel. He's a strong man. I could never endure that, Sergeant."

But while they were discussing Fidel's undaunted courage things changed. Gambler pointed, telling Baker, "They've got some broad. They're dragging her across the street."

Baker and his charges stared in stillness, wandering where the young lady figured in. Two soldiers, one on each side of a raven-haired young woman, physically lugged her across the street. She was fighting them every step of the way, but was no match for their physical superiority. When they reached the spot where the officer stood waiting, he talked with them, apparently instructing them what his plans were, after which they dragged her over to another post along the side of the street and shackled her much the same as they had Fidel. "How does she figure?" Gambler wondered aloud.

"We'll see," Baker replied, keeping his eyes glued to every move being made.

They didn't have to wait very long, either, to realize what the Jap commandant's intentions were. The two captors who had amused themselves torturing Fidel released the thong from around his head, then both reached up and grabbed a hank of his hair and twisted Fidel's face around so that he could see the girl they'd tethered to the other post. The officer turned on his toe and strutted to where she was bound to the post. He paused, swiveled his head, back and forth, studying the crowd's reaction, then grabbed a fistful of the garment she wore and ripped it straight down the middle. He shocked everyone's modesty when he flung the dress onto the ground, baring her nude body for everyone to see. She was screaming and crying and pleading for help, but no one was permitted to intervene. Those who tried were shoved back into the crowd by the Jap sentries.

Tillie was furious. He hoisted the business end of his BAR, intending to cut the beasts to bits. Once more, Baker stopped him. "As you were, soldier," he said in a firm yet subdued tone of voice. "Hold your fire."

"For Christ's sake, Sergeant," Gambler unloaded on Baker. "What the fuck are you made of? You're going to just sit here and watch this fucking circus? And not let us kill them bastards?"

Baker realized he had the makings of a mutiny on his hands, but he did not bend. "I said, 'As you were,'" he reiterated his earlier orders to Tillie. "That's insubordination. I won't hold for it. Shut the fuck up. I will call the shots. Is that clear?"

Gambler did not reply. He nodded and turned his watchful eyes back toward the village center, sulking like a child.

Will, however, had kept up his silent vigil. By the time Tillie, Gambler and Baker were through with their disagreeable face-off, there was a new development. The Japanese officer had slipped his sword from its scabbard and was gently jabbing the point of the blade into the young maiden's breast. Will alerted Baker, suggesting, "Sir, you'd best watch this. I don't know what to make of it. Is he a lunatic?"

Again, all eyes were on the roadway. Will could hardly comprehend what he saw. After teasing the young maiden with his saber, the diabolical beast in charge thrust its point against her throat on a pretense that he would slice off her head if Fidel did not cooperate. Will held his breath. He was speechless. His heart began to pound inside of his bosom and his hands were coated with sweat. He noticed that a streak of blood was streaming from a wound on the girl's breast. It infuriated him to think any human being could be so utterly barbarous.

"That's it," Baker announced. "We're going to take 'em on. I will not stand by and let them kill that child."

Tillie was elated, as was Gambler. Both Will and Farmer stifled their urge to celebrate, but Baker didn't waste any time making his move once he'd made up his mind. He pointed to the east, telling Will and Farmer, "Scoot on down the creek. Keep your heads down. I don't want to be seen until we hit 'em." He then latched on to Tillie and Gambler, ordering them to move in the opposite direction, explaining to the four of them, "We're going to catch their ass in a crossfire. On my signal you will jump out of this ditch and take it to 'em. Pick your targets in advance. Do your best to hit the Nips and miss the villagers. Got it? I want every goddamn one'a these sonsabitches laid out cold and dead when it's over. Okay?"

Everyone nodded their approval. "Get moving. Take your positions. We haven't much time. We're gonna rescue our scout in the process of righting a serious wrong," Baker vowed, sending them on their way. He watched carefully, making sure they took up the positions that he'd indicated, and seeing that they had, he glanced left, then right, before raising his hand above his head. When he was positive everyone was at the ready, he dropped his hand and jumped up onto the bank of the creek, pushing his way through the growth, the muzzle of his Thompson spitting fire.

Will leaped out of the ditch, and when he had cleared the leafy barrier he'd used for a buffer while they waited he drew down on his Thompson and cut loose on the first Jap that came into view. Farmer wasn't but a step behind him. But suddenly another Nip appeared as if from out of nowhere, coming from behind a hut, and Will caught a glimpse of him raising the muzzle of his rifle and taking aim directly at him. He flung himself down onto the ground and rolled forward, coming back up onto his feet, just as he pressed the trigger of his weapon. He saw the muzzle flash of the Jap's rifle, but Will had made a direct hit in the same instant. The Jap reared backwards, pitching his rifle into the air, then fell into a heap on the ground. So, Will turned his attention back to the center of the village. He could not believe what he saw. There wasn't a single Jap left standing. They'd killed every last one of them, or so it appeared. That was when Baker came running, shouting to Will, "One'a them sonsabitches is getting away. He went around that hut.

You go left, Munday, I go to the right. Find him. Kill him. No survivors. No prisoners. Got it?"

Will darted up the street, cutting to his left to veer around the hut Baker had pinpointed. Within a half a minute he was swallowed up in the jungle, where his field of vision was limited to a few yards, so he slowed his pace to pause and eyeball the surrounding woodland to make sure he wasn't the one being stalked. He saw and heard nothing, so he cautiously ventured ahead, taking short, tiptoed steps, while swinging his head back and forth to check his flanks. The word "sniper" popped up in Will's mind. Could his prey have shinnied up a tree? Was he possibly drawing a bead on Will? He'd heard that sniping was their specialty. He stopped again and took a gander up into every tree visible. Again, he saw and heard nothing. Baker came to mind. He wondered where he'd gone. He figured they both had to be within a short distance of one other. Inching forward, Will came to a small clearing in the trees, and just as he entered the aperture he heard the crisp snap of a rifle bolt coming from off to his left. Jerking his head in that direction, he spotted the prize he'd been searching for not more than fifteen yards away. He had Will in the sights of his rifle but instead of firing the weapon, he lowered it. Will figured he was a goner. He'd allowed the man to take his edge away, so he was shocked when the Jap failed to fire his weapon. By pausing, he'd compromised his edge; the element of surprise. There had to be a reason. Will cautiously took stock of his nemesis, giving him a once-over from head to toe. He was just standing there, his feet firmly planted on the ground, his legs apart, holding a rifle already affixed with a bayonet, staring at Will. Will scanned the weapon. The bolt was hanging open. He could only speculate, but that was an tattletale sign that the man had no cartridges. He and Will just stood there, staring at one another with dumbfounded expressions on their faces, but Will could read fear in the man's eyes. It figured. Will was scared. Why wouldn't he be? The kid looked young, almost too young to be a soldier. His eyes darted back and forth as though he was seeking some kind of guidance, and his chin was quivering. Will thought the young man even tried to force a grin, but if he did, it was not meant as a hand of amity. He hunched his shoulders, thrust his weapon forward, then lunged at Will, intending to stick him with the bayonet. Will hoisted the muzzle of his Thompson and squeezed off a three- or four-round burst, not bothering to take aim. He didn't need to. They were so close to each other that all Will had to do was point in the general direction and pull the trigger. The Nip staggered backwards. His rifle flew end over end through the air. He landed on his hind end, then sprawled out on the ground. Will cautiously approached his victim and, standing over the corpse, pointed his weapon again. He intended to make sure the "slant-eyed sonofabitch" was dead, but Baker came running into the clearing before Will could squeeze the trigger, asking, "Did you get him?"

Will stepped back and pointed to the object of his handiwork. He kept the muzzle of his Thompson aimed at the corpse, informing Baker, "Yeah. I got him. But I was thinking I should make sure he's dead."

Baker shook his head from side to side, suggesting to Will it was a bad idea. "He's dead. I'll attest to that. Save your ammo."

"Well, Sergeant," Will tried to influence Baker's to let him satisfy his whim, "this was for Duffy. You do remember Duffy, don't you?"

"Yeah," Baker came back, "how could I forget him? I'll say this, you killed that sonofabitch deader'n hell, Munday."

"Well, sir," Will responded, "you told us that day that we should take a good look at Duffy's remains and then we'd know what to do when the time came."

"So I did," Baker recalled, "and you responded exactly like I expected you to. You were an angry lad that day. You put your career on the line when you took me on. Now, you've had your revenge. Let's get back into the village and mop up. We've gotta get moving."

Will was in favor of that. He took off on a trot because he wanted to find Farmer and tell him Duffy's death had been vindicated. Somehow it seemed like the closure he needed, recalling the traumatic experience that was his introduction to the hazards of war. Settling that score was no longer unfinished business. The transaction was complete.

Chapter Twenty

Will didn't waste any time hightailing it back into the village. Baker, being the cautious mother hen, took his own sweet time and covered the rear, just on the chance there might be another sniper thereabouts. The village was a far cry from what it was when Will left to pursue the runaway Jap. The roadway was teeming with frolickers who'd obviously emerged from nowhere. There was at least ten times the people there'd been during the interrogation session, and unlike the somber faces of those who watched the affair, these folks were celebrating as though nothing had happened. It was a miniature Mardi Gras. The jubilant revelers had transformed the hamlet into a carnival. They were dancing. They were singing. They were shouting. But what Will heard over every other sound was a chorus of voices praising their benefactor; MacArthur. "MacArthur's back," they chanted, much to Will's surprise. What kind of deity was this man, he wondered, to deserve this awesome display of loyalty? MacArthur was a thousand miles from here, yet they saw his image in these young American soldiers. It was the message MacArthur had left three years earlier that mattered, not the messenger. Oh, they were thanking Tillie, hugging Gambler and… "Wait." Will paused, swiveling his head back and forth, up and down, left and right, to the rear. "Where's Farmer?" he wondered aloud. The country boy was nowhere in sight.

He wondered if, with things being in a turmoil as they were, he might've just missed seeing Farmer. The crowd was milling about in a frenzied fashion that almost made Will dizzy. He turned about and retraced his steps, coming upon Fidel, who was being treated for his injuries by several of the local ladies. "Have you seen Farmer?" he asked the Filipino scout. Fidel gave his head a negative wag to acknowledge Will's inquiry but said, "No, Mister Will. I haven't."

Will paused again, trying to look over the top of everyone, hoping he'd find his lanky friend, who, because of his height, should've stood head and shoulders above the celebrants. But he struck out. *Where'n the hell did he get off to?* he wondered. Spinning around, he spotted a small, elevated stoop on the frontage of a hut that faced the road. He headed that way, hoping to climb onto the perch and get a revealing view of the entire area, but once he reached, then mounted, the tiny platform and gazed out across the hordes of humanity that swirled below him he was disappointed. Farmer had vanished. Recalling the last time he'd seen his friend was when they jumped out of the ditch and charged into the village. Farmer had been right behind him. He knew that. So, he craned his neck and tried to hone his line of vision in on the spot abutting the creek where he thought their assault had originated. Twisting his body while craning his neck, he hoisted himself upon the railing and peered above the mingled mass of humanity that overflowed the street. He saw Farmer, then, stretched out on the ground not ten yards from the ditch. "NO-O-O!" he shrieked. "NO-O-O, NOT FARMER," he continued to bellow as he jumped down onto the ground and began to run as fast as his legs would carry him. He pushed Filipinos aside, elbowed his way through the throng, still screaming, "NO," every step of the way. And when he pulled abreast of where the country boy lay, he fell onto his knees and skidded through the loose soil, shouting at the top of his lungs, "Farmer! Are you okay? Talk to me."

Farmer moaned, then slowly turned his head so he could stare into Will's eyes. Will was shaking like a leaf in a whirlwind, and when he made a more thorough observation he saw that Farmer's eyes were glassy, and blood was oozing from the corner of his mouth, then dribbling down across his chin. Will slid his arm underneath Farmer's upper torso to hoist his head. That's when he sensed the warmth of Farmer's blood soaking the sleeve of his fatigue jacket.

"Farmer! Can you hear?" Will plied him for an answer.

"Un-huh," Farmer managed to respond, telling Will, "I'm hurt. Hurt bad. Gut shot." His eyes were searching for a sign of inspiration, his ears peeled for some words of encouragement. He was laboring to breath.

"You're gonna make it," Will tried to reassure him as he took Farmer's shirt in hand and tore the buttons off. He ripped it away and tried to examine the injury, but Farmer's midriff was bleeding so profusely that he couldn't even see the actual wound. He had a gut feeling that the wound was fatal unless treated by a qualified physician, or someone with a certain amount of medical expertise. "Fat chance," he muttered to himself. There couldn't be such a person anywhere near. So Will forged ahead with his deception, lying to Farmer, kidding himself. "You're gonna be fine. Just fine. I'm here, Farmer. Do you hear me? I'm here."

He didn't fool this medical corpsman, who understood his plight better than Will. "Naw," Farmer managed to mutter, "I ain't gonna make it."

"Sure you are. Don't talk like that."

"Naw. What about ... my mama?" he asked, still worshipping his beloved mother. "What'll she do? The farm? Oh-h-h, I'm cold, Will. So cold."

"Damnit, Farmer. Don't you quit on me. D'ya hear? Goddamnit, don't you quit on me."

Tears were streaming down Will's cheeks. Farmer had just enough stamina left to reach out his hand and squeeze Will's forearm. "Will? Will?" he called to him.

"Yeah. I'm here. Right here."

"D'ya suppose," Farmer asked in a faltering voice, "that I coulda made the grade?"

"Grade? What grade?"

"You know. What you said ... about me goin' back to school and becomin' ... a famous sawbones?"

"What do you mean, asking me a silly question like that? You're going to. Quit that past tense shit," Will began to rave, ignoring the fact that Farmer was dying. He knew, but he wouldn't accept it. Farmer tried to inhale a final breath, then a gurgling sound emitted from between his lips, and his body slumped in Will's arms. But death was not acceptable. Will wouldn't allow it. "And do you know what, country boy?" he continued to rattle on, almost incoherently at times, "When this war's over, I'm coming to get you and I'm going to kick your ass all the way to that schoolhouse. Yeah. You'll be famous. When you do open your private practice someday, Farmer, I'm going to deliberately break my goddamn leg so I can be your first goddamn patient. Do you hear?"

Farmer could not hear his delirious raving. He was dead. Will wanted this to be another one of his fantasies; not real. "It's a dream. A bad dream. This isn't happening," he tried to defer the inevitable. Oh, how he wanted this to be just another trip in his world of make-believe, the imaginary dimension where he called the shots and from which he could return as he pleased. It wasn't in the cards. He just stared off into space, refusing to look down, because he knew what he'd encounter; Farmer's death mask.

Will lifted his head and glanced around from side to side. He was the main attraction of a gathering he hadn't even been aware of. The townsfolk had lost some of their enthusiasm and were coming to grips with the reality of the scene. And a familiar voice penetrated his eardrums. "Munday," Baker called his name.

Will did not respond. It was as though his throat was paralyzed and he couldn't speak, or it might've been a form of involuntary protest; he didn't want to return to the reality of a war that held him captive and was responsible for his best friend's death.

"Munday. Listen up," Baker tried to garner his attention again.

"Everything's going to be A-okay, Farmer," Will rambled on, ignoring Baker.

Sergeant Baker was a professional. While he sympathized with Will's sorrow, he also realized it was his responsibility to turn Will's lust for revenge in the direction of those who were responsible; the Japs. He could hardly complete his assignment without Will. Losing Farmer was about the last straw. However brutal his response might've seemed, he had to deal with Will's indifference without delay. He understood Will's trauma. He also knew that being a nice guy didn't fit this scenario. He hoisted his leg and planted his shoe against Will's helmet, then kicked it completely off of his head and sent it rolling across the ground. When Will glanced up with a startled expression of shock on his tear-stained face, Baker informed him, "Farmer's dead. Deal with it, soldier. You're not dead, and we have a destiny to fulfill, and I need your help. Tell Farmer goodbye in as few words as you can and get on your goddamn feet and quit sniveling like a goddamn baby."

And then fate intervened, fortunately, for the two of them, because the fire in Will's eyes was hardly compassionate. He was an angry young man. Before he was able to take his feet the young lady who'd been intimidated and carved on by the Japanese officer knelt down on the other side of Farmer's lifeless body. She reached her hand out and placed it on Will's neck, offering him her condolences. "I'm so sorry. So sorry," she said in a soft, sympathetic tone of voice, after which she leaned across the corpse and kissed Will on his cheek.

Will was suddenly flustered, no longer angry. He was astonished to begin with over the fact that the girl spoke almost perfect English. And he was embarrassed because he'd seen her nude body tied to the post and had taken pause for a second look. He had never before seen a naked woman. It was an awesome sight. Even more flattering, he'd never been kissed. He raised his hand, slipped his fingers around hers, and squeezed. She looked him squarely in the eyes and repeated her token of sympathy, "I am so sorry. I can see he was your best friend. Why else would you cry?"

Baker figured that was an excellent spot to intervene and squelch what appeared to be a budding romance. "Okay, Munday. On your feet. We've gotta get moving," he barked.

Will was back in control. He slowly raised himself back onto his feet, then asked Baker, "What will... I mean, sir, what happens to Farmer? I can't just leave him here."

Fidel, who'd been watching the tail end of the episode, informed both Baker and Will that the villagers would see that Farmer had a proper burial and that they would try their best to notify those in charge that an American's remains were interred there.

Will nodded. It wasn't what he wanted to hear, but he knew that was how things were meant to be. He pivoted, moseyed over to where his helmet was lying on the ground, and picked it up. Still going through the motions of securing it on his head, he said to Baker, "I'm ready, sir."

Before Baker could round up his squad and move out he was propositioned by one of the local people to include him in the act.

Trying to downplay his role and dispel whatever suspicions the villagers might've had over him and his men's unexpected arrival, Baker played dumb, asking, "What act?"

Fidel grinned. He intervened, saying he'd already talked to the man and that the fellow had a proposition worth listening to. So, Baker said, "Out with it. What's on your mind?"

Again, Fidel cut in, advising Baker, "He speaks very little English. I will interpret."

Baker nodded his approval.

The man didn't appear to be Filipino. He actually looked more like a Jap. And as the exchange continued Baker learned that the man was, indeed, of Japanese extraction and that he'd come to the Philippines many years ago and had taken a wife and was a trustworthy individual who considered himself to be a Philippine national. That was music to Baker's ears. As the conversation unfolded, Baker learned that the man was quite familiar with the communications complex and that he had suspected when he first saw the Americans that their purpose for being there was to destroy it. The complex was, he thought, the only thing around worthy of an American incursion into the back country. Through Fidel's interpretation Baker learned that the complex had undergone radical revisions recently, and the man questioned whether Baker could accomplish his task without some inside help, which he offered to provide.

"What can he possibly do that we cannot?" Baker demanded to know.

After a moment's delay while Fidel spoke, then listened, and finally relayed the man's reply, Baker learned that they had cleared the forest completely away from the structure's outside barrier walls and had beefed up the defensive perimeter. He warned Baker that he couldn't even get close unless there was a distraction, and that he was the logical person to perform that task.

Exactly how the man knew all of this puzzled Baker, but he soon learned that the old man had a thriving produce business and that each week he would load up his oxcart with produce, make the long trip to the complex, and would offer his wares to the soldiers, all of whom were delighted to see him come with fresh food to supplement their meager rations of rice. He could, he vowed, not only be a diversion, but he could get inside of the structure.

Baker was caught between a rock and the proverbial hard spot. It was hardly his place to make such a decision. Yet, by ignoring the man's offer he might be doing the mission an injustice. This was, in Baker's estimation, like filling an inside straight in a high-stakes poker game. He was skeptical, however, whether Roul would agree. Roul was his own man. He did like to call the shots. Still, Baker figured there was nothing to lose by allowing the old man to tag along, providing he could keep the pace. That in turn brought up another option, one that Baker really loved, because the delays he's encountered had him behind schedule. The old man, who finally managed to get an introduction to Baker, said his name was Seto. He knew, he claimed, a short-cut that would save at least an hour, maybe more, and he vowed he could keep up with the others, telling Baker that all he had to do was walk. An oxen, he boasted, would do the work, and he boasted that oxen rarely tire out.

Baker threw his lot in with Seto, asking how soon he could be ready to move out. Seto surprised him. He said he'd been so sure they'd follow his advice that he had loaded the produce on his cart already and had only to hitch up the oxen before leaving. So, it was a done deal. Ten minutes later Baker and his men were saying their goodbyes to the villagers, who raised their voices in a rousing cheer when the Stopwatch segment headed up the road.

Will was still suffering his trauma over Farmer. He hadn't paid close attention to details while Baker hatched the plan with Seto, like Gambler and Tillie had, so he was more or less just tagging along, stumbling over his own feet in a dazed stupor. Gambler was set back a trifle when he learned that Seto might end up being the powder man, or at least playing a major role in the finale. He'd been looking forward to his maiden run to destroy something; anything. It was a hangup he revered. And Tillie was just Tillie, the hillbilly clown with an itchy trigger finger and nothing to shoot at. But he did boast to Gambler while they walked side by side that he thought he'd "Kilt at least three'a them bastards. Kilt 'em deader'n a doornail."

Will finally tired of playing the lone wolf. He picked up the pace to catch Gambler and Tillie. When he drew up alongside of them, Gambler glanced at him, then said, "I'm sure sorry, Munday. You know what I mean. About

Farmer. I know he was your best friend."

Will nodded his acceptance, but Gambler had a little more to say. "I guess I've been a real asshole. I was never very good to him and he never did me any wrong ... well, except when he wailed the tar outta me that morning, but I had that coming."

Gambler's confession came as quite a shock to Will. He realized that the cardsharp must've had some misgivings over his conduct when he saw Farmer stretched out cold and dead. "Yeah," Will agreed. "You did. Old Farmer, he worshipped his mama, you know."

"Un-huh," Gambler concurred.

"I think that ... well, if I make it through this thing ... I'll go to see her when the fighting is done," Will bared his soul.

The conversation ended when Baker urged them to move up, and "Keep the ranks closed. Little is good. Don't string out."

The interruption gave Will an opportunity to overtake Baker. He wanted to chat with him. In fact, he needed to. He couldn't help but ask himself how many times his sergeant had to bail him out of a predicament. And every time it had been he who was out of line, who was wrong, and Baker had been the sympathetic respondent of his discourse. When he fell into step with Baker, the sergeant acknowledged him, saying, "Things will look better another day, Munday. I've been where you just came from, more than once. It's the shits, I know, but time heals all things."

"Yeah," Will replied, recalling aloud, "You know, back that day in Guinea, when the Japs hit us, I took notice how those swab-jockies on the LCI just rolled with it, like it was no big deal. And I wondered shortly thereafter if I would ever reach a point of toleration. I guess I've been a real pain in the ass a few times, haven't I?"

"Well, yes. You have. But you're getting the hang of it," Baker replied, trying to make Will understand that he harbored no hard feelings. "You might've been wrong about your observation of those sailors. I don't think they were acclimated to it. It was a job they were trained to do and they did it. It wouldn't be fitting and proper for guys like you, who've been conscripted to serve, to accept toleration as a given. You're going home one day and this will be history. You'll discover that making that adjustment will be equally as difficult as the one you've been called on to make as a soldier. You're not a born killer. What you just did back there in that village was exactly what those sailors did. You went through the motions of doing the job you were trained to do, quite handily, I might add."

"Do you think the captain will be upset over us letting that farmer tag along?" Will asked.

"It's anyone's guess. I'll stand good for it. You know, this might surprise you, but I'm a Civil War buff. Yeah. You never figured your sergeant read books, did you? I have. Many books, but mostly about warfare. I've been hooked on the Civil Was since school-days, and that's where I discovered that a change in strategy sometimes pays off." Baker used the history book to justify him making a decision without a superior's approval. "I reckon I've read dozens of books on the subject. Anyway, during the battle of Shiloh, the Rebs had the Yanks pinned with their backs to a river when nightfall came. The battle had raged all day, with the Rebs about to make the kill. But the commanding general decided there was no hurry, it could wait until dawn, and they could use the interim period of darkness to care for the wounded and pick up their dead from the field. Well, dawn brought an unexpected surprise. When they probed the Union lines the Yanks counterattacked and drove them off. Why? Because, during the night the Union lines were re-enforced with several thousand men who were transported up the river on barges. The lesson is, when you have the initiative keep it, don't let up."

Will was a trifle amazed that Baker was such a learned man with history. But he wondered what the story had to do with today. And he asked.

"Well, this oxcart is our barge, Seto our re-enforcements. I don't know what to expect when we make our rendezvous tonight, but just suppose for a minute that all three teams don't get there on time, for any number of reasons, and we're short-handed. It won't matter if we have a half-dozen men, or a dozen, the assault is on. So, I really don't think Captain Roul will fault me for calling in the reserves," Baker elaborated.

Fidel had been probing ahead and no one had seen him for quite a spell. Seto and his oxcart were leading the parade because he knew the route and, Will discovered, Seto wasn't gathering any moss either. In fact, the oxen was setting the pace, and it wasn't a stroll. The huge animal set a rugged pace. The sun was setting in the west when Baker and his party reached the rendezvous point. Baker was pleased. They were the first ones to arrive.

"Hey," Tillie complained, "Where's everybody?"

Baker smiled, advising Tillie, "We're first on the scene. The other two squads will be along … soon, I hope. We've a lot of time to kill, much more than I thought we would have, when everything fell apart today. But thanks to Seto we got back on schedule. In fact, we're running hot."

Will moseyed over to the tree line and parked his carcass on a boulder. He was tired and still aching over Farmer. He just wanted to be alone for a few minutes to commiserate with his ego. Baker decided to tag along with Fidel, who said he was going to scout the fringe area that surrounded the compound. He figured they were about a half mile from the complex. Baker

302

suggested, just before he left the area, "Keep the noise down and fade into the woods if you hear or see anything unusual. Help Seto to get that cart and animal out of sight before you crap out. I'll be back in a jiffy."

Gambler jumped up onto his feet and told Will and Tillie, "Sit tight, you guys. I'll help the old man secure that oxcart. I want to look it over, anyway. It could be a useful tool."

Tillie hunkered down beside Will. They smoked and talked, particularly about Captain Roul. Will complimented Roul, admitting to the others that the captain was usually right about his projections and predicitons. He asked Tillie, "Remember what he said about Catherall?"

Tillie snickered. "Catherall?" he jibed Will. "You've gotta be kidding. Who's he?"

"He was talking about what lay ahead and he quoted a man named Catherall," Will explained. "Anyway, it's what he said that really hits home. He said the three foundations of learning were: seeing much, suffering much and studying much. And he went on to say ... you remember, it was after the air raid ... that we had seen and we had suffered, so now we had to study. That's what our training session was all about. Studying."

"Man," Tillie exclaimed, "how do you remember all'a that stuff? Shucks, I have trouble remembering what vittles I ate yesterday."

"Oh, I don't know. I just have a knack for it, I guess. Anyway, I was wondering if you feel as though you really absorbed what we were taught ... I mean about war and killing and the jungle? All of that stuff," Will asked him.

Tillie paused, hung his head, then casually replied, "Wal, Will. We was brung up in different worlds. Yeah, worlds. I've cradled a gun in the crook of my elbow since I was knee high to a grasshopper. I hadn't never kilt a person before, but I've did my share of killing wild game and, somehow, this isn't that much different."

"I isn't?"

"Naw. I just tell myself that them Japs is vermin, you know?"

"Vermin? How so?"

"Wal, I've heard tell they don't fret when they torment folks. I ain't had much book learnin', like you. I can't read. But the preacher man used to read the Bible in church on Sundays and I kinda gathered from what he said that killing people was a sin. But he also read us something about "a life for a life." And that's kinda how I look at it. Them Japs kilt a lot of folks at Pearl Harbor and I'm just following them Scriptures. I figure I done kilt at least three of them critters today. It's a payback sorta thing. D'ya see?"

"Yeah, I think I do. You're right about us being reared in different worlds.

303

We learned from each other. I have learned a lot from you, Tillie. And I've suffered even more. God, I have suffered. You have no idea of how much I hated to leave Farmer lying back there," Will lamented. "And I think I really did study back there in Guinea, because I can't even believe that I just boldly jumped outta that goddamned creek bed and commenced killing people like it was second nature. Not me. Not Will Munday. Nevertheless, I did it, and I can't say I'm the least bit sorry, either. In fact, right now I have no feelings about it one way or the other. I'm almost numb. It's like when you wake up in the morning and you're still fretting over a dream you had. Well, it almost seems like that was all just a dream today. That Catherall fellow was pretty smart, wasn't he?"

"Yup. Reckon so. Now, don't forget. When we get back to," and he paused, an expression of bewilderment dimming his face, "where are we supposed to go when we finish off that complex?"

"To some rendezvous point, I imagine. They'll tell us."

"Wal, anyways, don't forget you promised to read my letter and help me write some words to send back home," Tillie reminded him.

Will assured Tillie he had not forgotten and would be delighted to do it when they finished off the Jap installation and returned to some base where he could sit down and chat with him.

Baker and Fidel came dragging in a short time later, both breathless from the trek. Baker slipped the crumpled map from his breast pocket again and spread it out on the ground. He glanced around, asking, "Does anyone have a pencil?"

Will patted his breast pocket, smiled, then fished a nub from it and handed it to Baker.

Baker cocked his head, smiled in return, needling Will for being so predictable. "It figures," he said, "that you'd have a pencil, Munday. Okay. Gather around. Fidel, I'd like to have Seto in on this."

Fidel awakened Seto, who'd fallen asleep on the ground next to his oxcart, and ushered him to the gathering. When they were all in place, Baker took the pencil in hand and began to scribble near the center of the page. "This," he informed them, "is the area surrounding the complex. The timber is gone. There is very little cover within a hundred yards of the structure."

"Is it okay if we smoke, Sergeant?" Will interrupted him.

"Yeah. It's okay. In fact, let me bum a smoke from you, Munday," Baker surprised him.

"YOU?" Will asked with an look of astonishment. "I've never seen you smoke."

"Only when I'm keyed up, Munday."

He lit the cigarette, inhaled a drag of smoke, then glanced at the sky toward the west. "It'll soon be dark. We have to hustle with this, because those bastards didn't make our job any easier. So, here's what we're looking at. As best we could determine from a distance was that there are two lofty guard towers, one on each end. Both are equipped with Nambus," he explained, being interrupted at that point by Tillie, who inquired, "What's a Nambu?"

"A machine gun. Deadly weapon. Lots of oomph," Baker responded, then reminded Tillie, "We covered the Nambus down in Guinea. Evidently you didn't pay attention."

Tillie nodded, and grinned, and muttered, "Yup. I recall now."

Now that he'd put Tillie in his place again, he continued with his critique. "The way I see it, we're going to have to use Seto's oxcart to bootleg the explosives inside of the compound."

"Well, just how'n the hell am I going to blow the joint if my explosives are inside and I'm outside looking in," Gambler protested.

Fidel was keeping Seto informed about Baker's plans, so when the old man raised a hand to intervene, Baker asked Fidel, "What's he got?"

Seto went into a long-winded dissertation, waving his arms and almost shouting to Fidel, who finally shushed him so he could relay the message. "He says there is a bunker very close to the radio transmitter tower and he thinks it is their arsenal. It is his suggestion that we bury the explosives in his cart, leaving a fuse just out of sight, but near the side racks, where it can be lit without being too obvious. He believes he can put off selling his wares until after daybreak if he arrives after dark. He has come late in the day before, and they always have given him a pad to sleep on and let him conduct his business the next day," Fidel related Seto's long-winded tirade. After hearing it, Baker could understand Seto's enthusiasm.

Gambler, seeing his dreams shattered, jumped into the fray, asking Baker, "Don't you think we should wait until Captain Roul arrives to make a decision?"

"Hey. Wait up," Tillie offered, wondering, "Where are the other guys, anyways?"

Baker thrust his hand into the air, an open palm directed at both men, advising Tillie, "First things first. Yes. They are late. Yes. I'm worried. Roul originally projected we'd all meet before sundown in this location. It's sundown. Neither squad has shown up."

Will studied Baker's expression carefully, finally concluding that the sergeant wasn't simply worried, as he'd claimed, but was about to push the panic button. Zero hour was approaching, and Baker, with three of his regulars not including Fidel and Seto, was halfway convinced they might not show up at all. He tried to reason with Gambler, citing all of the pluses for using the oxcart and emphasizing all of the negatives for trying an assault from outside of the walls. Finally, after dwelling on the possibilities for a moment or two, he broke the bad news. "I hate to tell you guys this, but I have a hunch Able and Charlie aren't going to make the meet. We encountered several delays and still got here on time. I don't want to think about it, but I'm figuring that they, too, ran into Jap patrols, and, that being a possibility, they might not have fared out as well as we. It's sort of ... time to put up or shut up. C'mon, hustler," he chided Gambler, "you of all people know about odds. We're running out of time. We can't fold. This is a winner-take-all situation."

Gambler stared at the ground, trying to avoid everyone else's stare. Baker was right and he knew it. He just needed to deal with it. "Well," he managed to say in a disheartened tone of voice, "is that it? Is it really going to come to Baker squad against the whole goddamn world?"

Baker nodded, admitting, "It looks that way."

"Okay," Gambler fired back, "you'd better let a pro stuff that cart and set the charges if you wanta do this right."

Fidel explained to Seto that Gambler would call the shots about building a "two-wheeled ox-bomb," as he labeled the cart.

"C'mon, Tillie. Give me a hand," Gambler said, jumping to his feet. He grabbed the bag of explosives he'd toted for several days and hightailed it over to the cart. Seto jumped in line behind Tillie, figuring to help out if he could, leaving Will, Baker and Fidel remaining. Will was tired and told Baker, "I'm going to try to catch some Z's, unless ... you were thinking about having some grub, in which case I'd be happy to forego a nap."

"Hungry?" Baker asked him.

"Yes. I am. Well, sorta hungry. My gut's been tied up in a knot ever since we left that village. Early on I really didn't care if I ever ate again," Will replied, admitting he had misgivings he needed to deal with.

"It'll pass, Munday. But I guess we should have a bite to eat. It's almost dark. I've been stalling, hoping the whole gang would be here. They aren't coming," Baker remorsed.

Baker had only a few cartons of K's remaining. He yelled over to Gambler and Tillie, asking them if they wanted to eat, and when they dropped what they were doing to get their rations Baker told them, "Bring Seto along. He must also be hungry."

"Are we out of rations?" Will asked.

"Darned near. I brought just enough for us, figuring Roul would be here.

One of his Filipino volunteers was toting some extra rations for everyone," Baker broke the bad news to them.

Gambler, Tillie and Seto grabbed their share of the rations and sat down in a circle, facing Baker and Will. Fidel hung back, eating alone. Will thought this was as good a time as any for everyone to get anything off of their chest that was bothering them. Some idle chatter over dinner seemed appropriate. So, he asked Baker what their chances were of making it through the mission in one piece.

"Well, let me put it this way. You do want me to be honest with you, don't you?"

They all nodded in the affirmative.

"There probably are no odds. This assault was calculated to need at least a dozen men, two non-coms, one officer and a handful of Filipinos. Take a look around. There's one non-com, three of you, one Filipino and our guest of honor, Mister Seto," Baker informed them, trying to be as gentle as was possible. "And speaking of Mister Seto, Fidel, ask him what he intends to do once inside of the compound. It's time to plan our strategy. It's evident we're going to have to tackle it alone."

Seto bent Fidel's ear for the longest time again but finally did stop for a breath of air, at which time Fidel began to translate before Seto could resume his dissertation. "He says," Fidel repeated, "he should get there no later than eleven, else they might be suspect of him traveling alone so late at night. And in answer to your question about what he intends to do once he's inside, he says he will take his oxcart across the compound and park it right between the tower and the bunker that he told you about. Then he intends to tether his oxen to one of the upright beams of the radio tower on a pretense that he's going to settle in for the night."

"Hm-m-m-m, not bad for a first-timer. So, what comes then?" Baker pressed Seto.

Fidel went into another extended chin fest with Seto, finally cutting him off with the wave of a hand, and informed Baker, "He says he has no way to ignite a fuse. But he would be glad to do that if we will furnish him with matches. He doubts the Japs will pay much attention to him. Most of them will be in the barracks, sleeping. The ones who are up and about will either be in the transmitter room or manning the watchtowers."

Baker was troubled. "Does he fully understand that when he lights that fuse he'll have a very short time in which to get the hell out of there?" the sergeant asked.

Fidel relayed the question. Seto looked Baker in the eye but spoke to Fidel, telling the both of them, "I understand. Do not worry over me."

307

Everyone exchanged glances. Will wondered, *Doesn't he realize it'll probably be a ten-second fuse, and that isn't long enough to get his ass out'a there?* then answered his own query, telling himself, *Yes. He does. Roul sure as hell has his finger on the pulse rate of his countrymen. They are a gallant people.*

Gambler wouldn't hear of it. "No," he interjected a complaint. "No way. Seto is going to end up blowing himself to smithereens."

Although Seto might not have understood Gamblers words, he evidently interpreted the message. He reached out his hand and patted Gambler on the wrist, then bowed in a true oriental custom, and asked Fidel to relay to Gambler, "I appreciate your concern. You have been brave to travel so far to set us free. It is the least I can do to repay you."

Gambler was provoked. "He owes me nothing," he yelped.

But Seto just smiled, then pointed at Gambler's part pack of cigarettes and said to Fidel, "It has been many years since I have tasted an American cigarette. I wonder if this young man would share his pack with me."

Gambler fished the pack from his pocket and handed it to Seto, who promptly plucked out a cigarette and stuck it between his lips, pointing at Will's Zippo as if to ask for a light. Will flicked the cap open and spun the flint wheel until the wick was blazing, then held the flame underneath the cigarette dangling from Seto's lips. The old man sucked in a mouthful of smoke, then slowly exhaled it along with a pleasurable moan of satisfaction. "Arigato," he said, bowing to his hosts with a series of waist bends.

"Huh?" Gambler asked.

"He is thanking you in his native tongue; Japanese," Fidel explained. "He bows out of courtesy, a gesture which they consider to be a compliment."

They finished the remaining orts of food, crumpled up the cartons and shoved them into their packs. It was their last meal unless Roul showed up. But Will, like Baker, had bad vibrations about the possibility. It was now totally dark. There was a three-quarter moon, which was momentarily dimmed by a few thin clouds that floated aimlessly around in the night sky. Will just sat there haggling with his thoughts, trying desperately to dismiss from his mind what might've happened to the guys in Able and Charlie squads. But he couldn't erase the inquiry. He would've preferred to tumble into one of his trances, where he could surround himself with fond memories of happier days. That, too, failed him. He was still smarting on the inside over Farmer's death. Trying to put everything into perspective, he didn't think he would ever get over bidding Farmer goodbye, if of course he, himself, managed to live through the assault on the radio complex. His world was topsy-turvy. He could no longer commiserate with the past; his favorite retreats such as the soda fountain, his Land of Oz where his wishes were always granted and his make-believe hideout that sheltered him, all had forsaken him. Farmer was gone ... forever ... his remains having been left alone in a village where no one would mourn his passing or pause to pay their last respects when he was lowered into his grave, if indeed there would be a grave. It was just too much to handle. He pulled his knees up under his chin, dropped his arms around them, then hid his face and sobbed. He guessed he'd finally been overwhelmed by a terminal case of war's insanity. And he halfway hoped that he'd be put out of his own misery before the sun came up. There was really little left for him fret over. "That fucking jug of wine and the goddamned loaf of bread," he muttered.

"What did you say?" Baker asked.

"Oh, nothing. Just thinking out loud."

Chapter Twenty-One

"How long do you figure it'll take Mister Seto to reach the gate of the compound?" Gambler asked Baker.

"Oh, a half hour, maybe less. We'd better figure on thirty minutes," Baker replied.

Will had been dozing. The conversation stirred him from his slumber. Nothing had changed. He was still in limbo, waiting for the signal to proceed. "What time is it?" he inquired.

"Twenty-two hundred hours," Baker told him. "Everybody'd better start their engines. We'll be moving out in a half hour. So, listen up. When we reach the bluff overlooking the compound, Mister Seto will break off and head down the hill to the gate. He doesn't anticipate any problem getting inside, but they will stop him and give his produce a once-over before letting him enter. It's not likely they'll have any reason to doubt his purpose for coming. I will assign all of you to vantage points overlooking the complex. Now, are there any questions so far?"

There were none. Everyone urged him to finalize the plans. "Okay. Are you sure you have the oxcart primed and ready?" Baker quizzed Gambler.

"Yes. I'm sure. I figure the way I've got it packed they'll hear the explosion all the way to Tokyo," Gambler boasted.

Everyone chuckled. "Okay," Baker continued. "Now, I'm going to ask someone to make a contribution to the cause. I need one of your lighters to give to Seto. Who wants to part with their Zippo?"

Will reluctantly raised his hand, offered his lighter to Baker, wisecracking, "Here's my supreme sacrifice. I've been thinking about giving up cigarettes, anyway."

"Awe, go on," Tillie fired back. "Sacrifice, my butt. But seein' as how you're gonna quit, why don't you give me that part pack you've got stashed in your pocket?"

"I didn't say I was GOING TO quit. I said I was thinking about it," Will hedged.

"Knock it off," Baker intervened, reminding them, "we've got business to tend to. Now, it's obvious we're the only remaining squad; one out of three. We were lucky, it would seem, even though we had our share of problems getting here. But we made it in one piece, well ... scratch that ... almost one piece. We're one man short. God only knows what happened to Roul and Schuster. I'll give you your individual instructions when I post you up there. But I'm sure you've wondered what happens after we blow the joint. That gets a tad ticklish. The original plan was to meet here, where we started, then to fan out in pairs and work our way through the jungle in an easterly direction. Hopefully, our troops will be well entrenched on a beachhead come tomorrow evening. Just how long it might take to hook up with our forces is a guess. One thing is certain, we'll all have to dodge Jap patrols to get there, because they'll pull every damned unit out of these boondocks to intercept our guys."

"So?" Tillie asked, "D'ya want us to meet back here?"

"Yes. That's my thinking. There are two important things to remember. On my signal, you will concentrate your fire on the two observation towers. That will divert attention away from Mister Seto. Tillie, you'll take out the far tower with your BAR. It has the range. Munday will keep the near tower busy. Gambler and I will be positioned midway between you two. When the curtain rises, that being my signal, cut loose and don't let up until you hear and see that transmitting tower bite the dust. Now, does everyone understand?" Baker polled them.

Hearing nothing, he continued, explaining the second-most important thing to remember. "When the tower goes down, everyone pull back into the trees and haul ass for this spot ... right here," he directed them, adding, "The Japs won't be long regrouping, and they'll be out in force beating the bushes like a bunch of flies on horse dung. Speed. Think speed. Get the hell back here, pronto, so we can put some distance between us and them. Now, that's about it. If anything else does come up I'll keep you informed as we go. You know your assignments. Now, I'll just bet you're asking yourself whether or not this squad can cut the mustard by themselves. Well, I've got this to say. Not putting down any other squad, understand, because they're all good, but I'm thanking my lucky stars I have Baker squad right now. You won top honors back in training as far as I was concerned. Thinking back to that day on the beach when I first met all of you, it's a small miracle that fate threw you guys together. The captain once remarked that if we could divert your scrappy attitude toward the Japs and away from each other we wouldn't need so many men. Little did he realize that his observation was a forecast of things to come."

His closing message was greeted by an eerie silence. They all exchanged glances but said nothing. "Well, have a last smoke. We're moving out in ten minutes," Baker informed them.

Fidel held a hushed confab with Baker, then took his leave, heading out toward the compound. He was, Will supposed, going to make sure the coast was clear prior to Baker leading his small detachment up the roadway.

Will pulled a cigarette from his pack, bummed a light from Tillie, and gingerly sat his rump down on the ground. He cleared his throat, "A-hem," trying to garner Tillie's attention.

"Did you say somethin'?" the hillbilly asked.

"No. Not exactly. I just felt like talking. I was wondering something, Tillie."

"Yeah? What?"

"Are you scared?"

"Oh ... I don't know. Are you?"

"Yeah, sorta. I was thinking about that three's-a-charm stuff."

"What d'ya mean?"

"You know. They say that back during World War I they never kept a match burning long enough for the third man to light his cigarette."

"Yup. I've heard that."

"My mother used to say, when things came in threes, 'Three's a charm.'"

"Yup. I've heard that, too."

"This is number three. I mean, the third time we've tackled the Japs."

"How so?"

"Well, there was the air raid. You surely recall that. You got the only trophy that day. What did you ever do with that little Jap flag?"

"Still got it. Up under the straps in my helmet liner."

"I'll be damned. Well, anyway, the air raid was the first time. Then we took on that squad of Nips this afternoon. So, this is our third go at it," Will tallied the score. "So, when we hit the complex tonight, that will be three, right?"

"Ah, don't let numbers spook you, Will," Tillie dismissed the innuendo that 'three' might be a bad omen.

"I guess you're right. Well, it's about that time, huh?"

Will jumped up onto his feet, swung his Thompson around and grabbed it with both hands just when Baker barked, "Okay. Move out. Gambler? You take the point ahead of Mister Seto. Don't stretch out too far ahead of us. The rest of us will tag along behind the oxcart. When you reach the top of the knoll, hold up. You'll be just a short distance from the complex. We'll regroup there. Hopefully, Fidel will also be there."

Gambler headed on up the trail. Mister Seto, armed with a bamboo switch, which he laid across the oxen's backside to get him moving, came out from under the cover of the trees and followed behind Gambler. Baker grabbed Will's arm, telling him, "Get in behind Mister Seto. Maintain a distance of about fifty yards, so we're spread out a little." He then reassured Tillie, "Last isn't always the least," and told him him to follow Will's lead by fifty yards. Baker stalled until Tillie was almost out of sight before bringing up the rear.

The night was still, the air unusually crispy for the tropics. Will was glad he was walking alone. He wanted to solo so he could take another stab at hooking up with MaryLou.

His mind detoured to the soda fountain. He was elated. *It worked, it worked, it finally worked,* he rejoiced. Like magic, Will was jerking sodas, eyeballing MaryLou, who was seated on a stool at the counter, making eyes at him.

"Lime rickey," she said. "Can you mix a lime rickey?"

"You know better than that. There's no gin behind this bar," Will disappointed her.

"Okay," she said with a smile, accentuating that darling dimple that drove Will nuts. "A lime rickey. Hold the gin."

"Coming up," he replied, dashing to the backbar to fetch a wedge of lime. He threw the soda into the glass, added a dash of sugar, squeezed and tossed the lime into the concoction, and returned to the counter. "Here," he said with a wide grin, "one lime rickey for the most beautiful girl in the world."

"Watch where you're going, Will," Tillie yelped, shoving him aside when he almost collided the oxcart. Seto reined his oxen in and stopped to wait for everyone to catch up

"Oh," Will remarked, a glazed expression on his face, finally asking, "Gee, are we already on the hill?"

"Yeah," Tillie informed him, "we've been here. I passed you back there a ways. Man, you were really dogging it."

Will couldn't believe he'd been walking in a stupor that long and that Tillie walked past him without being seen. But except for Gambler and Fidel, everyone was present, so he supposed he must've spaced it.

"Where's Gambler?" Baker inquired.

"He had the point, Sergeant," Tillie reminded him.

"Well, he was supposed to stop about here," Baker complained.

Fidel came slinking down the roadway. When he got to where Baker was standing the sergeant asked him if he'd seen Gambler.

He hadn't.

"But you just came from up front. He had to have been between where you were and where we are," Baker informed him.

Seto, who'd been tending to his oxen, approached Fidel and asked if there was a problem. When Fidel told him the discussion was over Gambler, he jabbered like a chipmunk, pointing back down the road. Fidel waved him off, trying to quiet him down, and told Baker, "He says the young man who gave him the cigarettes should be with you because he turned back along the road a little while ago."

"Munday? Did you see Gambler?"

"No, sir."

"Tillie?"

"Nope."

"Well, Jesus Christ on a crutch. What else can go wrong?" Baker exploded, jerking his helmet off his head and flinging it onto the ground.

Will hustled over to pick up the helmet and cautiously handed it to Baker, confessing, "Sir, he might've slipped past me. It's dark, you know." Actually, Will was lying. He hated himself for caving into the urge to fantasize rather than be vigilant during the hillside climb. He didn't dare admit his folly, lest Baker really lose his cool. Will was as baffled as the others. Gambler's disappearance was as mind-boggling to him as anyone else.

Baker, although overwhelmed with frustration, rose to the occasion. He didn't relish the idea of tackling the job with half a squad, but it was put up or shut up time.

"Okay," he muttered, "it's almost 2300 hours. Mister Seto said he should be in the compound by that time. So, let's get moving." He asked Fidel to pass along the word to Mister Seto, and the old gent hotfooted it to where he'd left his oxen and cart, slapped the bamboo whip across the oxen's backside, and started his journey down the hillside.

Baker instructed Fidel to observe from the bluff to make sure Seto was allowed to enter the compound. He was afraid that by the time he posted both Tillie and Will, he might be late getting into position himself. When Mister Seto vanished from view, the remnants of Baker's dozen sought cover underneath an umbrella of trees, Baker leading the way, and ventured along the rim in search of a suitable site that would serve as a crow's nest overlooking the complex. Fortunately, Baker stumbled over a small outcropping that was just barely nestled in the jungle's edge, but positioned so that Will could carry out his assignment. "Here," he half-whispered. "Hunker down, behind these rocks."

Will scooted ahead, then crawled behind the outcropping Baker had designated.

315

"Munday?" Baker asked. "How far would you say this outcropping is from that tower?"

Will gave the area a quick once-over, then suggested to Baker, "I'd guess it's about ... oh, fifty yards, maybe."

"Yeah, that sounds about right. How did you do on the grenade range back in basic training?" Baker quizzed him.

"Oh, fine I think. I qualified."

"Yeah. And how far do you think you could pitch a hand-grenade?"

"Well, sir ... I'm not Bobby Feller. I was never much on sports. But I'd say I could throw a hand-grenade around fifty yards if I put my shoulder to the task."

How far could you throw it if your life depended on it?"

"Maybe a little farther."

"Your life does depend on it. When I give the signal to open fire I want you to lob two grenades right into that pillbox atop of those stilts, got me? That looks to me to be about a three-second toss. They'll never know what hit 'em."

Will stared out across the abyss that separated him from the tower. He glanced back at Baker. The monkey was on Will's back. "I can do it. Yes, sir. I can do it," Will assured him.

"Okay," Baker approved. "Get down and stay down. I'll try to make it back before the party begins. If I don't, well ... give it your best shot, Munday. I'll see back at our rendezvous point."

Will hated to see Baker leave. He felt like a bride jilted at the altar. Being alone didn't stir his inquisitive nature like it had so many times before. He looked out across the valley while he toyed with a numbers game. He estimated there had to be at least a hundred men in the garrison, perhaps more. It was probably a round-the-clock operation and as such had the equivalent of three staffs. Taking a quick head count of those he could see, there were two men in the tower nearest him, another two standing guard duty at the gate, perhaps a half-dozen floating around inside of the compound. He couldn't make out how many were manning the far tower but guessed they'd have two men there as well. It being late at night, he supposed, there were more men asleep in the barracks than awake, so he calculated that his estimate of a hundred men was probably close.

He was bored. There was precious little time left, so he purged an urge to transport his thoughts back to MaryLou. In fact, he chastised himself, it was he who really screwed up a half hour earlier by pleasuring his fantasies instead of keeping a watch on his surroundings while they made the ascent. He wondered why, if Gambler did venture past in the dark, he didn't acknowledge his passing to Will. That seemed odd. Then again, was it? Will also wondered if he might've gone AWOL? It wasn't likely. Where would he go? On the other hand, he wasn't overly thrilled about losing his starting job to Mister Seto, either. The more Will thought on the subject the more he came to realize that Gambler, being unpredictable, was capable of almost anything. He ruled out foul play. If the Nips had nailed him they would also have taken Will prisoner.

Mister Seto and his caravan arrived at the gate. He was challenged by the sentries, who walked around his oxcart, probing the interior with their bayonets, but more than anything they were just going through the motions of being sentries. One of them stepped back while the other one opened one side of the huge, wooden gate and beckoned Mister Seto to proceed. That put him temporarily out of sight behind the high barricade that marked the perimeter of the compound. So, Will turned his attention to other highlights. In the near corner he saw a tall, yellow-colored structure. He wondered what its purpose might be. Along the far left perimeter there were two buildings, which he suspected were the barracks, and almost to the far end, another building, that was well lit. He could make out two, possibly three, men grabbing a quick smoke on the steps. The occupants of the garrison made no effort to hold down the racket. A sound of voices wafted up to Will's hillside observation post on a gentle breeze.

Seto and his oxcart came into view again. He was now leading the animal with a rope, headed exactly where he said he'd go, to a spot between the base of the tower and a dirt-covered bunker that Will figured was the arsenal. The area around the base of the tower was shadowed by the bunker, so when Seto brought his rig to a stop Will had trouble seeing what was transpiring.

Hearing a noise coming from behind, Will swung the business end of his Thompson around, half scared he'd been found out, but it was only Baker making another welfare check. "How's it looking?" the sergeant asked as he slipped in beside Will.

"Mister Seto got in all right, and he tethered his oxen over between the tower and that bunker he told us about. But it's awfully hard to see what's happening. He and the animal, as well as the cart, are in the shadows," Will remorsed.

"Good report, Munday," Baker complimented him.

"Well, sir, I was wondering something. Look right down there, just inside of the compound. That yellow building," Will said, pointing at the structure. "What do you suppose it is?"

"I'd guess it's the generating plant. They have to have electric generators to power this place. Yeah, I'd guess that's what it is. Why?"

317

"Well, sir, I was thinking the same thing. I wondered if I could pitch a third grenade onto it. Now that you've confirmed my suspicions about it being their power source, the plan sounds even better. What do you think?"

"Damn, Munday. That's good. Take the light away from them. Un-huh. Well, I'd better move along and check on Tillie's welfare. That goddamn Gambler has me puzzled. I really could use another gun up here," Baker said, taking his leave. "Yeah, Munday. Go ahead," he murmured over his shoulder, "If you think you can lay a grenade onto the yellow building, go for it. I'll try to make it back one more time before all hell breaks loose." And with those words Baker was again out of sight.

Will began to make preparations for the assault. He pulled three hand-grenades off his belt, laid them side by side on the face of the rock directly in front of him and, after reconsidering the odds, laid another clip of ammunition on the rock. He eyed the tower again. Two men still manned the post. They weren't exactly tending to their business like Will thought they should be. They were clowning around with one another, and he could hear their voices over almost everything else. There were two Nambus dangling on their tripods. This looked almost too easy. Will was frightened that there was something he didn't know. He checked his grenades again, then made sure he had a round chambered in his Thompson. The wait was the pits. He tried to locate Tillie across the way but couldn't. He wanted to smoke a cigarette and couldn't so he shrugged, recalling he had no lighter. He wanted to know precisely what time it was but had no timepiece. He was positive it was later than eleven thirty. He didn't have much time remaining to enjoy the quietude, so he hunkered down a tad to catch some rest while he waited. He figured he'd made all of the preparations he could. But a movement caught the corner of his eye when he turned his head, so he quickly focused in for a retake of the compound, staring at the area where Mister Seto had tethered his oxcart beside the base of the transmitting tower. He squinted. There appeared to be two people there and his first thought was that one of the Japs was trying to dicker with Mister Seto tonight, rather than wait until dawn. But then he saw the unthinkable. He blinked, looked again, then mumbled to himself, "Damn. It's Gambler. He's in the compound ... talking to Mister Seto." Still, Will knew that Seto did not speak English and that Gambler did not speak Japanese. If they were, indeed, communicating with each other, he wondered how. He continued to monitor them, wishing Baker could've been there to see it with his own eyes. And then a good thing happened. He got his wish. Baker came sliding down beside him, asking, "Everything still okay?"

"No," Will surprised Baker. "Take a look down there, behind the cart by the tower. I know it's dark but tell me what you see."

"Well, Jesus Christ," Baker exploded again, apparently unable to rein in his temper. "It's Gambler. What the fuck is he doing there? How'd he get inside?"

Will hung his head, mulled over Baker's comment, then said, "Why am I not surprised? Did you really think you were going to screw Gambler out of his finale, Sergeant?"

"I should've known. In fact I should've tied a rope on him to keep him in tow. Gaddamn him anyway. He climbed into that oxcart when he turned back on the trail. That's the only answer. Mister Seto was in front and couldn't see him and you were too far back on the trail. He hasn't got a prayer, you know. Him or Mister Seto. Neither one of them have. I'll bet he's got a ten-second fuse on that bomb down there. When he, or Mister Seto, light that fuse they'll be lucky if they aren't blown to bits," Baker complained, then had second thoughts and asked Will, "What did you say? Did you ask, 'Why am I not surprised?'"

Will wagged his head in the affirmative.

"What prompted that? What do you know about Gambler that I don't?"

"That's it, Sergeant. You do know. He's a Gambler. He has to have the action. He couldn't survive without it. Gambling's his obsession. He did a complete reverse in character on this trip. It all began at the waterfall. After that, he turned into a really nice guy," Will explained, finally asking, "Are you surprised to learn that?" But he didn't level with the sergeant by confessing that his daydreaming might've been a factor that aided and abetted Gambler's stunt.

"Munday," Baker responded to his query, "I'm surprised at nothing anymore. And it's closing in on zero hour." He paused, squinted to catch the time of day, then told Will, "Ten minutes. I'll be right over there. By that clump of bushes on the crest. See them? Start keeping your eyes trained on that spot in a few minutes. Tillie is right over there. It's too dark to see him, but he's really not that far away. When the tower goes down, get the hell outta here. Haul ass and meet back at the rendezvous point. Got it?"

Will nodded and Baker departed for his final time, leaving Will F. Munday, the reluctant warrior, to fend for himself. He was surprised to discover his own change in comportment. He'd finally made the one-hundred-and-eighty-degree change in direction that transofrmed him from the role of the reluctant warrior into a dedicated lunatic. His hands were steady. They were not sweating. His heart was not palpitating. He didn't feel a need to urinate. He was primed like the fuse on Gambler's bomb to respond on command. It was a whole new perspective. He honed his vision in on the leafy clump of undergrowth where Baker had said he'd be. "C'mon, Baker.

C'mon. C'mon. Do it!" he muttered over and over again until he finally saw his big, lanky sergeant raise up his hand, arise to his feet, and that was when the unthinkable occurred.

"FIRE IN THE HOLE," Gambler screamed from somewhere inside of the Japanese compound.

"He wouldn't!" Baker muttered. "YES! He would! He did! He just hit the button on our stopwatch, that goddamned, crazy kid, anyhow. He finally drew that Royal Flush after he bet the farm."

Baker brought his Thompson down and took aim at the tower he'd assigned to be Will's objective, just as the explosion rocked the entire countryside.

POW-W-W-W-W-W!

Will fumbled with a grenade, finally pulled the pin, stood up and heaved it with all of his might toward the tower. He reached down and grabbed the second grenade just about that time the first missile made a direct hit on the target. He cocked his elbow and, standing there flatfooted, stared at his handiwork. The Jap sentries, who just moments earlier were toying with one another, went crashing toward the ground, trapped inside of the pillbox. He didn't pitch the second grenade. He knew he didn't need to, so he turned to eyeball his second option, the yellow building. Rearing back, he flung his arm forward and released the grenade from his grasp. He waited. He waited. "God," he mumbled to himself, "a goddamn dud?" It wasn't. He was just overly anxious and had lost his perception of time. It exploded on the thatch roof of the power plant, smothering every trace of light within the compound.

Will was heartsick over Gambler. They might've had their differences, but he now felt as though he was beholden to him, for a second time in that many days; the first time being in the cavern underneath the waterfall. He was a professional in everything he did, and Will hated it that he'd waited too long to heap some homage on him. Recalling the first night in camp back in New Guinea, Will remembered how Gambler had introduced himself, saying, "Bobby Belton's the name and gambling's my game," then going on to boast he liked big pots and bigger explosions. This explosion shook the earth clear up on the hillside where Will was stationed as well as splintering the tower's supports. It began to wobble, to twist, to bend, and when a second explosion detonated—the arsenal nearby that Mister Seto told them about—that was the finishing touch. It lit the entire valley up like Broadway in New York City on New Year's Eve, and nearly every structure inside of the walls came tumbling down. It was beyond awesome, but Will had lost his edge. Snuffing out the power plant was but a temporary reprieve. The bamboo and thatch structures, including the perimeter barricade, were all ablaze, an oversight on

Will's part, because the compound was once again bathed in light. In fact, the series of explosions illuminated the compound better than the portable generator system had. The Japanese regrouped and seized the offensive, returning fire that blistered the hillside where Will, Baker and Tillie were perched. The enemy marksmen had already spotted Will's nest on the hillside. They laced the entire area, their projectiles ricocheting off the rocks that, heretofore, had protected Will. Will snatched his Thompson, pocketed the spare clip he'd tossed on the face of the outcropping, and began to return fire. The explosion blew a gaping hole in the fortress wall, which provided the Jap soldiers with an ideal exit to vacate their ravaged post to counterattack. Will emptied his first clip on a dozen or so men who were already charging up the hillside, killing perhaps half of them. It was, he decided, "time to go," so he spun out of the rocky crag and, remembering Baker's orders to "haul ass," took off on a dead run, hoping the Nip sharpshooters wouldn't be able to see him in the trees. When he estimated he raced far enough to outdistance the Japs he paused to listen, hoping to hear a friendly voice, perhaps Baker's. What he heard was Tillie, who was screaming but still chipping away at the Nips. Will recognized the bark of his BAR over the other sounds of alien fire. But then he heard Tillie calling out in a mournful plea, "Cheezus. Oh, CHEEZUS." He swiveled his head trying to catch a glimpse of his friend just in time to see the lanky hillbilly tumbling down the hillside, arms and legs flaying about like a discarded rag doll. Tillie had been shot.

"Oh shit," Will screamed, recalling his promise to Tillie, "The letter. The letter. I never read his letter." But he had little time to dwell on that, because a bullet tore through his right knee cap and knocked him off of his legs. When he dropped he managed to break his fall with his hand, but when he tried to raise himself back onto his feet he discovered that his right leg was useless. Crawling, trying to retreat further into the forest, he called out for Baker. "Sergeant? Sergeant? I'm hit." All he heard in response was a sound of voices off in the distance; those of Japanese soldiers already searching the countryside for the interlopers who'd destroyed their complex. He knew he could not escape, so he rolled over onto his back, pulled his Thompson up onto his belly, took a firm hold on the stock, and leveled it in the direction from which the voices echoed. He figured he was as good as dead, and it was his intention to take as many of those sonsabitches with him as he could. A sound a twigs cracking underfoot cought his ear. The crunching noise was near, too near. He gripped his weapon, slid his finger across the trigger and braced himself for the onslaught. It was not what he expected. A voice called out, "Munday. Munday. Is that you?" It was Baker.

"Over here. I can't walk."

Baker loped over to where Will was sprawled out on the ground. He put his arm around Will's waist and hoisted him up onto one leg. "Munday," he half-whispered, "I'll help you. But you've got to help yourself. Put your arm around my shoulder and use me as a crutch. Let's go. They're closing in on us."

Baker took off, dragging Will along, zigzagging through the forest, trying to put some distance between them and their pursuers. It was slow going, and Baker was almost groping his way across the dark, shadowy landscape. Will heard voices resounding through the forest and could tell they were gaining on them. He told Baker, "Leave me. Go. You can't make it trying to carry me."

"Munday, shut the fuck up," Baker reproved him, advising him, "You'll never see the day I leave one of my men to fend for himself."

Baker's admonishment sparked Will's determination. He managed to limp along to keep the pace with Baker, until the sergeant misjudged his footing and the two of them tumbled down a steep grade, both finally rolling to a stop in a cluster of ferns. Will was moaning. Baker covered his lips with an open palm, saying to him in a soft voice, "Quiet. No sound. Lie still. They might pass us by. Sh-h-h-h."

Will was no longer armed. He'd dropped his weapon somewhere, perhaps when he first fell, but one thing was sure, he didn't have it on his person. And he had no intention of trying to recover it, either. Running through the thicket to stay alive had been his primary concern. Now, wracked with pain and bleeding profusely, Will realized his fate was in his sergeant's hands. Baker, however, was hamstrung to do anything about Will's discomfort at the moment. His paramount goal was concentrating on keeping Will quiet so as not to compromise their position. The Japanese patrol was just above them, combing the rim of the precipice they'd tumbled into. Their voices were quite audible. They were so close, in fact, that the crunching of their feet was even audible above their incessant chatter. The only thing Baker and Will had in their favor was the cover of night, because the Jap pickets were directly above them, where, had it been daylight, they'd have easily seen them.

Will's strength was waning. But Baker just whispered to him, reminding him to, "Suck it in, Munday. Quiet." After a tense moment in limbo, Will thought he detected the sound of their voices fading away, and he guessed he was right when Baker relaxed his vigil and tried to examine Will's ravaged knee. It was dark and difficult to see, but Sergeant Baker was able to determine that Will's knee was totally shattered, probably beyond mending.

Rather than share the bad news with Will, Baker tried to encourage him, saying, "I've got only one morphine, Munday. I'm going to try go stop the bleeding and wrap your leg. Then I'll give you the shot. It won't last forever. Hold still and stay quiet."

Baker tried his very best to be gentle, but in the darkness of the night it was difficult to see what he was going. Groping with his fingers, he managed to unwind a gauze strip from a packet he fished out of his first-aid kit. He ripped the corner off of an envelope of sulfanilamide and sprinkled a generous portion of the powdered white medication across the knee, then began to swirl the gauze around Will's leg, trying to wrap it snuggly so as to serve a dual purpose; that of a dressing and a pressure pack.

Will's head began to spin. His forehead was suddenly numb and he was very cold, even though the temperature was still quite warm. He opened his eyes and found he was staring up at the sky. It was magnificent—a star-studded ocean of glittering sparkles not too different from the heavens he'd focused on that first night back in Guinea. The three-quarter moon was wending its way through the cloud cover, and its faint beams of light filtered down between the foliage overhead and waltzed across Will's face. He tried to put things into some sort of perspective, recalling how he'd managed to weasel his way through any number of trials and tribulations since being inducted into the Army, by just regressing into his Never-neverland. He knew that it wasn't possible to steal time from the Grim Reaper, but he figured anything was worth a try. He would, he decided, concentrate his thoughts on visions of home, and in his mindset he was suddenly sitting at his desk back in the college classroom. English Lit, he thought. Yes. He loved it so. Especially poetry. He would sit with his nose buried between the covers of rhyme and just read, and read, and read. There was something calming about poetic verse.

Baker finished wrapping Will's leg, injected the needle of his morphine syringe into Will's thigh and squeezed the painkiller into his flesh. Relief was almost instantaneous. Will suddenly felt melancholy and the mood fit the scene he'd dredged up; a happy haunt in the halls of learning. Someone was reading to the class. It was something from Poe; sinister, dark, eerie verse that only that master of darkness could invent. No. He didn't want to hear Poe. He was, he suspected, dying. He didn't want to die, either. Not in a godforsaken place like this. But life was oozing out of his body, and he realized it was his moment to face death with some sort of courage and dignity, not "sniveling like a baby" such as Baker had once accused over Farmer's demise. And then another voice resounded through the classroom. It was echoing, coming from some faraway place. *Awe, yes,* Will thought, overhearing the words from William Cullen Bryant, another master of the depths but one who did eventually come to terms with fate. Who else knew the secret to impending doom any better than he? And the voice was reciting from Bryant's "Thanatopsis," particularly the final stanza, where the bard wrote, *"So live that when thy summons comes to join, the innumerable caravan which moves, to that mysterious realm where each must take his chamber in the silent halls of death...."* It was then that reality emerged and Will was standing face to face with the Grim Reaper, asking him, "IS IT TIME? IS THIS DEATH? DEATH? IS DEATH ACTUALLY THIS SIMPLE?" It was then that an apparation of Farmer appeared in Will's muddled mind. Farmer grinned at Will, that childish, countrified grin that made him so special, and motioned to Will to come and join him. And Will's thoughts drifted back to his home. The moon floated behind another cloud, leaving him forsaken, swathed underneath a shroud of darkness, alone and in despair. He heard his mother's voice calling to him, "Better come inside, Willie. It'll soon be dark. Supper's on the table."

Chapter Twenty-Two

On the calmest of days on the high seas any oceangoing vessel, regardless of its rated size in tons, will roll with the swells, making the footing on deck a trifle uncertain. November 18 was such a day, but Will F. Munday wasn't able to walk upon the deck. He was confined to a bed in a recovery ward aboard a huge hospital ship; his safe ticket home, providing some renegade Japanese submarine commander didn't take it upon himself to violate the rules of engagement by torpedoing the craft. Will didn't trust the enemy. He understood what they were capable of doing, and he realized that the huge red cross symbols that identified the floating haven were no guarantee of safe passage.

This would be his final voyage. He was weary of being a seafaring soldier, having served more sea duty than many a sailor; those dry-docked deckhands delegated to shore duty. Will had sailed to New Guinea aboard a troop transport, went ashore on a Higgins boat, trained for Stopwatch on an LCI, was ferried to the Philippines on a Navy seaplane, was bootlegged through enemy waters on the *Señora Rosita*, and now found himself steaming toward San Francisco on a floating infirmary. He'd had enough and was headed home, although he wasn't quite sure what the future held. There were considerations now that might change everything.

Will was bored. There was little he could do except to dwell on memories that would've been best forgotten. Occasionally a thoughtful nurse would bring a wheelchair and take him up onto the deck to soak up some sunlight. If he asked she might wheel him to the ship's library where he could, if he was a'mind to, write a letter, read a book, or take a snooze. There was a ship's store that offered all of the goodies he'd been denied for months; candy, chewing gum and other sweets that the nurse insisted were not permissible on his rigid dietary schedule. But Will had not rekindled his desire to read, nor had he written a single word to his loved ones. He was at a loss over what to say. Should he come right out with it; give them a forecast of what to expect when they first saw him? Or would it be best to let them get an eyeful, then draw their own conclusions at the time of the reunion?

Will did have an edge over many of his prostrate shipmates in that he had mastered the art of withdrawing into his mental cocoon to shut out the world around him. He was, in fact, on such a journey at the moment; wandering around in Never-neverland, trying to reconstruct the complicated tale he'd been told about his rescue, as it was relayed by a medic back on Leyte. According to the young pill roller who tended to his needs he was comatose for quite sometime. There was, the corpsman said, a sergeant who came dragging into the aid station carrying Will in his arms. He'd been dodging enemy patrols for days on end, traveling mainly at night to avoid them. But when Will asked the identity of the sergeant no one could tell him. He told Will the man left no name. He merely handed Will's dog tags to someone and vanished. They did, however, credit him with saving Will's life. He would surely have perished had the sergeant not been a sensitive, caring, well-trained individual. Will was, when he arrived at the station, suffering an acute case of malnutrition, was dehydrated almost to a point of dying, and his right leg was rotting with gangrene. It was necessary to amputate his leg just above the knee to save his life. Will's recollections of the journey were fuzzy at best. He did have vague memories, mostly of someone telling him repeatedly, "Hang on. I'll get you outta here." The fact that his Samaritan's identity was ignored seemed a shame to Will. Surely, he reasoned, it was Baker, but he couldn't be sure. Someone distinguished themselves, then blended into the surrounding crowd of khaki-clad warriors, never to be rewarded for his valor. Something about it seemed unfair.

Will wasn't a mixer. The scuttlebutt on board was focused on the homecoming. Trying to put everything into perspective was a chore. It was almost impossible for him to rationalize the fact that it had been only about four months since he had sailed under the Golden Gate bridge to begin his overseas tour of duty. It seemed much longer. And he recalled his journey by truck from Fort Ord that night, under cover of darkness, and walking up the gangplank to get on board. There'd been no fanfare. The departure was cloaked in secrecy. Now, he was hearing forecasts of an enthusiastic greeting at the pier; a "welcome home, hero" sort of thing, possibly with a brass band and a sea of flags fluttering in the breeze. Being one leg short, he wouldn't be in the first contingent to debark. Perhaps they'd get a thunderous welcome. The wheelchair cases would probably be put ashore after the commotion died down. He didn't actually care, one way or the other. Being a cripple was going to take some getting used to.

Will wasn't overly enthused about his future. His favorite nurse, the one who would take him for a ride now and then, warned him he was destined to spend some time in hospitals and rehab centers, where he'd be fitted with an artificial limb. He didn't think too kindly about sporting a "wooden leg," as he dubbed the device. But the nurse assured him he'd be pleasantly surprised how mobile he would become, because artificial limbs had substantially improved in recent years. He supposed that the war had something to do with that. It was the war, he thought, that opened a window for researching miracle drugs, such as penicillin. There were probably thousands of cases like his where men had lost a limb, so the technology figured. The trouble was he had been more than happy with his natural leg. And sometimes he thought it felt as though it was still there. Again, the nurse explained the trauma. Nerve endings on the stump were to blame, but, she told him, that would improve with time. He tried ever so hard to lighten the load with jokes. He'd ask her if an eye patch and cutlass was issued with the wooden leg so he could resemble a respectable pirate. She'd laugh with him, knowing he was hurting on the inside, displaying courage on the outside. He confided to her that he felt like a "freak." He'd be "stared at," perhaps even "pitied," and he couldn't live like that. So long as the war lasted he suspected he'd be "worshipped" by his peers; the conquering hero awarded a Purple Heart Medal. But he was historian enough to realize when the clatter of musketry faded into memory, he'd become just "another handicapped pain in the ass."

His misfortune brought back to mind a neighbor who lived next door when he was growing up. Will knew him as Mister Oldman. The old-timer rocked his way through life on a dilapidated rocking chair sitting on the front porch of his home. Each morning, he recalled, Mister Oldman's daughter would redundantly help him to his chair, then wrap his frail body with a quilt, give the rocker a shove and leave him alone with his thoughts. The old man would just sit there, trying to keep the chair in motion with his toes; caught up in a vacuum where he saw nothing, heard nothing and said nothing. Will had once inquired about the old man's welfare of his mother and she had simply replied, "The poor dear. He was gassed in the big war. He'll never be well. His health slips away with each passing day." But Will had never actually looked upon the man as anything special, so he had adequate reason to suspect he, himself, was nothing special in anyone else's eyes. He halfway contemplated he'd be the blunt of jokes, especially from the younger set, who weren't mature enough to comprehend the realities of an adult world. He remembered he'd poked fun at Mister Oldman, so now he would have to atone for those sins by trading places. "Move over, old man," Will found himself saying, "to make room for Will F. Munday."

Will's delayed mail finally caught up to him; six letters from MaryLou and a couple from his mother. He'd received them the previous day but didn't open any of MaryLou's letters. He was fearful that MaryLou might've had a change of heart. He worried that he'd misinterpreted her first letter, and that she really wasn't in love with him, or, even worse, she'd played a practical joke on him. He had taken time to read the letters from his mother. Things around home weren't exactly ginger, peachy, keen.

Your daddy isn't well, she'd written.

> *It is his heart. The doctors are hoping for a full recovery but I'm concerned. He isn't the same person. I think it's a result of too many beers for too many years. The heart attack must've opened his eyes. He told me that he has seen the errors of his ways and, although he didn't come right out and say this, I suspect he's hoping that his relationship with you can be mended. Hopefully, he'll live to see you come home.*

Will figured it would take something just short of a miracle to mend fences with his dad. One or the other of them would have to make the first move, and Will didn't think he could bring himself to do that. So, it would fall his dad's lot to extend a hand of amity. He decided to push it out of mind, at least temporarily, because he had more important concerns to address. If he intended to get his degree, there was another year of college to complete. That might present a problem, because, when looking back on his college days, recollecting some of the childish whims that accompanied it, he doubted he could knuckle down to such a routine again. He'd be bored by just listening to a henhouse of crazy coeds giggling, making eyes, strutting their stuff across the campus, all of them trying to reel in the prize catch of the season; the outstanding jock. He had nothing in common with them any longer. And when he factored in his handicap, that only enhanced the problem. If he couldn't accept them as they were, however juvenile that might've been, how could he expect them to accept him, a one-legged "freak"?

The war had broadened his horizons considerably. It had, for one thing, helped him to find himself; the real Will F. Munday. Taking a mental excursion back in time, he saw himself as a raw recruit, an antagonist of sorts, being whittled down to his size. The fact that he was only overseas a mere four months, and that his actual time in combat was probably total less than one hour if everything he did was tallied together, gave him cause to wonder what might've happened if he'd been in an outfit caught in a ongoing, day-in-day-out struggle. The strafing raid, although hairy, was of short endurance. They'd dispatched the Japanese patrol in the village in a matter of minutes. His biggie came when they assaulted the radio complex, barely an hour at best. It was just another quickie. Recalling Baker's history of warfare, Will was still a rookie compared to him. Nothing much made sense.

He really believed his future hinged on MaryLou. He needed to read her letters to sate his curiosity. But fear of rejection nagged him. He didn't think he could handle that.

Farmer came back to mind. "God," he murmured to himself, "I shore do miss that country boy." He doubted that he would ever shed his image of Farmer's pleading face when he asked, "D'ya suppose I could've?" And, what of the others, the rest of that rambunctious team of misfits? Oh, he remembered Tillie tumbling down the hillside, screaming, "Oh, cheezus!" He guessed he would still be able to hear that hillbilly's mournful call after twenty years had passed by. He hated it that he never had time to read Tillie's letter from home. Gambler? Oh, hell, he wasn't such a bad ass after all. He sacrificed himself; a needless sacrifice, but his way of doing things. Gambler needed that. And then Will smiled, remembering how Gambler had shouted, "FIRE IN THE HOLE," that last day of training in New Guinea, and of how angry Baker was over his stunt. Mister Seto paid the supreme price, too. That was a travesty, because he didn't even have to volunteer. It wasn't really his war, or was it? He was just a simple farmer who was caught in the war's wake, much like Private Will. F. Munday. As for the others, Will could only speculate their fate. Perhaps, if it was Baker who carried Will halfway across an island, he and the sergeant were the only survivors of the ill-fated mission dubbed Stopwatch. He'd tried to glean some information about Stopwatch from several different individuals but struck out. "Stopwatch?" they would ask. "What is Stopwatch?" The mission was a "never heard of it" fiasco, Will guessed. It was a rousing success in every sense of the word, but most of the principals perished in the process of carrying it through. To discredit the mission that opened the floodgate for the initial invasion of the island constituted a breech of honor, as far as Will was concerned, and by ignoring it, that's precisely what someone did.

Will's thoughts surfaced again. He was back on his bunk, staring at the bulkheads. So, he decided to tether his agony by opening, then reading, all six letters from MaryLou. He shook one such envelope to slide the letter away from the end, gingerly tore off the tip of the paper shroud, and cautiously unfolded the stationery. It said:

My dearest Will,
Your letter arrived today. Mother was almost as excited as I. She

has been teasing me day in and day out because I suddenly was so willing to retrieve the mail from our postal box. She calls me a 'lovesick kitten.' And I believe she is right. I have been a willy-nilly, sitting on pins and needles, waiting for your reply. I am so thrilled to learn that you care for me, and I am anxiously awaiting the day when you come home so we can explore the possibilities with each other.

The letter continued on the premise that she would wait for him, and that she would be faithful. She closed with,

All of my love, forever and ever. I shall pray for you and all of your friends.
Your MaryLou.

Will should have been exuberant. He wasn't. She'd just said almost every word Will had ever wanted to hear. That was the glitch. How could he be sure she'd still want him now that he was only a part of a man? She did not yet know he was a "freak."

Before he could open the second letter he heard the clatter of footsteps on the metal deck plates. He turned his head to encounter a naval officer approaching his bed. It was, he suspected, the ship's chaplain. When the man sidled up to Will's bedside, he reached out a hand and grasped Will's wrist, then began to deliver a canned missive, probably passages taken from a chaplain's handbook of encouraging words for wounded soldiers. But Will let most of what he said pass over his head. The gold cross on the chaplain's collar brought Farmer to mind. Actually, it triggered memories of a purple paper cutout shaped like a cradle that was emblazoned with Farmer's name. When he died, Will wondered, did his spirit get a free pass back home so it might get another glimpse of that cradle? Or a vision of the mother he worshipped with his heart and his soul? Or was it destined to forever dwell where the body is interred; at a remote gravesite on some soon-to-be-forgotten island five thousand miles from home? Farmer's death was a tragedy that would haunt Will all the days of his life.

The chaplain "Amen'ed" his prayer and took his leave, telling Will to "Keep the faith." Will was pleased to see him go. He wanted to be alone; to once again be swallowed up in melancholy, surrounded by those he loved, Farmer, MaryLou, his mother and, oh yes, Sergeant Baker, his benefactor many times over.

His favorite nurse sauntered up to greet him, but when she saw the forlorn expression he wore on his face, she asked, "Can I do anything to help?"

He nodded. "Yes," he said. "My mother always told me that big boys don't cry, but if I do not cry I think I will disintegrate into a million pieces. Tell me it's all right to cry."

She sat down the edge of the bed, took his hand in hers, and said, "The entire world is crying, why shouldn't you?" So, Will F. Munday finally let his tears wash away his agony.

Epilogue

I believe my chance encounter with a man named Will F. Munday was not a coincidence. There were powers beyond explanation that intervened to put me in the right place at the right time. I was driving through the Rocky Mountains to keep an appointment in Grand Junction when a winter storm turned the roadway into a treacherous skating rink. I elected to take pause in a small town; a pause that lasted almost a week. Not being accustomed to small-town living, I was at the mercy of the local merchants, whose hours were also dictated by the storm. The local motel did have a vacancy. I rented the room and freshened up a tad, then strolled over to the front window to take a peek at the lay of the land. It was still mid-afternoon, much too early to eat, but as luck would have it I spotted an American Legion Club just across the roadway. Being a member in good standing, I decided I'd mosey over there, have a couple of beers, then find a café.

When I entered through the front door of the club I saw the sign advertising their "Happy Hour," at which time drinks were two for the price of one, so I climbed up onto a bar stool and ordered a Presbyterian. The barmaid mixed me a double-header. I raised the glass for a sip before I realized I had taken a stool next to another patron. The chance meeting would change my life.

We struck up a conversation, and for some reason that I've never really understood, we shared a rapport that was difficult to explain. He began to pour his heart out to me, reliving a World War II adventure with graphic clarity. Little did he know that I was an author in search of material. I was so taken in by his candid memoirs that I just hung around town, paying a visit to the Legion Club every afternoon, making notes while he talked. On the fifth night I realized he was coming to the end of his tale. I was almost sorry to see our mutual exchange end, especially when the barmaid announced, 'Last call." I realized I had but a few moments to glean certain facts which I needed to tie some loose ends together. So, I prodded Will Munday for answers, asking, "What about Farmer? I mean, I guess, Farmer's mother?

You said you intended to go visit her. Did you?"

"Yeah," he said. "It was early in the day. I almost changed my mind and drove right on past when I reached the place, but something inside of me wouldn't allow it. So, I turned my car into the long driveway that led to a white Victorian-style house that was nestled in the midst of several outbuildings. My first observation was, the place did stink, just like I told Farmer it would. And just as I was shoving my leg through the doorway of my car, a big dog came running and like to tore it off. In fact, I think he would've had it not been for the lady of the house; Farmer's mother. She called him off, then squinted her eyes to get a better look at me, and said, 'Sport. That's no way to treat such a special guest.'"

"I asked, 'special guest? How so?' And she really bowled me over when she asked, 'You are Will, aren't you?' How could she have known? She did. I think it's a gift mothers have that menfolk never quite understand."

His visit was everything Farmer said it would be, right down to and including that big stack of flapjacks, and a cinnamon roll if he "cleaned his plate." After they'd finished eating she took him to the parlor, where they sat and chatted, her showing Will snapshots of Farmer as a tad, which she was taking from a tattered, cardboard box. Finally, she reached into the box and took out a small purple cutout that was shaped like a cradle. She raised it to her lips, kissed it and said, with tears welling up in her eyes, "It was his, you know. From the church." It was a traumatic moment. Will embraced her, and they cried together.

Will picked up his glass and swallowed the last trace of beer, then sat the glass back onto the bar top. I knew he was on the verge of leaving, and I had to know about Sergeant Baker. I tried to delay him, asking, "What about Baker? Did you ever find out if he was the man who carried you to safety?"

"Oh, that," he replied in a somber tone. "Yes. I did. Sergeant Baker was killed on Luzon shortly after the landing at Lingayen Gulf in early 1945." His voice choked, but he managed to add, "You know ... I wasn't the jurblowf who got him killed. You can bet some joker was a fault, though. He was much too cautious to get himself killed. Make no mistake about it, Sergeant Baker was the best non-com I ever encountered. He was a true leader of men. I owe my life and sanity to him."

Almost as suddenly as I met Will F. Munday, we came to a parting of the ways. He shoved himself off of the bar stool, painstakingly took his feet, and looked me squarely in the eye. "It's still there, you know," he said, rolling up his left shirt sleeve. "No matter how hard or how often I scrub that arm, I've never been able to wash away that trace of Farmer's blood. Sometimes my arm itches so bad it drives me mad. But it's an itch I cannot scratch. It's

Farmer, I think, touching base with me."

He started to leave, then stopped abruptly, and pointed at the calendar that hung on the back bar. "He died forty years ago today," he said, then sauntered toward the doorway. I took notice of the date. It was October 19, 1984, precisely forty years after that fateful day when Farmer died in Will's arms.

Unfortunately, he never gave me a chance to inquire about MaryLou. But a strange event then occurred. Just before he reached the doorway, the door swung into the room, and a lovely lady stepped into the club. She'd come to escort Will home. A gray tress of hair dangled pretentiously down across her eye when she tipped her head to kiss her man. He said something to her, she then glanced in my direction and smiled, accentuating a darling dimple in the cheek of her aging face. She slipped her arm about Will's waist, and the pair vanished through the open doorway.

I decided right then that the venerable lady who came in from the night was, indeed, MaryLou. And if she wasn't, well, what the hell! That would be just another misfortune of the reluctant warrior's war.

Cease Firing. Secure all weapons.

Author's Note

World War II began on December 7, 1941, with hostilities ending on Sept. 2, 1945. Will F. Munday's war began on December 7, 1941, and ended with his death in the fall of 1986. He was buried without fanfare in a grave provided for him by his grateful countrymen. His legacies are this story and the flag that draped his coffin. How sad! Indeed, how sad!

Peace is the happy, natural state of man; war his corruption, his disgrace.

—J. Thomson, Scottish Poet

The End